SHANNON GUYMON

taking chances

D1534216

SHANNON GUYMON

taking chances

Bonneville Books
Springville, Utah

The views expressed within this work are the sole responsibility of the author and do not necessarily reflect the position of Cedar Fort, Inc., or any other entity.

This is a work of fiction. The characters, names, incidents, places, and dialogue are products of the author's imagination, and are not to be construed as real.

ISBN 978-1-59955-205-7

Published by Bonneville Books, an imprint of Cedar Fort, Inc., 2373 W. 700 S., Springville, UT 84663
Distributed by Cedar Fort, Inc., www.cedarfort.com

Library of Congress Cataloging-in-Publication Data

Guymon, Shannon, 1972-
  Taking chances / Shannon Guymon.
    p. cm.
  ISBN 978-1-59955-205-7 (acid-free paper)
  1. Mormons--Fiction. I. Title.

  PS3607.U96T35 2008
  813'.6--dc22
                                    2008028162

Cover design by Nicole Williams
Cover design © 2008 by Lyle Mortimer
Edited and typeset by Allison M. Kartchner

Printed in the United States of America

10 9 8 7 6 5 4 3 2 1

Printed on acid-free paper

Dedication

To all the survivors of abuse, especially Edie. May you all know just how beautiful and precious you are in your Father in Heaven's eyes. And by the way, His eyes are the only ones that count.

And to everyone out there who struggles with that second commandment. I know I'm not the only one!

Other Books by Shannon Guymon

Makeover
Forever Friends
Soul Searching
Never Letting Go of Hope
A Trusting Heart
Justifiable Means

Acknowledgments

As most of you know who have read my books, I like to keep things light and funny. Sure, learn something, but when you put the book down, I want a smile on your face. So writing a story about sexual abuse is not something I ever thought I'd do. I've had relatives who have suffered this tragic, horrible evil, and I know it ruins lives firsthand. But I just didn't have a choice in the matter. One day I woke up with this book in my head, and it just wouldn't leave me alone until I got it down on paper. This was probably my pushiest book ever. Most books let me take my own time and work around nap times and bedtimes. This book was a temper tantrum-throwing two-year-old. (In the nicest of ways). It had to be written and it had to be written now. I just have the strongest feeling that there is someone special out there, who Heavenly Father loves so much, and that this book is for them. And I still hope that when you put this book down, that you have a smile on your face.

Thanks to all of those wonderful people in my life who support me and who encourage me. Thanks to my kids who put up with me being glued to the computer for too long. And thanks to my husband, Matt, for his constant support and kindness. And lastly, thanks to Kammi and Allison at Cedar Fort.

In the midst of winter,
I finally learned
that there was in me
an invincible summer.
—Albert Camus

Chapter 1

Maggie tried not to stare out her back mirror as she left St. George behind, but she couldn't help it. She shared a lot in common with Lot's wife. Well, except for the whole Sodom and Gomorrah thing. As the red rock turned slowly to gray, she could swear she felt some of the warmth leave her own body. She'd been born in St. George and she'd lived there her whole life. Except for the occasional art show and vacation, she stayed put. She loved St. George and its warm red rock cliffs and plateaus. She would miss hiking Zion's National Park and driving down to Lake Powell for the day. But most of all she was going to miss her mom and Terry. It was easy to leave when you knew you were coming back. It wasn't so easy knowing this was going to be for awhile.

She tried to focus on something less depressing than Alpine, Utah, and turned the radio on. John Mayer—bonus! She sang at the top of her lungs about changing the world for two and a half minutes and then got depressed again as soon as a commercial came on. She turned off the radio and blew her long brown hair out of her eyes. Fine, she would just focus on the positive aspects of uprooting herself and moving to Alpine. Okay, number one, *obviously*, the free house. A lawyer had contacted her two months ago and told her that she had inherited a house from her great-grandmother on her father's side. Her mom was nervous about her accepting it, but *hello*. Free house. So there were some family issues there. Obviously her great-grandmother had thought enough of her to put her in her will.

Okay, reason number two, she needed new inspiration. Maggie had been an artist since the first moment she picked up a crayon and was on the path to being a well-known, respected painter at the young age of twenty-four. She'd gotten amazing reviews at her last showing in San Diego. But when she had flown back from California and picked up her brush, she had just stood there, immobile. *Nothing.* There was nothing inside her wanting to get out. Nothing was flowing. Life just wasn't stimulating her anymore. She'd moped around her house for a month until her mother had told her to knock it off and go find her inspiration. Which worked out well with the house thing. She needed to go check it out. She could see what needed fixing in order to sell it or use it as a summer getaway when the heat hit triple digits in St. George.

So new surroundings, new inspiration, new everything. Which led her to reason number three for leaving. She was twenty-four years old and she was bored to death. It was time to stretch and give her spirit some exercise. Being in one place too long, either physically or mentally, made you weak. And weak was one thing she just wasn't ever going to be.

So, here she was, zooming up I-15, heading toward Alpine. Maggie sighed. *Alpine.* She'd looked it up on the Internet as soon as she found out about the house. It was described as a quaint little town with rich pioneer heritage and beautiful views. Oh, and a ton of rich people. Maggie frowned. She really didn't have anything against rich people. She happened to be one herself now. Her last painting had sold for $450,000. But she hadn't grown up that way. Her mom had raised her single-handedly since her dad had died before she was even born. They were used to living very simply. Her mom worked as a child psychologist for the state of Utah. She worked with children who had been abused and helped prepare them for testifying in court. Her mom lived for her job. Probably because it helped her deal with her own abuse as a child.

Maggie frowned and took a sip of her Propel. Reason number four for going to Alpine. Get a piece of her mom's past back, face her maternal grandmother, and retrieve the pictures of her mom as a little girl before Nathan Palmer had come into the picture.

She and Terry, her mom's husband for the last two years, had talked about it. Terry had been the one to suggest it. Part of the healing process for a lot of people who are victims of child sexual abuse is having a picture of themselves as a pure, happy, innocent child. They have to believe in their beauty and innocence. Her mom had come a long way. She was happy now, and she was healthy, but Terry insisted having that picture would be the final piece of the puzzle in her mom's healing. *Maybe.*

Maggie bit her lip and thought of Terry's last words to her before leaving that morning. "Sometimes your mom still hurts. She cries at night when she thinks I'm sleeping. Maybe she always will. But if she had something to look at . . . you know what I mean. But remember—no information."

Maggie had nodded, knowing exactly what he had meant. She wasn't supposed to give Letty Palmer, her mom's mother, any way to contact her. Terry didn't want her mom having to deal with any confrontations. Her mom had

had to rebuild her life after leaving Alpine. She had married a childhood friend, Maggie's father, but he had died of leukemia four months after their marriage. Lisa Tierney had moved to St. George and picked up the pieces as good as any eighteen-year-old could do. Maggie smiled sadly. And Lisa had done a pretty good job of it.

Maggie turned the radio on again and smiled. She could face anyone for her mom. Her mother had raised her to be strong. No one was going to mess with her when she got to Alpine. Her grandmother was going to hand over her mother's pictures or she was going to be very sorry. And as for her father's family—she wasn't sure. She knew from her mother that the two families had lived next door to each other. Her mom never had much to say about her in-laws. Any time she asked about her dad or his family, her mom's mouth would tighten and her eyes would turn sad. And she always said the same thing. "Sorry sweetie, but at your dad's funeral they made it very clear that they never wanted to see me again. But that's okay. I just feel sorry for them, because I am one of the coolest people I know."

That answer had always worked for her when she was younger, but as she grew older, she knew to ask different questions. *Like, did they even know they had a granddaughter?* Lisa would look away guiltily and shrug, or she'd change the subject. But when Maggie had been contacted by her father's family's lawyer, she'd had her answer. Her grandparents had known. They just hadn't cared enough to contact her. No big deal. So they couldn't care less if they had a granddaughter. Maybe she couldn't care less that she had grandparents.

Maggie frowned and rubbed her forehead. She'd grown up her whole life without relatives. Now she was getting the chance to meet some. Okay, so meeting her mom's mother was going to be nothing less than a nightmare. What did you say to the woman who knew her own daughter was being sexually abused by her stepfather and did nothing to stop it? Maggie felt a shiver run down her spine. It wasn't fear. She wasn't afraid of this woman. It was just plain dread.

She picked up the picture of her house she had put on the seat next to her and glanced at it. It was so cute. A little pioneer home with red brick, a black roof, and the most perfect white front porch. She knew from her mom that it wasn't too close to either one of her grandparents' houses. It was at least a mile down the road. She smiled a little. It looked like a place she could do some serious painting.

Maggie turned the radio back on and sang about putting records on and letting her hair down. She was ready to let her hair down. But was Alpine ready for her? She grinned and sang louder.

Chapter 2

Luke stared at the bright silver convertible BMW pulling up into the driveway next door and frowned. His frown deepened as he saw the tall, skinny woman step out of the car and stand with her hands on her hips as she stared up at the old Tierney house. She was grinning as if she were the queen of the world. Luke sighed. He already couldn't stand her. She had that careless, snobby look that had remodel written all over it. Just what he needed. Construction workers pounding and sawing and waking him up too early. Dust. Dirt. Nails in his tires. Garbage on his lawn, strange liquids in old pop bottles, and worst of all, Tuscany, Italy, right in the middle of the last of the pioneer homes in Alpine. Luke sighed and rubbed his hands over his five o'clock shadow. Mayor Benson was getting pretty sick of him showing up at every town council meeting complaining about losing the feel of old Alpine, but hey, Mayor Benson was his home teacher. He had to put up with him.

He watched morosely as the woman practically skipped to the back of her car, opened up the teeny trunk, and pulled something out. She stacked two boxes, one on top of the other, and tried to put a large easel on top of that. This woman was clearly nuts. Just from that alone he could tell she was impatient. She was so skinny she was probably a vegan member of PETA. He stared at her shoes. He wasn't sure from where he was standing, but they looked like hemp. The typical modern-day anorexic, save-the-rainforests, hemp-wearing pain in the butt. He blinked as she lost her balance and her boxes and her easel went flying into the old brick retaining wall. Her face crumbled and she looked like she was going to cry. *What a girl*. Luke sighed and ran lightly down the stairs and out his front door. He walked up to the woman still hunched sadly over the pieces of wood.

"Hey there. Did you break something?" he asked with just a slight hint of irritation in his voice.

The woman looked up at him in surprise. "Um, yeah. It's my fault. I was being stupid trying to get it all in one load. I just couldn't wait to get started. And now I'll have to make a trip into Salt Lake to get this fixed. Ugh!" she said and stood up, leaving the easel on the ground and wiping her hands on her pants. She stuck her hand out in friendly manner and tried to smile.

"I'm Maggie. You must be my neighbor. So nice to meet you." She smiled, shaking his hand just as good as any rookie police officer, or college football player for that matter. Luke winced at the unexpected crush of bones. She was kind of strong for being so skinny.

"Yeah, likewise. Listen, I've got some tools in my basement. I can fix your easel for you if you'd like," he offered grudgingly.

Maggie's eyebrows shifted up a notch. "No, thanks. I appreciate the offer though," she said, and turned around and lifted one of the boxes in her arms.

Luke frowned at her back. "Look at it as a welcome to the neighborhood gesture. This way I won't have to make you any bread," he said without even a hint of a smile.

Maggie snorted and looked him up and down doubtfully. "Um, no offense, but are you really familiar enough with tools to fix an easel?" she asked with an apologetic wince.

Luke stared at her in shock and looked down at himself. Okay, maybe he was still in a suit and tie, so what. Like that meant he was an idiot.

"Okay, I see how it is. Prejudicial judgments. No problem. Well, then, see ya around," he said with a slight bow, and turned back toward his house with a smile. *Bonus.* He offered, it wasn't accepted, he was off the hook. Now he could get out of his clothes and relax.

"Hey, wait a sec, there. What did you say your name was?" the woman called after him.

Luke hesitated and then turned slowly around. "I didn't. But it's Luke. Luke Petersen," he said, staring at her in a less than friendly way.

Maggie smiled at him winningly. "Listen, Luke. Sorry if I hurt your feelings there. Didn't mean to. Sometimes whatever I'm thinking just pops out on its own. But there is something you could do to help me. You know in that welcoming neighbor thing you just mentioned? Could you just grab my keys and open the front door for me? I've got my hands full here, and that would be really helpful."

Luke stared at her for a few seconds and then walked over to the BMW. No prob. One door and then he was done. He didn't want to fix that easel anyway. Forget that he'd gotten an A in woodshop. Or that his dad and grandpa had taught him everything they knew about craftsmanship. And they knew a lot.

Dang her. He grabbed the keys and walked quickly up the old stone pathway to the front porch. She told him which one was the house key and he shoved the key in, turned it, and then pushed the door open. And then stood there in surprise. The hallway was filled with three separate vases of flowers. Large bouquets of roses and daisies and gladiolas. *Wow.* He ignored Maggie standing behind him, waiting for him to move, and walked down the hall toward something delicious smelling. Something really good. What was that smell? *Pot roast.* Luke stood in the doorway of the kitchen and stared at the counter laden with baskets of rolls, a plastic-wrapped covered salad, and a big note that said the roast was in the oven and to take it out at five o'clock sharp. Luke glanced at the clock. It was three minutes after five. He grabbed the oven mitts and took the roast out, laying it on the waiting hot pads. He peeled back the tinfoil and stared at one of the most beautiful sights in the world. A perfectly cooked roast surrounded by carrots, potatoes, and those cute little onions. *Oh yeah.*

"Hey, you're vegan, right?" he asked over his shoulder.

Maggie walked into the kitchen and stopped in shock. "No way! Is that a pot roast?" she asked, and sort of skip-hopped over to the counter. She picked up the card Luke had read and turned it over, reading it aloud, almost to herself.

Hope you like roast!
This was one of your dad's favorite meals.
Welcome home.
Love,
Grandma and Grandpa Tierney

Luke stared at her curiously as she cleared her throat and rubbed her arms as if she were cold. She placed the card carefully down and sighed. She looked torn about it. Like she couldn't make up her mind whether she was happy about it.

She grabbed a fork sitting by the plate and speared a piece of meat, popping it into her mouth in a way no vegan ever would in this lifetime. Luke's face fell in disappointment as Maggie grinned, obviously deciding that she was happy about it.

"*Mmmmm.* You would not believe how good this is," she said and then took the serving spoon and heaped practically half the roast on her plate and at least three-fourths of the carrots.

Luke watched a little sadly as she sat down and whipped the napkin onto her lap. True, he didn't much like tall, skinny, strangely obnoxious women who didn't believe in his skills with tools, but at that moment in life he would trade his solitary sandwich and chips in a second to have some of that roast.

Maggie looked up in surprise that he was still standing there in her kitchen, staring at her food as if he were starving. "Oops, I forgot to say a prayer. Do you mind?" she asked, and folded her arms. Luke cleared his throat and folded his arms too, closing his eyes and praying she would offer him some roast.

Maggie smiled approvingly and closed her eyes. "We are so grateful for all of our wonderful blessings. Especially this amazing food. And please Lord, help my new neighbor Luke with his troubles and trials. Please ease his burdens and help him with his life." She closed the prayer and then smiled expectantly at him.

Luke stared at her as if she were a strange animal in a zoo. "Okay, I'm out of here," he growled with a little bite of anger in his voice.

Maggie jumped up and grabbed an extra plate. "Hey, I can't eat this entire roast by myself. Care to join me?"

Luke turned back and stared at the most annoying woman he'd met in a long, *long* time, and then looked at the roast. He could eat fast. "Do you have any ketchup?" he asked.

Maggie looked a little shocked but turned and opened the fridge. He stared over her shoulder and noticed that it was fully stocked. What a baby. She had her grandparents do her shopping for her.

"Yep! Here we go. Dig in," she said, and then ignored him and started eating. There was a certain, hearty gusto and passion for food that he hadn't seen since his college days. It was almost heartwarming. He dished up as much as he politely could and then sat next to her at the counter. He hadn't had a roast since his mom had left on his parents' mission. They had been gone for over two years. His dad had been called as a mission president in Honduras.

"Man oh man, this is incredible," he murmured a few moments later.

Maggie took a breath and then got up to get them both a glass of water. "It is good. Did you happen to see my grandparents come over this morning?" she asked, as she handed him the glass.

Luke shook his head. "Nah, I just got home from work right before you got here. Sorry. So hey, I guess I should ask you a little about yourself since we're sharing dinner now and we're neighbors," he said, trying to make an effort.

Maggie smiled and popped another carrot in her mouth. "I guess you should. Well, my name is Margaret Tierney, Maggie to my friends. I'm twenty-four years old. I just inherited this house, so I'll be camping out here for awhile. Umm, I like to paint. And I'm a black belt in Jujitsu. I'm single, no pets either. And I'm ready for a challenge. What about you?" she asked, going back for seconds.

Luke couldn't help it; he laughed. "*Margaret*? Are you serious? Who would name their kid *Margaret*?" he asked with a slight laugh. "That's kind of an old-fashioned name, isn't it?"

Maggie glared at him. "My mom wanted me to have a strong name so I could grow up to be a strong woman. Go figure. And by the way, laughing at someone because of their name is really lame," she said with a stern voice.

Luke tried to look apologetic and stopped smiling. *She was grabbing the rest of the carrots.* She should have mentioned how dang gluttonous she was, because he'd been staring at those carrots for five minutes and if he hadn't been being so polite, they'd be on *his* plate.

Luke had to force himself to stop glaring at Maggie. She was looking at him expectantly. The greet and meet. Got it. "Um, okay, yeah, my turn. My name is Luke Petersen. I'm twenty-seven years old. I'm staying in the house next door while my parents are on their mission, so I can keep an eye on everything. I'm the youngest of seven kids. I'm the manager of a bank down the street. And in my spare time, I like *woodworking*," he said and looked at her blandly.

Maggie raised her eyebrows and her mouth twitched. Almost as if she were trying really hard not to laugh at him. What—a—brat.

"You're a banker, huh? So that must be all those worries and troubles and trials I see on your face," she said knowingly.

Luke rolled his eyes. "Are you one of those girls who are really into horoscopes and reading palms and stuff like that?" he asked in mock sympathy.

Maggie laughed and speared the last potato. "Don't be an idiot. I just noticed you looked really tired and stressed out. Sorry if praying for you made you uncomfortable. I was just taught that if someone has a need, pray for them. No big deal. Man, this was good, huh? I've gotta get the recipe for that."

Luke sighed happily and stood up. "So, thanks. See you around," he said and turned to leave.

"Not so fast. Does this look like McDonalds? It's kind of rude to eat and run, don't you think?" she asked sweetly.

Luke looked back at her in horror. *What now?* She couldn't possibly require more conversation.

"I can't eat this whole cake by myself, now, can I?" she asked even more sweetly.

Luke turned to see what she was pointing at. A real, honest-to-goodness three-tiered, old-fashioned, homemade cake with white buttercream frosting. His stomach did a leap of joy. He'd better stay. He had a feeling that his new neighbor could eat the whole cake by herself easily.

"Of course I'll stay," Luke said heartily and bypassed Maggie to grab a dessert plate and the serving knife. He cut himself as big a piece as would fit on the plate and sat back down at the counter.

Maggie rolled her eyes and took just as big a piece and joined him. "So, in payment for this incredible dinner, I want some info. Give me the lay of the land on this part of town. Who are the neighbors? Who should I look out for? Give me the good, the bad, and the ugly. Shoot," she commanded and started snarfing cake happily.

Luke gave up and smiled as he paused to watch her eat. She was a master at it.

"Well, you know me now. I'm a great neighbor. I'm gone during the days, but I'm home at nights and on the weekends usually. No dogs, no bad habits. I'm the best. On your other side, you have Gwen McFeeny. Now, she has a ton of dogs. She's pretty nice but eccentric. On the opposite street, you have your Buhlers, the Carters, and the Brisbys. The Brisbys have three teenagers. Their two oldest boys are always gone for sports, but the younger daughter is always around. She's pretty sweet. The Carters have a four-year-old who likes to run in the street, so watch out for him. And the Buhlers are a retired couple who like to work in their yard. Easy. You moved into a really decent neighborhood. No big secrets. Nothing exciting. Just boring, old Alpine."

Maggie's face flinched at his last sentence. Luke's eyes narrowed at her. Something had bothered her about what he'd said. But what?

"No big secrets, huh? I wish," she said sort of sadly and then looked away. "Okay then. So tell me what you know about the Tierneys," she said and got up to get another piece of cake.

Luke glared at the cake but relaxed when he saw more than half was still waiting for him.

"Hmm, oh yeah, the Tierneys. Well, as you know, since she was your great-grandmother, she recently died. Sister Teirney was really cool. I liked her. She always made me brownies when she knew I was coming over. Her son and daughter-in-law, your grandparents, visited her a lot and made sure the walks were always clear and the garbage was always taken out and the grocery shopping was done. This last year was pretty hard on them I think. They brought in a nurse to help her in the end."

Maggie nodded and kept eating. "Okay, so now my . . . *grandparents*. Tell me about them," she said more softly.

Luke stared at her expressionless face and shrugged. "Well, they're *your* grandparents. Don't you know?" he asked, bewildered.

Maggie shrugged and got up to put her dish in the sink. "Not really. We haven't been close by any means. I don't even really know them," she said honestly as she turned the water on and rinsed the crumbs.

Luke stared in surprise at her back but did as he was told. "Frank and Bonnie Tierney. They live just a mile up the road. Up toward Sliding Rock. I don't know them really well, since they're not in our ward, but Sister Tierney talked about them all the time. I guess Frank and Bonnie have had it kind of hard. Their daughter, Ellie, died in a car crash when she was sixteen leaving a dance, and their son ran away from home when he was eighteen instead of staying in the hospital for chemotherapy. I guess he had leukemia. He'd already beaten it once before when he was a little kid. They say he'd still be alive today if he'd just stuck the treatment out, but then he ran off with . . ." Luke paused and stared at Maggie. "Your mother?" he asked.

Maggie sat back down in stunned silence. Her dad ran away from treatment that could have saved his life? Had her mother known? She shook her head to clear the distress.

"Go on, please," she motioned and looked away from Luke's piercing eyes.

Luke cleared his throat and pushed his plate away, no longer hungry.

"Sorry. I was just spouting off, but it's your family. It's your life. Look, if you want to know, just call them. It doesn't take a detective to know that someone who loves you or *wants to* love you made this dinner and filled your hallway with flowers."

Maggie looked down at her hands blindly. Yeah, but did she want to know them? Love them? She stood up suddenly, tired of the conversation.

"You're right, Luke. Well, thanks for stopping by," she said, standing as a hint.

Luke smiled in relief and popped up. "Yeah, no problem. Here's my business card if you ever need anything. My cell's on there. See ya around, *Margaret*," he said and walked down the hallway, letting himself out.

He walked quickly back to his home—his uncomplicated, relaxing, happy home—and couldn't wait to shut the door on Maggie Tierney. She was too complicated. Too everything. Maybe she would just lose his business card, he wondered hopefully. He slouched down on his couch and flicked on the television. Now, back to life.

Chapter 3

Maggie stared at the closed door and stood there for a few moments. *Wow.* So that was her neighbor. Luke Petersen. He was kind of cute if you ignored his innate grouchiness. His dark brown hair was slightly wavy and kind of appealing if you were into that kind of thing. And he was at least four inches taller than her. Since she was 5'10" that was saying something. She liked his eyes. They were a mixture of so many colors. She guessed they were hazel, but when she'd told him he couldn't fix her easel, she could have sworn they were bright blue. She'd have to make him angry again and see exactly what shade of blue they were. Of course when he had taken his first bite of cake, she could have sworn they were a bright green. Amazing.

And he was kind of funny for being such a grouch. Kind of like Oscar in a really nice suit. And he was the one person she knew who could eat as much as she could. She looked down at the business card in her hand. *Yikes.* A banker. She shrugged and shoved it in her pocket. She doubted they'd run into each other very much, but still. He was cute.

She walked back out to her car and grabbed her small suitcase and a few blank canvases. She had come prepared. She locked up the car and turned to look around her neighborhood before going in. She stared at the mountains. They were so different from her red rock plateaus, but there was something there. There was definite beauty and strength. She stared down her street at the quaint small homes and the perfectly manicured yards. It was all so . . . *nice.* Different, but nice. She didn't know what kind of inspiration she was going to get from nice, but she was giving herself six months to find it. She waved cheerfully at a couple walking a large dog down the street and went in the house. She set her suitcase down and looked around to explore. She started with the front room.

Living room, den? She wasn't sure what they called the front room a hundred years ago. Maybe just *front room*. It was tiny by modern standards but perfect for meeting with visiting teachers or anyone you didn't want seeing your messy kitchen. She hadn't known the house would be furnished. The couch was old. Maybe as old as the house and covered in a soft gold velvet. She ran her hands over the wooden back and smiled at the beautiful craftsmanship. She walked over to the ancient piano set up against the wall and picked up a slightly dusty picture.

A family. A little old lady with bright white, short curly hair surrounded by smiling people. This must be her great-grandmother, Elisabeth Tierney. She studied the people surrounding the woman. A man and a woman and two children who looked to be about fourteen and fifteen. She zeroed in on the teenage boy and knew immediately it was her father. Her mother only had one picture of her father since they had run away from home to get married—their wedding picture. Maggie didn't like to look at it much because her dad looked so skeletal and gray in it. He was smiling happily with his arm around her mother's shoulders but his eyes looked incredibly sad and tired.

But in this picture he was healthy and happy as if he didn't have a care in the world. He was as tall as his father in the picture and he looked strong. She couldn't believe how blonde he was; his hair was almost white. Well, she definitely got her looks from her mother. She stared closer at his eyes and stopped. She had her father's eyes. Bright, clear perfect blue. Her mom's eyes were brown. Hmm. Maybe there was something about the face too that reminded her of what she saw in her mirror. Something about the bone structure. Huh. *Her dad.* Maggie reached up and wiped a tear off her cheek and closed her eyes. He looked nice. He looked like someone she would have liked to have known. He looked like someone who would have loved her.

She put the picture down and turned to look at the picture hanging on the opposite wall. She stepped closer to get a better look. The picture itself was only about 16 x 24, but it had been matted and framed expensively. It was a painting of a girl with long, wavy brown hair and brown eyes. She was sitting next to a tree with her knees pulled up to her chest and her hands clasped over her knees. The girl had tears on her cheeks and sad eyes. Maggie looked at the picture and noticed the awkward shading and the untrained lines, but there was something there. There was love in this picture. And quite a bit of talent. Maggie smiled and turned to walk away when she noticed the signature at the bottom of the painting. She reached out and ran her hand over her father's signature. Robert Tierney, 1980. She looked back at the picture and realized who it was. *It was her mother.* Maggie felt as if her heart had stopped beating. She stood very still and took this image of a moment in her parents' life inside her. Her father had painted this picture of her mom as a girl. He had seen the sadness and the pain and he had cared. It was written right there on the canvas for anyone to see. Her heart ached for the two young people her parents had been, faced with trials and situations that most kids should never have to face.

She whisked more tears off her face and sighed. She would come back to this room later. Right now she needed to see the rest of her house. She turned and walked out of the room toward the stairs leading to the second story. The staircase was so old-fashioned. Her long, narrow feet barely fit on the treads. She ran lightly up the stairs and peeked in all three bedrooms briefly before walking back to the largest one. The bed was made with a beautiful handmade patchwork quilt and there were more fresh flowers sitting on the dresser. It was almost spooky knowing her grandparents had been here sometime today, putting fresh sheets on the bed and making her dinner. As nice as that was, she needed to change the locks. She grabbed her cell phone out of her pocket and dialed information. It took less than three minutes to schedule the locksmith for the following day. She walked over to the bed and noticed a small note sitting on the pillow. She picked it up and opened it carefully.

Dear Maggie,

We hope you enjoyed your dinner and that you like the house. Please call if you need anything!
(801) 543-6758.

Grandma and Grandpa Tierney

Hmm. It was just so surreal. Her fridge was stocked with tons of food, she'd had a wonderful meal just waiting for her to walk in the door and eat, and now, fresh flowers everywhere and clean sheets. No birthday cards. No calls on Christmas. But the nicest "welcome home" she could have ever imagined. It just didn't make sense.

Maggie shrugged and put the note down on the dresser. She walked over to the window and stared down into her backyard. Maggie stepped closer and her mouth opened in surprise. Her whole backyard was covered in flowers. Her grandparents hadn't spent any money on the flowers—it was all right here. Maggie turned and ran down the stairs and out the back door. She walked slowly through the yard, staring at the profusion of color. It wasn't a large yard by any means, but everywhere she looked there were flower beds—raised, surrounding trees, and following little rock paths. And a real, honest-to-goodness birdbath. She didn't know a lot about flowers, just that she liked them, but she recognized the roses and the zinnias and the daisies and the gladiolas. The color and smell were intense. She breathed deeply and closed her eyes, lifting her arms high above her head and smiled. She felt a warm breeze drift over her face as she let her arms drop. And then, for the heck of it, she did a back handspring, and then felt so good, she did one more. She laughed and turned around one more time, staring at her new backyard before walking toward the house. She was surrounded by extraordinary color, she had a beautiful home, her stomach was full, and for some reason she felt like she was getting closer to knowing a little bit more about her father. She grinned at her new world and walked back inside. She had made the right decision to come to Alpine. She couldn't wait to unpack her paints.

Chapter 4

The man and woman peeking through the hole in the fence straightened up and stared at each other with surprised smiles before turning and walking quickly back across the street. The man had to pull extra hard to get Barney, their Mastiff, to follow.

"Come on ol' boy. No playing in the flowers today. Maggie is there now. This is her home and she wouldn't want a mutt like you messing things up," he said with a happy laugh.

The woman grinned and slid her arm through her husband's. "Did you see her, Frank? Did you see her face? She might have Lisa's hair and coloring, but that's Robbie's daughter. She has the same look to her."

The man nodded and patted his wife's hand. "I saw. I saw. Man oh man, did you see the way she flipped her body around like she was some kind of circus star? I thought you said she was an artist?" he asked with a shake of his head.

Bonnie smiled and lifted her face to the wind. "She *is* an artist. I showed you those pictures on the Internet. But you know what else she is? She's *our* granddaughter."

Frank's smile slipped a notch, and he looked down at his wife in worry. "Now don't go getting your hopes up, Bonnie. You know this doesn't mean anything. She probably doesn't want anything to do with us. Her mom's probably told her we're the worst people in the world. Just hold back on planning a family reunion," he said more sternly than he felt.

Bonnie clucked her tongue and looked back at the house her husband had grown up in before turning the corner. "I know what I saw Frank, and you're not going to change my mind. I just saw an amazing young woman who

15

waves at strangers, and gets so happy at the sight of flowers that she jumps for joy. Now does that sound like someone who wouldn't want to know her own grandparents?" she asked with a snap in her voice.

Frank smiled and shook his head. "You might be right. You just might be right. Now that she's here, what are you going to do to keep Letty Palmer from finding out about her? What if she scares her off and she leaves?" Frank asked, his smile completely disappearing.

Bonnie frowned just as darkly. "I just got my granddaughter back, there's no way I'm going to allow Letty to scare her off," she said firmly.

Frank paused while Barney sniffed at a tree. "Maggie is Letty's granddaughter too, Bonnie," he said softly.

Bonnie crossed her arms over her chest and looked down at her feet. "There's being someone's grandparent biologically and then there's being someone's grandma. Letty's life is what Letty has made of it. Well, mine is what I'm going to make of it. And I'm going to do whatever I can to make sure that young woman feels at home here. This is Robbie's daughter, Frank! She's ours. And to be honest, I don't think Letty would care one way or the other even if she knew Maggie was here. You know that," she said without any heat.

Frank sighed and took his wife's hand as they continued walking home. "Letty Palmer is the saddest person I've ever known. Maybe knowing Maggie would be good for her," he offered.

Bonnie glared at a rock before kicking it. "Knowing Lisa would have been good for her too," she said simply.

Frank winced at the old memories and walked on, trying not to remember the past and its ugly history.

"Lisa Palmer. She was so beautiful, poor thing," Frank murmured softly.

Bonnie sighed and nodded in agreement. "From the looks of Maggie, I say Lisa did a good job raising her. She seems so happy and carefree. I wish Robbie could see his daughter. He'd be so proud."

The two walked in silence for a few minutes pausing here and there to let their dog explore and sniff.

"Robbie wants this, Frank. I just know he does. Forget about Letty and forget about the past. Our granddaughter is here now and she's a part of us. She'll come to us. I just know she will. Oh, Frank, I'll make my peach cobbler for her. Robbie always loved that best. And I could make some fried chicken and mashed potatoes. She's so thin, the poor thing; I don't think she ever eats. I hope she's not anorexic. We've got to fatten her up. Do you think she'll come for Christmas this year? Can you imagine?" Bonnie asked, her eyes lighting up as she dreamed of the future.

Frank laughed and put his arm around his wife's shoulders and squeezed her tight. "I can imagine, my dear."

The two held hands as they walked the mile back to their home. Neighbors and friends waved and honked as they passed the Tierneys and wondered what had happened to put such large grins on their faces.

Chapter 5

Maggie finished duct taping her easel together and set it up right in the middle of the backyard. She placed the canvas and picked up her brush. This was her favorite part. Picking colors. She liked to imagine that she had something in common with God when she picked up her brush. She'd seen his sunsets. She knew an artist when she saw one.

She felt yellow today. She dipped her brush and starting painting a sun drenched garden. True, the pieces she sold in galleries were bold and aggressive, more reminiscent of Gustav Klimt than anyone from the Impressionistic era, but right then, standing in her great-grandmother's backyard, surrounded by her flowers, her canvas called for a sun-drenched imprint of happiness. Maggie concentrated and hoped Monet was looking down from heaven and that he was maybe just a little bit jealous. The light was starting to fade fast, but she could finish later. She worked quickly to get the bones of the picture and then did what she always did. All of her pictures always had a person in them. For no reason at all, she decided to paint her father. She placed him right in the middle of the backyard, looking blonde and healthy and happy. And maybe a dog. She thought about the large dog the couple had been walking earlier and knew he'd be perfect. She worked on it for another hour and then sighed in contentment. Most of the time she just painted for pure enjoyment. Kate, her agent, would visit her every few months and take pictures to put on her website. She had showings twice a year now, although Kate was pushing for more. But she didn't want to turn her joy into drudgery. Maggie put her arm down and studied what she had just done. She tilted her head and couldn't wait to finish. The way the light shimmered through the leaves onto the flower petals was just delicious.

She picked her canvas up and her paint box and walked back into the house.

She laid the canvas on the table and immediately started washing the acrylics out of her brushes. She stood at the sink with the cold water running over her hands and brushes and stared into the backyard as the sun set and the shadows overtook the flowers. There was something about this house that was grabbing hold of her. It was like two arms were reaching out and embracing her in a way she'd never felt before. She loved the house she had just bought a year ago in St. George. And her mom's little two bedroom house by the golf course was cute and comfortable. But this was different. She couldn't put her finger on it, but she was going to figure it out before she left. She turned the water off and dried her hands as she stared out the window and thought about her first day in Alpine.

She already loved her house and even though she didn't know her grandparents, at least she knew she loved their cooking. She loved all the flowers in her yard and she loved the sense of homecoming she was immersed in. For whatever reason life had brought her here, she was glad. She felt a sense of excitement and wasn't even sure why. Painting was the best feeling in the world, and feeling her energy and her creativity spark again was incredible, but it was even more than that. She walked through the house and out onto the front porch so she could sit and watch the sunset.

She sat down and stared around her new neighborhood at the microcosm that was now her new life, and she felt a great sense of gratitude. To her great-grandmother Tierney, to her father, to her mother, and to God especially. She sighed happily and listened to the crickets and people driving by and calling out to each other. As she sat in the shadows of her porch, she was content to be unnoticed as she drank in the feel of Alpine. For now.

Chapter 6

Luke stared as the silver convertible glided up to the house next door. Maggie Tierney had only been in town two weeks, and already things were different. Okay, she hadn't started remodeling. *Yet.* But everything felt different. It reminded him of chemistry. You add one wrong ingredient, and not only does everything change, but that change could include an explosion.

He stared at her from his upstairs window as she hopped out of the car and shut the door with her hip. She actually looked around and smiled at nothing and no one in particular. *Who did that?* Luke watched morosely as Maggie took her bags of whatever into the house with her. He frowned and then frowned even more deeply when he realized that he was hoping she'd come back out. He turned away from the window in surprise. *What was he doing?* Okay, yes. She was attractive. Maybe even more than just attractive, but so what. She was so annoying. Just yesterday when he had gone to get his mail, she had run out of the house as if she had been waiting for him and asked him dumb questions about everything from plumbing problems, to Alpine history, to gardening.

Luke walked downstairs to make himself dinner. Maybe she was lonely? Maybe she had just wanted someone to talk to? He wished she'd just find someone else to ask. Every time he got around her, it made him feel . . .

Luke stopped suddenly and closed his eyes. *She made him feel.* And react. Even if it was just feeling annoyance or irritation or, *okay,* amusement. Maggie could be funny. He had to give her that. He opened the fridge and frowned again. He wasn't sure if he wanted to feel anything though. Feeling just led to pain and he'd had enough of that in the last year. *Plenty.*

Luke pulled out some ham and cheese and shut the door when he heard the doorbell ring. He groaned loud and long as he walked quickly to the door, squinting through the peephole. *Maggie!* He swung the door wide open and looked at her curiously. What in the world could she want now? "Hey."

"Hi, Luke. I noticed your car, so I figured you were home. I brought you over something. I was in a cute little health food store today getting vitamins, and I remembered how you're always talking about vegans and hemp and PETA and everything, so I saw this, and I just knew I had to get it for you," she said, holding out one of the sacks she had carried in from her car.

Luke raised his eyebrows and looked suspiciously at the bag held out to him. He hadn't gotten a present in a really long time. He reached out and took the bag and opened it up. Huh. *A T-shirt?* He pulled it out and dropped the bag by his feet and unfolded the white T-shirt and turned it around. It was a picture of a butchered cow with writing in blood red. *I'd rather die than eat meat.*

Luke looked from the T-shirt to Maggie's wide innocent eyes and frowned. He wasn't buying it.

"So you saw this and just knew I'd want it. That's it?" he asked politely.

Maggie smiled cheerfully. "Well, I've never met anyone who talks about PETA so much. Or remodeling for that matter. Next time I'm in Salt Lake, I'll try and find you a T-shirt with Italian architecture on it." She couldn't help bringing up those early misconceptions he had asked her about a few days after she moved in—he was such an easy target.

Luke's eyes turned to slits. *She was teasing him.* Who did she think she was, teasing *him*?

"Well, *gosh.* Thanks, Maggie. You're just a real sweetheart, aren't you?" he said acidly.

Maggie held a hand up to her mouth but just nodded mutely. She mumbled a "see ya later" and turned and fled. Luke walked out on his porch and watched her make her way back to her house and couldn't help hearing her laughter. She was giggling all the way back to her house, at his expense.

Luke felt his lips quiver, and he looked down at the shirt bunched in his hands. It was kind of funny. And it's possible he might have deserved it. Point taken. He'd lay off the hemp/PETA/remodeling accusations in the future. He glanced back at Maggie's house and felt his lips curve up. Maggie Tierney. There was definitely some chemistry there. The question was, was he willing to take a chance on everything blowing up in his face—again? He walked back in the house and put his new T-shirt on. And for some reason, for the rest of the night, he was *almost* in a good mood.

Chapter 7

Maggie laughed all the way back inside her house and then collapsed on a kitchen chair. The look on his face was priceless. She'd been wanting to take him down a peg or two ever since the day they had met. Now, maybe he'd lay off all of the assumptions about her and get to know her. Because for some reason, grouchy, rotten personality aside, she kind of wanted to get to know him. That, or she was just a sucker for crazy-colored eyes.

She pushed the hair out of her eyes, still smiling, and decided she felt like painting. She didn't want to waste the high she was in, so she grabbed her gear and headed to the backyard. She automatically looked up to Luke's window, next door. Sometimes, she'd look up and see him staring down into her yard. He didn't seem to be looking at her though. It was more like he was staring at her canvas instead. As if he couldn't believe she was really painting. He wasn't there now. He was probably cutting his new T-shirt up into rags.

Maggie laughed softly and then got to work, forgetting all about Luke, his crummy personality, and everything else in the world. The only thing that mattered was the vision in her mind, transforming itself into the painting before her eyes.

She worked late into the evening, later than she should have probably. But when she hit her stride, it was almost painful to stop. She laid her brushes down and stared up into the sky at the wisps of red and gold turning into gray and sighed happily. It had been a good day. Her painting felt like it was just flowing out of her. She grabbed everything but her easel and headed inside. She cleaned up quickly and then made herself a quick dinner of chicken salad from her dinner the night before. After devouring the salad, some garlic bread, and a bowl of ice cream, she almost felt human again. She took her dishes to the sink to rinse them out and paused in surprise. Someone was walking out of the shadows and into her backyard. The person walked right up to her easel and picked it up. Maggie stared in shock as the person turned around with her easel and started walking off with it. Maggie sputtered and squawked and then ran for the back door. No way was anyone stealing her easel.

She ran as fast as her long legs could take her and tried to do it quietly. She was going to tackle this psycho and give him something to remember her by. She whipped past the privet hedge and leaped over the small bench. The thief turned his head for a second but it was too late. She was already airborne. She tackled the thief and went rolling with him, cringing as she heard the snapping of wood.

"What the heck!" yelled a masculine voice.

Maggie popped up and went into her fighting stance with her arms up and her knees slightly bent. She stalked around the intruder until she had cut him off from escape.

"Bring it," she said in as menacing a voice as she could muster. She'd practiced situations like this with her mom down at the martial arts studio more times than she'd like to remember, but this was her first real encounter. She felt the adrenaline whipping through her system and bared her teeth. He was tall, but she could take him.

"Are you stinking nuts? What is this? Some Jackie Chan movie? Just relax," the man commanded in a gruff voice.

"Luke?" Maggie asked, shocked and surprised. She lowered her arms and stepped closer, looking at the man's face. It was dark, but she could make out his wavy hair and strange eyes.

"Luke, what do you think you're doing coming into my backyard and stealing my easel? *I saw you do it with my own eyes.* Are you insane?" she demanded, and forgot about Jujitsu and went straight for her hands on her hips and her toe tapping.

Luke glared right back. "Not as insane as you! What if I was a real thief and I had a gun? You'd be dead. Dang, Maggie, don't you even think?"

Maggie's eyes glittered in fury and she stepped closer as if she were going to kick him in the jaw. "I'm totally willing, right now, to show you what I can do to an unarmed man."

Luke cleared his throat and decided to change tactics.

"Hey, I had no idea my life was in jeopardy here. I just happened to see you out my back window painting and noticed the crummy repair job you did with *duct tape*, and thought I'd just go the extra mile as a good neighbor and fix the stupid easel whether you wanted me to or not. And now, thanks to you, the thing's even more shattered," he accused, pointing to the pile of wood that was once a very expensive and treasured easel.

Maggie's mouth opened in shock that he was turning this entirely around on her. What nerve.

"I believe I told you I'd rather you *didn't* fix my easel," she said tightly, tapping her toe even faster now.

Luke looked down at her foot and back to her face. "Look, your foot is going to fall off if you don't slow down. Please, for the love of Pete, don't karate chop me. Just follow me. I'll show you my wood shop, and then if you don't trust me to touch your precious easel, I won't. I'll leave you and your duct tape alone. I promise," he said with his hands up and with as sincere an expression on his face as he could muster.

Maggie glared at him and glanced at her easel. She groaned and knelt down by the wood. "I loved this easel. It was a present from my mom when I was sixteen. It was her way of saying, 'I stand behind you. I'll support you in your dreams.' She has such a hard time expressing herself and this easel was her way. Now it's ruined," she said sadly.

Luke stared down at her and waited a second before bending down and picking up every piece of wood he could find. Maggie got up and followed him toward his house. He walked into a side door, and she followed him into the kitchen and down into the basement. His house was old like hers and had a few too many cobwebs. She reminded herself she needed to check out her own basement. She rubbed her shoulders as she felt the cool air. He flicked on a light and walked down a hallway to the last door. He opened it and turned on the light and then turned to see her face.

Maggie's mouth fell open. It was every woodshop teacher's dream. It had saws of every kind. Sanders and tools she couldn't even name. Benches and saw horses. And in the corner a beautiful chest of drawers someone was obviously in the middle of making.

"Are you? I mean, did *you* . . . um, did you do that?" she asked, motioning toward the chest of drawers.

Luke shrugged and placed her easel and all of its abused pieces on an empty table. "Yep, and before you start apologizing, just let me say one thing. It better be good. So get started," he said.

Maggie laughed and shook her head. "Okay, okay, so maybe I misjudged you. But hello, I look up and here's this banker guy offering to touch my best easel. Come on, give me a break," she said, shrugging with a grin.

Luke shook his head and leaned against a bench, crossing his arms over his chest. "Nah, that just isn't going to cut it, I'm afraid. I'm sure you can do better than that."

Maggie snorted and shook her head. "Don't push it. I can still get you for trespassing, stealing, and mental cruelty. So how about you just fix my easel like a good neighbor, and we'll call it even?" she said, raising an eyebrow.

Luke grinned all of a sudden. "Mental cruelty, huh? What are you? A lawyer? But fine, *fine*, I don't want a lawsuit on my hands. I'd win of course, but I'm too busy these days working on my chest over there. That was some tackle though. I haven't been hit that hard since I played football in high school," he said, looking at her with new respect.

Maggie grinned proudly. "Trust me, you don't want to mess with me. My mom raised me to take on anyone. And just to warn you, I have a taser and I know how to use it," she said, walking over to the chest and running her hands over the smooth wood.

"I'd like to meet your mother. She sounds like a very interesting person. She'd have to be to raise you," he said.

Maggie looked at him quickly, looking for the insult but couldn't see it in his face. She shrugged and agreed with him. "Yeah, you could say that. She's the most amazing person I know."

Luke started to say something when they both heard the faint sound of the front doorbell being rung.

Luke winced and motioned for her to follow him. Luke walked tiredly up the stairs, and Maggie followed closely behind him. He acted like he already knew who was ringing the bell. And that wasn't a happy look on his face. She stood behind him as he opened the door. She peeked around his shoulders to see a beautiful blonde woman standing in the doorway. She was gorgeous and so petite. Almost like a china doll. Her hair was down past her shoulders and perfectly straight. Her brown eyes were warm and looking at Luke in what Maggie could only describe as adoration. She was dressed in simple jeans and a T-shirt, but Maggie could tell they were expensive. She was just darling. She had no idea why Luke wouldn't be thrilled to death to open his front door to this woman.

"Hey, Luke. I knew you'd probably be sad today, so I thought I'd come over and keep you company. I made you some oatmeal raisin cookies—your favorite," she said and stepped toward Luke, holding the plate toward him.

Maggie could actually feel all of Luke's muscles tense up next to her, almost as if he were getting ready to run for it. She frowned and sensed that something was wrong.

"Hey, Jennie. Sorry, but this isn't a good time. Maggie, my new friend, is over and we kind of have the whole night planned out."

Maggie watched with interest as Jennie's mouth fell open in shock, and Luke moved out of the way so Jennie could see her. Luke turned and smiled at her grimly as he raised his eyebrows slightly. Code for *just go with it*. Maggie rolled her eyes and sighed. Luke put his arm around her shoulders and brought her in close to his body.

"Jennie, this is Maggie Tierney. Maggie, this is Jennie Benchley."

Jennie stared at her as if she were a grimy, dirty, disease-soaked leach. "I've heard of people in mourning doing crazy things, but this is just sad, Luke. Maggie did you say? Maggie, listen. I'm going to make this crystal clear for you. This poor man that you're taking advantage of is the sweetest, most loving man in the world. His heart has been shattered. He is not ready for *friendship* yet. And your being here today of all days is just taking advantage of a man when he's at his weakest. I'd appreciate it if you left. *Now*," she said, frowning at Maggie darkly and holding her plate of cookies as if they were weapons.

Maggie blinked in surprise, and she turned and looked up at Luke. He looked at her so pleadingly she felt an incredible urge to save him. She saw Jennie's toe start to tap and thought, *What the heck?*

"You could be right, Jen. But then, if you knew Luke the way *I* did, you'd see that he *is ready* to be my friend, and that he's been ready for a long time. I don't think he'll be needing your cookies anymore," she said in a bright voice that was more suited to teaching kindergartners than fighting off a territorial woman.

Jen's face froze and her brown eyes looked like they were about to explode. She turned away from Maggie, completely ignoring her, and focused on Luke again.

"Luke, don't you think Melanie is looking down from heaven right now and wondering what you're doing? She's only been gone six months. What would people say? I brought over some of Melanie's scrapbooks. They're in my car. I thought you and I could look through them together. I mean, this was supposed to be your wedding day. I'm not sure what people would think if they knew that you were spending the evening with another woman," she said in a strangely soothing voice.

Maggie looked quickly at Luke and saw the harsh pain on his face. She felt her heart break for him. So he'd obviously been engaged and even more obviously, his fiancée had died somehow. No wonder he was grouchy. But whatever heartache he was experiencing right now, this woman wasn't helping. Luke needed help. And as his neighbor . . . well, she was just a naturally neighborly person.

"I'm sorry, Jen. Now's not a good time. But thanks for the cookies," Maggie said and promptly took the plate out of Jennie's hands and closed the door squarely in her face. She and Luke watched as it took a moment for Jennie to realize what had happened and to stomp back to her car and drive away on squealing tires.

Maggie pulled the tinfoil off the cookies and picked one up. "Good timing. I'm starving," she said, and took a bite.

Luke's shoulders relaxed, and he started grinning. He surprised her by chuckling, and then shocked her by bending over and laughing helplessly. Maggie had seen this before so she just gently patted him on the back while he wheezed and got himself under control. She put the cookie and the plate down on the hallway table and leaned against the wall as Luke got his breath back.

"Sorry, but those cookies are just nasty," she said, wiping crumbs from her mouth.

Luke looked at her and smiled. It wasn't his usual grouchy, sarcastic smile either. It was big and genuine. Maggie smiled back. *Good.* They were friends now.

"That was the nicest thing anyone's ever done for me," he said sincerely and with a touch of awe in his voice.

Maggie shrugged and tried not to blush. "It was the right thing to do. I hate to see anyone pitied to death. Want to tell me about it?" she asked simply.

Luke looked down at his feet for a few seconds and sighed. "Of course not. But I guess I owe you. I've got some ice cream in my freezer, if you're not too full from dinner?" he offered.

Maggie laughed. "One thing you should know about me, Luke. I'm never full." She followed him into his kitchen and couldn't help snickering at the lace curtains and flowered wallpaper.

Luke shrugged. "Hey, it was my grandmother's house and she loved this kitchen. My mom refuses to change a thing about it. My mom and dad use this as a rental. Their house is up by the rodeo grounds. I didn't want to stay all three years in such a big house though, so I stay here. I go up a few times a week to check on the house and do yard work. It's not much for free rent," he said, opening the freezer and grabbing two small cartons of Ben & Jerry's.

Maggie grabbed the Cherry Garcia before Luke had turned around with the spoons. When he saw her hands cradling the ice cream possessively, he glared at her. "Man, I've got to watch you like a hawk," he said as he picked up the plain chocolate.

She took the spoon he held out to her and sat down at the small wooden kitchen table. She snagged one of the other chairs and kicked her feet up on it, slouching back.

The two ate in harmonious silence for a few minutes before Luke broke the silence. "I was supposed to get married today. Our invitations hadn't been sent out yet, but they were ordered. The honeymoon had been scheduled. It was all set in stone. Six months ago, Melanie flew down to Arizona to stay the weekend at some spa down there. When she came back she complained of not feeling well. Her mom and dad rushed her to the hospital, where she died two hours later of internal bleeding and an infection. I was up in Salt Lake at a meeting and didn't even get to say good-bye."

Maggie's eyebrows shot up and her spoon paused in its descent. "Internal bleeding?" she whispered.

Luke nodded and took another bite, closing his eyes at the memories. "Yeah.

She had flown down to Arizona with one of her best friends. They both had some liposuction done, from what I understand, and something went wrong. She just had to look perfect for the wedding pictures. That was Melanie though. Perfection. She couldn't stand getting B's. She couldn't stand coming in second place. It was always top of the class for Melanie. That's why I guess we waited so long to get engaged. Melanie wanted her master's degree in business first. She had her whole life planned out and being the best was just always part of the plan. And she couldn't stand the thought of not being the thinnest, most beautiful bride ever. Don't get me wrong. She wasn't stuck up or rotten or obnoxious. She was accepting of everyone else and their faults. She just couldn't give herself a break. And she died for it. And now, ever since, I've had Melanie's younger sister Jennie, whom you just met, doing her best to comfort me and be there for me and help me through this dark time in my life. Along with everyone else in Alpine. I'm thinking maybe I should move just to get away from the constant shower of pity and kindness and cards and cookies," he said, stabbing his ice cream viciously.

Maggie winced for him. "You're a walking car wreck. People have to stop and stare. It's what they do. They don't mean any harm by it," she said, tilting her head a little to look at him.

Luke nodded. "That's it exactly. I'm so tired of the gawking and the pity. Can't I just move on with my life?" he asked.

Maggie shook her head. "People don't like that much either. Take Jen for instance. If you moved on, where would that leave her? She's still mourning her sister. She's not ready for you to move on. And FYI, I sensed a little more than almost sister-in-law concern there. I think Jen means to comfort your heart by stepping in," Maggie said gently.

Luke rolled his eyes. "You're only the millionth person to point that out. I swear I'm not an idiot. I don't know why people assume that."

Maggie smiled and picked a cherry out of her carton. "For what it's worth, I'm really sorry. I know things like this take a long time to get over. If you ever want to show me some of her pictures or go see her grave together, I'd be happy to go with you," Maggie said.

Luke stared at her in surprise. "Really? I mean, you'd do that? It's just so hard sometimes. My mom and dad are gone, and all of my brothers and sisters are great, but they're so busy with their own families, and I can't handle talking to Melanie's family. I just feel like I'm drowning when I'm with them now."

Maggie nodded. "Have you gone to her grave since the funeral?" Luke shook his head guiltily. Maggie frowned. "Hey, there's no right or wrong when it comes to mourning. You just deal with it the way you deal with it. Why don't we take some flowers from my yard over to the cemetery sometime? I bet they'd make her grave look beautiful," she said, taking another bite.

Luke nodded his head. "Look, I don't even know you. I mean, we just met and here you are talking to me about Melanie and offering to go to her grave with me, and it's just so strange. I mean, doesn't this freak you out just a little?" he demanded, staring at her.

Maggie smiled and laughed softly. "My mom's been a grief counselor, a rape crises counselor, and she's worked all the hotlines. I've grown up with grief. Me and him are pretty good buddies. Sometimes it's just easier to tell a complete stranger how you're feeling than someone who knows you. No biggie," she said and stood up to look for the garbage can. She found it under the sink and threw her carton away.

"Well, whatever it is. Thanks. I really appreciate it," he said gruffly, looking down in embarrassment.

Maggie grinned and crossed her arms over her chest, studying him. "Come on. Show me a picture of Melanie. I've got to see what kind of woman was able to snare you," she said, motioning for him to get up.

Luke threw his carton away and walked out of the kitchen into a small family room. He picked up a large photo album and sat down with it. Maggie sat next to him and opened it to picture upon picture of a beautiful, small, blonde woman who looked at the camera with the confidence of polish and style. Maggie waited for Luke to take control but realized he couldn't. So she started turning the pages and pointing to things of interest. "Wow, she was really stunning. Oh, look at you two! *So cute.* I can't believe anyone voted you prom king, Luke. Oh my heck, you on a mission!"

Maggie went through the pictures, laughing and smiling and trying to open the door for a little happy to sneak back into Luke's memories. He sat in complete silence as Maggie talked and talked. When she came to the end, she shut the book and put it on an end table beside her.

"What has been the hardest thing for you?" Maggie asked, looking at the grim person beside her.

Luke blinked a few times and then looked up at her. "Knowing I didn't love her enough. If I'd loved her enough, she would have known that she didn't need to be perfect. She would still be alive," he said simply, and then stood up.

Maggie frowned but didn't say anything and stood up too and walked with him to the front door. Maggie smiled and took his hand in hers, shocking him with the physical contact. "It's going to be okay, Luke," she said, and walked out the door and into the night.

Luke stared out after her and blinked hard a few times until the moisture in his eyes disappeared. His mom and dad had told him that six months ago, and he hadn't been ready to understand that then. He could almost believe it, though, when Maggie said it. He shut the door and walked back downstairs to the wood shop. He had work to do.

Chapter 8

Maggie spent the next day dealing with the movers, who showed up at noon. She smiled as she saw them drive up to her house. If she were a more organized person, they would have arrived at the same time as she had, two weeks earlier. But when she made up her mind to do something, she just did it. Little things like clothes and her computer and all of the stuff that made up her life weren't so important anymore. But she was still glad they were finally here. Now it was final. She was here all the way. She ran outside to meet the movers and spent the next few hours unpacking.

Maggie ran to the local grocery store for Propels, Spicy Hot Doritos, and ice cream after everyone left. She had to have the necessities of life or she just couldn't function. She stared happily at all the people milling around the store and tried to picture her father knowing these people and being a part of their lives. It made her feel good being around the same places he had been. She threw her groceries in the car and took a little tour of Alpine. Alpine, being Alpine, it didn't take too long. But what she saw made her feel a little melancholy. It was good to be here because she knew Alpine was a part of her dad. But Alpine was also a part of her mom. And not a good part. She drove home without any music and thought about what kind of hell it must have been to live in a perfect little town and to have such an imperfect, hideous life. She wondered if her mom would ever be able to come back to Alpine. She had been nervous when Maggie had told her she was moving here for awhile. Maggie had even considered just listing the house with an agent and forgetting about it, sight unseen. But something inside of her had told her she needed to come.

Maggie breathed in deeply and let it out slowly. If she had been abused by her stepfather for years on end, and this was the place it had happened, she'd never set foot back anywhere near here. The thought made her sad. Maybe she could find some good here for her mother. Maybe Alpine could be part of her healing. Maggie pulled into her driveway, turned off the car, and stared up at her house. How could she feel so much peace when her mother had had none? Maggie got out of the car and walked into the house, setting the bags on the counter. Alpine was still a mystery to her. She was going to figure it out though. One way or another.

Maggie had a quick snack and then took a long bubble bath. She blow-dried her hair until it was glossy and full and then dressed in a pair of old shorts and a paint-spattered T-shirt. She felt like painting. Good thing the movers had arrived with her extra easel. She set up in the backyard and tried to get the same happy, excited, warm feeling back. She closed her eyes and lifted her head to the sun, and felt a little of the pressure and sad thoughts leave. She rolled her shoulders around and breathed in the floral-scented air. She started to focus more on the home she was in and the people who had lived there and loved there. She concentrated on the feeling of her father in the same garden she was standing in and all of a sudden, she had her yellow back. She opened her eyes and picked up her brush. She spent the next two hours working on getting the fluid feeling of the sunshine just right. She glanced down at her watch and frowned. She had lost track of time again. She always did that. She rolled her shoulders and bent down into a deep body stretch, releasing all the tension in her spine. She flopped down on the soft green grass and shaded her eyes with her arm. She looked up at what she had painted and smiled in satisfaction. She'd need another day on it, but it was there. She closed her eyes happily and dozed for a moment, letting the warmth of the earth mix with the warmth of the sun to give her a unique embrace of elements.

"I always suspected artists were lazy," she heard a growly, low voice say from somewhere above her.

Maggie shaded her eyes and looked up at her intruder. *Luke.* "Are you home already? Give me another twenty minutes," she said, and put her arm back in place over her eyes.

Luke smiled down at the woman, snoozing in the sun like a cat. He'd never met anyone so completely comfortable in their own skin. He couldn't even imagine pulling up some grass for a nap. It didn't exactly sound bad, but he still couldn't imagine it. He stepped over her long body and walked toward the canvas. He noticed this easel didn't have any duct tape on it. He narrowed his eyes in the sunlight to see what she had been working on that had exhausted her so completely. He stepped closer as his eyes widened in surprise.

She was good. More than good. He'd been watching her paint, night after night, and had thought she was what she looked like. Some rich kid, who was kind of strange and annoying, putting on that she was an artist just to get some attention. But that's not who Maggie was at all. In just a few weeks he'd found out that regardless of whether or not she was rich, she was incredibly strong, fearless, kind, and now, *obviously*, an extremely talented artist. He glanced behind him at the woman and really looked at her. Of course anyone who had the guts to shut a door on Jennie Benchley was someone he wanted to know, but there was more to it than that. He wanted to get to know this person. He suddenly felt intrigued, and he hadn't felt intrigued in so long he had almost forgotten what it felt like. *Almost.*

"Do I have crud on my face or what? What are you staring at?" she asked in irritation.

Luke ignored her and turned back to the picture. "Who's the man in the picture?" he asked, sticking his hands in his suit pants pockets and leaning in closer to study her brush strokes.

Maggie turned over on her stomach and kept her eyes closed. "My dad. He died before I was born. My mom says he died before he even knew she was pregnant with me."

Luke smiled at the picture. She had painted a young man of about twenty years of age. He looked happy and open to the world. He looked kind and good somehow. How do you paint someone *good*?

"I'll give you a hundred dollars for this painting," he said in all seriousness.

Maggie smiled and turned back around to look up at her new neighbor. "That's quite a bit of money. What would you do with a painting like that?" she asked, sitting up and crossing her legs.

Luke forced himself to turn away from the picture and face her. "I'd like to hang it in my bedroom so I could see it when I wake up. I'd kind of like to remember that bad things happen sometimes but that the sun still comes out if we're willing to walk out into the garden and feel it," he said softly, looking away from her.

Maggie smiled sadly and stood up. "Tell you what. I'm having a sale today, so I'll sell it to you for fifty bucks. We'll call it a good neighbor discount," she said, putting her hand out to shake on it.

Luke looked at her hand and grinned. "Deal!" he said, and shook her hand before turning around to grab his new picture.

"*Uh—uh—uh!*" Maggie screeched at him. "Hello! I'm not done, you doofus. Art takes time," she chided him, pushing him out of the way and standing in front of the picture protectively.

Luke frowned. "It looks finished to me."

"If I even think you're going to snatch this painting, I'll call an architect I know and have this house turned into a Tuscan villa before fall," she said, smiling evilly as Luke's face paled at the threat.

Luke shrugged and put his hands on his hips. "You wouldn't dare."

Maggie arched an eyebrow. "Oh really? Go ahead. Put one finger on this picture. Just a pinky. That's all it would take."

Luke grinned at her and shook his head. "What a brat. Fine. I can wait. Do you have any plans this weekend?" he asked, almost nervously.

Maggie's mouth fell open. No way was she being asked out on a date. Luke saw her expression and looked away in embarrassment. "Relax. I was just thinking. Well, actually, since last night, I've been doing a lot of thinking and if you meant it, and you're serious, maybe, um, maybe you could go with me to Melanie's grave this Sunday after church. I mean, if you were serious, because if you weren't, that's okay. Really," he said, almost stammering.

Maggie's face relaxed and she smiled kindly at what it must have taken for him to come over and open himself up enough to ask her to go with him. "Of course I was serious, Luke. I've been going to the singles ward. What time does your ward get out?"

Luke sighed in relief and looked her in the eyes. "We get out at twelve, same time as you. Thanks, Maggie."

Maggie nodded her head and watched him turn away to go home and realized she didn't want him to leave just yet. "Hey, I'm starving. I was planning on running down to Olive Garden for some pasta. Do you want to join me?"

Luke turned back with a bright open smile. "Are you paying?"

Maggie laughed and grabbed her brushes and paints. "Sure. You got yourself a free dinner, but go change out of your suit first. I'll meet you out front in ten minutes."

Luke grinned. "I'll wear my new shirt," he said and ran out of the yard.

Maggie watched him with a smile and laughed at the mental picture of him eating dinner while wearing the grossest T-shirt in the world. Scary.

She cleaned up her brushes and laid the painting on the table before grabbing her keys and heading out front. They drove to the restaurant and bickered fiercely over song choice the entire way. Maggie smiled at the joy he seemed to derive from their battles. She could tell everyone had been treating him a little too gently since Melanie's death. He needed to be treated like any normal man. She'd have to remind herself to give him a hard time as much as possible. It made his eyes go clear and bright green.

They both ordered lasagna with side orders of spaghetti and had a contest to see who could eat the most bread sticks. Maggie won by three. They both burst out laughing when a man tripped and fell into a waiter after reading Luke's T-shirt.

On the drive home, they talked about only superficial stuff like their favorite music, their favorite movies, and their favorite foods. When they got home, they looked at each other in strained silence.

"Did we just have a date?" Maggie asked Luke, biting her lip.

Luke smiled. "If it was, that means I get a good-night kiss, right?" he asked, stepping toward her.

Maggie held her hands up and backed up. Way up. "There's my answer. Definitely *not* a date. But still fun. See ya around, Luke," she said and walked quickly toward her porch.

Luke laughed and watched her retreat. "Fine, have it your way. But for not being a date, it was the best time I've had in over a year," he threw over his shoulder as he turned to walk back to his own house.

Maggie turned around in surprise and watched him go. *A year?* She frowned sadly. Poor Luke. She should have come to Alpine sooner.

Chapter 9

Sunday arrived quickly. They rode to the cemetery in silence, each one deep in their own thoughts. Maggie smiled at the quaint little town cemetery set on a hill.

"This was where the early fort used to be. They built it up here so they could spot the Indians sneaking up on them," he told her as he parked the car.

Maggie got out of the car and turned in a circle. He had parked at the very top. There were sculptures of bronze pioneer children, along with old headstones.

"This is the oldest part of the cemetery. I brought you up here so you could see that." She had been so focused on the graves that she hadn't even notice anything else. It was gorgeous. The cemetery sat in such a way that you could turn in a 360-degree angle and see all of Alpine. The little valleys, the green hills, and the strong mountains. It was glorious.

"It's beautiful, Luke. Thank you." She was already planning on bringing her paints and brushes for a visit as soon as possible.

She followed Luke as he meandered here and there, pointing out old family plots and interesting grave stones.

"Sorry, I didn't take you for a native Alpiner. With your tan skin and all that brown, wavy hair, I thought you were some transplant," she said skeptically.

Luke smiled and ran his fingers through his hair. "Nope, my roots run deep here on both sides of my family. Pure pioneer heritage. I get my dark hair and skin from the pretty little Indian girl my great-great-great-great-grandfather fell in love with. Her genes skip a generation here and there, but it pops up every now and then. My sisters all hate me for it," he said with a satisfied chuckle.

Maggie grinned. "So cocky. It is a nice combination with your eyes. Did you know your eyes are like a mosaic? I would love to paint your eyes. They're kind of blue right now, even though you're not mad. Must be that Indian blood giving you magical eyes," she said, stepping closer to look up into his face.

Luke laughed in embarrassment. "I know. My mom says I have shaman eyes. Come on. You have Alpine pioneer heritage too. The Teirneys are all over here. I'll show you your grandmother's grave," he said, walking quickly away from her. Maggie grinned, realizing she had embarrassed him. *Silly.*

He showed her the new grave. The grass still hadn't grown in all the way where they had placed it. She studied the name and the dates and appreciated the rose carvings in the stone, but for some reason she couldn't feel a connection to this hard piece of rock. She felt more connected to her great-grandmother at home in the garden. She placed a small bouquet of pink roses on the grave and knelt down to touch the name.

"I wish I could have known her. Just from her house I get the feeling she was lovely."

Luke nodded in agreement. "Lovely describes her perfectly. Very kind and very good. I miss her," he said, and brushed some leaves off the marker.

Maggie stood up and sighed. It was so strange to miss someone you never knew. "So the Tierneys were here with your family in the beginning. That's so interesting. Maybe we share some relatives. Maybe we're cousins!" she said, grinning at him.

Luke frowned at the thought and walked on. "Now don't forget the Palmers on your mom's side. They're over here too. I guess that's your grandfather's grave. He died about five or six years ago," he said, pointing out the grave that had a fresh bouquet of white carnations on it. "See, there it is. Nathan Palmer."

Maggie went instantly cold as he took her hand and pulled her over to see the man's final resting place. This man was dead. She knew he couldn't hurt anybody anymore, but something made her want to turn and run, except she never ran away from anything. She walked to the edge of the stone and read the marker. *Beloved Husband and Father, Nathan Palmer.* She looked up and away from the lie of the words, sickened that anyone could write that on this man's stone.

"Maggie, are you okay?" Luke asked in concern at the complete change in her demeanor.

"Yeah, I'm great," she said tonelessly as she looked back. "This man wasn't my grandfather. He was my mother's stepfather. They legally changed her name to his when my grandmother married him, but her real dad's last name was Jenner."

Luke looked at Maggie in awkward fascination. She looked like she was going to spit on the man's grave. She glared down at the marker for a moment and then so nonchalantly, it almost seemed like an accident, kicked dirt over the words on the marker. He stared after her as she walked away. But it hadn't been an accident. He could tell Maggie hated this man. He stared down at the man's grave and couldn't figure out why. He hurried to catch up to her. There was so much about Maggie he wanted to know, but the mystery of Nathan Palmer could wait.

"Hey! You're going in the wrong direction. Melanie is over here!" he yelled after her. She was walking so fast she was almost to the edge of the cemetery.

Maggie turned back and retraced her steps in embarrassed silence. They walked silently toward a discreet marker that had a new feel to it as well. She placed the roses to the side of the marker and knelt down, pushing a leaf to the side.

"Melanie Anne Benchley. Treasured daughter, beloved sister, and cherished friend to all," Maggie read out loud. She looked up at Luke's face and noticed he had turned and was looking at something in the horizon. She reached up and pulled his hand down, causing him to kneel beside her.

"What do you think of her headstone, Luke? I think it's really pretty. Whoever picked it out did a really good job," Maggie said, trying to get Luke to look at the grave.

Luke sat back on his hands and looked at Maggie instead. "You know, Melanie had this way about her. She was so organized. Everything fit into place with Melanie. She even organized me. I remember the first time I noticed Melanie. We were sitting in seminary. I think we were both sixteen, and she leaned over the aisle and said, 'Hey, Luke. I'm free Saturday night. Why don't we go to the movies or something?' And so we did. She kind of planned everything. She took care of everything, all the details, all the decisions. We were engaged before I even realized what happened. It was kind of along the lines of, 'We should really move to the next level, Luke.' And the next day we were picking out rings and picking out invitations," he said, still looking away.

Maggie frowned and studied his face. He looked so disgusted with himself. Something wasn't right. "Do you feel maybe you were pressured into a relationship with Melanie?" Maggie asked gently.

Luke sighed and closed his eyes, leaning back on the grass and pillowing his head on his hands. "This is just between you and me, right? No part of this conversation will leave this cemetery. Right?" he asked, peeking at her.

Maggie smiled. "As if you had to ask."

"I can't call it being pressured, because I never felt the strain of it. I was just organized into it. She had everything set up and I just kind of walked onto the stage, so to speak. I tried dating other girls every so often, but they'd leave for college, or go on missions, or meet someone else. And Melanie was always there, coming over with cookies, bringing me soup when I was sick, and writing me the longest letters on my mission. You would not even believe the letters and the packages I got. She was incredible," he said honestly.

Maggie picked the grass from around the gravestone and blew it all away. "Luke, were you in love with Melanie?" she asked.

Luke groaned. "Yes and no. I mean I *sort of* loved Melanie. I just didn't think I should marry her. A week before she left for Arizona we had a big fight. I took her out to dinner in Salt Lake, and I told her that I thought we were making a mistake. I told her that we should call off the engagement and just be friends. Well, she had a total breakdown right there in the restaurant. Screaming, crying, hysteria. I'd never seen her so emotional before. That was the thing about Melanie. You never saw her really happy or really sad. She was always, just *okay*, you know. So it scared me when she lost it. I did everything I could to calm her down and then I told her we could just go ahead with the wedding. She accused me of wanting the perfect woman, and she said I thought she wasn't good enough for me. Which is so wrong. What it really comes down to, she went down to Arizona to be *more* perfect *for me*," he said, his voice breaking.

Maggie sighed and looked down at her lap, feeling her heart break a little bit for Melanie and for Luke. "You're going to feel guilty the rest of your life, aren't you?" she asked sadly.

Luke rubbed his eyes and sat up. "Do you think I want to? Don't you think I want to be happy? Part of me is. Part of me is so relieved I'm not married to Melanie, I feel like running down the road and jumping for joy. But then I feel like complete crap, because she's dead! That's how I got out of my engagement. Death. I should have had the guts to tell her I didn't love her that night. She would have been sad for awhile, but she'd be alive," he said, almost yelling.

Maggie winced and patted his knee. "Maybe, maybe not. You said last night that Melanie was kind of hard on herself. Maybe she would have gone anyway, Luke. Maybe whether or not you broke up with her, she would have done it. Most people don't just wake up one day and say, dang, I feel like a little plastic surgery. It's usually something they've been thinking about for awhile," she said.

Luke snorted. "How would you know? Have you ever had plastic surgery? Have you ever had lipo?" he demanded.

Maggie shook her head and looked away. "Nah. But my mom has. She kind of feels like there's always something wrong with her or with the way she looks. Like she's not as good as other people. It's not her fault—she was abused as a child. It goes with the territory. So yeah, I've been around the plastic scene. It's a big leap. You have to come up with a ton of money and then you have to get to a point where you're able to let someone cut you up in order to look better. It's kind of a jump. You said she went a *week* later? If it was at some ritzy spa, I bet she had that appointment set up for a long time," she said, picking a rock out of her flip-flop.

Luke flicked some grass off his jeans. "Huh. You really think so?" he asked quietly.

Maggie sighed in relief. "Yeah, I do. But if you don't believe me, call her mom. Tell her you just want some information about the spa and ask her when Melanie set up the appointment."

Luke looked grim and then pulled out his cell phone. Maggie stared in surprise. She hadn't expected him to do it right then in front of her.

"Hey, Marlene? This is Luke . . . Yeah, I'm okay, thanks for asking . . . Yeah, Jennie stopped by the other day . . . oh, Maggie? She's a friend . . . Oh no, she's just a friend. Nothing like that . . . Um, well tell Jennie I'm sorry, but uh Marlene, the reason I called was because I wanted some information about the spa Melanie went to. I know you and Mike are filing a lawsuit against them, but the question I have is, do you know how long ago Melanie made her appointment with them? . . . Are you serious? Really? That was before we were even engaged . . . Well, yeah I know, I realize that, but . . . okay Marlene. Listen, tell Mike I said hi. Thanks, bye," he said and disconnected.

He stared at her in shock. "She made that appointment almost a year ago."

Maggie let the breath she had been holding in out and stood up, reaching her hand out to help him up. "Don't feel bad, Luke. You're just not a girl. You don't understand stuff like this. Do you feel better knowing it didn't have that much to do with you?" she asked as he stuck his sunglasses on.

"You have no idea," he said, his voice cracking slightly.

They walked quietly back to his car. He went to open her door for her but then paused. He leaned his hip against the car and looked down at her.

"You know what, Maggie? This is going to sound really strange and it might freak you out, but I'd really appreciate it if you'd be my friend. You've done more to help me out in the last week than anyone has in a long time and I don't take that lightly. I just feel like maybe I can start over with my life. You have no idea how weightless I feel right now. I . . . if there's anything I can do for you. Just one word, that's all it would take," he said seriously.

Maggie grinned and patted his cheek as if he were a little boy. "You're a sweetie. But undying gratitude just isn't my thing. I don't need a vow of service, I just need a friend right now too."

Luke shook his head and laughed. "Maggie you are one of a kind, you know that? But I have to warn you. Being my friend is kind of dangerous. I'm into cliff jumping, four-wheeling, skiing, and rock climbing. I can't just sit around all day and watch you paint. And I don't do girly crap, so don't even try it."

Maggie huffed her cheeks out. "Who asked you to? And I'm one of the best skiers I know, thank you. I've been hiking and climbing rocks since I was born. But I've never been four-wheeling," she said, almost nervously.

Luke grinned and opened her door for her. "You are in for something amazing, Maggie. We could go to Little Sahara next Saturday if you don't have any plans," he said, walking around the car.

Maggie sat down and smiled, weak with relief that Luke had made it over this hurdle. She was so glad, she'd even go four-wheeling. "How much sand am I going to get in my teeth?" she asked with a frown.

Luke laughed. "So much you'll never be the same again. It's life changing."

Maggie smiled back at him and rolled her window down. She had a feeling that Luke Petersen was going to be life changing.

Chapter 10

Luke dropped her off at her house and waved out the window. Apparently he had a sudden urge to go see one of his older brothers. Maggie went in the house and right for the kitchen. She had the munchies like nobody's business. She grabbed her sunglasses, her chips, and a book she had bought last week and headed out to her porch swing.

She sat down and got as comfy as she could. She decided she'd be taking a ride into town tomorrow to pick up some cushions first thing. It wasn't too bad if you sat up completely straight. She sighed and looked around before she opened her book. She glanced up and down the street. She kind of wanted to meet a few neighbors besides Luke. She didn't see anyone but she could hear someone yelling out commands to some barking dogs next door. It had to be Gwen McFeeney.

Maggie squirmed on the hard wooden seat and gave up. She laid her book down and got up. She walked quickly next door and around to the backyard. She opened the gate and let herself in.

"Hello! I'm your new neighbor," she called out in greeting.

At least a thousand dogs broke out into cacophonous barking so loud she had to cover her ears. And then she heard the running and Gwen's urgent yells. Maggie turned and ran for it. She opened the gate and made it through just as bodies hit the wall. She stared at the gate in horror, wondering if her neighbor was breeding dogs for illegal fighting. Her heart rate was twice what it was at her last 5K race. She ran her hands up and down her arms and walked backwards, keeping her eyes on the gate in case it gave way under the pressure of all that canine fury. She made it to her own yard when Gwen came out her front door.

"You! Where do you think you're going? You can't just walk into my back-yard like that. Are you crazy?" she demanded.

Maggie was starting to think she was. Or maybe her neighbor was. Either way, she hated getting yelled at. "Yep, that's me, crazy Maggie," she said, trying to sound normal and calm her breathing down at the same time.

She stared at the woman walking toward her and smiled. Luke was right. She was eccentric. Her hair was cut so short, the Marines would be proud of her. She didn't wear a speck of makeup, but even so, there was a stark beauty about her face. With a face like that, she should have been in expensive silk. The delicate bone structure was at odds with the butch hairstyle and the pajama bottoms and T-shirt that read "BACA" and had two fists on the front. Maggie remembered that the acronym stood for Bikers Against Child Abuse and thought this woman might have some things in common with her mom. She liked her instantly.

"Sorry if my dogs scared you. They're completely harmless. They just get excited around strangers is all," she said, walking up to Maggie and stretching out her hand.

Maggie shook her hand firmly and grinned. "Isn't that what Michael Vick said?"

Gwen laughed and shoved her hands in her pockets. "Don't get me started on Vick. So you're the new chick on the block. I was wondering what was going to happen to the old place. Glad to see someone's going to take care of it."

Maggie nodded and looked back at her house. "Yeah, me too. I didn't know my grandmother, but I feel like I'm getting a sense of her, if you know what I mean."

Gwen looked at her carefully. "Your *grandmother*, huh? Elisabeth never mentioned a granddaughter. Where you been?" she asked as she took a ciga-rette out of her pocket and lit up.

Maggie eyed the cigarette and moved upwind from the smoke. "Actually, she's my great-grandmother and I've been in St. George. It's a long story, but I guess there were hard feelings between my mom and my dad's family. But I'm here now," she said, wishing she had brought her bag of chips with her.

Gwen sniffed and took another puff. "I happen to like long stories myself. So tell me about yourself. What's your name, what do you do, all that stuff," she said, waving her hand in the air.

Maggie coughed on the smoke and stepped farther away. "I'm Maggie Tierney. I'll be here for awhile, and I paint for a living," she said, keeping it as simple as she could.

Gwen nodded and looked at her strangely. "Maggie Tierney from St. George. Huh. You're not that Maggie Tierney that painted the *Woman and Child at the Well* are you?" she asked doubtfully.

Maggie stared in surprise. Although she was becoming well-known in certain art circles, it was very rare to run into someone who recognized her name. "Yeah, that's me," she said.

Gwen still looked doubtful. "I mean the artist that sold that one painting last year for $475,000? The one where the tears on that woman's face look like you could touch them. That one?" she said questioningly.

Maggie smiled and understood. So many people looked at her and didn't believe a twenty-four-year-old could paint well. "It was one of my favorites. I almost didn't let it go, but the man who bought it had just lost his wife and he said it reminded him of his Nancy. He was a rich old guy who made his money off of real estate developing. He still emails me and tells me everything his friends say about it when they come over to his house," she said, smiling in satisfaction.

Gwen relaxed and smiled at her. "No way. I got a real artist living next door. Do you paint dogs?" she asked, taking another puff.

Maggie smiled apologetically. "Nope. I just paint what comes. I did just paint a picture that had a dog in it, but that's pretty rare for me, to be honest. I like painting people. That's my thing."

Gwen shrugged. "To each his own. I'll take dogs over people any day."

Maggie whisked more smoke away from her face and heard her stomach growl. "Listen, I'm about to expire from lack of calories. Do you mind if I grab my bag of chips? I just left them on my front porch. Don't go anywhere. I'm not done talking to you," she warned, and then waited for Gwen's wave of her hand before darting back to snag her chips. She walked back and offered the bag to Gwen first before inhaling what she could get in her mouth. They walked over and sat on Gwen's front steps and chewed in comfortable silence.

"So tell me about the neighborhood. I asked Luke Petersen to tell me, but he just gave me names. Is everyone pretty cool, then?" Maggie asked, while her mouth was still full.

Gwen rolled her eyes. "Never ask a man a question like that. Always go to a woman for the details. I'll give you the rundown. Me, I'm the best. And you'll notice my dogs don't bark at night."

Maggie smiled and nodded. "That's right! They don't. You've trained them very well."

Gwen smiled proudly. "That's what I do. I breed purebred Schnauzers and train them. I make pretty good money doing it too. I'm forty years old, I'm single, and *happy* to be so. I teach the seven-year-olds in Primary on Sunday, and I love paintings of dogs," she said with a twinkle.

Maggie smiled but glanced at the cigarette butt lying on the sidewalk. "Oh that. Yeah, I smoke. Doesn't mean I don't go to church. It helps me relax. No big deal. Plus, as long as I smoke, I get the stake president for my home teacher. You start walking the straight and narrow and watch out. You get home teachers who don't show up until the last day and don't bring treats," she said, trying to make a joke of it.

Maggie wiped crumbs from her mouth with the back of her hand. "Interesting. Do you mind if I try converting you to the strait and narrow or would that offend you?" she asked out of curiosity.

Gwen laughed and grabbed another chip. "I'd be hurt if you didn't try. I've tried quitting. It's no use. But I'm always open for suggestions. I surely would like to make it to the temple one of these days before I die."

Maggie smiled and knew she'd be on the Internet that night looking up the newest cures for nicotine addiction. "So tell me about the other neighbors. Luke said the Brisbys have a few teenagers and that the Carters have a four-year-old and that the Buhlers like to work in the yard. Did he get it right?"

Gwen nodded. "Yeah, there's not much to say really. The Brisby kids are really pretty great kids. The two older boys can get out of hand, but good hearts, all of them. The Carters are a cute little couple. That little boy of theirs keeps them hopping more than all ten of my dogs. Man, he's a cute little rascal, though. Now the Buhlers rub me the wrong way, but that's just me. They're a little self-righteous and rude, but hey, every street has one, right? You might like them, so I won't say anymore. But you'll like it here. It's a good place," Gwen said with a sweet note of gratitude in her voice.

Maggie looked at her thoughtfully. "What about Luke? You didn't mention him," she said as she tried to stuff five chips into her mouth at once.

Gwen laughed at her and shook her head. "Forget it. He's gorgeous, but he doesn't even date since that girl of his went off and died on him. He used to be real funny and happy. But he's closed up. It would take a miracle to break through to that one. I wouldn't waste my time if I were you. He's a lost cause. Now if you're interested in a social life, there's a good singles ward for this area," she said, wiping her hands on her pajama bottoms.

Maggie winced and nodded her head. "I know. I've been going the last few weeks. Me and the single scene don't seem to go together, though," she said self-consciously.

Gwen looked at her sharply. "Why? You're a beautiful, talented young lady. You'll probably be obese by the end of the week with the way you eat, but I know plenty of young men who would jump at the chance to go out with you," she said sternly.

Maggie laughed and grabbed a handful of chips. "You've been hanging around dogs too much. Guys take one look at me and immediately see a *friend*. I've only had one serious boyfriend before and I'm twenty-four," she said with a blush.

Gwen frowned at her. "What's your story? A girl doesn't look like you and not have a social life. Spill it," she commanded.

Maggie cleared her throat and looked down at her shoes. "I go out occasionally, but I can't seem to fully connect. It's complicated. But to make a long and painful story short and painful, my mom was sexually abused as a child. I didn't find out about it until I was about sixteen. My mom has made it her focus in life to raise me to be strong and independent—you know, someone who wouldn't be victimized like she was I guess. She's raised me to be fearless and honest and for some reason, men shy away from that. None of my relationships seem to work out. I think having guys around when I was younger made my mom kind of uncomfortable. Of course that was when I was younger. She actually met a really nice man a few years ago and got remarried. Since then, she's relaxed a lot, but nothing's changed. It's just me. Men are looking for feminine, pretty girls they can take care of. I'm not that feminine, and I don't need anyone to take care of me. So here I am," she said, embarrassed that she had said so much.

Gwen nodded her head in understanding. "I get ya. And I can understand your mom. I was a victim of sexual abuse too. My older cousin," she said without any emotion. "That's why I stick with dogs. They love you, they obey you, and they don't hurt you. It's what works for me. But I can see a husband and children for you. You're a special type. I can see why men would be put off by you. But not *all* men. It would take someone really strong to be with someone like you. Otherwise you'd mow them down. He'd have to be secure to take you on, but it's not impossible. You'll see," she said and stood up. "I hate to eat and run, but I've got a yard full of dogs needing to be fed and put through their paces. Come by sometime and meet them," she said, smiling.

Maggie stood up and smiled back. "I'll do that. It was really good to meet you, Gwen." She meant it.

Gwen smiled back. "Yeah, that wasn't so bad, was it?"

Maggie walked back to her house and threw the empty chip bag in the garbage can. She still didn't feel like going back in the house so she sat on her front steps to watch the goings on of the neighborhood and hoped to meet more of her neighbors.

She was a people person and as an artist that's where she got her inspiration. She turned her head, looking down the street and noticed the same couple she had seen her first week with the large dog walking toward her on the opposite side of the street. She wondered if they were the Buhlers. The man was tall with graying brown hair and the woman had short, almost spikey blonde hair.

She smiled as she watched them. From the way they held hands and walked in sync with each other, she could tell they'd been together for awhile. Their dog was just plain huge and even from across the street she could see the slobber. As she studied the couple, it took her a moment to realize they were studying her right back. She lifted a hand and waved at them. They both stopped immediately and waved back. Then they looked at each other as if they weren't sure what to do next. Maggie laughed softly as she watched them. Would they come over and chat, or would they keep going? She was about to call out to them when Luke drove up and honked his horn.

Maggie stood up, forgetting about the couple and walked over to Luke's driveway.

"I thought you were going to hang out at your brother's house?" she said as he opened the door and his long lanky legs appeared.

Luke slid out of his car and shut the door. "I forgot he was just called to the bishopric. He'll be busy until tomorrow. He just lives on the other side of Alpine though. I'll catch him later. You would like him. He's married and has three kids, and he's only two years older than me. Crazy."

Maggie shoved her hands in her back pockets and glanced back across the street. The couple with the dog were still there, kind of talking to each other. *And kind of still looking at her too.* She smiled again before turning back to Luke.

"So I just met Gwen. She's really cool. I'm going to get her to stop smoking," she said with a grin.

Luke leaned up against his car and laughed. "Of course you are. I'm not even going to doubt it. What else did she say?"

Maggie felt a glow in her heart as she watched Luke's eyes change from blue to green. She walked over and leaned on his car too. "Oh just that I better stick with the singles ward and stay far away from you. She says it would take a miracle to thaw your cold heart and that I'd better not even look in your direction."

Luke frowned and looked shocked. "She said that, really? Dang, and we're friends."

Maggie held up her hands. "Oh no, don't take it that way. She was just trying to look out for me and you too, I think. I got the impression she didn't want me to throw myself at you is all."

Luke's jaws tensed and he glared at Gwen's house. "Just so you know, you're welcome to throw yourself at me anytime."

Maggie's smile faded and she blinked in surprise. "What happened to you and me being just friends? Remember, two hours ago at the cemetery? You and me skiing and four-wheeling, stuff like that?" She asked in confusion.

Luke grinned at her and stood up. "Think of it as friends with benefits. And the best part of all, Jennie Benchley will be scared to death of you," he said in a voice so full of delight Maggie had to smile.

"What's a big, strong man like you doing, being afraid of a cute, little blonde like Jennie?"

Luke shuddered. "You have no idea."

Maggie watched him curiously. "So are you afraid of me?"

Luke paused and looked down at her, *really looked at her,* and she felt a blush creep over her face.

"I'm only afraid of what would have happened if you hadn't moved in next door," he said quietly.

Maggie's heart melted almost instantly. "Luke, don't be offended, but I'm starting to think you might actually be kind of sweet."

Luke's eyes turned bright cerulean blue, and he smiled as he shoved his hands in his pockets. "Takes one to know one."

Maggie burst out into a full on blush and made a lame excuse before hurrying home. She shut her front door and leaned on it, as she whisked her hair out of her eyes. Her heart was beating fast for some reason and she had no idea how Oscar the Grouch had suddenly turned into a man she could have a very serious crush on. He was smart, good looking, funny, and for some reason, he really got her. She just might be in trouble.

The next day she was in the front yard weeding the flower beds when Luke drove up. She waved at him over her shoulder and went back to work. She wanted to finish the front yard before dinner. Luke honked his horn at her though to get her attention, so she stood up and walked over. He hopped out of his car with two bags of groceries.

"Listen, are you hungry? I've been dreaming of fajitas all day and it's dumb to make fajitas for just one person. Plus, I think I owe you a couple dinners. Come over after you're done in your yard, and we'll pig out. If you don't mind watching *Heroes* that is," he said in a rush as if he were nervous she'd say no or something.

Maggie smiled up into Luke's eyes and felt the now familiar jolt of wonder as she watched how his eyes changed color as he looked back at her. "I would have never taken you for a *Heroes* watcher. You look more like the PBS special type."

Luke sneered at her and didn't even bother to reply to that. "I'll yell over the fence when it's ready. You know, if you're done weeding, you could paint for an hour before dinner," he said pointedly.

Maggie sighed dramatically. "The creative process cannot be forced. You just make sure you have the fifty dollars ready, buddy."

Luke laughed and started walking away. Maggie ran up to him and grabbed his arm. "Hey Luke, do you see that couple walking down the street. I know you can't see their faces now, but do you know who they are? This is the millionth time I've seen them, and they look like they want to say hi, but they're shy or something. Is it the Buhlers?" she asked pointing down the street.

Luke turned and looked at where she was pointing. "No, not the Buhlers. Maggie, I could swear that's the Tierneys. They have a Mastiff just like that. Yeah, that's them."

Maggie's jaw dropped as she stared after her disappearing grandparents. "Holy crap, that was my grandparents. For the last few weeks, *I've been waving at my grandparents*," she said as she looked down the empty street.

Luke turned toward Maggie and put his arm around her shoulder. "Hey, it's okay. They're just curious. They probably don't want to pressure you or scare you off. They're really nice people," he said in a kind and warm voice.

Maggie leaned into his one-armed hug. "It's just so weird. You come from a big family, so you might not understand, but for my whole life, it's just been me and my mom. That's it. And now I have grandparents, and they just walked past my house! Should I run after them? I never really thanked them for all the food and the pot roast. They probably think I'm an ungrateful brat or something," she said, looking up at Luke.

He stared back down at her and rubbed her arm. "It's up to you. They're probably just as nervous as you are. They've never had a grandchild before. I mean, just think of it. Their son died so young and you're a part of him. It's obvious they'd love to meet you."

Maggie sighed and broke away from Luke's embrace. "This is going to make me sound like a complete chicken, *and you know I'm not*, but maybe you could go with me and introduce me to them sometime?"

Luke's eyes warmed and his eyes turned a cobalt blue. "Of course. How about next Sunday? That'll give you a week to get used to the idea."

Maggie looked back down the road and tried to be excited about it. "Okay. Thanks, Luke. You're the best neighbor I've ever had," she said sincerely.

Luke walked back toward his house. "Right back at ya," he said, and turned and disappeared.

Chapter 11

Maggie shoved her gardening gloves in her back pocket and walked inside her house and shut the door. She walked into her front room and picked up the family picture sitting on the piano. Before, her eyes had only been for her dad, but now she studied the couple in the picture standing behind Elisabeth. Luke was right. She had just seen her grandparents. She should have known. She put the picture back down and sat down on her gold couch and closed her eyes. Could she really just go and meet her grandparents on Sunday?

She reached into her jeans pocket and pulled out her cell phone. She scrolled down to her mom's number and punched the button.

"Hey, Mags! How's it going? I was planning on calling you tonight in case you were in a frenzy of painting," Lisa said in a happy voice.

Maggie slouched down on the couch and kicked her flip-flops off to put her feet up.

"Oh Mom, it's pretty incredible. But yeah, I've already been painting and I have two more pictures in my head wanting to come out. *Tons* of inspiration here."

"Honey, are you okay? Is something wrong?"

Maggie groaned and closed her eyes. "Mom, I just saw my grandparents. I haven't spoken to them or anything, but I'm going to find out where they live and go over this Sunday and introduce myself. Any advice?"

Lisa stayed silent for awhile before answering. "Honey, I can't give you any advice when it comes to your dad's family. I just know they loved Robbie more than anything in the world. So I'm sure they'll fall in love with you immediately. What's not to love?" her mom said with a laugh.

Maggie frowned and thought of a few things. "Well, I just feel nervous for some reason. It's just so weird to be twenty-four and meeting your grandparents for the first time."

"Of course it's weird, but you can handle it. You can handle anything, Margaret, right? And besides, if you find that you don't like them, that's okay too. But I think your dad would like you to get to know his parents. He loved them very much," Lisa said softly.

Maggie blinked at the tenderness in her mom's voice. She'd always been so closed when the subject of her grandparents had come up. *Hmm.* "Well, okay. I'll let you know how it goes."

"So anything new about your neighbors? Anyone interesting?" Lisa asked.

Maggie smiled. "You could say that. I told you about Luke, right? I really thought I was going to hate him at first, but he's turning out to be kind of sweet. He's fixing my easel for me. I accidentally broke it trying to get it into the house. And then I met my other neighbor, Gwen McFeeney, just now. She raises show dogs. She is really cool. You would love her. She reminds me of you a little."

Lisa laughed. "Well, it sounds like I don't need to worry about you then."

Maggie chatted with her mom for awhile and then hung up, feeling better about everything. She stood up and stretched before walking over to the window to shut the blinds and paused as she saw a car drive up in front of Luke's house. *Uh-oh.* She shook her head in admiration at the determination of Jennie Benchley. This time it looked like she had brought over a whole casserole. From the grim smile on Jennie's face, Luke was in for it.

Maggie thought longingly of her flower bed and then sighed. Luke needed her. She ran quickly out the back door and vaulted over the fence into the back of Luke's yard. She ran to the side door and let herself in. She was only slightly out of breath as she walked into Luke's kitchen. She saw the steak marinating and the vegetables out on the cutting board, but no Luke. She tilted her head up and heard the faint sounds of someone taking a shower.

Maggie sighed. She could still finish her weeding. Jennie would just ring the doorbell and then leave when no one answered. She grinned as she heard the doorbell right on cue. She went to Luke's fridge and opened it up. She deserved a drink after that amazing leap she just made for nothing. No Propel, so she grabbed a water. She was just taking a sip when Jennie walked in the kitchen.

"You!" Jennie said with so much loathing that Maggie choked.

"Me." Maggie wheezed, putting the bottle down and wiping her mouth. "So do you always just walk uninvited into people's homes? Or is this a special occasion?" she asked, loving the way Jennie's brown eyes snapped.

"What are *you* doing here? My mom talked to Luke recently and he said specifically that he was *just* friends with you and that he was in *no way* interested in you. *At all*," she said spitefully.

Maggie grinned and walked over to the sink to wash her hands. She picked up a red pepper and started chopping it into thin slivers.

"You see the thing of it is, Jen, there's friends, and then there's friends with *benefits*. Luke and I just happen to have a beneficial relationship. What about you, Jen? What kind of relationship do you think you and Luke have?" she asked out of curiosity.

Jennie crossed the room and placed her still-warm casserole dish on the stove. "Luke and I have an amazing relationship. We share a deep bond that someone like you wouldn't be able to understand, okay? So let me make things clear to you. Luke might be trying to get over Melanie by hanging out with you, but he knows, and I know that he and I . . ."

"Sweetie, why aren't you wearing an apron? I don't want you ruining your shirt," Luke said, walking into the kitchen and successfully interrupting whatever Jennie was about to say. He grabbed an old-fashioned blue cotton apron out of a drawer and put it around Maggie's waist for her, tying it with slow, deliberate movements. He rested his hands for a moment on her waist before turning to look at Jennie.

"Hey, Jennie. I didn't know you were coming over tonight," he said in a friendly voice that somehow felt cold at the same time.

Jennie smiled brightly and took the tinfoil off the casserole. "Hey, it's *Heroes* night. I couldn't let you watch your favorite show without your favorite dinner. Tuna noodle casserole. Melanie told me just how you like it."

Maggie winced, feeling kind of bad for Jennie. She kept cutting the peppers as Luke walked over and bent over to sniff the potato chip- laden warm, gooey dish.

"Jennie, *wow*, thanks for thinking of me. But Maggie says I need to watch my cholesterol. I'm getting close to thirty now and she says it's never too early to start worrying about my heart. She's going to be cooking for me a lot from now on. I'm so sorry," he said, walking back to stand by Maggie. He nudged her leg with his a couple times before she got the hint.

She put the knife down and turned to smile pleasantly at Jennie. "Oh, yeah. I'm the queen of good health, and it's my mission in life to make Luke the king. Tuna noodle? Definitely not on the menu," she said, wiping her hands on her apron.

Luke nudged her again and she frowned at him. *Oh!* She caught on slowly to this stuff. She put her arm around his waist and leaned in for a cuddle.

"Someday if I'm lucky, I'll be making healthy meals for our children," she said and looked adoringly up at Luke.

Luke grinned down at her and kissed her forehead. "Too true. So what's new with you, Jennie? Are you seeing anyone new now? I know Devon was heartbroken when you two split up a few months ago," he said, with his arm still securely around Maggie's waist.

Maggie looked up and moved a strand of Luke's wavy hair over his ears, trying to play it up. He grabbed her hand and kissed her fingertips as Jennie explained that she and Devon didn't have that much in common and how she'd always seen herself being with an older man. Someone who was mature and stable and *needed* her.

Luke winced and nudged Maggie's leg again. Maggie was stumped. Here they were glued to each other's hip and Jennie was still going for it. Time to step it up.

"That's so interesting, Jennie. And to think I love Luke because he's one of the most immature men I know. I mean, how can you sit back and relax with someone who acts like your dad? You and I must have completely different taste in men. I swear when I saw Luke laughing so hard he had noodles coming out of his nose, I knew he was the man for me. We're two of a kind," she said, looking up at Luke with laughing eyes.

Luke grinned back down at her and his eyes turned bright green. Maggie stopped grinning and reached up and traced her finger over his eyebrow. "Your eyes really are amazing," she said softly, wishing again she could paint him right at that moment.

Luke turned slightly red and Maggie came out of her trance, coughing in embarrassment. *Oops.* "Um, so Jennie. Thanks for stopping by but *Heroes* is just about to start and Luke has to start grilling these peppers. I'll walk you to the door," she said, taking her apron off and handing it to Luke.

She took the casserole and gave it back to Jennie and then took her by the arm as they walked to the front door.

"So do you have a key or what Jen? How did you get in?" Maggie asked, dropping Jennie's arm and opening the front door.

Jennie took the key out of her front pocket and dropped it into Maggie's outstretched hand.

"You're a real witch, you know that. Luke will drop you in a second as soon as he realizes how . . . *sloppy* and . . . *messy* and . . . *pushy* you are," she said, sputtering as she walked out the door. She turned and glared at Maggie one more time. "And you're not even half as pretty as Melanie! You don't even wear makeup or do your hair for heaven's sake!" she screamed, turning around and running to her car.

Maggie shut the door slowly and blinked in surprise. Huh. *She wasn't pretty?* Her mom had always told her she was. True she didn't wear that much makeup. She knew how, she just always forgot to. Her hair? Maggie pulled a long strand of wavy, brownish, golden hair out and looked at it. It looked okay to her. She walked slowly back into the kitchen and noticed that Luke really was out in the backyard grilling the steak. She finished chopping the peppers and took another sip of her water before walking out to join him.

"Saving you from obsessed women is starting to be a full-time job," she said as she pulled a lawn chair over and collapsed theatrically on it.

Luke sprinkled some seasoning on the steak and shut the door to the grill. "Don't be snide. Admit it, my spell has already started working on you. No woman is immune to me," he said with a slightly sad smile.

Maggie smiled sadly with him. "Well, if it makes you feel any better, I was able to get your house key back from Jennie," she said as she pulled it out of her pants pocket and tossed it to him.

Luke grabbed the key out of the air, shaking his head in irritation. "So walk me through this. I leave you with strict instructions to finish painting my picture and the next thing I know, you're chopping peppers in my kitchen like little miss homemaker," he said, sitting down next to her in a patio chair.

Maggie grinned and took another sip of water. "Let's just say I saw Jennie drive up and so I came running to the rescue. *Literally*. It wasn't easy, but hey, what are neighbors for," she said, leaning her head back and closing her eyes.

Luke studied her with a slight frown on his face. "You know she's wrong, don't you? You really are quite beautiful," he said in a quiet, serious voice.

Maggie blushed and opened her eyes to squint up at him. "You heard that?"

Luke winced. "Me and half of Alpine. She's right about one thing though. You're very different from Melanie. She was pretty in a very controlled, stylish way. You're beautiful in the same way a spring morning is. You just . . . *are*. I hope she didn't hurt your feelings," he said, looking at her from out of the side of his eyes.

Maggie shrugged and sighed. "What you see is what you get."

Luke looked at her intensely. "I sincerely hope so," he replied in a strangely serious voice.

Maggie looked at him sharply, but he had turned his face away from her.

"Come on, let's get the peppers going. The steak's ready," he said and got up.

Maggie followed him inside and watched as he stir-fried the peppers and onions and sliced the steak into extremely thin slices. He warmed the tortillas and put a plate full of fajitas together. "Grab those TV trays will ya?" he asked and disappeared into the family room.

Maggie grabbed the TV trays that had to be from the 1950s and followed him. He set everything up, they said a quick prayer, and he turned the TV on.

"It's just starting! Man I love this show."

Maggie felt bad she didn't leave any fajitas for leftovers, but they were good. She and Luke spent the next hour arguing over which character had the best powers and having a seriously decent time. She patted her stomach and stretched at nine o'clock. Time to head home.

"Thanks for dinner, Luke. I better take off," she said, pushing her tray out of the way and carrying her plate to the kitchen. She rinsed it off and put it in the sink. She turned around and found Luke standing in the doorway looking at her funny.

"What? Do I have fajita in my hair?" she asked, running her hands through her hair.

Luke shook his head and walked closer to her. "Nope, nothing's wrong. I was just wondering something. Are you ready for the benefits part of this friendship?" he asked, pushing her hair out of her face and tracing her cheekbone.

Maggie's eyes went wide in surprise and she stepped back a little. "Um, are you serious?" she asked in a squeaky voice.

Luke stepped forward. "Well, obviously. You have to admit, with our little performance for Jennie, we work pretty good together. Besides, a little hug here and there, holding hands every now and then, a little kiss here and there. Sometimes, it's just . . . *nice*," he said, grabbing her hand and pulling her back toward him.

Maggie cleared her throat. "Luke, I've gotta be honest with you. I don't have the best track record with guys. I've only had one serious boyfriend before and all the other guys I've dated seem to turn me into their best friend by the second date. Instead of wasting time with me, maybe you should be . . . *beneficial* with a different girl," she said nervously as he intertwined his fingers with hers.

Luke gazed at their joined hands and shook his head thoughtfully. "Here's the thing. You're the only friend I have that's a girl. And the girls I do know, I have no desire to be beneficial with them. We know for sure we're friends now, so we'll just take the beneficial stuff slow. Like, we could start out tonight with a simple hug. That's not asking too much, is it?" he asked, looking at her with an adorably hopeful expression on his face.

Maggie smiled and relaxed slightly. "Okay. Yeah, a hug is no big deal. I can handle that," she said and straightened her shoulders. "So where do you want my arms?" she asked.

Luke gave her a crooked grin and shook his head. "You're perfect, you know that? How about I walk you home first, and we'll see where the arms end up," he said, pulling her out of the room and down the hallway to the front door.

Maggie laughed lightly at herself and followed Luke out the door. She didn't even care when he grabbed her hand as they walked back. It was no big deal. She was cool with it. *Friends with benefits.* She had no idea it was this easy. They walked the short distance to her front door in less than a minute.

"I honestly think it's been three months since I was hugged by anybody. Just basic human contact is a necessity, don't you think?" he asked, glancing at her.

Maggie snorted. "Is that a line? Dude, I already agreed to the hug. Don't oversell it."

Luke laughed and grabbed her in a huge hug, rubbing her head with his chin. Maggie laughed too and wrapped her arms around his back. She breathed in the smell of his freshly laundered T-shirt and the faint smell of cologne and felt wonderful. They stood there sort of rocking back and forth a little, and she felt herself relax into the embrace. She could do this. This was really okay. It was actually . . . really pleasant. She felt a very light kiss on the top of her head and looked up.

"Caught ya. I think kissing hair is definitely not happening until week three," she admonished him sternly.

Luke grinned at her. "That only makes me wonder what happens during week fifty-two."

Maggie blushed and pinched him. He sighed and held her tighter. "Do you feel that? It's human connection. I can't believe I'm hugging my neighbor, whom I just met less than a month ago, and that it's the best hug of my life," he said in a bewildered voice.

Maggie smiled and let her head fall on his chest. "It's not so bad, is it? I should really start hugging my neighbors more often."

Luke smiled into her hair and let her go slowly. "Well, thanks for coming to my rescue yet again. I never realized I needed a knight in shining armor until you showed up. But, man oh man, am I grateful you got here when you did," he said and let his hands slide down her arms until just their hands were touching.

Maggie tilted her head and looked up at him. "Don't look now, but I could swear you're wearing a set of armor yourself. I might look like a knight, but I have a feeling that my inner damsel will be showing herself sometime soon," she said, still thinking of her grandparents.

Luke squeezed her hands and then let go. "The mutual rescue society. That's us. Good night, Maggie," he said and then looked like he was going to lean in and kiss her cheek but changed his mind at the last second and turned and walked away. Maggie smiled and waved at him before letting herself into the house.

She turned on her outside lights, locked up, and went upstairs to wash her face and get ready for bed. That night she fell asleep with a smile on her face.

Chapter 12

Maggie woke up the next morning feeling refreshed and energetic. She hopped out of bed and threw on her running clothes. She had to get rid of all of her excess energy or she'd end up being a nervous spaz all day long.

She ran smoothly down the road toward the park. She didn't want to run up her grandparents' road in case she ran into them. For some reason, she really wanted Luke with her when the introductions were made. She turned to the right and decided to run up toward the rodeo grounds. Luke said his parents had a house up there, so she'd go try and figure out which one it was. She ran past kids walking to school and other runners. Everyone she ran past smiled and waved to her. It made her feel like a real Alpiner.

She made it up to the rodeo grounds but couldn't for the life of her figure out which house was Luke's. It didn't matter which one it was, she could tell his parents were well-off. She ran back down to the city center and headed toward the park. She ran past a beauty salon and paused. She walked back and peeked in the window and thought about what Jennie had said to her last night about her hair and makeup. She was going to meet her grandparents for the first time in a few days. Maybe she should look her best.

"You know, you can go inside. Looking's only fun for awhile."

Maggie jumped and turned around. A cute little redhead stood beside her, with a laughing grin on her face and a two-year-old on her hip. He was adorable. He had chubby rosy cheeks and a darling little Dutch boy haircut.

"Oh my heck! That is the most precious little boy I've ever seen," Maggie exclaimed, wanting to reach out and touch him.

"And for that you get twenty percent off your first visit. I'm Sophie, the co-owner here. I'm just opening up. Why don't you come in and glance through a few magazines," she said.

Maggie looked down at her sweaty shirt and bit her lip. "I'm not sure you should let me in your salon. I might scare off all your nice clients," she said, following Sophie in anyway.

Sophie laughed and waved what she said away as if it were a fly. "Let me just set Adam down and I'll get you something to drink," she said as she walked toward the back of the salon where Maggie could see a little kid center. It had little slides, games, toys, a seesaw and a mini-tv/dvd player. *Cool.* Adam went right for the coloring books. Maggie smiled.

"Here we are," Sophie said, handing her a bottle of water. "You look a little parched."

Maggie grinned and opened the bottle, drinking the whole thing. "You would be right. Thanks."

"So what brings you to my door? Are you in the mood for a makeover? Do you just need a trim or highlights? What are you feeling like?" she asked, motioning for her to sit down in a comfortable chair.

Maggie sat down and threw her empty bottle away in the wastebasket to her side. "Well, here's the thing. I'm meeting two important people for the first time this Sunday, and I kind of want to look nice. For my dad's sake anyway. And this girl last night told me I wasn't very pretty, so I'm kind of feeling a little insecure. I'm not sure what to do. Do you do makeup too?"

Sophie frowned. "Someone told you that *you* weren't pretty? Oh that's it. I'm on it now. You're going to walk out of here looking like a million bucks. That's *crazy*! Anyone can tell you're more than pretty. Anyone can do pretty. It's a lot harder to be beautiful. And your face is just incredible. You're like a cross between Sandra Bullock and Scarlett Johanssen. Was it someone I know? Please tell me the girl's name wasn't Daphne," she begged.

Maggie laughed, liking her. "I don't know any Daphnes yet. I just moved here a month ago. No, her name was Jennie Benchley, and she's kind of upset with me because she thinks I'm stealing her man," Maggie said as she picked up a magazine and thumbed through it.

Sophie looked surprised. "Jennie, huh? Interesting. And I bet I know which man you'd be stealing then. Luke Petersen. Am I right?"

Maggie sighed. "You got it. What's your take on that, if you don't mind my asking?"

Sophie pushed her hair out of her eyes and winced. "That one's tricky. Melanie was a *really* big deal here in Alpine. She and Luke were like the *It* couple. So polished and successful and beautiful and on the fast track to the ultimate life kind of thing. When Melanie died so suddenly, Luke was just devastated and Jennie just jumped in with both feet. We've all come to the consensus that she's kind of been in love with Luke on the sly all along. We were kind of thinking Luke would give up and just pick up with Jennie, but if you're telling me that you're giving her a run for her money, well, then I'm all for it," she said with a strong nod of her head.

Maggie smiled weakly. "I don't know if I'm giving her a run for her money, but I do know that Luke isn't interested in Jennie in the way she wants him to be. But me and Luke, we're just friends right now. Sort of, anyway. Well, it's kind of complicated."

Sophie laughed. "*Right.* Well, why don't you run home and take a shower and then come right back? I'll get everything ready and when you get back, we'll start your makeover," she said, smiling in excitement.

Maggie smiled and stood up. She could tell Sophie sincerely enjoyed her job. This could be fun.

"Okay, I'm sold. Give me fifteen minutes. I just live around the corner," she said and left with a wave of her hands.

She sprinted all the way home, waving as Luke pulled out in his car to go to work. He looked like he wanted to talk to her for a moment, but she didn't have the time. She was getting a makeover and for some reason, she was really excited about it. She took a quick shower and threw some clean clothes on. She ran a pick through her hair and ran back out the door. She speed-walked the half a block back to the salon and was back in the door within fourteen minutes.

"No way! I didn't even believe you. You must be the fastest woman alive," Sophie said, putting Adam down and walking toward her. "Well, have a seat, my friend. The party is about to start."

Maggie took a breath and sat down, while Sophie put a drape around her shoulders. Sophie lifted her hair and looked at her for a few minutes in silence before talking.

"You have beautiful, thick, wavy hair. People pay me a lot of money to make their hair look like this. Seriously. I perm, I color, I tease, and it takes hours to get results that look like what you were born with. I'm not going to change a thing. Sorry. I'm not even going to give you highlights. You already have natural ones. I don't think I've ever seen such amazing hair. Where did you come from?" Sophie demanded.

Maggie blushed and shrugged. "St. George. I'm outside a lot. My mom calls it honey hair."

Sophie nodded. "Well, you do need a trim, so I'll shape you up and put some product in your hair that will give you more waves. And then we'll do your makeup. We're definitely waxing your eyebrows. I say you're out of here in under an hour. This will be a walk in the park," Sophie said with a smile.

Maggie relaxed as Sophie talked and trimmed. Sophie told her all about

Alpine—past history and current. Maggie sensed she had a gold mine of information so she went for it.

"Do you now the Tierneys by chance?" she asked as nonchalantly as she could.

Sophie glanced at her in the mirror as she squeezed some pomade in her hand and started working it through her hair.

"Do you mean Frank and Bonnie? Oh yeah. Everyone knows them. They're the salt of the earth. Bonnie comes in once a month for a trim. You should have seen her hair before I got a hold of her. Basic bob. Boring brown. So sad. I gave her some spike and white blonde highlights and you'd think she was reborn. That woman walks around town with her head up and a sparkle in her eye now. Bonnie's great. And her hair is amazing. It just really suits her personality," she said, grabbing the hair dryer.

Maggie jumped on that. "Personality? What kind would you say she has?" she asked before Sophie could turn on the dryer.

Sophie looked at her carefully. "These people you're meeting on Sunday and wanting to impress—would it happen to be the Tierneys?"

Maggie blushed. "Maybe it would."

Sophie raised her eyebrows and waited. Maggie gave in. "Okay, they're my grandparents and I've never met them before. Ever. It's a long story," she said with a shake of her head.

Sophie's eyebrows rose at least an inch. "You're the Tierneys' granddaughter? You? The one who's the famous artist? Oh—my—heck. Are you kidding me?" Sophie blurted and laid her dryer down, now totally forgotten.

Maggie looked away nervously. "Um, how did you even know about me? Who told you?" she asked.

Sophie shook her head, looking her up and down with new eyes. "I can't even believe this. You're Maggie Tierney. And you're sitting down in front of me in my own dang salon. This is unreal."

Maggie frowned at her and Sophie shook herself. "Okay, okay. Sorry, it's just you're kind of a legend. When Bonnie and Frank found out that you existed, you've been the only thing they can talk about. I guess when Bonnie's mom made her will out decades ago, she left her house to your dad and she never changed it. Well, the lawyer did a basic search after she died and you popped up. Bonnie says you're all over the Internet. She was telling me you had an art show in Seattle last year where you sold all the paintings in less than two hours. And not one of them was under a hundred thousand dollars. This is just wild," Sophie said, grinning at her.

Maggie cleared her throat. "So what you're saying is that my grandparents did *not* know I was alive until Elisabeth Tierney died?" she asked in a surprised voice.

Sophie blinked. "Well, of course not. If Bonnie and Frank had known they had a granddaughter, you wouldn't have been able to get rid of them. They're very loving, giving people. You're lucky. I could tell you horror stories about relatives that would curl your toes. I shouldn't, *but I could,*" she said under her breath.

Sophie stared at the blow-dryer and shook her head. "You know what? Let's just let your hair air dry. The waves are glossier that way. Come over here and we'll get started on your eyebrows and makeup. That way we can talk better."

Maggie got up and followed Sophie over to a different station. She watched with a smile as Sophie got her son, Adam, a juice box and a cheese stick from the back room. Sophie then grabbed some long clips and put sections of Maggie's hair up.

"This way, when your hair dries it will have a lot of lift at the root but still have the air-dry look. You'll see. So where were we? Oh yeah, *you*. Spill it," Sophie commanded and got the wax out.

Maggie zoned out whatever it was Sophie was doing and talked about growing up without any relatives at all and how shocked she was to find out that a great-grandmother from Alpine had left her a house.

Sophie frowned in concentration as she applied the wax very carefully. "Okay, so help me fill in the blanks here. Would your mom happen to be Lisa Palmer then?"

Maggie licked her lips and stared at her nails. "Yes. She was their next door neighbor. She and my dad were childhood friends."

Sophie paused and looked sadly at Maggie through the mirror. "Please tell me your mom ended up happy and okay."

Maggie bit her cheek and wondered what the town of Alpine knew about her mom and what they thought about her. Now was obviously the perfect time to find out.

"So I'm being honest with you here," Maggie said, looking directly into Sophie's eyes. "I'd like you to be completely honest with me. What have you heard about my mom? What does everyone say about her?" she asked in a quiet but firm voice.

Sophie took that instant to pull the wax strip off of her eyebrow. Maggie screamed in surprise. "Holy crap! You could have warned me!" she yelled, rubbing the hairless spot and glaring at Sophie.

Sophie shrugged. "Stop being a baby. Do you want to hear this or not?" she asked, concentrating on placing the next strip. "Now I'm not the town gossip or anything, but most of the information dirt road comes my way. From what Bonnie and a few other people have said, your mom was one of the most beautiful girls in Alpine. Bonnie said she was heartbreakingly beautiful. Well, I guess Letty, your mom's mother, got remarried after her first husband took off. I think she said your mom was just a young girl, like around eight or something. Well, this new husband, Nathan Palmer, was a real charmer. He moved in and made friends faster than you could say snake in the grass. A few people didn't take to him, but Bonnie says most of the town was fooled.

"Robbie and your mom grew up being friends, like you said, but when her new stepdaddy got in the picture he put a stop to that. He didn't allow her to have any friends over and especially not a good-looking neighbor boy. Bonnie and Frank didn't think much of it at the time, because they were protective parents too. But something was just off, she said. Bonnie told me she'd be out in the yard doing some weeding, and she'd see Lisa walking *real* slow coming home from school, like she didn't want to go home. Well, one day she called Lisa over and talked to her for a few minutes, and she said Lisa looked miserable. More than miserable even. Scared and sort of hopeless. Bonnie said she started thinking maybe Nathan was abusing her, but when she brought it up to Letty, Letty threw Bonnie out of the house and refused to ever speak to her again."

Maggie felt almost ill hearing about her mother's ordeal. "Why didn't my grandmother go to the police? Why didn't she go to the Church?" she asked in a hard, brittle voice.

Sophie paused and put her hands on Maggie's shoulders. "*She did.*"

Maggie lowered her head and pinched the bridge of her nose with her two fingers. "Just give me a moment, please," Maggie asked. She heard Sophie walk over to her son and talk to him about his drawings. She heard the beginning of Disney's *Cars* start and she breathed a little. She lifted her head and saw Sophie standing next to her with the most beautiful glazed donut she had ever seen.

"Here. You need this," she said.

Maggie grabbed the donut gratefully and took a bite just as Sophie ripped the eyebrow strip off. She almost choked on her donut. "Okay, no more waxing," she said with her mouth full.

Sophie shook her head in derision. "You are such a wimp. Man, Bonnie and Frank are going to be so disappointed to learn you're a big fat baby."

Maggie laughed and took another bite. "Excuse me? I'm a black belt in Jujitsu. I am not a baby. I'm just not into being tortured. Huge difference."

Sophie laughed and picked out the makeup she was going to use. "Honey, unibrows went out with the cavewomen. If you want to give Jennie a run for her money, you're going to need a beautifully arched brow. End of story. Now, do you want me to keep going? Or should we save the rest of the story for another time? I know this is hard," she said, looking kindly at her.

Maggie nodded and motioned with her hand to keep going. "Okay then. Well, Bonnie told me that she tried to talk to Lisa every chance she got after that, but Letty and Nathan were there constantly, making sure Bonnie never had the chance. But she did go to the bishop about it. She told him her worries, and so he called Lisa in and she denied it. And he called Nathan in, and of course he denied it. And that was that. Bonnie said she watched Lisa grow thinner and thinner and sadder and sadder, and there was nothing she could do about it. Bonnie told me that Lisa tried to run away four or five times, but the police always brought her back. It was right after Lisa turned eighteen that she ran away with your dad. By then, he was really sick. It just about killed Bonnie and Frank when Lisa called them four months later and told them their son had died," Sophie said, tilting Maggie's face back as she applied foundation.

Maggie closed her eyes sadly. "So does everyone think my mom was abused?" she asked.

Sophie paused but then resumed. "No. Bonnie hasn't told too many people her suspicions. Nobody would believe her anyway. Like I said, everyone thought Nathan was a friendly, all-around American good guy. He was charming to everyone. If you don't mind my asking, how was your mom abused? Was it physical or sexual?"

Maggie winced and tightened her grip on the arm rests. "Sexual. My mom hasn't told me a lot of the details. She said she didn't want me to be traumatized. But I think I am just the same, you know. She did tell me one time that the reason she could never tell anyone is that he told her he would kill her mom if she ever did. It was the one thing he could use to control her."

Sophie's face turned white and she picked up the blush brush. "Why didn't she tell her mom? Her mom could have called the cops on him, and he would have been gone."

Maggie's face turned hard and her eyes went cold. "*She did*. Letty Palmer knew it was happening all those years and did nothing to stop it."

Sophie gasped and covered her mouth with her hands. "No. No, she couldn't! Her own mother?"

Maggie breathed in deeply and let it out. "She told my mom to stop making up lies and that she should be respectful and obedient to her *father*. It went on for nine years. Can you imagine being in hell for nine years, with no way out?" she asked quietly.

Sophie shook her head, heartsick. "I'm so sorry. For your mom, for your dad, for you. For anyone who has had to go through that or deal with the results."

Maggie nodded. "That's the thing. It's not just the victim who's victimized. It's their children who will hurt too. It's their spouses and their loved ones. Nathan Palmer threw a rock in the pond and the imprint of his evil is still out there. Heck, I'm twenty-four years old and I'm scared to death to have a real relationship with a man. All because of him," she said, looking up in surprise. "*Oops*. You know what, there's something about you that just makes me want to spill my guts. I did not mean for that to come out," she said, turning red with embarrassment.

Sophie laughed and wiped a tear off her cheek as she picked out a light peach lipstick.

"It's okay. This conversation is just between you and me and that's where it ends. Besides, I don't gossip about my friends," she said with a kind smile.

Maggie smiled back and sighed, feeling a little bit better.

"So don't leave me hanging. What happened after that? Why didn't your mom tell your grandparents about you?" she asked.

Maggie frowned. "My mom doesn't like to talk about the Tierneys very much. I guess they had a big fight at the funeral. My mom didn't even find out she was pregnant until three months later. I guess she didn't feel like sending the Tierneys a Christmas card saying, 'Hey, by the way, you're going to be grandparents.' My mom doesn't hate them or anything, but by the time emotions had cooled down a lot of time had passed."

Sophie nodded in understanding. "Wow, your mom had to do it all on her own. I look at Adam and I have no idea how single parents do it. I mean, I bring him to work with me sometimes, but that's like only twice a week. Sam's mom watches him sometimes and I just don't work that much anymore. Me and my mom own the salon together and she just had a baby last year so we've hired on a few more stylists."

Maggie nodded, ignoring her face in the mirror and whatever Sophie was doing to it and concentrated on her cuticles. "Yeah, she's pretty strong. But wow, growing up, talk about protective. Men just weren't a big part of my life. But then she met Terry at work. He's a cop and he is *amazing*. He makes her laugh and giggle. You should see them together. He just loves her to death. And she loves him too. It's just a relief to see her so happy," she said with a smile.

Sophie nodded. "Wow, we are so alike, it's scary. My mom just got remarried too after being single forever. I have a new baby sister who's adorable. It just makes you appreciate how hard life is sometimes but how worth it is in the end. I know I look at my own life, and it hasn't all been a walk in the park, but knowing that I can go home at the end of the day and be with a man who loves me more than anything else in the world, I don't think I'd change a thing."

Maggie nodded with a frown. "I don't know if my mom would agree with you, but I can see your point."

Sophie winced. "Sorry. Sexual abuse isn't worth anything. Nothing so evil and damaging and traumatizing could be. I just meant that whatever road brings us to our soul mates, is a road worth taking."

Maggie smiled. "I'll let you know when I meet mine. I don't know who could put up with me though," she said.

Sophie snorted and motioned her to look in the mirror. "Yeah, you're a real burden on the eyes. Don't be an idiot."

Maggie glanced in the mirror and paused as she was about to say something.

She closed her mouth and leaned in closer. Sophie took the clips out of her hair and fluffed her hair out. Her hair didn't look so messy anymore. It was glossy and super wavy and pretty. *And her face.* Being an artist, she knew the power of color and line. And Sophie was definitely an artist. Her eyes looked huge and exotic. She wouldn't have recognized herself.

"You know it's easy to do. Just use an eyeliner and mascara. You can't get more simple. It's just the basics. Light foundation, a little blush, eyeliner, and brown mascara, and a little taupe eye shadow to highlight those blue eyes of yours. Nothing to it."

Maggie smiled in embarrassment. "I've never looked like this before. It's just not me. I'm the type that wears blue jeans and T-shirts. I put my hair in a ponytail if I'm feeling adventurous. My mom would die of shock if she could see me," she said, studying herself.

Sophie grinned. "Honey, you're twenty-four and you've got Luke Petersen interested in you. It's time to step up your game. Welcome to womanhood."

Maggie groaned. "I don't think I'm ready."

Sophie took off the drape and laid it on the chair. "Trust me, you're ready. I sure wish I could see Frank and Bonnie's face when you show up on their doorstep. Just promise me you'll come back for a manicure and tell me how it goes."

Maggie smiled and walked over to the cash register. "That's a promise. It's been really great meeting you, Sophie. I'm so glad I ran past your salon this morning."

Sophie grinned and rang her up. "Me too. I'm giving you my special friend discount."

Maggie took a bill out of her wallet and handed it to Sophie. "Good! Because I'm giving you my special friend tip. I'll see you soon," she said and walked out, laughing at Sophie's shocked face.

Chapter 13

She walked sedately back to her house, not wanting to mess up her makeup or hair. As she got to her street, she noticed an older couple working in the yard across from her house. *The Buhlers.* She walked over to introduce herself. The woman stood up as she noticed they had company.

"Well, you must be our new neighbor," the woman said, slipping her gardening gloves off and holding a hand out.

Maggie smiled and shook the woman's hand. "That's right. I'm Maggie Tierney. And you must be the Buhlers," she said, shaking the man's hand too.

They seemed like a nice couple. Living in St. George, she was surrounded by a population of senior couples so she felt right at home.

"I'm Alice and this is Dan. We were good friends with Elisabeth. She was a dear lady. We sure do miss her. It's so strange though, you being her great-granddaughter and never coming to see her. *Even once*," Alice said, eyeing her closely.

Maggie blinked and put her hands in her pockets. "I can see how you'd think so. Well, I better get going. It was nice meeting you both," she said, and turned to walk across the street.

Dan stopped her with a question though. "How does a granddaughter who never visited her grandmother inherit such a nice, expensive home, if you don't mind my asking?" he said in a cool tone that immediately rubbed Maggie the wrong way.

Maggie turned back to the Buhler's and smiled politely. "Actually, I do mind. Have a nice day," she said and turned and walked away.

She tried to ignore the huffy sounds coming from Dan and Alice and squared her shoulders. She should have expected something along those lines. It probably did seem strange to everyone that a virtual stranger should inherit such a beautiful old home. Too bad she didn't feel like telling everybody her life story. Almost everybody, but not quite.

She let herself into her house and immediately went for her paints and canvas. She might be able to finish Luke's picture. She shoved her now gorgeous hair back in a rubber band and pushed all irritation and annoyance out of her mind. She concentrated on thoughts of her dad and happy sunny, healthy days. Three hours later she dipped her brush in black paint and signed the picture. She looked at what had appeared and smiled at her dad. He looked good and he looked happy to see her. She kind of felt bad knowing she would be saying good-bye to him so soon. But Luke needed a little sunshine in his life. Actually, he needed a lot.

Maggie sighed in contentment. She went to grab her digital camera to take some shots of it. After rinsing her brushes and putting her paints away, she set the canvas on the kitchen table and looked at the clock. She couldn't believe it was already five o'clock. She was about to die of starvation. She walked over to open the fridge door when the doorbell sounded. She ran to answer it, hoping it was Luke with some food.

She opened the door to a UPS man holding a large envelope. She signed for it, thanked the man, and then shut the door. More paperwork from Kate to go through. As she turned to throw the envelope on her hallway table, the doorbell rang once again. She sighed irritably and pulled the door open only to smile happily when she saw who it was.

"Luke! *And my easel*. I knew you could fix it," she said with a grin, taking the easel from Luke's outstretched hands.

Luke winced. "Yeah, you had so much faith in my skills. But what do you think? It looks just like new. And I put a coat of varnish on it. Amazing, huh?" he asked proudly.

Maggie looked the easel over carefully and smiled happily. It was perfect. "Luke you are an amazing craftsman. You have my eternal gratitude," she said, putting the easel down carefully.

He was still dressed in his suit from work and he looked at her in a faintly disappointed way. "Maggie, I worked until midnight last night and all I get is eternal gratitude? Come on, we're F.W.B. now. I'm pretty sure that's worth a hug," he said, looking pathetic.

Maggie grinned and threw her arms around his neck. "Luke, how could I have ever doubted you? You are without a doubt the best," she said and kissed him heartily on the cheek.

Luke grinned and held her close. "That is so much better. So tell me, what's the deal with the hair and makeup? You look like you have a hot date," he said suspiciously.

Maggie let him go and rolled her eyes. "Well, after hearing how ugly I was last night, I figured I'd better go in for a little makeover. I don't want to scare my grandparents off when they meet me."

Luke ran his hands through her glossy waves. "First off, you could never be ugly. Ever. Just forget everything Jennie said. But just so you know, this isn't meet the grandparents. This is a photo shoot in St. Tropez," he said, studying her face intently.

Maggie blushed and pushed her wavy hair back from her face. "I know. It is different. I'm not used to doing the glamour thing. But I ran past this cute little salon by the park, and I met Sophie. She invited me in and the rest is history. She said it was time to step up my game," she said, sounding very unsure.

Luke cupped her face in his large hands and looked at her almost tenderly. "You do look beautiful, but you looked just as beautiful last night with pepper stuck in your teeth. This is just hitting everyone over the head with your magnificence."

Maggie pulled away and blushed. She hated compliments. "Hey, I've got something for you too. Come and see your present," she said, waving him along the hallway. Luke followed her to the kitchen and went right to the table where his picture lay.

"It's incredible, Maggie. I've never seen anything like it. The way you painted your dad's face, it's almost as if he's getting ready to talk to you or something. It's beautiful," he said in awe.

Maggie grinned and laid her hand on his arm as they looked at the picture. "This is definitely one of my favorites."

Luke carefully placed the painting back on the table. "I really appreciate the gesture, Maggie, but I can't accept it. It's too much. I googled you at work today and you don't even sell pictures for less than a hundred thousand dollars. Your last picture went for, what was it? *A half a million?* And you were going to sell this to me for fifty bucks. You're sweet, and kind, and generous, but you could get a lot of money for this," he said sadly, staring at the painting wistfully.

Maggie frowned at him. "Look, my agent Kate sells my paintings for a lot of money. *I* sell my paintings for whatever I want to sell my paintings for. But if money is an issue with you, then I won't sell it to you. It's my gift to you. I want you to have it, and it will hurt me deeply and irreversibly if you don't accept this part of me. I want you to have a sunny day every morning you wake up. Please. *Take it,*" she said earnestly, grabbing his hand in both of hers.

Luke looked torn. He looked at the picture and he looked at Maggie. He sighed and shook his head. "You make it really hard to be decent. How can I say no? But what if three months from now you decide you hate my guts and want it back?" he asked doubtfully.

Maggie let go of Luke's hand. "This isn't junior high, Luke. You think I'd pour my soul out into this painting and give it to you just to change my mind later and want it back? Do you even know what the word *gift* means?" she asked in exasperation.

Luke blushed and grabbed her hand back. "How about a simple thank-you then, instead?" he asked.

Maggie sighed and looked up at her ceiling. "Is that really the best you can do?" she asked sadly.

Luke's eyes turned bright green and Maggie had just a second to think, *uh-oh*, before he swooped down and pulled her into his arms, leaning her gently back before brushing his lips very lightly over hers. He opened his eyes, staring into hers, and it was only because his eyes were turning such an amazing color that she forgot to stop him when he kissed her again. This time not as soft but still very sweet. Maggie knew she wasn't the most experienced kisser and couldn't help wondering if he was grading her. She pulled away, blushing to the top of her hairline.

Luke smiled at her. "Sorry, but that was almost a dare," he said with a shrug.

Maggie ran her hand over her lips unconsciously and then cleared her throat. "This whole benefits thing. It's going to take me awhile to get used to it. I told you I'm not very good at this stuff."

Luke frowned and crossed his arms over his chest. "What do you mean you're no good at it? What are you saying?"

Maggie glared at him. "Stop being nice. It's annoying. All I'm saying is that me and kissing just don't work. I get nervous, I don't know what to do, and it's just horrible, okay?" Maggie sputtered at him. She didn't tell him that her last boyfriend had broken up with her because he said that she would never relax with him and that kissing her shouldn't be such hard work.

Luke's eyes turned a soft, almost grayish blue color. "Is that it? *Really?* Well, then I've changed my mind completely."

Maggie looked up at him, a little stunned. "Okay then. So we'll just be friends *without* benefits?" she clarified.

Luke snorted and shook his head. "Are you crazy? No, I mean I've changed my mind about going slow. I think you just need some practice is all. You just have a lot to catch up on. Just think of me as your remedial kissing instructor."

Maggie laughed and punched Luke in the arm. "Get out of here. Seriously. Get out," she said, pointing to the door.

Luke grabbed her finger and pulled her into a hug. "Don't be scared of me, Maggie. Just promise me that if you ever get the urge to kiss me, you give in to it. Just do what feels comfortable. No pressure," he said, rubbing her back soothingly.

Maggie relaxed. Just a little. "You know, my best friend in high school told me that's exactly what her boyfriend told her too. They have three children now," she said accusingly.

Luke laughed. "My point exactly. Come on. Enough of this mushy stuff. Let's get out of here. We can't waste all of Sophie's efforts. And I get to be seen with the most gorgeous woman in Utah."

Maggie laughed and blushed at the same time. "If it involves food, I'm there."

Luke leaned in quickly and kissed her again on the lips. "Lesson number one. Always be prepared to be kissed by me. Now go get changed. One of my college buddies plays in a band, and he's got a show tonight up in Salt Lake."

Maggie grinned in excitement. "Cool! But are you sure there will be food?"

Luke sighed dramatically. "Just the best food Salt Lake has to offer. Now hurry or I'm calling Jennie," he said seriously.

Maggie rolled her eyes. "I dare you."

She ran upstairs and threw on a slim-fitting black silk shirt and a bright red wrap around top. She didn't even bother looking in the mirror before flying downstairs.

She locked up and they drove to Salt Lake talking and laughing the entire time.

"You know, if someone had told me after meeting you that first day that I'd be sitting here with you a month later thinking you were funny, smart, and just about perfect, I'd think they were crazy," she said as she got out of the car.

Luke joined her and slipped his arm around her waist as they walked into the building.

"And if someone had told me that the PETA loving, hemp wearing, Tuscan addicted woman I'd met a month ago would turn out to be the most beautiful, sweet, incredible woman I'd ever met, I would have believed every word," he said as he leaned down and kissed her forehead.

Maggie laughed happily and felt something click into place. She wasn't sure what it was, but whatever it was, it felt right. They spent the evening listening to the best Jazz she'd ever heard and eating truly delicious finger foods for almost three hours straight. It was the best date Maggie had ever been on in her life.

Chapter 14

The rest of the week went by fast. *Too fast.* Maggie wasn't sure she was ready when Sunday arrived. So she was glad when Luke came over after church and cancelled on her. He had forgotten a family get-together at one of his sister's. He invited her to go with him, but she made her excuses and sent him on his way. She would spend the rest of the day psyching herself up to meet her grandparents tomorrow. According to Luke and Sophie, the Tierneys were the nicest, kindest, best people in the world. *So why was she so nervous then?*

She decided to take a long drive and drove the Alpine loop. She parked her car at a lookout and found a good spot to sit and look at the world. She stayed there for an hour just thinking. Thinking mostly about her future and what she really wanted. Did she really want grandparents? She had to admit that deep down, she craved having grandparents. Her mind wandered to other areas too. Like did she want a boyfriend in her life? And if so, was Luke going to be able to put up with her? She wasn't the easiest person in the world. She had the bad habit of being painfully, sometimes rudely, honest. Most guys she had dated stuck around for a second or third date, but fourth dates were extremely rare. Which led her to her next train of thought. Was she up for a broken heart if Luke wasn't up to the challenge of dating her?

She threw some rocks down the mountain and sighed. That was the thing about life. There was just no use guessing. You always had to find out on your own.

She drove back home in a contemplative mood. But she was ready for Monday. She was ready to meet her grandparents. At least she thought she was.

The next morning was just as beautiful as every morning she'd had in Alpine. Nothing out of the ordinary. No birds singing at her window. No rainbows in

70

the sky. Nothing to signify that this day was any different from any other day in her life. But as she stood up and stretched, the tingle of nerves ripped down her back letting her know that today was different. She smiled grimly. Today she would reconnect a severed line of her family tree. She just hoped it didn't hurt too much.

She puttered around the house and ate way too much junk food as she waited for Luke to get home from work. She even tried to recreate the same look Sophie had given her for her makeover. The second he drove up, she was out the door and to his car before he even had a chance to open his door. He stood up with a welcoming grin.

"Dang, I could get used to this. Being greeted after a hard day's work by a beautiful woman just makes life worth living."

Maggie rolled her eyes. "You sound like a 1950s sitcom. Now are you still planning on going with me over to my grandparents? Because I really just want to get this over with," she said, shifting from one foot to the other nervously.

Luke sighed and leaned on his car door. "Maggie, just take a breath. You're about to implode or something. If the anticipation is getting to you, let's just go right now."

Maggie didn't say anything, she just walked around to the other side of Luke's car and let herself in. Luke sighed noisily and joined her. They drove in silence down the road to the house her father grew up in. Luke parked across the street and reached over and grabbed her hand before she could get out. "Listen, if you feel like you need to leave, just nudge my leg a little. I'll think of something," he said with a wink.

Maggie took a deep breath and nodded. "Thanks, Luke. Really, thanks for this. I know I could do this on my own. But I'm just so glad I don't have to," she ended in a whisper.

Luke's eyes crinkled up and he smiled slowly at her. "You *can* do this. And remember, these are nice people. You don't need to worry," he said and opened his door. He walked her across the street and up to the front porch of a nice stone house. He rang the doorbell and then pushed the hair out of her eyes.

"Smile. You look beautiful."

Maggie winced but tried to smile. She could hear footsteps getting closer and closer. The door opened and the woman she had seen so many times walking past her house stood in front of her, looking as if she were about to have a heart attack. Her hand went to her heart and her eyes were huge.

"Frank! *Frank!* We have company," she yelled over her shoulder.

"Maggie?" she said and then grabbed Maggie by the shoulders, pulling her in close and bursting into tears all at once.

Maggie tensed up immediately. She just wasn't used to that much physical contact. Her mom had never been a hugger, so she just was never sure where to put her arms. She patted her grandmother's back awkwardly as she saw Frank run down the hallway toward them.

"Well, who is it for heaven's sake? What's all the fuss a- . . . " Frank said and stopped mid-word. His face went slack in shock, and he came to a halt in front of her.

Bonnie pulled back and turned to face Frank. "Come meet your granddaughter. Maggie's come to see us!" Bonnie said on a sob.

Maggie felt horrible making her grandmother cry so hard but felt even worse when Frank started wiping his eyes with his sleeve. He moved Bonnie aside gently and pulled Maggie in for a huge bear hug. Maggie's eyes went wide as she started to feel panicked. Frank didn't act like he was ever going to let go. She tried to signal Luke with her hand, but he was way ahead of her.

"Frank. Do you remember me? Luke Petersen." Luke held out his hand and forced Frank to let go of his granddaughter.

Maggie immediately stepped back to stand by Luke's side. After shaking Frank's hand, Luke put a protective arm around Maggie. Mostly to protect her from any more hugs.

"Well, why don't we sit down and get to know one another?" Luke asked as everyone just stood there for a minute not saying anything, just looking at each other.

Bonnie jumped. "Absolutely! Come in the family room. I just made a peach pie. You'll love it, Maggie. We grow our own peaches. Your dad would make himself sick eating so many peaches every year. Just give me a second. *Don't go anywhere.* Frank, get the picture albums," she ordered and ran from the room.

Frank did what he was told and disappeared the opposite way his wife went, leaving Luke and Maggie to find the family room on their own.

Luke grinned at Maggie. "See, it's okay. They're just a little nervous and excited. It's sweet," he said, pulling her down the hallway as they looked for the family room.

Maggie stepped closer to Luke. "I know, they're very sweet, but they keep hugging me. I'm not even used to hugging you yet. I've had more hugs in the last week than I've had in the last six months," she said, completely serious.

Luke looked at her in surprise. "That is so sad. Just stick close. If they go in for anymore hugs, I'll step in with a handshake. Just try and relax. Try and get to know these people. They knew your dad the best. They can tell you all about him," he said as he found the family room and pulled her toward a large, brown leather couch.

They sat down in the middle and waited. Luke pointed out some pictures on the wall of her dad and his sister. She was too nervous to get up and study them though. A minute later, Bonnie appeared with a tray of peach pie served on beautiful china plates. Maggie couldn't help smiling. It looked delicious, and she was starving to death.

"Wow, this looks amazing," she said, taking the plate being held out to her. Frank appeared next, holding about seven picture albums in his straining arms.

"Here we are. I wasn't sure which ones to bring so I brought as many as I could carry," he said as he set them carefully on a chair. Bonnie handed him a plate and they both sat down in the chairs opposite Maggie and Luke.

"We're so glad you stopped by Maggie. We were hoping you would. Weren't we, Frank?" Bonnie said, ignoring her pie and just staring at her granddaughter.

Maggie took a bite of pie and closed her eyes in appreciation. Luke groaned in delight.

"Bonnie, this is the best peach pie I've ever had," he announced.

Maggie nodded her head in agreement. "I wish you could teach me how to make this. I'd bake it every day," Maggie said fervently, taking another bite.

Bonnie looked like she'd just been given a free ticket to the celestial kingdom. "Really? I would love to teach you how. It's so easy. Maybe you could come over some time and I could walk you through it," she said, starting to tear up again.

Maggie frowned and looked to Luke for help. Luke smiled encouragingly at her.

"Isn't this great? It's like a mini-family reunion," he said, trying to get the conversation back on track.

"Oh, and thanks for the roast and the flowers. I got your notes. It was really sweet of you to go to so much trouble for me," Maggie said, looking down at her plate with a frown. She'd eaten her slice already.

Bonnie was already placing another piece on her plate before she even looked up. "Wow! Thanks," she said, and dug in.

Bonnie's smile was huge. "I should have known you would want two pieces. I swear Robbie could eat a whole pie. I hated it when he got sick. He always enjoyed food so much, and the chemotherapy made him nauseous all the time," she said sadly.

Maggie looked up questioningly. "I'm glad you brought that up, actually. Just so you know, and to get to the heart of the matter here, I really would like to have a relationship with you both. I think it would be incredible to have grandparents. And I would love to get to know my dad through you. But we need to start off honestly. I need to know what happened that was so bad that I had to grow up without you in my life," Maggie said, putting her plate down and clasping her hands in her lap.

Bonnie and Frank looked surprised at her forthrightness, but Frank smiled. "She's just like Robbie, isn't she? Right to the point. No messing around. Well, she's right. It's always better to start with a clean slate. Clear out all the muck and begin anew."

Bonnie nodded sadly and looked down at her hands. "We didn't even know you existed until my mother died a little ways back. If we'd known, Maggie, you have to know that we would have wanted to be a part of your life. Please believe that," she said, looking pleadingly at her.

Maggie smiled and nodded. "I do believe that. But I want to know *why*," she said, reaching out and finding Luke's hand waiting for hers. She felt stronger instantly and was able to look her grandparents in their faces.

Frank sighed and patted Bonnie on the knee. "It was my fault, Maggie. When your mom called us and told us Robbie had died, we were just heartbroken that we didn't get a chance to say good-bye to our boy. You have to understand, we loved your dad so much. He was the sweetest, kindest, most tenderhearted boy anyone had the privilege of knowing. And when he up and left with Lisa, well, it just about killed us. The doctors told us he had a chance of beating the leukemia if he would just stay and do the chemo. But he flat-out refused. He was eighteen, so he checked himself out of the hospital, went home, packed his bags, and left with your mom. All within about three hours. And that was the last time we ever saw him. At the funeral when we saw Lisa, we were pretty angry. We blamed her for everything. We shouldn't have. But we did. We said some things we shouldn't have said and we're sorry. No one knows just how sorry we are. A few years after Robbie died, we tried to find Lisa and tell her that, but she just kind of disappeared. We couldn't find her anywhere. We could have hired a detective, but money was tight for us back then, what with the hospital bills and funeral bills. So we just waited it out. We figured she might come back and visit her mother. But she never did. We haven't seen Lisa in over twenty-four years," Frank said, looking puffy around the eyes.

Maggie looked away and out the window into their backyard. She could see all the fruit trees and the large garden. She wasn't sure what to say.

Luke cleared his throat and squeezed her hand comfortingly. "I think what Maggie wants to know, is what exactly you said to her mom. Lisa's a very private person and doesn't talk about it," Luke said, completely making it up, but hitting it on the head anyway.

Bonnie bit her lip and looked at Frank before talking. "Frank's wrong. It wasn't his fault. It was my fault. He just doesn't want you to hate me. I'm the one who talked to Lisa after the funeral. Frank was so ill after the service that he was having heart palpitations and had to lie down. I'm the one who cornered Lisa and screamed at her. I told her she had ruined our lives and that she had killed our son. I told her I never wanted to see her again, as long as I lived," Bonnie said.

She broke down crying so hard that Frank had to lead her out of the room.

Maggie stared sightlessly at the spot where her grandparents had been just seconds before.

"Honey, people who lose loved ones, and who are grieving as much as they were for your dad, shouldn't be judged too harshly," Luke whispered softly, scooting closer to her and putting his arm around her shoulder.

Maggie gave in and leaned back into his chest, feeling the warmth seep into her cold arms instantly.

"What do I say to that, Luke? My dad's parents told her that she *killed* him. She's had to carry that burden all these years. Do you honestly think we can move past this?" she asked in a whisper, her eyes huge with distress.

Luke kissed the side of her face gently and rubbed her arms. "I *know* you can move past this."

Maggie groaned and fisted her hands on her knees. "But how?"

Luke caressed her hair and hugged her for a moment. "The Atonement, Maggie. He can heal this if you'll let him. This can be healed in such a way that you can have a wonderful relationship with your grandparents. But only if you choose to. Anger and resentment won't take the words back. They won't heal your mom's heart. Just listen to them for now. We'll go soon, but I want you to give them a chance. You can do that, Maggie. Can't you?"

Maggie sighed and closed her eyes. "If you only knew what my mom has been through in her life. She needed my dad's parents so much and instead of helping her when she needed them the most, they blamed her. I don't know, Luke. I just don't know," she whispered.

Frank and Bonnie walked slowly back into the room, looking nervously at Maggie and Luke.

"Sorry, Maggie. Bonnie just gets emotional sometimes. But we just want you to know that we love you. We don't know you yet. But we love you. You're Robbie's daughter. You're a part of us and we just want a chance to get to know you. We were so excited when we found out you were moving into the house; we thought you'd just put it up for sale and forget about it. But you came home. We don't want to pressure you—we know how upsetting this probably is for you. But we're here and we're not going anywhere. Just please, let us be a part of your life," Frank said as Bonnie's eyes welled up again.

Maggie swallowed and stood up. "I came today because I wanted to meet you. I'm glad I did. I'd like to talk to my mom before I see you again, though. Thanks for the peach pie. It really was the most delicious thing I've ever tasted," she said politely, and then walked to the door and out into the sun. She walked to Luke's car and waited for him to come out the front door. She wondered what he could possibly have to say to her grandparents, but was too wrung out to care at the moment.

As she leaned up against the car, wishing the sun would warm her up, she noticed a woman standing in the yard next to her grandparents. The woman was standing as still as a deer, just staring at her. Maggie looked away and then gasped and looked back. She stared right back at the woman knowing instantly this was Letty Palmer. Her *other* grandmother. She was close enough to shout out a greeting to her, but she remained perfectly quiet. She stared in grim dread as the woman started walking slowly toward her. Maggie noticed that she had the same wavy golden brown hair as she and her mother had. Her face was thin and her high cheekbones jutted out almost painfully. Her mouth was thin and compressed in a tight line across her face. But her eyes were what sent shivers down Maggie's back. Letty Palmer's eyes were so bright they were almost glowing.

Maggie started backing up when she heard Luke run up to her.

"Luke, can we go right now, please," Maggie whispered urgently.

Luke nodded and opened the door for her. Maggie practically jumped in and shut the door quickly, locking it too.

Luke walked slowly around to his side and let himself in. Maggie watched as Letty Palmer came to the edge of her yard and stopped, looking straight into the car and right at her.

Maggie looked away and leaned her head against Luke's shoulder as soon as he sat down. "Please hurry, Luke. Please just start the car, put your foot on the gas, and leave this place. Please," she begged quietly.

Luke looked at her in surprise, but did as he was told. "What's the matter? I thought that went pretty well, all things considered."

Maggie ignored the question until they were a few blocks down the road and she couldn't see her grandmother in the mirror anymore.

"Didn't you see her?" she asked, looking straight ahead.

Luke glanced at her and then back at the road. "You mean the woman standing in the yard?" he asked, and then he winced. "Letty Palmer. Sorry. I was so caught up with the Tierneys, I forgot about the Palmers. Why didn't you go say hi? She was right there; heck, we could have gotten all the family reunion stuff over in one day."

Maggie leaned over as if she were in pain and leaned her head on her hands, bunching her hair in her fists.

"What! What is the matter, Maggie? Are you sick? Was it something I said? Was it something your grandparents said? *I'm pulling over*," he said, and parked his car on the side of the road. "We're not going anywhere until you tell me what is hurting you so much," he said grimly, putting his hand on her shoulder.

Maggie lifted her face and wiped a tear off her cheek. "Remember I told you my mom was abused as a girl? I think I mentioned it," she said as she turned toward him, her eyes brightened by tears.

Luke frowned and nodded. "I remember you said something about it, but you never really said what or how or who or anything. Did her mom beat her or something? Is that why you wanted me to leave so fast?" he asked softly.

Maggie leaned back and closed her eyes, not even caring when she heard Luke undo his seat belt and scoot over so he could put his arm around her. Maggie swallowed and took a breath.

"My mom was sexually abused as a girl by her stepfather, Nathan Palmer, for over nine years. And my grandmother let it happen," she said quietly.

She heard Luke's intake of breath and opened her eyes. She turned to look at him and was surprised his eyes looked dark gray.

"I'm so sorry, Maggie. I don't know what to say," he said and reached for her hand.

Maggie nodded. "What is there to say? There really should be greeting cards for this but there's not. I think Hallmark should be ashamed of themselves for not having a whole aisle just for people in this situation. I could send one to my mom that says, 'Hey, so sorry your life has been damaged by the worst evil known to mankind. But I'm here for you.' Or you could send me one that says, 'Hey, would love to have a close relationship with you, but I understand that you're somehow emotionally stunted when it comes to men because you're terrified of what a dangerous thing physical intimacy can be.' Or I could even send one to my grandmother that says, '*You evil, horrible witch. If you ever come near me or my mom I'll . . .* ' " Maggie, said, choking on her tears.

Luke pulled her over and she laid her head on his chest as she wept. She raised her head minutes later and stared in horror at the mascara, eye shadow, and lipstick that she had so carefully applied that was now smeared in a wet mess on Luke's expensive button-up shirt.

"I am never wearing makeup ever again," she said and looked up to see Luke's pale green eyes looking at her tenderly.

"Yes, you will. But why don't we go home and change real quick. And then we need to get some food in you." He leaned over and kissed her cheek softly before driving home.

Chapter 15

She ran to her house to wash her face while Luke changed into jeans and a blue-striped polo shirt. She got back to the car the same time Luke did. They drove quietly to the restaurant in Sandy, listening to music and holding hands.

"Ruby River Steakhouse? I've never been here." Maggie's stomach growled so loudly, Luke burst out laughing.

"I think this occasion calls for some serious pigging out. We're ordering all the appetizers you can dream of, the biggest steak they make, and at least two desserts," he said as he opened the door for her.

Maggie smiled in gratitude. "I will hold you to that. You'd think peach pie would have a little staying power."

They were seated immediately and ordered four appetizers as soon as the waitress appeared. They were soon surrounded by cheese and bacon potatoes, fried onions, chips and dip, and garlic bread. Maggie jumped in with so much relish, Luke decided to sit back and wait a few minutes before venturing his hand into the fray.

"So do you want to talk about it?" he asked as he sipped his water.

Maggie sighed and felt so much better she had something in her stomach that she even smiled. "I don't really know what to say. I think I need to call my mom tonight and get some answers out of her. I just hate making her remember the past, you know? She's so happy now with Terry. I don't want to cause her anymore pain."

Luke nodded and took a bite of bread. "But Maggie, maybe if you had all of the answers, you could move on too."

She nodded, silently agreeing with him. "I don't know if I can do it, Luke.

The whole *grandparents* thing. There's no way I can go back to their house knowing *she'll* be there watching me and waiting for me. She looked like she expected me to go over and talk to her. How can she expect that?"

Luke frowned and grabbed a potato. "Maggie, this is your life and you're the one in control of it. If you feel like you want to have your grandmother and grandfather in your life, which as your friend, I hope you do, then have them come to your house or meet them for lunch somewhere. You only have to do what you feel ready for and what you're comfortable with. If seeing Letty Palmer is too hard, then don't," he said simply.

Maggie scooped up as much pesto and cheese dip as she could possibly fit on one chip and skillfully maneuvered it into her waiting mouth. Luke smiled in admiration.

"You make it sound so easy. You're so logical and sensible, I love that about you. I think you're right," she said as she finally started to relax.

Luke grinned and tried to copy her with the chip trick, but just ended up spilling half his cheese dip on his shirt. Maggie laughed and got another chip.

"Good. So we have a plan. You call your mom tonight, get all the facts. Then maybe tomorrow or the next day, give your grandparents a call and maybe go out to lunch with them? If you pick a neutral spot, I think it will be a little less emotional," Luke said, wiping his shirt with his napkin.

Maggie nodded. "Okay. And thanks for today. When I was sitting on that couch today, I just remember feeling so grateful you were with me. I needed you today. *So much.* And it's kind of scary for me to need people. Thanks, Luke," she said sincerely, and smiled at him.

Luke smiled back and grabbed her hand across the table. "Like I said before, we're the mutual rescue society. Come on, you can't have forgotten about Jennie so fast."

Maggie grinned. "I'll be on my deathbed someday, and I will still remember Jennie Benchley. I'm not sure if anything will be able to erase her imprint from my mind," she said with a laugh.

Luke raised his eyebrows. "I bet I can."

Maggie laughed. "You're welcome to try."

Luke shook his head at her. "Now you've done it. There's another dare and you know I love a good dare."

Maggie and Luke laughed and ate and talked and then ate even more. When their desserts were served, Luke groaned. "I just don't know if I can do it. I think I'm going to gain a hundred pounds just hanging out with you. Five years from now I'll be a contestant on the *Biggest Loser* and you'll still be skinny and gorgeous. It's not fair," he said, shoveling chocolate fudge-covered cake into his mouth.

Maggie snorted and took a large bite of strawberry cheesecake. "Whatever. But if you're worried, come running with me tomorrow. It'll be fun."

Luke rolled his eyes. "I lift weights, I hike, and I play basketball with my buddies. Running is only for people who have no idea how to have fun," he sneered.

Maggie gasped in outrage. "Are you insane? Did you know I get most of my ideas for my paintings when I run? Running and creativity go hand in hand. What's more fun than inspiration?" she demanded.

Luke looked at her in derision. "One word. Basketball."

Maggie reached over and snagged a bite of Luke's cake. "And that's what you get."

Luke grinned and pushed the rest of the cake toward her. "You are welcome to it. I'm about to explode in a very graphic and disturbing way. Save yourself if you can move fast enough. Or at least cover your eyes," he said dramatically.

Maggie laughed and pulled the cake toward her.

Luke smiled, watching as she gleefully ate. "So what's been the hardest thing for you, growing up as the child of an abuse victim?" he asked seriously.

Maggie's smile faded and she lowered her fork as she thought about it. "Wow, you're the first person who's ever asked me that. I'd have to say there's been a few things that are tough. But for me, it's hard knowing that I've had such an amazing, good, safe life when my mom had the exact opposite. Where I had a mom who loved me and would protect me with her life, she didn't. Where she had to grow up at a very young age, I still feel like I'm thirteen sometimes. I guess it's survivors guilt to some degree."

Luke rested his chin on his hands and studied her. "But you said your mom's really happy now with her new husband. Does that make it easier?" he asked.

Maggie shrugged and took a sip of water. "It should, huh? When my mom met Terry it was like she was falling in love for the first time. She was so excited and happy and would just walk around the house smiling all the time. And I really like Terry. I remember talking to him one time when my mom was getting ready for their date, and I was kind of grilling him. I was real tough, and I was trying to scare him a little, you know? Like the talk where the dad usually says, 'If you hurt my little girl, I'm coming after you with my rifle' sort of thing. Only I was twenty-one and it was my mom and I might have said something about how I'd use every penny I had to ruin him if he ever hurt her. And I'll always remember what Terry said. He said, 'I know you're worried, because I know what your mom's been through, and I know that it will be hard for her to even have a relationship with me. But I'm going to promise you right now, that if she's willing to give me her widow's mite, everything she has in her heart that she's able to give me, then that is more than enough for me.' He said, 'I'll take care of her, Maggie. I love her and I'll protect her.' "

Maggie paused and cleared her throat for a moment. "And that's when I knew I could relax. I could trust him with my mother. Some of my first memories as a child are of waking up at night and hearing my mom cry. Terry says she only cries every now and then. But he's asked me to do something. He wants me to get a picture of my mom as a happy little girl. *Before* Nathan Palmer came into the picture. He wants my mom to have that memory of herself as an innocent, untouched happy child. He says it's important to her healing process. I saw my grandmother today, Luke. I looked into her eyes. And I'm sorry, but I can't do it," she conceded, twisting her napkin into knots in her lap.

Luke frowned and looked pensive. "We'll find a way. You don't have to do it tomorrow. Let's just work on one thing at a time. And right now, that's you. Let's just get you to where you can be with your grandparents and be comfortable. And let's work on getting you comfortable with the thought of me in your life. After that, then we'll get your mom's picture. We don't have to fix everything all in one day," he said with an encouraging smile.

Maggie laughed. "What do you mean, I need to get comfortable with you? *I am!* Heck, you're now my new best friend, I've hugged you like a million times and you've even *kissed* me. If I get anymore comfortable, we'll be picking out china patterns together," she said, finishing off the last bite of chocolate cake.

Luke shrugged. "It's something you said in the car. You said you felt emotionally stunted because you were scared of how dangerous physical intimacy can be. I don't want you to be scared of me. Because I've got to tell you, when I look at you, I see china patterns. All over the place. I just feel somehow that if you can make peace with what happened to your mom, then you can feel free to move to the next level with me," he said seriously, his eyes a stormy dark green.

Maggie winced and sighed heavily. *Why did he have to be so perceptive?* "We can always just window shop for china patterns, right?" she asked.

Luke shook his head. "Window shopping is for cowards. This is real life, sweetie. For the first time in a long while, I know what it's like to feel free. I want you to feel the same way. Because when I look at you, I see an achingly beautiful girl, who's so talented and so smart and so good and kind and giving. But she's scared," he said, leaning back against the bench cushions.

Maggie stared at him in surprise. "Look, my mom raised me to be strong, but strong doesn't mean I don't get to be scared. I think I have a right to be scared. I think it's okay to be cautious. Okay, yeah, I'm twenty-four. I might have overdone the caution, but this is *my* life. I'm doing the best I can. I'll make peace with what happened to my mother when I'm good and ready. Why are you pushing me?" she demanded almost angrily.

Luke frowned back at her. "Because *this* is too important. You're too important! You and me, Maggie. I feel it so strongly. Don't you feel like every minute we spend together we're more and more connected? Can't you feel this happening between us? If you can, then don't you think it's worth it to get past this?"

Maggie gulped and looked away. "Just slow down Luke, you're freaking me out."

Luke frowned. "Okay. I get it. I'll back off. I just know that you're a very up-front person who is painfully honest with people. I thought you could take a little honesty," he said in disappointment.

Maggie glared at him. "There's honesty and then there's too much too soon. Let's just back up and start again, okay? Forget the china patterns, forget secondhand victimization. Let's forget everything and just pretend that life is easy and simple for just a moment. Can't we?" she pleaded.

Luke smiled wistfully. "No. We can't. And I don't want to. The problem with make-believe is that you have to wake up some time. And by the time you do, you've lost your chance at having something worth so much more. Come on. Let's go," he said, standing up and throwing some bills down on the table.

Luke held her hand as they walked to the car, but they drove home in complete silence. Halfway over the point of the mountain, Maggie scooted over as far as her seat belt would let her and leaned her head on Luke's shoulder.

Fifteen minutes later he stopped the car in his driveway. Maggie lifted her head and sat up straight. "You're right, I do feel it. For some reason, we are connected."

Luke let out a large sigh of relief. "Good, I'm glad that's settled. Come on, I'll walk you to your door. You've got a phone call to make, and I have some china to order," he joked.

Maggie watched him walk away as she locked the door. His brief but warm good-bye hug had left her feeling bereft for some reason. She turned on her outside lights and walked up to her room. She flopped on her bed and threw her arm over her eyes. She could put it off until tomorrow, but she knew her mom had work in the morning. She could put it off until tomorrow night, but then, she would just have to deal with the weight of thinking about it for another twenty-four hours. She groaned and reached for her cell phone.

She listened to the phone ring and hoped her mother didn't pick up. But her mom always picked up when she called. Always.

"Honey! I'm so glad you called. Terry and I were just talking about driving up to Alpine to see your house. What do you think? Are you up for a little company?" Lisa asked, her voice sounding excited.

Maggie's mouth opened in shock. Her mom wanted to come back to Alpine? *Unreal.*

"Mom, first off, you're not company. You're my mom. I could be living out of my car and I'd still have room for you to visit. Of course you and Terry should come. I would really love that. I want you to meet Luke. He's my neighbor I was telling you about. He's really nice but at the same time he can be grouchy and *pushy*, but he's really up-front, which I love. And he came with me to meet my grandparents and he was just amazing and he took me to dinner afterwards. I really, *really* like him," she said, smiling at herself at how goofy she must sound.

Lisa laughed in delighted surprise. "Oh my word, you don't know how long I've waited to hear that. I'm definitely coming now. I've got to meet this guy. He must be incredible. Let me guess. He's tall, blonde, and blue-eyed. He's into martial arts like you. He's a musician because you like creative people. And he's really poor because he gives all his money to build schools and wells in Africa. Am I close?" Lisa asked, half serious.

Maggie snorted loud and long. "You have never been so wrong in your life. He is tall though. But he's dark and his eyes are kind of multi-colored. Sometimes they're green, sometimes they're blue. They're shaman eyes," she said, smiling.

"Dear, that's called hazel. It's pretty common, actually."

Maggie rolled her eyes, even though her mom couldn't see her. "Mom, I think I know what hazel means. Just wait. You'll see what I mean when you meet him. And he's not a musician. He's a banker. But he does like woodworking in his spare time. And he's definitely not poor. You should see his car. It's kind of posh," she said, wishing she could see her mom's expression.

Lisa made humming noises over the phone. "Well, that's just odd. It sounds like you picked somebody the complete opposite of yourself."

"There's not a whole lot of choice involved here. It just feels so . . . inevitable. I don't mean that in a dreary sort of way. I'm not sure how to describe it except, that for some reason, this person I just met has come to be very important to me. If he took off and left tomorrow and I never saw him again, I think my heart would hurt every single day of my life. It's nothing to do with how similar we are, it's just that . . . he fits me," she said lamely, not knowing how to express herself

"Are you getting ready to sing a Celine Dion song?" Lisa asked seriously.

Maggie laughed and groaned at the same time. "Come on, Mom, help me out here. You know my track record with guys. I just don't want to mess this up."

Lisa laughed. "Honey, you're doing great. Any girl who has a guy going with her to meet her estranged grandparents and then taking her out to dinner is doing something right. I don't want to scare you or anything, but as your mother, this sounds kind of serious. *And that's okay.*"

Maggie sighed and closed her eyes. "Now you sound like Luke. He's already talking china patterns."

Lisa made more humming noises. "I have to meet him. Terry and I can't get time off until next week, but we are there."

Maggie smiled, excited that she would see her mom soon. "I'll warn him," she said, and talked to her mom about her visit with the Tierneys. She didn't bring up anything serious though. She mostly talked about the peach pie. She figured if her mom was going to be coming to Alpine, she'd save that painful conversation for a face to face. She disconnected ten minutes later and automatically felt better. Luke was right: she needed to deal with all of her issues. But maybe her issues could wait just one more week.

Chapter 16

Maggie got up the next day and went running again. She ran all over the other side of Alpine, which took maybe twenty minutes, and then ran back toward her house. She needed to find a Jujitsu studio fast. She needed to get some of her pent up energy out, and running was only doing so much. She slowed to a walk as she came to Sophie's salon and looked in the window so she could wave if she saw her. A blonde girl with a toddler on her hip was standing in the doorway and yelled back in to the salon.

"Sophie! Does she look like a model who needs to gain a few pounds?"

"Yeah!" someone yelled back.

Maggie frowned at the woman, and started to walk away.

"*Uh-uh.* Not so fast. You're wanted inside," the blonde woman said in a bossy way.

Maggie pointed a finger to her chest and looked around to see who this girl could possibly be talking to when Sophie stuck her head out the door.

"Hey, Maggie. Are you here for your manicure? Because trust me, you *desperately* need one today," she said, raising her eyebrows in a meaningful way.

Maggie squinched up her nose and looked at her cuticles. They were pathetic, but there was no emergency. Was there?

"Why don't I run home and take a shower first. I can come back later today. I've got some things I need to do," she said, starting to walk backwards.

Sophie shook her head and the blonde woman opened the door wider. "Honey, if you know what's good for you, you'll get your rear inside."

Maggie bit her lip and walked past the two women standing like soldiers at the door. She had no idea women in Alpine took their nails so dang seriously.

She sat down in the chair Sophie indicated and held out her hands. Sophie grabbed some tools and got to work.

"So my mom and the Benchleys are in the same ward. You'll never guess what Marlene told my mom on Sunday after Relief Society," Sophie said as the blonde girl sat down next to them, leaning her chin on her hands and looking rapt.

"Oh, this is Jacie. She's cool. She's been my friend forever and she agrees with us. Luke needs to be Benchley free."

Maggie nodded in complete agreement. "Nice to meet you, Jacie. So what did Marlene say to your mom?" she prodded.

Sophie shook her head grimly and grabbed a file. "Well, all I can say is you must have rubbed Jennie the wrong way, because from what I can tell, she has just declared holy war all over you. I think she realizes finally that Luke isn't going to happen for her. But now that Luke is ready to move on, she says *she's* going to find the perfect girl for him. She's told everyone that will listen that you're an evil witch and that you're using some kind of mind control over him to take over his life. She says you won't let him eat anything but health food, you won't let him see any of his old friends, and that you're already planning to marry him and have his children," Sophie said, looking at her questioningly.

Maggie burst out laughing and shook her head. Jacie traded looks with Sophie as they waited. Maggie got herself under control and then told them everything that happened from the first night she met Luke to her leap over the fence, to her taking back the keys to Luke's house.

Jacie and Sophie were grinning from ear to ear by the time she stopped talking. "You are something else, girl. We could have used you in high school, huh Jacie?" Sophie said with admiration.

Jacie grinned and sat back. "Daphne would have been contained so much better if we'd had Maggie. Crud, where have you been?" she demanded.

Maggie smiled and shrugged. "St. George. So what can Jennie even do? Really? I mean, she's just ticked at me, but it's Luke's life. I don't care if she tells everyone in Alpine I'm a weird food-crazy brat. Would anyone even believe her?" she asked with a shake of her head.

Sophie and Jacie exchanged glances. "Well, actually, yeah. They probably would. You see, the Benchleys are kind of like Alpine royalty. Their dad was the mayor for a few years. Their mom, Marlene, was PTA president forever, and Melanie was like the princess that everyone liked. She raised money for orphanages in South America and she spent her summers reading to senior citizens who were bedridden. She was just kind of perfect. And she loved Luke *so* much. It was almost like she worshipped him. And when she died, Alpine mourned in a big way. And Luke was practically theirs, you know. They feel a little possessive about him, which is kind of understandable. So if Jennie goes around and tells everybody that there's some conniving witch going for Luke, well, all I can say is watch out. Things could get tough for you," Sophie said with a frown.

Jacie nodded and looked perplexed. "I actually *like* Jennie. She was my science partner in school and if it wasn't for her, I'd still be in summer school. Who'd have thought that sweet little Jennie could turn so mean over a man," she murmured.

Maggie frowned, feeling out of sorts. She'd never had a whole town hate her before. "So what should I expect? Are they going to toilet paper my house? Steal my morning paper? Bar me from the town parade? What?" she asked, watching as her nails went from plain and colorless to bright lime green with tiny diamond-like jewels on the tips. *Cool.*

Sophie shook her head. "This is Alpine, honey. It doesn't work that way. They'll try killing you with kindness. But I wouldn't worry about that. Jennie's plan is to take Luke away from you. She's already got a list a mile long of women she'd rather see Luke with. From what Marlene was telling my mom last night, she doesn't care who he ends up with as long as it isn't *you.*"

Maggie winced and felt glum. "Dang, and I've only been here a month."

Jacie laughed and got up to grab her son who was climbing over the play wall. "I can't wait to see what you do in a year."

Sophie smiled encouragingly. "You've got a fight on your hands, but you look to me like someone who can take care of herself."

Maggie let her breath out slowly and tried to smile. "I'm too good at taking care of myself. That's my problem."

Sophie smiled hesitantly like she wasn't sure what she meant by that, but she didn't pry. Maggie talked for a few more minutes before leaving. She walked home and was surprised at how much better her bright, neon lime green fingernails made her feel. She needed to figure out how to deal with Jennie and Marlene Benchley though. Should she warn Luke, or just sit back and watch the show? If Luke was serious about wanting to be with her and all of those china patterns, then he could withstand anything Jennie threw his way. He'd been withstanding Jennie for a few months already and doing a good job of it. *But that was Jennie.* There was no telling who was going to show up on his doorstep now. *But maybe she should be grateful to Jennie.* Now she'd know if Luke was trustworthy. If not? Well, then it was better to know now.

Maggie felt better and went in the house to shower and eat some breakfast. She made herself a huge ham and cheese and salsa omelet and decided to sit on her front porch and eat it so she could watch the little world of Alpine go by her door.

She was halfway through her omelet when a dark green Range Rover drove up to her house. She watched curiously as someone got out of the car, carrying a large box. Maggie blinked in surprise as she realized it was her grandmother, Bonnie Tierney. Her eyebrows lowered as she recalled her last words to her grandmother. She had made it very clear that *she* would call *them* after she sorted things out with her mom. And yet here she was. Huh.

Bonnie walked carefully up the walk to the stairs and had to rest for a second before slowly making the climb to where Maggie was sitting.

"So, what's in the box?" Maggie asked in a polite tone.

"Ack!" Bonnie sputtered and moved the box out of the way of her face. "Oh, Maggie. I'm so sorry. I didn't realize you would be sitting out on your porch this morning. I figured you'd be painting or something," she said, blushing and looking flustered at being caught.

Maggie almost smiled. "Nope. I'm a porch sitter. I like to see the world go by sometimes," she said, wondering what was in the box.

Bonnie placed the heavy box down on the porch and lifted a paper plate of snickerdoodles off the top and handed them to her. There was a note taped to the cellophane.

"I was just going to drop these off for you since we didn't get a chance to go through them yesterday, what with my hysterical crying jag getting in the way of a good visit."

Maggie smiled and felt her heart soften a little for her grandmother. "You brought me the photo albums?" she asked, ignoring the box and lifting the plastic to take a cookie.

"Yep. All twelve of them. I should have had Frank bring them over but he had an appointment with the chiropractor this morning. He's got a bad back. So here I am. How do they taste?" she asked, watching as Maggie finished one cookie and took another.

Maggie waited to swallow before answering. "Delicious. You are a terrific cook, I have to say," she said honestly.

Bonnie grinned and leaned up against the porch post. "Thanks. Robbie loved those cookies. He'd always ask for them after school. I haven't made them much lately though. It felt good."

Maggie smiled and patted the spot next to her. "Pull up some plank and have a cookie with me, since you're here," she said.

Bonnie looked pleased and sat down immediately and took a cookie. Maggie reached over and took the forgotten note and opened it up. "Let's just see what this says now. Hmm. 'Dear Maggie, thanks for dropping by yesterday. Please enjoy the cookies and the photo albums. Call us anytime. Love Grandma and Grandpa.' "

Maggie cleared her throat. She was kind of touched. *Grandma and Grandpa.* How nice was that?

"I called my mom last night. She's planning on coming up to see me next week, so I thought I'd wait and talk to her about everything that happened before when we can do it face to face," she said, hugging her knees.

Bonnie smiled sadly and held her half-eaten cookie in her hand. "That's probably wise. Frank and I would love to see her if she's willing. We could come here or go somewhere else if she doesn't want to come to our home," she said carefully.

Maggie studied her grandmother's grim face. "I know what happened to my mom."

Bonnie looked at her quickly and then looked away again. "Oh, I didn't know if she'd told you. She never really told me, I just, somehow . . . *knew.*"

Maggie nodded and sighed, putting the plastic back over the plate. "I'll tell her you want to see her," she said, changing the subject. She felt too raw to talk about her mom's past anymore.

"Maggie, just so you know, I'm not sure how you're going to feel about this, but I was at church on Sunday. The Benchleys are in my ward and Marlene and Jennie were saying some unkind things about you. I just want you to know that I set Marlene straight. Just between you and me, that woman won't say one more thing about you if I have anything to do with it," she said in a brisk but surprisingly tough voice.

Maggie grinned. "You had a throw down with Marlene Benchley over me?" she asked, delighted with her grandmother.

Bonnie sniffed and whisked some crumbs off her linen capris. "Honey, nobody but nobody is going to mess with *my* granddaughter. You just got here. If anybody thinks they're going to scare you off, well, they just have to go through me first," she said, her cheeks turning rosy.

Maggie laughed and clapped her hands. "Oh, I would have loved to have seen that. Thanks!" she said, feeling immensely better knowing her grandma had her back.

Bonnie smiled and patted her granddaughter's knee. "Well, I've got Marlene taken care of but Jennie's all yours. There won't be any vicious gossip going around but from what I heard last night, Luke's in for it," she said worriedly.

Maggie shrugged and leaned back on her hands. "I'm not scared. If Luke's worth having, he'll still be standing when all the smoke clears."

Bonnie chuckled and stood up. "You are just like your dad, you know that? Your dad never once ran from a fight. He was always one to jump in. Usually to defend someone else though. Well, I've got to get going. I've got a hair appointment this morning. I have the best hairstylist in town. I'll have to get you her card. Sophie is a genius with hair," she said and walked down the stairs, waving her fingers over her shoulder.

Maggie watched her grandmother walk away and grinned. Grandmas were really kind of cool. They made you cookies and they stuck up for you. She could get used to this. She stood up and went in the house with her cookies and plate and came back for the box of photo albums. She would save those for tonight when she could cuddle up with a blanket and concentrate. Right now, she needed to do something. She looked around her house and decided to tackle the basement. She knew she had one, she just wasn't sure what was in it. As a responsible homeowner, she probably should find out.

She spent all afternoon going through boxes and making a pile for DI and a pile to take upstairs. She found a box of old clothes that must have been from the 1950s that she couldn't wait to try on. She adored vintage. Another box held really old sun dresses. She took her treasures upstairs with her and decided to take a Propel out on the front porch with some cookies and a sandwich. It was almost time for Luke to get home from work, and she wanted to tell him about her call with her mom.

She munched happily on her ham and cheese when she noticed a young teenage girl across the street sweeping the front porch of her house. She looked kind of sad in a mopey, slightly depressed, teenagerish way. Maggie smiled and remembered her own adolescent angst. She said a tiny prayer of thanks for making it to her twenties as she walked across the street to meet her neighbor.

"Hi there. I'm Maggie, your new neighbor, and aren't you just beautiful," she said with a friendly smile.

The girl looked shocked and taken aback. "*Me?* Beautiful?" she asked in a stunned voice.

Maggie grinned. "Of course you. I have two perfectly good eyes, don't I? Have you ever done any modeling?" she asked, studying the young girl carefully. She wasn't what the world or fashion magazines would call beautiful, but she had an old-fashioned simplicity to her face that was refreshing and beautiful in its own way. She reminded her of a pioneer girl. Maggie's eyes rounded as she got an idea.

"Nah, I've never modeled. Are you kidding me?" the girl asked suspiciously.

Maggie shook her head. "What's your name?"

"Cheyenne," the girl said, looking at her strangely.

Maggie put her hands in her jeans pockets, still studying the girl. "Cheyenne, I'm an artist and I would love to paint you. I pay pretty good, but you'd have to ask your mom and dad," she said, deadly serious. She was already picturing Cheyenne in one of her great-grandmother's sun dresses standing on Cemetary Hill, maybe looking over her shoulder with the wind in her hair. Maggie smiled, already excited at the possibilities.

Cheyenne blushed and leaned on her broom. "You're an artist? Really?"

Maggie grinned, not offended. No one believed a girl in her early twenties did much except go to the mall and hang out with friends. She didn't mind surprising people.

"Yeah, really. But first tell me about yourself. I want to know everything," she said.

The two girls spent the next forty-five minutes sitting on the porch and talking about everything. Cheyenne had two older brothers who were football players on the Lone Peak football team. Her mom was a nurse and worked most nights and her dad was a pharmaceutical sales rep and was gone except for the weekends. So that left Cheyenne on her own a lot. Maggie asked about her friends, and she had a few, but since she didn't drive yet, she had a hard time being with them. Her mom paid her to clean and cook, so she felt good about that. She was halfway to earning enough money for a down payment on a car for when she turned sixteen next month.

Maggie liked Cheyenne. She reminded Maggie of herself at that age. So unsure and kind of lonely. Maggie knew she just needed a little boost to her self-esteem, and modeling for her would be a good start.

They watched as Gwen came out of her house and walked to the mail box. Maggie decided to be the ultimate neighbor and call out to her.

"Hey, Gwen! Come chat with us!" she called out. Cheyenne looked shocked and sort of intimidated, but Maggie had a feeling Cheyenne could use a little female bonding.

Gwen walked over immediately, holding a pile of letters in her hand.

"Hey, Cheyenne. Don't let Maggie scare you now, she's just one of those strange people who don't realize that regular people just don't chat much anymore. Least of all with their neighbors," Gwen said with a grin.

Maggie rolled her eyes with Cheyenne. "Gwen, now don't go upsetting me. Or I might call the Buhlers over to talk too," she said, watching Gwen's horrified expression with a giggle. Cheyenne giggled softly too.

"They don't like us much. They think my brothers are too big and noisy."

Gwen snorted and sat down next to them on the porch. "They don't like dogs either. Enough said," she said with disgust in her voice.

Maggie wisely decided to keep her fear of dogs to herself. "So Gwen, did you know lung cancer is a horrible way to die?" she asked conversationally.

Gwen laughed and shook her head. "You think you're funny, don't you?" she said.

Cheyenne's face had turned white with shock as she looked back and forth between the women. Maggie winked at her. "Come on, Gwen. You know you want to quit."

Gwen smiled. "Of course I do. Just not as much as I want to keep smoking."

Maggie frowned and watched in interest as Luke drove up in his car and parked in his driveway. She figured on talking for a few more minutes before walking over to join him. She watched silently though as a large SUV drove up and parked right behind Luke's car. It was filled with six energetic teenage girls and one very curvy, very attractive woman.

Maggie's face turned to stone as she realized what was happening. This was Jennie's first wave in the battle for Luke. They must have been on the lookout for him. She stared in silence, wishing she could hear what was being said. She, Gwen, and Cheyenne didn't say one word as the girls started washing Luke's car. The beautiful woman directed the entire production as Luke stood back with a pleased grin on his face.

From where Maggie was sitting, the woman looked to be about her own age. But where Maggie was thin and muscular, this girl was the exact opposite. Eve must have looked like this girl. She had long, glossy, strawberry blonde hair and her face could have been on the cover of *Bride's Magazine* she glowed so much.

Gwen lit a cigarette and blew the smoke over Maggie's head. "Hmm. If you don't get your rear over there and neutralize that situation, Luke's going to be way out of your reach," she said direly.

Maggie glared at Luke. "That's what you think," she said sourly.

Gwen coughed a little. "Cheyenne, honey, does one of your brother's have binoculars? Could you run and grab them for me? Maggie doesn't believe that that expression of joy on Luke's face means anything. She needs a closer look."

Maggie frowned and leaned her elbows on her knees. Luke better wipe that joy right off his face if he knew what was good for him.

"It's just nature, Maggie. Don't take it personally. I raise dogs, so I know all about it. Pretty girl, good-looking guy. One plus one equals two. End of story. Unless of course you want to walk on over there and do something about it," Gwen said, not unkindly.

Maggie huffed as Cheyenne appeared with the binoculars and handed them to her. She put them to her eyes and zoomed right in on Luke's face. He hadn't looked like this when Jennie had shown up at his door. But right now, Luke looked like he was in heaven. He was talking animatedly to the woman as the girls soaped and rinsed his car. He was laughing. She focused on his eyes, but wasn't quite sure what color they were. They seemed to be just his regular hazel color. No gleaming bright greens or bright blues. Surely, if he were interested in this woman, his eyes would tell the truth.

"I bet that girl's waist is twenty-six inches," Gwen interjected, making Maggie lower the binoculars and glare at her.

"So what? I have a twenty-five-inch waist. What's the big deal?" she asked snottily.

Gwen snorted. "Honey, do you have any brains in there at all? Hips are the big deal. You might have a tiny waist, but your hips are just as narrow. That girl over there has something *artists* call contrast. It makes men notice. I'm telling you, you better hustle," Gwen warned.

Maggie groaned and gave the binoculars to Gwen. "What? I'm just supposed to walk over there and he'll forget about *her*?"

Gwen looked at her like she was an idiot. "No, you have to substitute his visual feast with something concrete. Just walk up and give him a hug. It marks your territory and cancels her out. Nothing to it. If more people just paid attention to dogs, life would be so much easier."

Maggie laughed. "Mark my territory? Are you serious. Like a dog?"

Gwen looked like she was trying to hold on to her patience. "Not like a dog. Like a woman. Better hurry though. Looks like those girls are almost done, and that's when she's going to hit him up for dinner at her house or something. Time's running out," Gwen said, blowing smoke rings over her head.

Maggie stood up and held her hand out. "You want a show? *Fine.* Give me all your cigarettes and promise not to smoke for at least twelve hours and I'll do it," she said calmly.

Gwen looked up at her in horror. "Are you serious?" she asked.

Maggie looked over her shoulder at Luke who was looking way too happy. "I'm as serious as it gets."

"Fine! Here, you evil thing. Take them, but you better put on a good show," Gwen warned, throwing her cigarettes at Maggie.

Maggie caught the carton one handed and shoved them in her pocket. She smiled at Cheyenne and walked across the street. She was just a little irritated when Luke didn't even notice that she was coming his way. *What?* An attractive woman ruined your peripheral vision?

"Hey, Luke! I didn't know you were home already," she said a few feet away from him right before she walked right up to him, threw her arms around his neck, and did something unheard of for her—initiate a kiss. She pressed her lips as firmly and possessively as she knew how against Luke's mouth and smiled against him as she felt his surprise. It didn't last too long as he wrapped his arms around her waist and kissed her back with enough enthusiasm that she forgave him for smiling so much at the woman standing behind her.

Luke finally pulled away, grinning his head off. "Today is turning out to be the best day ever. I'm getting kissed *and* my car washed for free. Tell me I'm not dreaming."

Maggie pinched him. *Maybe harder than she should have,* just so he knew for sure he was awake.

"So who are all your nice *little* friends?" she asked as she turned to face the woman who was Jennie's idea of a perfect match for Luke.

Luke smiled and walked her over to the girl. "Maggie, this is Rebecca Layton. She's my best friend Daren's little sister. Rebecca's the Beehive advisor in her ward and they're doing drive by service projects. Isn't that a great idea? They're just driving around town looking for someone who needs a little help. I'm lucky. I just barely got home, and they showed up," he said, shaking his head at his good fortune.

Maggie smiled sweetly at the silent woman standing in front of them, who looked a little nervous now.

"Rebecca. What a lovely name. That is so interesting you just *happened* to be driving by Luke's house. It's almost unreal," she said as she bent over to pick up a sponge and hand it to her. As she did, Gwen's cigarette's fell out of her pocket and onto the soggy grass. Luke and Rebecca stared at the cigarettes in surprise. Maggie hurried and picked them up.

"Oh, these aren't mine. I'm just holding them for a friend," she said, hating the blush that was slowly creeping up her face.

Luke noticed all the Beehives staring in horror at Maggie and the pack of cigarettes in her hand and cleared his throat. "Well, we all know smoking is against the Word of Wisdom. I hope your friend realizes how unhealthy it is," he said loudly for the benefit of all the impressionable twelve-year-old girls.

Rebecca tore her eyes away from Maggie and the cigarettes still clenched in her hand and focused on Luke. "Well, Luke we're done here. Thanks so much for letting my girls get a little service in. Oh, and I forgot to tell you, Daren is coming by the house tonight. You should come over and play a little basketball with him. He was telling me just the other day how much fun the two of you used to have," she said, as she flicked her gorgeous glossy hair back over her shoulder.

Maggie rolled her eyes. This girl was good. She wasn't doing the direct assault like Jennie had. She was using basketball and her brother to move Luke into her territory. Well, like she told her grandmother, she'd just wait to see if Luke was still standing after the smoke cleared. She'd had no idea at the time just how smoky it was going to get.

Luke glanced at Maggie first before answering. "Um, that sounds like fun. Tell Daren to give me a call tonight. It's been awhile since we've talked some serious smack," he said, looking happy.

Rebecca grinned and turned back to her girls. She had just moved ten paces ahead.

"Come on, girls. Let's pack up. There are more people in Alpine needing someone like us to make their day better," she said cheerily.

Maggie picked up a discarded towel and walked it over to Rebecca. "Oh Rebecca? You forgot this. And by the way, good job there. Tell Jennie she's smarter than I thought," she said and walked away as Rebecca's mouth fell open in shock.

She walked back to where Luke was standing and smiled brightly. "Wow, that Rebecca is *so* darn cute."

Luke's eyes brightened and he grinned at her. "Uh-huh. She certainly is. Did you know she was the first girl I ever kissed?" He asked as he waved merrily at the departing SUV.

Maggie frowned and kicked a stick with her toe. "Actually, no, I was completely unaware of that."

Luke pulled her toward him and tilted her face up to his. "I'm so loving this jealousy thing you've got going," he said, laughing as he pushed her hair behind her ears.

Maggie had never pouted before in her life, but she felt a full-on pout cross her face. "You are sadly mistaken. This is what you call amusement at a smart man, being taken in by lots of big white teeth and too much hair. You're just imagining things. But just out of curiosity, what happened between you and Rebecca? I mean, since she was your first kiss and all. There's got to be a story there."

Luke pulled her in and hugged her, rubbing her back and chuckling at the same time. "Rebecca dumped me in the eighth grade for a ninth grader who had his very own dirt bike. Ever since then, I've been immune to her charms. She didn't just break my heart, she shattered it, stomped on it, and then lit it on fire. I love a clean car just as much as the next man, but I just don't think I could ever trust her again," he said, leaning back and looking down into her face, his eyes twinkling at her.

Maggie sniffed and looked away. "Well, she does sound kind of shallow."

Luke smiled warmly at her and then kissed her cheek. "Exactly my point. Come on. You can come keep me company while I heat up this casserole. You wouldn't believe it, but this girl I went out with a few times in high school dropped by the bank today and said she was just thinking of me and how we should get together sometime," he said, picking up the casserole dish off the porch.

Maggie sighed and shook her head at the power of an angry woman. "I believe it," she said and followed him to his door. She looked back over her shoulder first and gave Gwen and Cheyenne a V for victory sign. She wasn't surprised to see that Gwen had the binoculars firmly plastered to her face. Cheyenne waved back excitedly though.

Maggie grinned and walked through the door Luke was holding open for her.

Chapter 17

"So care to tell me when you started smoking? Is this a new thing, or an old, wicked habit I'm unaware of?" Luke asked as he walked into the kitchen and laid the casserole dish on the stove.

Maggie got two plates out of the cupboard and handed them to Luke. "Sorry about traumatizing those Beehives. I had just barely torn them from Gwen's claws when you showed up," she said as she watched Luke dish up an extremely large amount of . . . *something*.

"Um, Luke? What is that? That is not a tater tot," she said, walking over to look at what seemed to be little spongy looking squares, scattered over what could only be whole wheat noodles in a very watery-looking green sauce.

Luke poked around a bit before putting half of what was on his plate back in the casserole dish.

"This would be an honest-to-goodness, tofu something, something, casserole," he said, sounding morose.

Maggie put her hand to her mouth and giggled. Jennie must have warned all the girls Maggie was siccing on Luke to focus on health foods. Poor baby. She put her plate back down on the counter and shook her head.

"You know what? I just forgot, but I've got a couple chicken breasts marinating back at home," she said, backing toward the door.

Luke looked so forlorn, Maggie *almost* had pity on him. "See ya," she said, turning around to leave.

"Wait right there. Now let's be fair. I fed you just yesterday and that's no small job. Can't you invite *me* to dinner?" He asked as he quickly put the tinfoil back in place.

Maggie turned back and leaned her hip against the doorjamb. "I don't think so. What if your ex-girlfriend calls and asks you how you liked your yummy dinner? She must have gone to a lot of trouble to make that for you. It would be heartless not to eat it," she said, trying not to laugh.

Luke squinched up his nose in disgust but picked up a fork and took a bite from his plate. She watched him chew and chew and chew and chew. He held up his hand a minute later and walked to the kitchen sink. He spit it out and washed it down the garbage disposal.

"Sorry you had to see that, but I just couldn't do it. So what kind of side dishes are you making to go with your chicken?" he asked, clapping his hands together and looking at her hopefully.

Maggie laughed and gave in. "You are so naughty. I'm *never* making you a casserole. That's two now that have gone uneaten. Poor Jennie and now, who was it you said made this for you?" she asked sweetly.

Luke grinned and shrugged. "Her name is Maddy. Really cute girl by the way," he said as he walked happily past her toward the front door.

Maggie shrugged and ignored the crack about how cute his ex-girlfriend was. "Hold it mister. I don't hang out with bankers. Go change into normal people clothes, and I'll meet you back at my house," she ordered, walking past him.

He grumbled a little but ran up the stairs in record time. Maggie got home and put the chicken breasts in the oven and started the salad. She really hadn't thought of any very exciting side dishes. Of course she still had half a plate of snicker doodles. Thank you, Grandma!

Luke let himself in the house and walked into the kitchen dressed in an old T-shirt, long shorts, and tennis shoes. He really was looking forward to playing basketball later. He made himself right at home and started chopping the tomatoes.

"See, we'll be eating healthy tonight. I just don't understand why some people equate green and slimy with healthy. If you can't eat it, how can it help you?" he complained as they worked companionably side by side.

Maggie smiled and shook her head. He had no clue what was coming his way. She could only imagine what types of yummy health food he was in for. They ate outside on her patio table and talked about their day. She told him about her mom coming to see her and her grandmother's visit.

Luke was just reaching for a third snickerdoodle when his cell phone went off in his pocket. He grabbed it before Maggie could fully enjoy "Life is a Highway." She reminded herself she needed to get a new ring tone.

Luke talked for less than a minute and then stood up. "Bye, Maggie. Daren's waiting for me. Thanks for dinner!" he said and took off.

Maggie smiled after him and remembered the man she had first met. Luke had gone from a cranky, depressed person, to a man running to his car so he could go play with his friend. She laughed to herself as she picked up their empty plates and headed inside. It was amazing what letting a little light in could do for the soul.

She cleaned up the kitchen and took all of the photo albums into the family room off the kitchen. She ignored the couch and lay on her stomach and spread them all out before her. They were numbered in big yellow post-its. Her grandmother was either very organized or very thoughtful.

She opened it up and gazed at her grandmother in the hospital holding a small, red little baby, while she beamed at the camera. There was a young girl of about two or three sitting on the hospital bed with her—her aunt who had died so young and tragically. She turned the pages and watched as her dad slowly grew up. He was so blonde that the top of his head looked like a flashlight in some pictures. She smiled sadly, remembering how she'd always wanted to be a blonde like all of her friends in elementary school. Well, she definitely carried the gene somewhere inside.

She turned the page again and saw a picture of her dad playing in a little plastic pool with a little girl of about the same age. The girl had long brown, wavy hair and bright happy brown eyes. There was a whole page of pictures of the two playing together. She pulled the plastic back carefully and lifted the edge of the picture off the sticky page. It came off surprisingly easy. On the back of the first one was an inscription. *Robbie and his little friend Lisa.*

Maggie laid the picture back down and rested her chin on her hands. Her mom and dad, right there in front of her. It was almost too bittersweet to see the faces of her young, beautiful, innocent, and happy parents and know that life would hold so many disappointments and heartaches for them. She turned the pages and watched as her dad and her mom grew up. She felt a great weight lift off her as she realized that here was what Terry wanted. She didn't need to go to her grandmother Palmer and ask her for anything. She had her mom's childhood right in front of her. She decided she would go down tomorrow and make color copies of everything and put them in a picture book for herself and her mother. She'd wrap it up and give it to her mom when she drove up next week.

Maggie smiled sadly and wondered if this would be the last step in her mom's healing. She hoped so. She got up an hour later to grab some tissues and a Propel. She was getting dehydrated from the tears that kept slipping down her cheeks. She wasn't *really* crying, not like her grandmother had the other day, it was more like her heart was just so full, it kept overflowing.

She grabbed the last picture album at ten o'clock and opened it as she decided to sit on the couch after all. Her elbows were getting sore. This album wasn't very heavy. It was only filled halfway. She got comfy and opened the first page. She flipped to the next page and it was a picture of her dad at the prom with a beautiful girl with long blonde hair and bright blue eyes. *Not her mom.* And the way her dad was looking down at this girl, he looked like he was in love with her.

Maggie frowned. She had assumed her dad and mom had been high school sweethearts. Not according to this picture. She looked at the other pictures and noticed the blonde girl in pictures with her dad at a baseball game and on a camping trip. *Interesting.* Maybe her grandma and grandpa could tell her more about this girl and how her dad went from being in love at the prom to marrying her mom a couple months later.

Maggie sighed and turned the page. It was of her dad laying in a hospital bed. He looked so stoic, so resigned almost. He didn't look anything like the young boy in the other albums. His eyes were older and more serious. She sniffed and blew her nose. No seventeen- or eighteen-year-old should look so burdened. The next picture was her dad's graduation. He was smiling with his arms around his mom and dad, but his eyes told another story. His eyes were filled with a desperate kind of resolve. Maggie closed her own as she turned to the last page. She gasped as she saw pictures of a funeral. How tragic to go from high school graduation to a funeral. Someone must have taken these for her grandparents because they were in most of them. Her grandfather was weeping openly in most of them and her grandmother looked like everyone she was hugging was actually holding her up. Maggie felt her own tears start anew and she reached for another tissue. She wiped her cheeks and turned to the back of the last page. There was only one more photograph. It was of her mother, looking a lot like she did now, only younger. She brought the picture up close to her face since the tears had blurred her focus. It was a close-up of Lisa throwing a single white rose onto the top of her dad's casket. Her face was gray and terrified. She looked completely lost and hopeless.

Maggie looked closer at the picture and frowned. Standing behind her mother and to the side was her grandmother Palmer, she was sure of it. And with her, a man, looking at her mother with an expression so filled with yearning she felt ill just being a witness to it more than twenty years later.

Maggie shut the book and pushed it away from her, drawing her knees up and feeling horrified at seeing her mother's abuser. He looked so normal. *So nice.* He'd been attractive and wearing a good suit and looking just like everyone else. Except for his eyes. The eyes were the window to the soul, and his eyes looked like perdition.

Maggie stood up and rubbed her arms, feeling cold and haunted. She tried to think of good things. She thought about how happy her mom was with her career and her marriage. She thought of how her dad was now free from cancer and in heaven. And she thought of herself, here in Alpine, finding her way. She had to admit, she was happy to know her dad's parents. She was kind of excited to have a relationship with them. But could she really live in the same town as her grandmother Palmer? She winced and walked into the kitchen to get a glass of milk. She didn't know the answer to that yet. In the picture, as Letty Palmer had stood behind her daughter, she hadn't looked at all sad that such an amazing and good young man had died. She had looked strangely appeased.

Maggie shook her head to clear her thoughts and put her glass in the sink. She knew the only thing that could cleanse her mind was the scriptures. Her very own magic eraser. Bad memories? Read the scriptures. Bad thoughts? Read the scriptures. Bad anything? Read the scriptures. Maggie walked upstairs and fell onto her bed, reaching over onto the nightstand for her favorite set of scriptures. Her mom had given her some really fancy, expensive ones for Christmas, but the ones she had used all through seminary were the ones she always turned to when she was sad or needing help. Sometimes she could just flip the pages and turn right to what she needed to hear most. Right now she could use some inspiration. She flipped them open and put her finger down on section 50 verse 35 of the Doctrine and Covenants. She read, "And by giving heed and doing these things which ye have received, and which ye shall hereafter receive—and the kingdom is given you of the Father, *and power to overcome all things which are not ordained of him.*"

Maggie blinked in surprise and read the passage two more times just to make sure she really understood what it meant. She couldn't believe this had been here all this time, just waiting for her to read it. She was given the power to overcome anything *not* ordained of God. Her mom was given the power to overcome anything not ordained of God. Everyone in the world could have the power to overcome anything horrible, or evil, or unfair, or sad, or wrong. *If we do the things we have received.* Maggie thought about that. She had actually received a lot. The gospel of Jesus Christ was amazing in its immensity and yet brilliant in its simplicity. Follow Christ, keep the covenants she had made, basically just do the things that she knew she should do, and she could overcome this.

Maggie sat up in bed and really pondered this. She knew she had been given a key from Heavenly Father. This was important. No, *she* hadn't been sexually abused as a child. She'd never been abused, period. But the imprint of Nathan Palmer's evil still touched her somehow. She felt it's cloying stain seep onto the edges of her soul sometimes. And she hated it. She hated that he was dead and he still had the power to ruin, to degrade, to affect anything to do with her. Luke had felt it. He knew she was scared of starting a serious relationship. She'd always been scared. How nice would it be to not be scared anymore?

Maggie sighed and laid her head on her knees. She'd been doing everything she knew how to do, hadn't she? She did a mental checklist of her sins and virtues. She definitely had more virtues than sins. *What could possibly be holding her up?* she wondered as she opened her scriptures again.

The doorbell sounded downstairs and she immediately smiled, thinking of Luke. He probably wanted to tell her all about how gorgeous Rebecca could make three pointers or something obnoxious. She peeked out her bedroom window and saw a car parked in front of her house. Not Luke. Not Jennie—that wasn't her car. It wasn't the car her grandmother had driven that morning. Who could it be? It was after ten o'clock at night. Way too late for a social visit. She walked quietly to the front door and looked through the peephole. She reared her head back in dismay. It was Letty Palmer. She was standing on her front porch, looking very calm and almost stone-like. Maggie's heartbeat sped up three notches and she looked one more time just to make sure it was who she thought it was. The woman's intense eyes seemed to be looking right at her through the tiny hole in her door.

Maggie felt goose bumps break out on her arms and a cold sweat break out on her forehead. She was not ready for this. Not now. Not yet. Maybe not ever. Especially after seeing that picture of her mother at her father's funeral. Something was very wrong with this woman and she knew down to the tips of her toes she did not want to invite her into her home. She felt like this home was her sanctuary, a safe and good place where she felt her dad's and her great-grandmother's love. She could not let this woman inside. Maggie backed away from the door as Letty rang the doorbell once again. Maggie felt lightening bolts of electricity race along her veins as the sound ricocheted off the walls around her, but she kept moving backward until she reached the kitchen. She sat in her great-grandmother's kitchen chair and hugged herself as she heard the doorbell ring again, more insistently this time. She covered her ears with her hands and felt like calling her grandma Tierney. She could just picture Bonnie now riding to the rescue and chasing Letty Palmer away. She would too.

Her mom had raised her to be strong and to fight her own battles, but this was something else. This wasn't a battle. This was just too hard. She leaned her head against the cold tabletop and prayed that Letty Palmer would just go away and leave her alone.

A few minutes later she heard a rap on the back patio door directly behind her. Maggie let out a scream and leapt up from the table, turning in horror to see her grandmother Palmer's face staring right at her. But it wasn't Letty. *It was Luke.*

Maggie grabbed her chest, where her racing heart was trying to rip itself free. She stumbled to the door and opened it. Luke immediately pulled her tight against his chest and held her as she shuddered uncontrollably.

"I'm so sorry I scared you. I knew if I went to the front door you wouldn't open it. I just got home and saw Letty Palmer standing on your front porch. I had to check and see if you were okay. And you're not," he said softly.

Maggie shook her head and held on to Luke's T-shirt. It was sweaty and gross, but at least it brought her back to reality. Reality was, Luke was here. Letty was gone. She was okay. *She was okay.*

"Sorry for screaming like an idiot there. I thought she had come to the back," she mumbled, starting to feel embarrassed.

Luke rubbed her back and arms, making the goose bumps disappear. "Knock it off, Maggie. Even superheroes hang up their capes sometimes. Come on, sit down. You're still shaking. Why don't I make you some hot chocolate?" he said and turned her toward a chair and pushed her down into it. He looked through her cupboards for what he needed and set about making hot chocolate from scratch. He was actually warming the milk in a pan on the stove and using baking coco and sugar and vanilla. She smiled a little and thought about telling him about the canister of hot coco mix in the pantry but kept silent. It was kind of sweet.

"So tell me all about Rebecca. I bet she plays a mean game of basketball," she said, trying to calm herself down and think about anything else besides her grandmother.

Luke glanced at her over his shoulder and smiled. "There's that jealousy again. You know I love that. And you're right, she was there. She made every single free throw. She's incredible. I will never know why she didn't get a basketball scholarship. Life is so unfair sometimes," he said wearily.

Maggie glared at his back and leaned back in her chair. "Wow, *three hours* of basketball. You must be exhausted, you poor baby," she said in a sweet voice that wasn't exactly natural.

Luke's shoulders shook like he was laughing, but when he spoke his voice was normal. "Honey, it takes a long time to eat strawberry shortcake. Oh my word, you've never seen so many ripe strawberries in your life. And strangely enough, Daren had to leave early, so I felt obligated to eat his share. It takes awhile, Maggie. You understand, right?" he asked, as he continued to stir the milk.

Maggie ground her teeth and thought of all the horrible things she could do or say to Luke. "That's it. I want my painting back," she said, crossing her arms over her chest and feeling extremely annoyed.

Luke burst out laughing and took the hot chocolate off the burner. He walked over to the pantry and searched around until he found the marshmallows and sprinkled a generous handful on top. He brought her over a steaming mug and placed it on the table in front of her. He leaned down and kissed the top of her head and sat down with his own mug.

"I'm sure you do. But if it makes a difference, the whole time I was eating, I was telling Rebecca how much I liked you and what a talented artist you are and how sweet and generous and down to earth you are. I think Rebecca got a little sick of hearing so much about you," he said, blowing on the milk.

Maggie sniffed and took a sip. It was delicious. She smiled and took another sip. "Holy cow, Luke. This is pretty good," she said in surprise.

Luke frowned immediately. "And why wouldn't it be? Dang, Maggie, have some faith."

Maggie sighed and took another sip and relaxed a little. She didn't feel so cold anymore. Luke always did that. He was always warming her up somehow.

"So did you crush Rebecca's hopes or did you give her something to hold onto?" she asked looking at him over the rim of her mug.

Luke gave her a half smile and shrugged. "Well, you know I'm irresistible to women. But I think I made it pretty clear where my interests lie," he said, looking right at her.

Maggie blushed and took another sip. "And where's that?" she asked.

Luke tilted his head and took a sip. "Where they've been since the night I saw a beautiful woman smash a perfectly good easel because she was too impatient to make another trip to her car," he said, smiling and sitting back in his chair.

Maggie smiled back at him. "Good. Because my interests lie in the direction of a man who's inclined to steal perfectly taped-up easels, and who's inclined to disregard perfectly good casseroles and who has the bad habit of always coming to my rescue," she said, reaching over the table and squeezing his hand gratefully.

Luke grasped her hand and they held hands for a few warm and wonderful moments.

"You've been crying," he said abruptly, his voice turning hard as he sat up, staring at her intensely.

Maggie licked her lips and tried to turn her face away. "It's nothing, Luke. Really."

Luke shook his head. "What happened? Was it Letty? Did she say something to you through the door?" he demanded.

Maggie shook her head. "No, it was nothing like that. I told you my grandmother Tierney dropped off a ton of picture albums this morning. I just went through them tonight. It was wonderful, but kind of hard too. I feel so torn up and raw inside right now. And then when she started ringing my doorbell, I just couldn't handle it. Not after seeing all the pictures. Not tonight," she said, feeling sad again.

Luke winced and rubbed her thumb with his. "Oh, Maggie. I'm sorry. I wish I had been here with you. But that reminds me. When I drove up, I saw Letty lean down and put something on your doormat. Do you want me to go get it?" he asked.

Maggie let the air out of her lungs slowly. She didn't want whatever it was her grandmother wanted to give her. "Okay, yeah. If you wouldn't mind," she answered.

Luke left to get whatever it was as she finished her hot chocolate. She stood up and put her mug in the sink and turned when she heard Luke come back in the room. Luke was standing in front of her, holding an open brown paper grocery sack, with a strange expression on his face.

"You better take a look," he said, setting the bag on the counter and stepping away from it as he covered his mouth with his hand. He looked like he was about to start laughing.

Maggie frowned at him and peeked inside. She couldn't tell what it was from the top so she lifted out the small box and felt her mouth drop open. A box of nicotine patches. Her grandmother Palmer had shown up on her doorstep late at night, ringing the heck out of her doorbell, to give her a box of nicotine patches.

She looked up and caught Luke's eye as they both burst out laughing. Maggie collapsed in a chair as Luke grabbed his sides, he was laughing so hard.

Maggie couldn't stop giggling for the life of her. Luke was even worse. He leaned over the kitchen counter as he struggled to control his laughter.

"Rebecca must have been on her cell phone the whole time we were eating dinner," Maggie finally said, wiping even more tears from her already puffy, red eyes.

Luke sighed, still chuckling softly. "Nah, she probably just sent a text out to everybody she knew, and one of those persons decided they'd better notify Letty of what her granddaughter was up to. Looks like she doesn't approve of your choice in addictions," he said with a grin.

Maggie leaned her head back on her chair and sighed. "Why is it no one believes you when you say you're just holding something for a friend?"

Luke poured more hot chocolate and sat back down at the table with her. "It's sad, isn't it, what this world has come to. But just be aware, that your grandmother Palmer has just made her first step into your territory. This just means she's coming back," he said, with no sign of laughter in his voice.

Maggie stopped smiling and nodded. "It's so strange. She doesn't even know me. And under the circumstances, I'm shocked she would come to my home. And on top of that, to call me to repentance. *Scary*," she said, looking worried.

Luke frowned and pushed his mug away from him on the table. "She's probably been thinking of an excuse to come see you. Maybe this is her way of trying to *help* her way into your life. Or, on the other hand, she might see herself as the light on the hill and she wants to call you to repentance and bring you back into the fold. Or the last option. She's embarrassed by you and wants to tell you off for smearing the family name. Either way, be ready," he said, studying her quietly.

Maggie looked away and pushed hair out of her eyes. "I need a break. I need to get away and have a little fun. Everything's been too deep and too sad lately," she said, feeling homesick for St. George.

Luke smiled suddenly and sat up straight in his chair. "You didn't forget our date this Saturday, did you?"

Maggie shook her head at Luke like he was a naughty three-year-old. "Um, yeah, since you've forgotten to actually ask me out. So remind me again what we were going to do?" she asked, feeling worried for some reason.

Luke laughed and stood up. "Four-wheeling. Be ready Saturday morning by eight o'clock. Wear jeans and wear tons of sun block. I'll take care of everything else," he said and walked to the back door.

Maggie stood up and gave him a quick hug. "I'll be ready. And thanks. *Again*," she said staring up into his clear blue eyes.

Luke leaned down very slowly in case she wanted to back up and kissed her lightly. "My pleasure," he said, and disappeared into the night.

Maggie watched him go and then shut and locked the door. She put his mug in the sink and rinsed it and the pot with water. She was exhausted and went straight up to bed. She wasn't exactly looking forward to four-wheeling. Of course she had a few days to come up with an excuse. Or maybe she'd just go . . . and then spend next week picking sand out of her teeth. There was always the off chance that she might actually have some fun. Unlikely, but possible if she was with Luke.

Chapter 18

The next few days flew by and before she knew it, she and Luke were driving four-wheelers at a place called Little Sahara. There was only one part of the day where she actually feared for her life, and that was when Luke went up a hill so steep and so high that she knew in her heart he couldn't make it and they'd end up tumbling back down the hill with a large and heavy four-wheeler pulverizing them on the way back down. But they made it, and she forgave him an hour later when he handed her an ice-cold Propel.

They spent the day with Luke's older brother and his family. Luke's brother Tim and his wife, Jaden, had three kids who stayed in the non-adventurous areas, so she didn't really get to talk to them until lunch time. They'd been married five years and had twin boys who were four and a darling little girl who was three. Maggie was in awe of anyone having that many kids in so few years, but Tim and Jaden acted like pros. And they seemed so happy. She immediately felt comfortable around Tim. He reminded her of Luke in the way he talked and his dry sense of humor, but with his pale skin, light brown hair, and pale blue eyes, he and Luke didn't look like brothers at all. Luke had mentioned he was the only one who had ended up with the Indian genes. She couldn't wait to meet the rest of his family and see for herself.

She took the sandwich and apple Luke handed her and went and sat next to Jaden who was busy trying to give all her kids a juice box. Jaden was half-Japanese, half-American, and she was flat-out gorgeous with her long, dark hair and exotic eyes.

"So what do you think so far? Are you hooked for life, or are you counting the minutes until you can get home and take a shower?" Jaden asked, smiling at her as she cut a peanut butter and jelly sandwich into quarters. Maggie smiled and thought about it. "I'm definitely having fun, but I'm not sure if I'm hooked. Although, the day's not over yet," she said, knowing Luke was only feet away and listening to every word she said.

Jaden laughed and waited until Luke had walked over to help his brother set up an umbrella for the kids to play under.

"Okay, you can tell me the truth now. Shower?"

Maggie grinned and nodded. "I'm already visualizing hot, clean water. So what about you? Are you hooked or do you just love your husband so much you'd spend a whole Saturday playing in the sand?" she asked right before taking a bite of her ham and Swiss sandwich.

Jaden leaned back in her chair and grabbed a handful of grapes. "When it's just me and Tim, it's a lot of fun. I can be just as crazy as he is. But when it's the whole family, it's hard to completely relax because there are just so many people here and some of them go over board on the alcohol. I have nightmares of some-one running over my kids and me killing the idiot with my bare hands. So if that answers your question," she said wryly.

Maggie nodded and looked around. It was amazing that so many people drove from all over Utah to be here all at once. And she hadn't even known it existed.

"So Maggie, just so you know, me and Tim totally approve," she said, pop-ping grapes into her mouth and moving her son's juice box away from the edge of the portable table.

Maggie looked at her questioningly. "Approve? *Of what?*" she asked, grin-ning as Luke and Tim started wrestling and fell over in the sand.

Jaden laughed and grabbed the camcorder, getting the whole thing on tape. "You know. *You and Luke.* You're perfect for him. I mean, we all loved Melanie. Who wouldn't? But you are so *not* perfect. In a good way. And that's what Luke needs," she said, giggling as Tim shoved a handful of sand down Luke's pants. Maggie snorted her Propel out her nose as she laughed at Luke's expression. Man, he was in for an uncomfortable ride home.

She turned and looked at Jaden with one eyebrow raised. "I'm *so* not perfect? And that's good?"

Jaden cleared her throat in embarrassment. "Okay, that came out wrong, but it was meant as a compliment. You're just natural. You're you. You're not hiding anything or putting on a show. You make people want to relax around you. Luke could never totally relax with Melanie. It was hard watching them together. She was *so* put together. Her hair was perfect, her makeup was perfect. She would never have agreed to go four-wheeling. And poor Luke, well . . . you know Luke. He can put on a good banker face, but that's not really him. *That's* him," she said pointing to Luke who was giving his older brother the wedgie of a lifetime. The two women giggled and watched as Tim's kids joined in, jumping on their dad and uncle. Jaden kept the camcorder going and grinned the whole time.

"What I'm saying is, you're good for him. He's happy with you. He doesn't have that stressed out, tense look he always had with her. Don't get me wrong. I really liked Melanie. I just didn't like her for Luke. You, I like for Luke," she said, putting the camcorder down and taking a bite of her sandwich.

Maggie smiled. "Thanks, then. That's nice to know."

Jaden smiled back and then looked serious though. "*However*. Luke's mom and dad won't understand about the smoking thing. Seriously. His dad's a mission president. Now I'm a convert to the Church so I get how it's hard to quit, but if you want to make this work with the family and everything, you've gotta kick it. Luke is an RM, and he has a strong testimony. He won't marry anyone unless it's in the temple," she said, looking uncomfortable but determined to say what needed to be said.

Maggie choked on her sandwich and had to take a quick sip of her drink. "Excuse me?" she sputtered.

Jaden pushed a stray strand of black hair over her ear and winced. "My friend Tara called me last night and told me she had heard from her friend Danielle that Rebecca had seen you smoking a few days ago right in front of her whole class of Beehives."

Maggie sighed and pushed her sunglasses firmly back into place. This was starting to get ridiculous. She told Jaden about Gwen and her goal to help her kick the habit and why she had taken the pack of cigarettes in the first place. She told Jaden what Sophie had told her of Jennie's mission to free Luke from her evil grasp and finished by swearing on all the sand in Utah that she had never smoked in her life.

Jaden handed her a brownie and nodded. "Okay, I believe you. This Jennie thing is kind of serious though. You've got to nip that in the bud or I won't be adding your name to the Christmas present exchange list."

Maggie rolled her eyes and took a bite of the brownie. "Yummy! Did you make these?"

Jaden nodded proudly. "Of course, and thanks for noticing."

Maggie took another bite as she thought about what to do. "You know, I'm just not used to this . . . *girl* stuff. I've never had to out-maneuver another girl for the affections of a boy before. I honestly have no idea how to stop Jennie, except to tell the truth," she said bleakly.

Jaden studied her doubtfully. "Didn't you go to high school?"

Maggie laughed. "Of course. I just didn't do the whole social thing very well. I told Luke I needed remedial relationship classes. It's true," she said.

Jaden hummed for a minute as she thought. "Well, I usually pretend I'm Switzerland in all of the relationship messes Tim's family gets themselves into, but I think I'll step in on this one. It's like seeing the United States go up against Greenland or something. Sorry, but you're no match for Jennie. Jennie Benchley is a master at social manipulation. But with me on your side, you might just have a hope. Besides, everyone knows throwing Rebecca at Luke was nothing. She was just throwing smoke. If she was serious she would have called Sage. Luke had a *huge* thing for Sage Warnick. He dated her before he went on his mission, but she moved to New York to do an internship while he was gone. She married someone not so nice a month before Luke got home from his mission and that's how Melanie slipped in. But Sage is divorced now. *And* she just moved back to Alpine. She could be a serious threat," Jaden said, looking worried.

Maggie frowned and looked over at Luke who was playing airplane with his nephews. All this talk about social manipulation and fighting back and fighting for Luke gave her a headache. Why did it have to be so hard? Life was hard enough as it was. She secretly decided to stick with her original plan, which was to wait and watch and see who Luke wanted to be with. As much as she liked Luke, she honestly didn't want to even think as far ahead as marriage or Christmas present exchange lists. She was just trying to get comfortable with the idea of dating him. She let Jaden talk on and on. For all her talk about being Switzerland, she sure seemed excited about jumping in and thwarting Jennie. She was relieved when Luke grabbed her by the hand and helped her up.

"Come on. Enough chick chatting. We've got a few hours of fun left," he said, pulling her toward the group of four-wheelers parked by Tim's trailer.

Maggie smiled and went with him. She spent the next four and a half hours going up and down every sand dune Luke could find. And in the end, she had to admit, she had a great time. They got home later that night, after dark, tired, dirty, and not smelling all that great.

Luke kissed her on the top of her head and asked her to go to his ward with him at nine the next morning.

Maggie took a very long, very hot, very bubbly bubble bath and scrubbed every inch of herself. She leaned her head back in the water and smiled. It was good to be clean.

Chapter 19

Maggie dressed in a gypsy skirt and a gray silk scoop-necked T-shirt with strappy high heeled sandals for church the next day. She decided to wear her hair up in a messy twist so she could wear the earrings her mom and Terry got her on their honeymoon to Italy. They were long, dangling swirls of bright silver. Perfect.

She went downstairs and got a bowl of cereal and read her scriptures. She walked out the door fifteen minutes later to find Luke leaning on his car, waiting for her.

"Am I late?" she asked, glancing at her watch.

Luke gave her a half smile. "You're the type who likes to sit on the back row, am I right?"

Maggie laughed and got in the car. "Of course. That way I can play with all the babies who sit back there too."

Luke smiled and drove quickly to the church. He took her hand as they walked in and headed for the front. Most of the seats were taken so they had to sit on the very front row where the bishop and his two counselors smiled speculatively at her and Luke off and on for an hour. Maggie wished heartily they had gone for the back row. After the meeting it was no surprise that Luke dragged her up the stairs to shake hands with everyone.

"Maggie, this is Bishop Williams; his first counselor, Brother Black; and his second counselor, Brother Fennel. Everyone, this is Maggie Tierney, my new neighbor and very good friend. She's been going to the singles ward since moving here a little over a month ago, but I convinced her we had the best bishopric in the world," he said with a happy smile.

The bishop grabbed her hand first, pumping it up and down so happily, Maggie laughed.

"Sister Tierney, I can't tell you how pleased I am to make your acquaintance. Anyone who can put a smile that big on Luke's face is a friend of mine too."

Maggie laughed and shook everyone's hand in turn. It was like that for the next two hours as well. Some people gave her strange looks, but she just put that down to Jennie's texting. She was surprised that their lesson in Sunday school wasn't on the Word of Wisdom. She ran into Gwen in the halls as she walked her Primary class to the drinking fountain and grabbed her arm.

"Did you know I have half the town of Alpine upset with me for my smoking habit now? I got a box of nicotine patches on my doorstep the other night," she whispered.

Gwen laughed so loud everyone in the hallway turned to look at them. "Now you know how I feel. That's priceless. And by the way, I went the whole twelve hours without smoking. You should be very proud of me."

Maggie smiled. "I am. What else can I do now so you won't smoke for twenty-four hours?" She couldn't help asking.

Gwen looked gleefully thoughtful for a moment. "I'll get back to you on that," she said and went back to ordering her class around like a bunch of overgrown puppies. But from the looks of the kids, they loved Gwen just as much as her dogs did.

After church Luke took her home, where she found an invitation to lunch stuck on her front door, put there by Bonnie and Frank. The invitation included Luke as well. She turned and looked up at Luke with a lift of her eyebrow. He had been reading over her shoulder and smiled down at her.

"What do you think? Are you ready?" he asked, pushing a wisp of hair out of her eyes.

Maggie pursed her lips. "Yeah. I am. I still want to find out from my mom what really happened, but in the mean time, I'd like to get to know my grandparents. I just hope my other grandmother doesn't waylay me," she said, frowning.

Luke rubbed her back. "You're tough, Maggie. Even if she did, you can handle it. Heck, anyone who can tackle a burglar in her backyard going sixty miles an hour can handle anything," he said, stepping back and walking down her steps.

"Hey, you're invited too. And I happen to know my grandmother is an awesome cook," she said entreatingly.

Luke smiled and shook his head. "No buffer this time. You don't need me there," he said, shoving his hands into his pockets.

Maggie leaned her hip against the porch post and smiled beseechingly. "I might not need you there, but what if I want you there?" she asked.

Luke grinned, and his eyes brightened to a light green for a few seconds. "Sorry, Maggie, but I've already been invited to lunch by someone else," he said, looking slightly uncomfortable about the fact.

Maggie stood up straight but kept her smile firmly in place. She would not give him the satisfaction of even the appearance of jealousy. "Well, have a good time, then, and tell Sage I said hi," she said and turned around to go inside.

"Hold it! Stop right there. How did you know I was going to lunch with Sage? And how do you even know about Sage in the first place?" he asked grimly, walking back toward her purposefully.

Maggie squeaked and took the keys out of her pocket to unlock her door. If she got inside before he reached her, she was safe. His hand came out of nowhere and took the keys out of her hand. He turned her shoulders and tilted her head up so they were eye to eye. His were bright emerald green. Maggie stared for a second, wishing for her paints for the millionth time.

"Out with it, Margaret," he said in a voice her stepfather, Terry, would approve of if they were interrogating a criminal.

Maggie sniffed and looked at his ear so she wouldn't have to be blasted by so much green. It made her lose her concentration.

"I've never met Sage. I just happen to be aware of the fact that Jennie Benchley is on a crusade to, um . . . give you other options as far as your social life is concerned. Jaden mentioned yesterday that Sage would be turning up next. It's no big deal. I know that she was very important to you. I really do hope you have a nice lunch," she said, licking her lips and looking back up at Luke.

Luke's mouth formed a thin hard line as his hand fell away from her face. He turned and leaned up against her front door as he stared off into space.

"Jennie's been behind all of this? And you knew about it the whole time?" he asked.

Maggie picked at some peeling paint on the door casing and nodded. "Yeah, pretty much everyone in town knows about it. Sophie told me first, and then my grandmother warned me, and a lady at church in the bathroom an hour ago told me. So, yeah. You're probably the last person to know," she said softly, not knowing if he was mad or not.

Luke looked grimmer and grimmer. "Why didn't *you* tell *me*?" he finally asked.

Maggie winced. "Well, you were kind of enjoying it. Admit it, all that beautiful female attention and free food? Come on, what kind of girl would I be to ruin that for you?" she asked defensively.

Luke glanced at her and rolled his eyes almost imperceptibly. "The kind of girl who wouldn't let a good friend be made a fool of," he said quietly.

Maggie straightened up in shock. "Now wait a second there. That is not true. And how are *you* a fool in any of this? You're practically King Solomon here. I'm the one Jennie wants to run out of town because I'm not good enough for you. How are *you* the fool? You're the one who gets LDSsingles.com on his doorstep every day," she said, getting angry herself.

Luke pushed away from the door and walked away from her a few steps. He finally turned back around and his face looked slightly less hard. "Sorry. I hate people meddling in my life. I just wish you had told me what Jennie was up to. I wish you'd let me in on it. Here I was thinking . . . it doesn't matter," he said tiredly.

Maggie frowned and sighed. "Look, go have lunch with your ex-girlfriend. From what Jaden said, you two really had something special at one time. Don't feel bad because Jennie set it up. Just enjoy yourself."

Luke glared at her with eyes practically shooting green sparks and walked away. "Thanks for your blessing. Nice to know you couldn't care less that I'm seeing a beautiful woman I used to be in love with. I guess I know where we stand now. Enjoy your lunch with your grandparents," he called back over his shoulder and walked away.

Maggie stood there with her mouth open, staring after Luke. She didn't understand him. Couldn't he see she was trying to stay out of his way and not be jealous? Wasn't that what he needed right now? She felt like screaming and tearing her hair out at the same time. Instead she kicked her porch and went inside her house in a huff. She was in her room, changing her clothes before it dawned on her what he had just said. *He knew where things stood between them.* Had he just broken up with her?

Maggie's mouth fell open and she sat down on her bed. *Holy crap.* She ran to her window as she heard Luke drive away and wanted to wrench her window open and scream for him to come back so they could talk this out, but it was too late. He wasn't in the mood for talking anyway. He was in the mood for being totally ticked at her. And she wasn't even sure why. She sighed and went to her closet to grab a pair of jeans. She went downstairs and cut a bouquet of daisies for her grandmother and went out the door, locking up before she got in her car. She waved at Gwen and her herd of dogs before driving down the road. She hoped this lunch with her grandparents would go smoothly. She really didn't want to see her grandmother sobbing her heart out ever again.

She drove up to their house and sat in her car, staring at her Grandmother Palmer's yard. She didn't see anyone lurking in the bushes, but you never knew. She didn't want a surprise attack. She got out of her car and walked as quickly as she could to the front door and rang the bell. As soon as her finger left the button, the door flew open and both of her grandparents stood in front of her beaming. She was swept up in hugs and cheek kissing before she could even show them her bouquet of daisies.

"I knew you would come to lunch. What healthy young woman doesn't want a good Sunday dinner?"

Maggie smiled a little self-consciously. "Actually, I am starving. Thanks for inviting me over," she said and pulled the flowers out from behind her back to hand to Bonnie.

Bonnie smiled and then looked like she was going to tear up, but Frank cleared his throat loudly and took her by the hand.

"While Bonnie is putting dinner on the table, I wanted to show you this. Come over and see what your dad did when he was just fourteen years old. You've gotta see this," Frank said, leading her toward the office.

Maggie followed him in and waited for him to turn the light on. He motioned for her to turn around. She did a circle and looked at where Frank was pointing and saw a painting on the wall. It was the size of some of her larger paintings. She stepped closer and tilted her face up. It was a painting of Alpine. She recognized the mountains and the green hills. He had painted his hometown as an aerial view. She smiled as she saw individual houses, people, farms, and the park.

"Wow, he was only fourteen. I guess I know where I got my talent from," she said as she ran her finger softly over her father's signature.

Frank smiled with pride. "He won first place in the school's art contest that year."

Maggie turned and looked at her grandfather. "You still miss him, don't you?" she asked softly.

Frank's eyebrows drifted down and he stared at his feet for a moment. "Every day. Sometimes it's hard not to think about all the things we could be doing together. We used to love hunting and fishing together. He was a great kid to be around. I just wish I could have known him as a man," he said, trying to smile.

Maggie nodded. "After looking through the picture albums, I've been missing him too. And I never even knew him." She felt sad all of a sudden.

Frank put his arm around her shoulders and led her out the room. "You know him. Heck, you're so much like him, it's scary. You have his talent, his goodness, his honesty and his bright wonder and joy in life. It's been a real blessing having you here, Maggie. It makes losing Robbie a little easier to bear," he said as they walked into the dining room.

Maggie smiled at Frank and went to grab a dish from her grandmother. "Here, let me help you." She grabbed the hot dish of corn and put it on the table.

They all sat down and Frank said the prayer. Maggie grinned at all the food on the table. Her grandmother had made enough to feed the whole neighborhood. She took some corn, two homemade biscuits, some salad, and then she held her plate out to her grandfather so he could put a hot, gleaming slice of ham on it.

"This looks amazing, Grandma," she said, and took a bite as she tried to ignore the sniffling coming from Bonnie. It seemed like every time she called her grandmother "Grandma" she started tearing up. Maggie didn't feel like calling her Bonnie; that just seemed disrespectful.

Frank dished up his plate and his wife's and then they all got down to the business of eating.

"Now dear, I don't want to alarm you, but my visiting teacher Joan was telling me that Sage Warnick is back in town and that Jennie Benchley has been after her to get together with Luke. I like to mind my own business, but well, it's just that you're my business now, and I hate to see you lose your cute little boyfriend because of sour grapes," she said, looking worried and kind of upset.

Maggie frowned and wiped her mouth with her napkin. Frank stepped in before she could answer though.

"Honey, now you're worrying about nothing here. I remember that Sage girl. She's not half as pretty as Maggie. If Luke's the man I think he is, none of this is going to matter." He winked at Maggie and took another biscuit.

Maggie winced. "Well, actually, he's with Sage right now having lunch," she confessed.

Bonnie and Frank looked at each other with alarm on their faces. Bonnie put her fork down and looked at Maggie with her brows drawn together.

"Sweetie, I hope that if things don't work out between you and Luke that you'll still stay in Alpine. I would hate for anyone to make you feel like you're not welcome here. I know sometimes when things don't work out socially between people that relationships can become strained," she said, looking to her husband for backup.

Frank sighed. "Well, that just takes the cake. That Luke is the dumbest kid I've ever known. Doesn't he know you're a famous artist? He must need glasses if he can't see that you're the prettiest girl in town. I'm going to have a talk with him." He looked fierce.

Maggie looked back and forth between her two grandparents and laughed. They looked at her in shock.

"No, no, I'm not laughing at you. I'm just laughing because this is so not like me or my life at all. I don't date. I don't have people fighting over me and for me and about me. I feel like I've stepped into a soap opera. But to ease your minds, nobody can run me out of Alpine. Luke Petersen could date every ex-girlfriend he's ever had and I wouldn't leave. I'm not saying I'm staying forever, but I'm going to stay until I'm good and ready to leave. And please, Grandpa, don't talk to Luke. He and Jennie and Sage and whoever else need to work this out on their own. I'm just going to stay clear of it if I can," she said, taking a huge bite of her buttery biscuit.

Bonnie and Frank visibly relaxed and smiled at each other. "That's my girl. I remember that first day when I saw you do that backflip in the air. I knew right then you had guts," Frank said with a smile and then froze.

Maggie frowned. "Wait a second. How could you see me do a backflip? I was in my backyard," she said, puzzled.

Bonnie was blushing bright red as she knotted her napkin in her hands. "We were walking our dog that day, and we walked across the street to see what you were doing in the backyard. We thought maybe you might be painting or something. We weren't trying to spy, we were just really curious. It was the first time we'd seen our granddaughter. I hope you don't hold it against us."

Maggie shrugged. "No biggie. If I had a granddaughter I'd never seen before, I'd sneak a peak too."

Bonnie and Frank smiled in relief and the dinner went smoothly from there on. The doorbell rang as Bonnie cleared the table to make room for the angel food cake she had made. Frank excused himself and went to answer the door. He called for Bonnie to join him a minute later, leaving Maggie to sit by herself at the table, smiling at her surroundings. This was how she pictured it. Dinner with grandparents. Good food, pleasant conversation, and the feeling of acceptance and love surrounding everything. Warm. That's how'd she paint this picture. Lots of warm tones and light.

Bonnie and Frank came back into the room, looking different than when they had left. Gone were the happy smiles and in their places, tense unhappy frowns. They both sat down silently as Bonnie sliced the cake.

"Um, is everything okay?" Maggie asked, taking the dessert plate from her grandmother.

Bonnie sighed and handed a plate to Frank before sitting down.

"Maggie, I don't want to upset you, but Letty Palmer was just here and she wants you to stop by her house before you leave. She said she has some things she wants to say to you," Bonnie said, looking ill.

Frank sighed even louder than Bonnie did. "I told her you wouldn't go to her house and that we didn't want her coming over while you were here. She's not very happy with me about that, but you need to feel comfortable coming to our home. I don't want you to be harassed," he said, looking angry.

Maggie frowned and lost her appetite for the light, fluffy cake that she had been salivating over just seconds before.

"Did she say what she wanted to talk to me about?" she asked quietly.

Bonnie shook her head. "I told her if she had anything to say to you, that she should tell me and that I would pass it along. Then, if you felt like talking to her you could. But she didn't like that at all. Letty can be . . . she can be kind of forceful sometimes."

Maggie closed her eyes for a second. First her house and now here at her grandparents'. Luke was right. Letty was determined to see her one way or another.

"Well, I'll just get this over with then. That way I won't have to make myself sick thinking about it or worrying about it. Some boundaries need to be set. And I'm the one that has to set them," she said, standing up and pushing away from the table.

Bonnie and Frank stared at her in surprise. "My goodness, you sounded just like Robbie. Didn't she, Frank?" Bonnie whispered.

Frank nodded and stood up with her. "I'll go with you," he said, looking grim but sure.

Maggie smiled and walked over and kissed her grandfather on the cheek. "I'll be right back. You two enjoy your desserts and this will be over in a few minutes," she said, and walked away while she could. What she really wanted to do was grab her car keys from the hallway table and make a run for it. But Letty would just be pounding on her door later with a book on social etiquette or something else to reform her. Nope, now was the time to just get it done.

She walked out the door and straight over to the house next door. Letty was sitting on her front porch in an old rocking chair, waiting for her.

"I've been waiting for weeks for you to come over. It's about time," she said coldly.

Maggie walked right up to the woman and stared her straight in the eyes. There was no trace of fear or hesitation about her. She stood straight and tall and she didn't waver.

"You shouldn't have. You have no right to expect anything of me or from me. You gave up your rights to be my grandmother when you turned your back on my mom. Don't contact me again. Don't bother my grandparents at their home again. I don't want anything to do with you. Period," she said firmly and with no emotion in her voice.

Letty's cheeks turned red and her silver bright eyes stared right into her.

"I have every right to expect everything of you and from you. *I'm your grandmother*. You can't wish that away. My blood runs through your veins just as much as Bonnie Tierney's, and there's nothing you can do about it. You just had a nice Sunday dinner with them. Well, you can come in and sit down with me now. I plan on getting to know you and for you to get to know me. I don't know what lies and filth your mother has filled your ears with but it's time you grew up. Make up your mind for yourself instead of letting other people do it for you."

Maggie's eyes widened slightly but other than that, her face remained impassive.

"Answer me one question then, as long as we're talking about the truth. Were you happy my father died?" she challenged, staring into the bottomless eyes of her grandmother.

Letty looked taken aback by the question and then looked away. "The truth?

Yes. Yes, I was glad Robert Tierney died. Lisa stole my husband's heart away from me and the good Lord took her husband away from her. It was fair and right. Justice was done," she said, slapping her knee and looking austere.

Maggie nodded her head once and then stepped closer to her grandmother. She bent down so they were eye to eye.

"If you contact me again in any shape or form, I will get a restraining order against you. Since this is the last time I will be talking to you I want to make this crystal clear. You are an evil, twisted woman who sacrificed her daughter to the perverted desires of an even more evil man. I don't know how you justified what happened to my mother. I don't know if it was out of love for your husband or out of hatred for your daughter, or both. But for whatever reason, you stood by and let a young, innocent child be abused. The rationalization doesn't matter. Do you hear me? Your excuses don't matter. Because *you* let it happen. *You.* And I don't want to know you. Not now. Not ever." She turned and walked down the steps and back to her grandparent's house. She felt her breath coming faster and faster and her heart beating quickly. She'd done it. She'd said what she'd been wanting to say ever since her mother told her what had happened to her so many years ago.

"Don't you turn your back on me, Margaret! There's no law in this world that will keep me away from you. Go ahead and get your restraining order. It won't make a difference. You're *my* granddaughter!" Letty shouted after her.

Maggie refused to turn back and look at Letty Palmer. She let herself back into her grandparents' home and right into the arms of her grandmother who was waiting for her. She cried a little but wiped her face just minutes later. She raised her head and took the tissue being held out to her by her grandfather.

"Thanks. Sorry. I'm really not emotional. You can ask my mom. I think I've cried more in the last month than I have in the last five years of my life," she admitted.

Frank and Bonnie nodded and stood protectively by her.

"We heard what she shouted at you. We want you to know that we'll do what we can to keep her from you. But in the end she'll do what she wants. That's the way she's always been, I'm afraid," Frank said.

Maggie shrugged and sighed. "Well, I said what I had to say. And I meant it. I just don't understand how she can expect a relationship with me after what happened to my mom. You'd have to be completely irrational," she said, shaking her head.

Bonnie rubbed her arm. "Sweetie. Don't you trouble yourself over it. Just work on settling in here. Paint your paintings and fall in love with Alpine the same way your dad did when he was young. Things will work out with Luke one way or the other, and Letty will settle back into her own little world again. You'll see, this will blow over."

Chapter 20

Maggie said good-bye to her grandparents and left a few moments later with half of the angel food cake wrapped in tinfoil. She didn't bother looking over at her grandmother Palmer's house. She could feel the weight of Letty's eyes on her. She drove home and collapsed on her couch in the family room, throwing her car keys onto the carpet. She massaged her temples and tried to forget how full of hate Letty's face had been when she had mentioned her mother. *How could a mother hate her own daughter?*

She stretched out on the couch and tried to figure out what to do. She couldn't paint. Not feeling like this. She couldn't sit and read either, she was too keyed up. She could go for a drive. Maybe she'd drive up the canyon and walk around the tiny lake up there. That's what she needed. A little fresh air and exercise to clear her mind.

She reached over and grabbed her keys off the floor and stood up. She reached her front door just as the doorbell rang. She grabbed her hand back and felt ill. If it was her grandmother, she really was going to file a restraining order. She looked through the peephole and then stepped closer. It was a man. And it wasn't Luke.

She opened the door slowly and looked at the man standing in front of her. He was too good-looking for words. His hair was dark, dark brown like Luke's, but where Luke's hair always had that tousled look, this man's hair was gleaming as if he'd just stepped out of a shampoo commercial. He wasn't as tall as Luke, but he was still taller than her. And he was strong. Not like a body builder, but like a rock climber. His forearms were ripped. But it was his face that had her instantly suspicious. He was gorgeous. No other word for the man, but perfectly, unreasonably gorgeous. And she knew what that meant.

"Well, tell Jennie she hit it out of the ballpark with you. Where did she even find you? She probably had to search the whole state of Utah to find someone as beautiful as you are. I'll hand it to her though. If I were a weaker woman, I'd be throwing myself at your feet right this second. But she's just going to have to be smarter. I can spot a fake a mile away. Sorry, buddy. Tell Jennie thanks but no thanks," she said and smiled brightly before shutting the door.

The only problem was, there was a rather large boot in her way.

"Now don't get pushy or I'll have to hurt you," she said, being completely serious.

The man had the gall to smile at her. "Maggie, is it? Listen, Maggie, I don't know who Jennie is, but tell her thanks for me. I've never been complimented quite so well or so mistakenly."

Maggie frowned at him and opened the door again, leaning on the door frame. "Excuse me? You're saying Jennie didn't send you over here?"

The man grinned and pulled out his wallet, opening it up to show her his police badge. "Sorry to disappoint you. I'm Cooper Christiansen. Terry knew I was coming up here for the weekend to see my parents and asked me to drop some things off for you. I'll just go grab them if you don't mind," he said, his eyes twinkling as he turned and walked back to his car.

Maggie's mouth fell open as she realized what she had just said to the man. Her face turned bright red in horror, and she felt like turning around and running for her bedroom. He could just leave the stuff on the porch, and she could hide from her complete and total humiliation. Or she could apologize and act like an adult here. *What was she, a coward?* She cleared her throat and walked out and down the porch and to the man's car.

"Do you need any help?" she asked, wishing her voice didn't sound so small and wimpy.

Cooper shut the trunk to his car and laughed. "Nah, I don't think I need much help. He just wanted me to give you this and a hug from him," he said, raising an eyebrow.

Maggie stared at the pack of Propel and Spicy Doritos the man held easily in his hands. And then she started to laugh. At herself and the situation and everything in between.

"Oh my heck, you must think I'm some crazy nut. I am so sorry, Cooper. You have no idea how sorry. Please forgive me and ignore and forget everything I just said to you."

Cooper laughed with her and leaned against his car. "Are you kidding? I hope I never forget. You just made my year. So are you ready for your hug? It's from Terry and he'd be really offended if you didn't accept," he said, looking very serious.

Maggie smiled and shook her head. "Please don't sacrifice yourself. Terry isn't your boss, is he?"

Cooper smiled and nodded. "Yep and he's a good one. But even if he wasn't, I really wouldn't mind." There was an appreciative gleam in his brown eyes.

Maggie turned her head and blushed, and noticed Luke's car drive up. She watched as he got out and then walked around to the other side of the car and opened the door for someone else. She frowned as that someone turned out to be a petite woman with dark, mahogany brown hair cut into a razor sharp angled bob. The woman was holding Luke's hand and laughing up into his face. And he was grinning right back at her. Maggie felt a shaft of pain rip through her heart and she silently conceded the race to Jennie Benchley. She had won. Luke was safe from her. She looked away from Luke and back to Cooper.

"You okay there?" he asked softly.

Maggie smiled weakly and leaned up against Cooper's car with him so she wouldn't have to see Luke kiss his new girlfriend.

"Yeah. I'm great. Sorry, you were saying?" she asked, completely forgetting.

Cooper glanced at Luke and Sage and back at her. "I was just about to give you a hug, but I could go a step further and make it a little more interesting if that would help you out?" he asked, motioning with his head toward Luke.

Maggie blushed and was about to say no, but changed her mind. *Why not?* Luke had just made it very clear where things stood. Maybe she should salvage a little pride.

"Okay, I'll go for it. And by the way, tell Terry he's getting a huge Father's Day gift this year," she said, smiling shyly at Cooper.

Cooper smiled and stood up from the car. "Okay, let's give them a show," he said and took her by the hand and pulled her in for a hug, but instead of a hug, he picked her up by the waist and twirled her around before dipping her back so far that she gasped. And if that wasn't enough, he kissed her so close to her mouth, that it was still technically on the cheek, but close enough to where anyone watching *probably* wouldn't know that. Cooper let her up a few very long seconds later as she laughed and turned even redder.

"Wow. Thanks, Cooper," she said, smiling as if she had just won the Miss America Pageant.

Cooper grinned and shrugged. "Any time. Listen, Terry mentioned you were moving up here for a few months, but when you come back home, I'd love to see you again," he said.

Maggie couldn't stop grinning for the life of her. She just wasn't used to beautiful men paying her any attention. Forget one of them actually asking her out.

"I'd like that, but I don't know when I'll be back in St. George. Hey, you're just trying to be nice, aren't you?" she asked, shoving her hands nervously in her pockets.

Cooper chuckled softly as he studied her face. "Trust me, I'm not being nice." He took out a business card from his wallet and leaned over to grab a pen out of his car and wrote something on the back.

"There's my home phone number. I'll be waiting to hear from you." He handed her his card before he picked up the forgotten Propels and chips and then handed them to her as well.

She stood and watched him drive away with a dumbfounded look on her face. How strange could one day get? All but dumped by one man, a showdown with a grandmother, and then she was asked out by one of the most attractive men in the world. Life could not get any stranger.

"Stop drooling. I hate to see a perfectly intelligent woman lose her brain over a pretty face." Gwen was standing next to her.

Maggie laughed and shook her head as if she had been in a trance. "Did you see him? Was he not the most beautiful thing you've ever seen?" she demanded, opening the bag of chips and offering some to Gwen.

Gwen took a few and grinned back at her. "If I hadn't sworn off men, I'd be very tempted to chase that car down like one of my dogs."

Maggie choked on Propel as she stared at Gwen with a worried frown. Gwen laughed at her.

"Don't be an idiot. I'm not a lesbian. I just swore off men and chose to love canines instead. And there you were plotting to take away my cigarettes *and* my alternative lifestyle."

Maggie laughed shakily, still looking at Gwen suspiciously.

Gwen frowned. "Stop it."

Maggie laughed for real and took a chip, motioning for Gwen to join her for some porch sitting.

"You've sworn off men. So how's that working for you?" Maggie had to ask as they sat down together and opened up a cold Propel for Gwen.

Gwen shrugged. "Well, I'm forty years old and I have a successful business that I love. I'm financially stable and I'm happy. So far, so good." She took another handful of chips.

Maggie sighed and munched for a moment. "I might as well swear off men. I have never had good luck with them. I either do or say something that scares them off."

Gwen smiled affectionately at her and took a sip. "You're just a free spirit. Men don't usually go for that type. Some do, don't get me wrong, but most don't. That man that just left? He looked like somebody who goes for free spirits," she said with a wistful smile.

Maggie perked up. "Yeah, he did, didn't he? He told me he wants to ask me out when I go back to St. George. Can you believe that?" she asked in awe.

Gwen snorted. "Do you really have no mirrors in your house? Are you one of those obnoxiously fake modest types who just want everyone to tell them over and over how beautiful they are? Because if you are, I'm out of here," she said, looking at her in irritation.

Maggie looked at her like she was an alien. "What are you talking about?"

Gwen laughed and shook her head. "You are such an idiot. But I'm really starting to like you, so I'll let you in on a little secret. You're beautiful. Stop being so surprised when men ask you out or act like they're interested in you. It's annoying."

Maggie rolled her eyes and grabbed some more chips. "Whatever. If you want to talk beauty, you're the one we should be talking about. Your bone structure is *exquisite*. I'd really like to paint you if you're willing?" she asked in a wheedling voice.

Gwen blushed and turned away. "Would my dogs get to be in it?"

Maggie sighed and tried not to groan. "Maybe just one. I'm not painting ten dogs," she said firmly.

Gwen pursed her lips and considered. "Yeah, I could do that. Cheyenne told me today at church that you want to paint her too. Looks like you're working your way through the whole neighborhood."

Maggie frowned and glanced away. "Not quite," she said, thinking sadly of Luke's eyes and how desperately she had wanted to paint him.

"Oh, stop wallowing. If you want to go talk to him, *go talk to him*," Gwen said in disgust.

Maggie looked at her sharply. "I really don't feel like talking to Mr. Buhler right now. But you're welcome to go over if you feel like it."

Gwen laughed and threw a chip at her. "Don't get smart with me girl. You know I'm talking about Luke. Too bad you messed up there. I warned you though, didn't I? I told you he was coldhearted. Too messed up by that girl dying on him. I told you to stick with the singles ward. But no, you wouldn't listen. And now look at you. Sitting on your front porch looking like someone just kicked you in the face." She sounded disgusted.

Maggie sighed and leaned back on her hands. "Yeah, well, hindsight and everything."

Gwen took another sip of her drink and leaned back too. "You said a mouthful. Look, there he is now," she whispered as Luke walked down his porch with the striking brunette close by his side.

Gwen and Maggie stayed perfectly still and perfectly quiet as Luke opened the door for the woman and then went around and got in the other side. He drove away without looking in their direction even once.

"Oh, he's mad. Did you see the way he wouldn't even look at you? Wow. I would hate to hear what's going on inside his head right now." Gwen stood up.

Maggie closed her eyes and sighed before standing up too. "Well, we'll never know, will we? How about we get started tomorrow at nine? Come over after breakfast so you can change. I have the most darling dress I want you to wear."

Gwen looked at her in horror. "I gotta wear a dress? I can barely bring myself to put on a skirt for church."

Maggie raised an eyebrow and looked at her scathingly. "A big girl like you scared of a little lace. Come on, do you want to be art or not?"

Gwen thought about it and then gave in. "Fine. I'll see you tomorrow morning. And by the way, I haven't smoked even once today. I've decided to take Sundays off," she said proudly.

Maggie beamed at her and clapped her hands. "That's wonderful, Gwen! Brilliant. Hey, I happen to have a box of nicotine patches, if you'd like them?" she asked, motioning toward her house.

Gwen shrugged self-consciously. "Sure. I could use all the help I can get." She waited while Maggie ran in and grabbed the box.

Luke drove back as Gwen opened one up and slapped it on her arm. "Well, I'm out of here. Good luck," she said, and walked quickly away, holding her package of patches tightly to her chest.

Maggie smiled after her and then watched as Luke walked slowly toward her. Not smiling. Not even a little bit.

"Hey," she called out, trying to smile in a carefree, friendly manner. Or at least like someone who hadn't just had her heart broken.

Luke walked up to the bottom of her porch and looked up at her. "So who's your boyfriend?" he asked in a voice she hadn't ever heard him use before. He sounded so cold and uncaring. Almost like a banker.

Maggie shrugged. "His name is Cooper, and he works for my stepfather. He was just dropping off a little treat for me since he was up here seeing his mom and dad."

Luke's cheek clenched tightly. "Is—he—your—boyfriend?" he ground out slowly.

Maggie glared at him and crossed her arms over her chest. "Like—I—would—tell—you—after—seeing—you—smile—your—new—girlfriend—to—death," she said just as slowly and with just as much venom.

Luke glared at her. "Look, we're not in kindergarten here. I saw you kiss him. Just tell me once and for all what he means to you," he asked almost politely.

Maggie looked at him in exasperation. "I don't even *know* him. And I did not kiss him. He was giving me a hug from Terry. He went a little overboard. End of story. Although he did say he wants to ask me out when I get back to St. George," she added, watching with interest as his face grew harder and his eyes deeper green.

"Of course he does," Luke said grimly, looking almost angry.

Maggie shook her head in confusion. "So what's the deal with the third degree? You don't see me grilling you over everything you did with Sage," she accused, looking away from Luke and toward the mountains.

Luke took a step up, toward the porch. "Just out of curiosity, why aren't you?" he asked her quietly.

Maggie blinked a few times and then shrugged. "It's none of my business. Right? It's not like we're in some serious committed relationship or anything. Right?" she said calmly, though her heart started pounding faster.

Luke took another step toward her. "I thought I made myself clear the other day when I told you who I was interested in."

Maggie sighed. "Was that before or after you agreed to go to lunch with your ex-girlfriend?" she asked.

Luke frowned and took the last step toward her, bringing him within one foot of her.

"After. If you don't want me to see other girls, why don't you tell me? If you want a committed relationship with me, why not say so? If you want to be with me, *just say it*," he demanded, his voice growing louder and more intense.

Maggie turned toward him and knew before she even looked that his eyes would be shooting sparks at her. "Is this some kind of test? You know I'm not good with this sort of thing. I don't know how this works. I don't know what to do! I know I like you. I know I would like to get to know you better. But I think I'll just wait and see how many more ex-girlfriends you have waiting in line to invite you over for lunch. I'm just like everyone else in the world. I don't want to get hurt," she said, ignoring his outstretched hand.

Luke grabbed her hand anyway. "Sage spent the whole time talking about her ex-husband, who she's still very much in love with. I brought her back to my house so I could show her the painting you gave me. I was going to bring her over and introduce her to you, but you were too busy being twirled around and kissed by Orlando Bloom," he said testily.

Maggie's mouth twitched. "Watch it. He'd beat you up for that. He's a cop," she said in Cooper's defense.

Luke gritted his teeth. "Whatever. Look, let me make this easy for you. Do you want to come over and have some ice cream or not?" he asked, dropping her hand and putting his hands on his hips and looking moodily at her.

Maggie smiled. "I thought you'd never ask," she said, reaching for his hand.

Luke sighed and then smiled crookedly. "You're killing me, Margaret. You know that, right?"

Maggie leaned her head on his shoulder as they walked to his house. "Yada yada yada. Are we talking milkshakes or banana splits?" She asked as Luke laughed and put his arm around her. Maggie was surprised to find that Luke's arm made her feel instantly better. She had no idea why Gwen called Luke cold. He was the warmest thing she'd ever known.

Chapter 21

"Okay, right there. Do not move, Gwen," she said sternly and picked up her brush. Gwen was kneeling on the grass, looking out over the little Alpine valley. She was wearing an old-fashioned sun dress that could have been worn a hundred years ago. The cotton was faded and thin in places but still held its charm. Maggie smiled and got to work.

"Tilt your head down, just a titch if you don't mind," she called out.

Gwen did what she was told and sighed. "Do I get paid for this?" she asked sullenly.

Maggie smiled and glanced at her. "I'll pay you in Nicorette Gum and patches. How about that?" she said.

Gwen snorted and pulled at the grass in front of her. "It just seems so unfair that all I get is nicotine gum, and you'll be getting a million dollars."

Maggie grinned and dipped her brush. "It won't be a million dollars. Now stop complaining. You're making that crease between your eyes look like a crack in your face."

Gwen huffed out her breath but smoothed her expression quickly. "So how'd it go with Luke last night?"

Maggie shrugged and kept painting. "He kissed me breathless and then asked me to marry him. You know, same ol' same ol," she said, laughing at Gwen's expression.

Gwen glared at her. "You are a brat."

Maggie rolled her eyes. "And you are nosey. Now get back into position or I'm just going to buy you regular gum and not the good stuff."

Gwen sighed and moved back into place. "And to think I could be with my dogs right now."

Maggie switched brushes and stopped to stare at Gwen before dipping her brush. "I've been thinking of this anti-man thing you have going. I know this really neat guy. He's super good-looking, very nice, and he'd be perfect for you. He happens to be a huge fan of beautiful bone structure," she said, glancing at Gwen to gauge her expression.

Gwen looked up in surprise. "Hey, I'm not anti-man, I'm just anti-getting hurt, used, and taken for granted and so on and so forth."

Maggie paused and tilted her head, looking out at the valley. "No risk, no reward, Gwen. His name is Joe and he's Terry's brother. Terry's my stepfather. Joe's been divorced for about five years now. He has two teenage boys, thirteen and fifteen. He's an amazing father by the way. And he really is great looking. Tall and thin, but he works out. He's about your age and he has sandy blonde hair, but I can't remember what color eyes he has. Brave enough to be set up?" she asked, leaning down close to her canvas.

Gwen looked uncomfortable as she stared off into space. "I don't know, Maggie. I haven't been on a date for ten years. Honestly, I haven't. I'm just not the type men like to be set up with. I'm going to have to say no. Thanks, I appreciate it, but no. It's for the best," she said kind of sadly.

Maggie looked up and studied her friend. "Better for whom? Joe? I don't think so. His wife left him to raise their two kids alone after she fell in love with one of her chat room buddies. His two boys haven't seen their mom in years. And from what Terry has said, Joe has tried dating women, but they all just want to have fun. Nobody seems to want to settle down anymore. He's looking for a strong woman who knows how to stick and who he can love. Someone who can help him raise his two boys would be nice too. From what Terry was saying, they've been giving him fits lately." She smiled to herself.

Gwen looked interested and sat up straighter. "Teenagers are just like dogs. They need a lot of boundaries and a lot of love and even more treats. I'd be happy to talk to him about it anytime," she said eagerly.

Maggie bent down so Gwen couldn't see her grinning. "Well, I talked to my mom last night on the phone and Joe's coming up with my mom and Terry tonight. He's coming to look at some dirt bikes he wants to buy for his boys. They'll all be staying at my house. How about you come to dinner either tonight or tomorrow, because I'd really like to introduce you to my mom. I just know she's going to love you. And when you meet Joe, if you're not interested, fine. But if you are, then why not give it a try?" She tried to sound as blasé as she could.

Gwen bit her lip and thought about it. "I don't know. I mean, I could try it. But I'd probably need to wear some makeup or something. And I've never been good at doing my hair either. Could you help me out with that?" she asked in a small voice that Maggie had never heard from Gwen before.

Maggie stood up straight and looked over her canvas at her friend. "Nope,

I can't help you with that. Sorry. But I know someone who can. And I forgot to mention it to you, but one free trip to see Sophie is included in my modeling fee. We're almost done here anyway. I'll just drop you off at Sophie's on the way home for a consultation. What do you say?" she asked, crossing her fingers behind her back.

Gwen looked at her, her cheeks turning rosy and her eyes sparkling delightedly. "I haven't been to a salon in years. Do you really think she could do something with me?" she asked hopefully.

Maggie shook her head at her friend. "Hello? Don't you have any mirrors in your house? I hate to break it to you, but it's really annoying when naturally beautiful women act all modest when they should be showing off the cheek bones the good Lord blessed them with," she said with a smile.

Gwen laughed and dipped her head. "Yeah, maybe you're right. So tell me more about this Joe guy," she said, lifting her face to the sun.

Maggie smiled and told her everything she could think of, embellishing only here and there when she felt the need. An hour later, Maggie walked out of the salon, leaving Gwen sitting nervously in a chair while Sophie buzzed around her head like a fairy on caffeine. She couldn't tell who was more excited about the upcoming transformation, Sophie or Gwen, but they were a match made in beauty salon heaven.

Maggie went home and rinsed her brushes and put her canvas away. She thought about Gwen and Joe being together. It wasn't a sure thing at all. Joe's ex-wife had been a glamour girl to the nth degree. Gwen was so the opposite of that. She'd met a few of the women Joe had taken out and they were all feminine and pretty. She worried about what Joe would think of Gwen. Gwen had a delicate beauty that she tried to hide and did a pretty good job of it too. She wasn't sure what Sophie could do with spiky graying hair, but she believed in miracles and Sophie was capable of anything. It wasn't even really the way Gwen looked that worried her. It was Gwen's dichotomy of fragility and strength. She understood it, because her mom was the same way. They were so good at putting up walls and protecting themselves. They'd been hurt before and they would do anything to stop it from happening again. Even if it meant shutting out people. Gwen's gruff exterior might just put Joe off. But if Joe was anything like Terry, then there was a chance.

Maggie frowned and wondered if she had done the wrong thing. Knowing her, she probably had. But just getting Gwen to even think about something or someone else besides her dogs had to be a step in the right direction. The worst thing that could happen? Gwen could hate her. The second worst thing? Gwen making her watch all ten dogs while she went on her honeymoon.

Maggie laughed to herself and spread her brushes out to dry. The doorbell rang and she tensed up immediately. She told herself to knock it off and walked to the front door. It was only twelve o'clock and Gwen wouldn't be done yet. Luke was at work. It could be her grandma, *or the other one*. She took a breath and looked through the peep hole. Sage Warnick and Jennie Benchley. *Perfect*.

She opened the door with a welcoming smile on her face. "Well, if it isn't Jennie Benchley. What a wonderful surprise," she said, sounding only slightly insincere.

Jennie pouted angrily but stayed quiet. Sage smiled brightly back at her and stepped forward. "I know we haven't had a chance to meet, but I'm Sage Warnick. I just wanted to come over and apologize to you if you got the wrong impression yesterday. I was told by Jennie that Luke really wanted to get back together with me. Well, of course I found out yesterday that that was far from the truth. Luke told me all about you and how much he cares about you. I wouldn't be surprised if . . . well, I'll just leave that to him. But Jennie and I just wanted to stop by and apologize. I think Jennie's under the mistaken impression that Luke needs help with his love life. I think we both know that that's not true. Isn't that right, Jennie?" Sage asked, turning to smile grimly at the girl standing miserably next to her.

Maggie's eyebrows shot way, *way* up and her mouth opened in surprise. *Sage—was—awesome.* She waited for Jennie to say something and while she sputtered and stammered, she felt a smile bloom on her face. Today was turning out to be really good.

"I just thought that Luke needed more options."

Maggie frowned. *That was it?* That was her big apology?

Sage frowned at Jennie and turned back to Maggie. "Here's my number. I just moved back to town, and I would love to go to lunch with you anytime. I can't wait to hear about your last art show. Luke showed me the painting you did for him. I got tears in my eyes. I literally cried, it was so beautiful. Well, we won't keep you. Jennie was telling me how busy she was this morning. I always say you can't be too busy for friends though. Call me!" she said, and walked down the porch steps.

Jennie stayed behind for just a few seconds before joining Sage. She leaned over and whispered coldly. "Don't even think about going shopping for any white dresses. Luke will wake up any second and realize you aren't good enough for him. And I can't wait to be there when he does." She then called out cheerily. "Bye, Maggie. Please do call! I know a great restaurant you would just love," she said loudly enough that Sage smiled approvingly at her.

Maggie laughed softly and shut the door. Well, she liked Sage. And she had to respect Jennie. She was no wimp. She went upstairs to change out of her painting clothes so she could go to the grocery store and get everything she needed to make dinner for her guests that night. She couldn't wait to see her mom. They had a ton to talk about.

Chapter 22

Maggie took the grocery sack out of her car and slammed the door. Cooking for six people took a lot of food and a lot of muscles. She had both. She walked to her front door as she tried to find her house key and smiled at the lady walking down the sidewalk toward her. She was stunning. She hoped Luke didn't see her. That'd be just one more lunch date he would go on. She had long, light ash blonde hair cut into layers with long wispy bangs. She was wearing the cutest little sundress. Kind of like the one . . . *Gwen had been wearing.*

Maggie forgot her keys and stood stock still in shock as the woman walked slowly up to her and stood silently waiting for her to say something.

"*Gwen?* That can't be you, is it?" she whispered, feeling her groceries slip from her hands and hit the floor. The woman just smiled serenely and folded her arms, still not saying anything.

Maggie stepped closer and looked into her face. Sophie had highlighted Gwen's amazing cheekbones and used a lip liner to outline her now voluptuous lips. It was the eyes that were the star of the show though. Sophie had accentuated them while at the same time achieving that natural look. The combination of the makeup and hair was almost too much. Gwen looked like a completely different person. She could be in a witness protection program and never be found.

"Is that a wig?" Maggie finally asked, her eyes still wide with shock.

Gwen flipped her hair over her shoulder as if she'd been doing it her whole life and smiled wickedly. "Hair extensions. They're all the rage in Hollywood. Sophie was telling me everyone's doing them now."

Maggie shook her head and walked around her friend looking at every angle. "Gwen, you look amazing. I don't think I've ever met anyone as pretty as you are. I mean, I noticed the bone structure right off, but this . . . this is just ridiculous," she said, shaking her head in wonder.

Gwen grinned and pushed her new bangs out of her eyes. "Sophie says I'm the best transformation she's ever done, and she says she's done some really extreme makeovers."

Maggie grinned at her and laughed. "She is getting a huge tip. That girl is a genius. But there's one thing I forgot," she said, pursing her mouth and tapping her lip with her finger. "I forgot to mention that as part of the modeling fee I'm paying you, you get one free outfit. We have to go soon, though, since I need to make it back in time to make dinner. Can you run to the mall with me?" Maggie asked, starting to jump up and down in excitement. She felt just like the professor in *My Fair Lady.*

Gwen winced. "I've been gone all day as it is. I need to feed my dogs and they need some exercise. I don't know, Maggie. Trust me, the hair and makeup is enough. She gave me tons of samples of makeup too so I can do this on my own. Did you know I can look like this every day?" she asked in surprise.

Maggie laughed. "Well, duh. Come pick out something from my closet then. You're coming to dinner at my house tonight and you are *not* wearing pajamas. Pajamas are fine for getting the mail and everything else you do all day long, but not for meeting Joe."

Gwen rolled her eyes and didn't budge when Maggie grabbed her hand. "I am not a size zero for crap's sake. I'm not borrowing anything from you. I'll just wear my church skirt. I'll look fine," she said, sounding just like she always did, but looking like a model when she said it. Maggie grinned at the change.

"Fine. *Fine.* But if you show up tonight covered in dog hair and looking like your dogs dressed you, then you're in huge trouble," she said, shaking her finger in Gwen's face menacingly.

Gwen frowned at the finger and batted it away. "I have some stuff I haven't worn in awhile. I can dig something up. Stop worrying. You're acting like my mom," she grumbled and walked away.

Maggie picked up her sack and watched her go. She couldn't wait to tell Luke. *Or,* she could just wait and see his face tonight. That would be priceless. Maggie ran in the house with her groceries and put them away quickly before running right back out the door and all the way to Sophie's salon. She burst through the door and stopped in disappointment. Sophie was with someone, cutting her hair. A cute little lady with the quintessential granny perm.

Sophie caught her eye and motioned for her to have a seat. "Don't go anywhere. You owe me tons of money," she said, her eyes twinkling merrily.

Maggie laughed and picked up a magazine. Ten minutes and three articles later, Sophie waved good-bye to the woman and came and sat down next to her.

"I don't know what you've done with Gwen, but whatever you've done, keep doing it. She was so open and ready for change. She told me I could do anything I wanted! I was in heaven. I remember talking to her oh, about five years ago, and offering to do her hair and you know what she said? She told me that whenever she got sick of it she just hacked it off herself. *And she was serious.* But I tell you what, after I was done with her, she walked out of here a new woman. I could retire now. I really could. Today I did my greatest work. I will never be able to top that." She sounded in awe of herself.

Maggie didn't even laugh. She believed her. "I will pay whatever you want. You deserve every penny."

Sophie grinned. "I know. And honey, those extensions aren't cheap. I'm just happy you're a millionaire. If you weren't, I'd feel bad," she said handing her the receipt.

Maggie's eyes did widen in surprise, but she paid happily and left Sophie a large tip too.

"Hey, before you go, tell me what's going on in the war for Luke Petersen's heart?" Sophie asked as she put the money in the till.

Maggie sighed and sat down on the arm of one of the chairs. "I'm not really sure. Sometimes I feel like we're going to be together forever and then he turns around the next day and goes out with an ex-girlfriend. I just don't know. I'm not good at this stuff, so I feel like I'm just floundering around in deep water without a life vest," she said, frowning at her nails. She already had a chip!

Sophie leaned her chin on her hands and nodded. "Actually, I think that's pretty typical. I was the same way with Sam. Men are just confusing. But don't give up on Luke. I was talking to Jaden just yesterday, and she was telling me that she thinks you're the one."

Maggie perked up right away. "Really? Cool. I better tell Luke," she said, standing up and heading for the door. "Sorry I can't stay. I've gotta rush home and get everything ready for my parents. They're coming to dinner tonight," she said happily.

Sophie smiled at her. "Go with my blessing then, but just call me sometime. We can go out to lunch," she said with a friendly wave.

Maggie grinned and left. Having friends was fabulous. She ran home and started making the potato salad, Terry's favorite. Luke told her she could borrow his grill, so she could barbecue some ribs. She slathered them with sauce and put them in the fridge to marinade. She could wait and husk the corn later, so that left only the dessert. She had rushed through shopping so fast she had totally forgotten about dessert. She sat down and thought of the best dessert she'd ever had and immediately thought of her grandmother's peach pie. Maggie sat up straight. She could just call up her grandma and see if she wouldn't mind her coming over and picking some peaches. She might not mind. And then, maybe if she was lucky, she would give her the recipe.

Maggie took out her cell and grabbed the note from her grandmother that she had stuck to her fridge with a magnet and dialed the number.

"Hello?"

"Hi, Grandma? It's me, Maggie," she said nervously.

"Well, of course it's you. Who else would call me grandma?" Maggie could swear she heard tears in her voice.

Maggie cleared her throat as she drummed her nails on the table top. "Um, I was wondering something. Would you mind if I came over and picked some peaches from your trees? My mom and stepdad are coming up for dinner tonight, and I wanted to make them something really special."

Bonnie gasped, making Maggie sit up and clutch the phone. She'd probably offended her.

"Honey, why don't you come over right now and I'll walk you through the whole thing," Bonnie said excitedly.

Maggie grinned and stood up grabbing her car keys. "I'm almost there," she said and hung up.

She ran for her car and made it to her grandma's house in four minutes. She ran to the door and didn't even look at her other grandmother's house she was so excited. She reached the front door and didn't bother knocking, just opened it up and went on in.

"Hey, Grandma! I'm here," she called out, throwing her keys on the hallway table.

Frank popped his head out of his office and smiled at her. "Hey, sweetie. Your grandma's out in the back picking some peaches. She said to go on back."

Maggie smiled and gave her grandpa a quick hug before going out the back patio door. She saw her grandma immediately up on a ladder with a bag slung over her shoulders.

"Hey, I was supposed to do the picking. You're hogging all the fun," she protested with her hands on her hips.

Bonnie laughed and climbed down the ladder. "Well, get your fanny on up there if you think you can do a better job," she retorted, hopping down the last step and handing the bag to Maggie.

Maggie practically ran up the ladder and picked way too many peaches. She pretended not to see Frank taking pictures of her and Bonnie from the patio.

"So did my dad have to pick the peaches every year?" Maggie asked, climbing down the ladder when her bag was full.

Bonnie smiled sadly. "Oh yes. We picked them together and then he'd help me can them. He was so helpful. I've never known a more helpful child. Of course, he did have a selfish ulterior motive. That boy would come home from school during the winter and open up a can of peaches and sit there at the kitchen table and eat the whole thing! That boy was an eater. I think Frank and I spent more on groceries feeding your dad than most families with four children do."

Maggie laughed as they walked back into the house. She watched carefully as Bonnie showed her how to scald the peaches. Maggie thought everything looked pretty easy except for the pie crust. She was glad her grandma was helping her with that part tonight. She'd hate to feed her mom a flop. And she could always practice later. Like tomorrow and the next day. An hour later they pulled out the world's most beautiful pie.

Maggie just stood and stared at it. "It's amazing. I don't know if I want anyone eating it now," she said.

Bonnie laughed and called out to Frank. "Frank! Bring that camera and come take a picture of Maggie's first pie," she said.

Frank appeared seconds later, smiling like any proud grandfather. He took a picture of Bonnie and Maggie holding her pie proudly. Maggie wasn't sure, but she was betting that that picture was going to end up in a picture album sometime soon.

"Well, I can't thank you enough. Free peaches *and* a free cooking class all in one. I really do appreciate it," she said, using the pot holders Bonnie was letting her borrow to pick up the still hot pie plate.

"Honey, it was fun for me. Like I said, I would love to teach you how to make all of your dad's favorites. I'll teach you how to make cinnamon rolls next time," she said as she opened the front door for her.

Maggie stopped in wonder. "*Mmmm.* Homemade cinnamon rolls. I can *not* wait. Thanks, Grandma," Maggie said and walked out the door.

Bonnie called after her. "Sweetie, don't forget to tell your mom to give me a call when she has the time. I'd like to talk to her before she comes to visit."

Maggie nodded her head and waited for her grandfather to open the car door for her to place the pie carefully on the seat.

"Now no sharp turns, young lady, or that pie will be everywhere," her grandfather warned before hugging her tightly.

Maggie grinned and waved good-bye. "See ya soon!" she yelled out and then drove away. She didn't even notice Letty Palmer standing by her hydrangea bush listening to everything they said. If she had, she would have noticed the fearful look that crossed her face at the mention of Maggie's mom coming to town.

Chapter 23

Maggie opened the door to her mom and Terry with a shout of happiness.

"Mom! Terry! I'm so glad you're here," she said, and was swept up into the arms of her stepfather. Her mom kissed her briefly on the cheek and ran her hands down her hair.

"So pretty. My beautiful daughter. Now what smells so dang good?" Lisa demanded, walking past her and following her nose to the kitchen.

Terry moved aside and allowed his brother Joe to come in. "Maggie, you know Joe," he said, and followed his wife.

Maggie smiled at Joe and shut the door behind him. "Welcome to my humble home, Joe."

Joe laughed and gave her a bunch of flowers. "For you."

Maggie took the flowers and smelled them. White roses. *Sweet!*

"Hey Joe, now listen. I have a friend coming over for dinner. I want her to meet my mom. They have a ton in common. But here's the thing. She's really pretty, so don't make a fool of yourself over her. No staring at her all night or asking her out. Just give her some space," she said, trying not to smile as he took offense.

"Maggie, you turkey. You know I wouldn't do that. I'm a gentleman. I don't care how pretty she is, I wouldn't make a fool of myself."

Maggie looked at him doubtfully and raised an eyebrow. "Well, whatever. I'm just saying, watch yourself." She turned and left him fuming in the entry.

Luke arrived next, through the back door. "I set up the grill, so we're ready for those ribs," he said, looking totally at ease in spite of the fact that her mom and stepfather were staring at him with a lot of suspicion and interest.

135

Maggie rushed forward, grabbing Luke's hand for a quick squeeze. "Mom, Terry, this is my most wonderful friend, Luke Petersen. He's also my neighbor," she said, dragging him forward.

Lisa shook Luke's hand and from his wry expression she could tell her mom was giving him quite the squeeze. Which was nothing compared to Terry's handshake. She winced for him as he wiggled his fingers painfully afterward.

"It's a pleasure meeting Maggie's family," he said politely, not showing any fear.

Terry stared at him speculatively. "Luke Petersen. Any relation to Jared Petersen?"

Luke grinned. "Oh, you could say that. He's my dad."

Terry relaxed immediately. "*No way.* Your dad was *my* dad's mission companion. Topeka, Kansas, right?"

Luke nodded his head and stepped closer to Terry now that he figured Terry wouldn't try to hurt him anymore. "You know my dad always talked about this one companion he had from St. George who was a rodeo star. He said that Tom Wilson was the most honest, hardworking, humble man he'd ever met. Tell me your last name isn't Wilson," he said.

Terry shocked everyone and himself when he choked up and said, "Tom Wilson *is* my dad and he still talks about what an amazing missionary Jared Petersen was. Does your dad live in Alpine? I would love to meet him," Terry said, his eyes lighting up.

"Sorry, Terry. My dad's on another mission right now. He's the mission president in Honduras. They still have a year left, but I can give you their e-mail address. I know he'd love to hear from your dad. He still loves your dad so much. This is amazing. What a small world," he said, slapping Terry on the shoulder.

Terry sniffed back some emotion and pounded Luke on the back. "You come from good stock, Luke. The best," he said, and then turned and looked at Maggie, catching her eye, as if to say, *Don't mess this up.*

Maggie grinned and shook her head. Lisa, although less loud, still grilled Luke as politely as she could. Luke was a good sport and answered every question thrown at him to the best of his ability.

They were all out in the backyard when Maggie noticed Luke look strangely. He looked like he was seeing a ghost or . . . a vision.

Maggie smiled before she even turned around. She knew it had to be Gwen. She turned around and felt her own mouth drop a little in surprise too. Gwen had been holding out on her. Gone were the dog hair covered pajamas. She was wearing a simple summer skirt that flowed and shimmered around her hips and a simple cotton top with ruching around the waist, making her waist look teensy. Gwen was fabulous. But she looked a little nervous, so Maggie ran to her side.

"Gwen! I'm so glad you could make it. Come meet my mom and Terry."

She grabbed her hand and dragged her to where everyone was standing. She turned her head and whispered quickly, "Stop looking like you're about to jump twenty hurdles. These people are nice and all they know is that they're meeting my beautiful neighbor. Now smile!"

"Mom, this is Gwen. Gwen, Lisa Wilson," she said, making the introductions. She had to kick Luke in the shin so he would stop staring with his mouth open. He blinked and shut his mouth slowly. Maggie noticed Joe noticing Luke's reaction, and tried not to giggle as he looked a little nervous.

"And Gwen, this is Joe, Terry's brother. I believe I mentioned he was coming up to look at some dirt bikes for his two boys," she said, dragging a suddenly very heavy woman behind her.

Gwen finally looked up into Joe's face, blushing like any sixth grader at her first valentine's dance. "Hi Joe. It's, um, it's nice to meet you," she said, stumbling only a little bit.

Maggie watched with pride as Joe stared at Gwen as if he'd never seen a woman before.

"I hope you don't mind my saying so, but you are the most beautiful woman I've ever seen," he said, and then looked at Maggie guiltily. "I guess you hear that all the time. I'm sorry. It's just, if someone told me to picture a beautiful woman in my mind, I'd have to picture you." He blushed suddenly as he heard his brother snicker behind his back.

Maggie turned her head and glared at her stepfather. His laughter immediately stopped.

Gwen's eyes widened and she stared at her feet, totally caught off guard. Maggie stepped in and put her arm around her friend's shoulders. "Oh, Gwen gets that all the time. Heck, look at Luke. When Gwen comes in the room, he can barely put two sentences together. But Gwen's so humble, she doesn't even think she's pretty. Crazy, huh?"

Joe looked in shock at Gwen. "How could you not think you're beautiful? Gwen trust me, I've seen a lot of pretty women in my day, but you . . . you are something special," he said honestly.

Gwen looked up from her toes and stared in surprise at Joe. "Really?" she asked hopefully.

Joe nodded and held his hand out to hers. "I'm Joe Wilson. I am so glad to make your acquaintance," he said humbly.

Gwen giggled and shook his hand. "You're very sweet," she said, still blushing.

Maggie grinned to herself and kicked Luke one more time. "If you don't stop staring at Gwen, I'm going to have to hurt you," she whispered as she dragged him over to the grill.

Luke rubbed his shin and shook his head. "Gwen looks like a girl! I mean, she looks like a woman, Maggie. I would have never believed it. I mean, she's really pretty," he said, still stunned.

Maggie smiled proudly and flipped the ribs. "Honey, that's why they call me the miracle worker. I can do wonders." She caught her mom's eye and winked. Lisa laughed and shook her head at her daughter.

Everyone got plates of food and sat in the lounge chairs. Maggie had some soft music playing on her CD player as everyone chatted and got to know each other. Terry hogged Luke's attention the whole time, and Joe sat by Gwen's side the entire night telling her all about his children and his home in St. George. Maggie was fine with that because it left her mom all to herself.

She told her mom all about Bonnie and Frank and even about Jennie Benchley and all of the ex-girlfriends she'd had to deal with. Lisa laughed and smiled and enjoyed listening to her daughter.

"Mom, Bonnie and Frank really want to talk to you while you're up here. I think they want to apologize to you," she said as they went in the kitchen to cut the peach pie.

Lisa leaned on the kitchen counter and looked thoughtful. "Wow, it's been so long Maggie. The last time I saw them was at your dad's funeral. Are they still mad at me?" she asked softly.

Maggie frowned. "I don't think so, Mom. I just wish I knew what really happened. I mean, I feel like I just have half the story. Do you think you and I can talk tonight? Just you and me? I have a lot of questions," she said, looking worriedly at her mom. She didn't want to dredge up any pain for her mom, but she didn't know any other way to do it.

Lisa looked up and smiled sadly at her daughter. "Sure. It's past time as it is. How about right after dessert? I know a beautiful place we can go for privacy," she said, helping Maggie with the plates.

Maggie sighed in relief. "Thanks, Mom."

They took the dessert outside, and Maggie grinned as everyone stopped staring at Gwen long enough to *oooh* and *aah* at her pie.

"And I made it! Well, with a little help and advice from my grandma, but I seriously made this." She dug in to her own slice with a vengeance.

Luke took a bite and walked over to her and leaned down and kissed her on the cheek. "Darling, this is the best. You are the queen of pie," he said, smiling at her.

Maggie grinned back and took another bite. "Thanks, Luke. I'll let you have the last piece just for that."

Terry frowned and walked over. "Now wait a sec there, honey. I'm your stepdaddy. I think I deserve a second piece of pie more than your boyfriend here. Remember that time I ran over to your house in the middle of the night just because you thought you heard a noise? Remember that? I definitely deserve that last piece." He was staring Luke down and inching toward the pie plate.

Maggie and Lisa exchanged looks and laughed. Joe stood up and grabbed the last piece of pie. "Sorry, fellas. Nobody's getting this last piece of pie except for Gwen here. And I'll take you both on if you have a problem with that." He puffed his chest out and made Gwen giggle in embarrassment.

Luke and Terry stared at Joe with total disgust. Terry sighed in embarrassment for his brother. "Fine, Joe, we'll arm wrestle you for it. Just put it down over there, and if you can drag your sorry butt away from that cute lady, we can see who the real man is," he said, pushing his shirt sleeve up to his elbows.

Joe laughed and practically threw the pie down, he was so fast to join his brother at the table. Gwen grabbed the pie plate and joined Maggie and Lisa as they watched three grown men arm wrestle and laugh and hurt each other all in the name of peach pie. The three women divided the piece into three equal pieces and watched the entertainment.

Ten minutes later they picked up the discarded plates and left the men to their pie-free macho contest.

"So Gwen, Maggie tells me you raise and train dogs. That sounds like an interesting career choice," Lisa said, smiling in a friendly way over at Gwen who kept looking nervously out the window.

"Oh, well, yeah. I love my dogs. And my dogs love me. Besides what you see tonight, I'm really not good at this . . . stuff. Maggie gave me a makeover because I modeled for her and well, it's nothing short of a miracle," she said in a gruff, embarrassed voice.

Lisa looked at her closely, walked over, and sat down with her. Maggie smiled contentedly as she watched her mother pull Gwen's whole life story out of her within a half an hour. By the end of the night, Lisa and Gwen were fast friends.

An hour later, Gwen told Joe good night and promised to see him tomorrow. Luke gave Maggie a quick kiss on the cheek before whispering in her ear something about a pulled shoulder muscle.

Terry whispered something in Lisa's ear about an old elbow injury and disappeared upstairs to soak in the tub, leaving her and her mom alone.

Lisa smiled at her daughter and motioned for the door. "Come on, Maggs. Let's go for a ride," she said, standing up.

Maggie stood up and followed her mom toward the front door. "I'll meet you at the car. I just have to run upstairs and grab something for you. I'll be right down," she said, and ran upstairs. She grabbed the photo album she had made for her mom of all the pictures of Lisa as a child, and then ran downstairs and outside to meet her mom by the car.

She gave her mom the car keys and sat back as Lisa drove past the Tierneys' house and Letty's house and up the street until it ended in a small one-lane road.

"This is what you wanted to show me?" she asked, looking around doubtfully.

Lisa got out and shook her head at her daughter. "Don't be a goober. Come on. We've got a little hike."

Maggie looked back at the sun that was getting ready to set and followed her mom down the road. Her mom hopped a little fence and started walking uphill. They walked in silence for a quarter mile before Maggie broke the silence.

"So where are you taking me? Should I start leaving bread crumbs or something?" She was starting to feel a little nervous. She'd heard of mountain lions in these hills.

Lisa chuckled but didn't look back. "No bread crumbs are necessary. I just wanted to show you my special place. This is the place I would go after school sometimes so I wouldn't have to go straight home. I would come here to be by myself and to feel safe. I could come here and imagine a life where I was happy and where I was loved." Lisa said this so quietly that Maggie had to strain to hear her.

Maggie followed her mom as the colors of the sky started to appear, spreading pink and purple across the clouds as if someone had taken a bucket of paint and thrown it as hard as they could, mixing the colors and sending out small streams of gold.

Maggie heard the rushing water minutes later. "A waterfall? *In Alpine?* Are you kidding me?" she said in wonder.

Lisa looked back and grinned. "Oh, all the old Alpiners take it for granted. They don't realize what an amazing thing Sliding Rock is. Or they do, but they keep silent about it so everyone else in the world will leave it alone." She walked up a twisting path leading toward the mad rushing sound of water.

Maggie smiled and followed her mother as she started walking faster and faster. She saw the waterfall seconds later and stopped and stared. She had to paint this. It was magnificent. It was beautiful. She could see why her mother had come here for refuge.

They climbed up a few rocks and picked one that was still bright with the setting sun.

"This was my rock. See there? You can still see my initials." Lisa pointed out the small name etched in the rock so many years ago.

Maggie ran her finger over her mother's small, messy name and wondered how old she had been when she had first sought sanctuary here.

"I'm so glad I came back." Lisa closed her eyes and tilted her head back as she listened to the water.

"This is where I first heard God's voice telling me not to give up, to keep going. I could hear him in the sound of the water telling me that he loved me and that som day everything would be okay again," she said in a musing voice.

"And he was right. Always remember that Maggie. God knows the end from the beginning. If he tells you it's going to be okay, believe him."

Maggie wrapped her arms around her knees and studied her mom. So beautiful, so strong, and yet delicate too. Like stained glass.

"Mom, could you tell me about when you and my dad decided to run off and get married? Could you tell me why Dad's parents were so mad at you?" Maggie asked.

Lisa sighed and opened her eyes, reaching for her daughter's hand. "Your dad was the most amazing man I've ever known. He might have been only eighteen, but he was so mature and so Christlike. I will always love him, Maggie. I always will. Did you know he was in love with a beautiful girl named Christine? Oh my word, she was cute. I was kind of jealous of her because she had the prettiest long blonde hair. You should have seen the two of them together. They were bright and happy and in love with each other. The rest of us seemed kind of dull next to them."

Maggie looked at her in surprise and a little bit of horror. Had her mother wrecked her dad's relationship with Christine? Lisa glanced at her and smiled sadly.

"Well, one day, it was during the last part of our senior year, and I was up here throwing rocks, and Robbie walks up out of the blue and sits next to me. And he's really quiet. And I say, 'Hey Robbie. Are you okay?' And he said, 'No. No, Lisa, I'm not. I'm dying.' He told me that the doctors said that if he went through with the chemo and radiation this time that he would have twenty percent chance of survival. And then he looked at me, and I'll never forget it. His eyes were so sad and he said, 'But I'm not going to make it this time.' I still remember the way his voice sent goose bumps down my arms. He knew. I really feel that he knew his time was up and that he didn't have very long." Lisa sighed, picking up a rock and throwing it into the rushing water.

Maggie stared at her mom and tried to picture her mom and dad sitting right here where they were so long ago. "Why didn't he tell his mom and dad?" Maggie asked, picking up a rock and running her fingers over it.

Lisa sighed and rested her chin on her knees. "He did, Maggie. But the thing about parents and their kids is that parents never want to see their children's mortality. It's too much like hell. But Robbie knew it was coming. He had just broken up with Christine. He didn't want her mourning for him or wasting her life on a dying man when she should be out having fun and being happy. Oh, I felt so bad for him. It broke my heart to listen to him cry over her. He was so in love with her. I heard she got married a few years later and had a couple kids. Poor Robbie.

"Well, we talked a lot that afternoon. He told me of all the things he had wanted to do and be, and I told him of how I just wanted to be free and safe from my stepfather. And that's when he said it. He said, 'Let's do it.' He told me how he'd always cared for me and how he'd always been my friend, even when I pushed him away all those years. He asked me to let him do this one last good deed before he died." Lisa stopped so she could get her voice under control. She took a few deep breaths and then rubbed her hands over her eyes.

"He said we should get married so my stepfather would never have any power over me ever again. So we planned. I guess looking back on it, I should have said no. I should have talked him into taking the chemo. But Maggie, *he knew*. He knew his time was up. And maybe it was selfish, but I knew that if I married Robbie, I'd be free. I could finally be free. So we met back here every day for the next week and planned everything. How, when, where, all of it. And we did it. We took off a few days after graduation. He did go in for one last checkup for his mom and dad's sake. They tried to force him to stay, but he was eighteen, so he just left. We drove down to Las Vegas and got married, and for a few months Robbie did really well. But then, he started to get weaker and weaker and quieter. He was in a lot of pain in the end. I think that last day was hard for him not being near his mom and dad. He called them on the phone, but they were too mad at him to listen. They kept begging him to tell them where he was so they could come get him and take him to the hospital. But he refused. He just wanted to tell them good-bye and that he loved them, but they were too upset to listen." Lisa bowed her head and wiped her eyes.

Maggie breathed in deeply and let it out slowly, seeing both sides of the story. Devastated parents just wanting every chance for their child to live. Her dad, knowing he was dying and just trying to do one last good thing for her mom.

"Well, he died that night in my arms. I've never felt so helpless or scared. He cared for me as a friend, but he should have had his mom and dad there holding him. He should have had Christine there holding him. And he had to make do with me. *Poor Robbie*," she lamented, openly crying now.

Maggie cried with her mom and reached out and squeezed her mom's hand comfortingly.

"Oh Mom, it was his choice. Don't feel bad," she pleaded.

Lisa sighed and wiped her eyes with her sleeve. "I do. I still do. But the one thing that makes me feel better is you. I gave Robbie a daughter. We decided to consummate the marriage (not that either one of us really wanted to) so that my mom or stepfather couldn't find us and make us annul the marriage. Well, Robbie told me that because he'd had leukemia before as a kid and he'd already been through chemotherapy, that it was almost certain that he was sterile and he wouldn't be able to have kids. So of course we didn't use protection. We were both too embarrassed to go in a store and buy it anyway.

Well, a few months after the funeral, when I found out I was pregnant with you, it was like a miracle. For him and for me. For him, because a part of him would live on. For me, because I now had a reason to live. I had a reason to try. I had a reason to get help," she said, wiping her eyes and sniffing.

Maggie frowned and pushed her hair out of her eyes. "What do you mean, you had a reason to live? Were you thinking about . . . about suicide?" she whispered, feeling sick just saying the words in conjunction with her mother.

Lisa looked at her daughter and nodded matter-of-factly. "Yeah, Maggie. I did think about it. I thought about it a lot. At the funeral, when Robbie's mom and dad yelled at me in front of everyone and blamed me for killing their son, I just felt shattered inside. Like maybe they were right. I had no one. I had nothing. I was completely alone in the world, and I was so sad and so screwed up. But when I found out I was pregnant, I started going to church and I started doing what I should have done from the very beginning. I talked to my bishop. I told him everything that had happened to me. *Everything.* And he was amazing. He just listened to me and he prayed for me and he got me into counseling the very next day. He really did. He and his wife kind of adopted me after that. They had me over for Sunday dinner and family home evenings and his wife, Cheryl, went to all my doctor appointments with me. It was like having a real family for once. Bishop Bullock was transferred with his job back east a few years after you were born, but if it weren't for him, I just don't know, Maggie. I just don't know. I firmly believe that God sends people into our lives at times to act for him. I made it because these people were willing to help a poor abused girl. They signed me up for parenting classes. They helped me get an apartment and a job. They did for me what I couldn't do for myself. Sometimes I feel like they saved my life," she said, rubbing her arms as the temperature started to drop.

Maggie ignored the cooling air and reached into her forgotten bag, taking out the picture album. "Here, Mom. When I moved up here, Terry asked me to get a picture of you when you were a child. He said it would help you finish your healing process," she said, softly handing the photo album to her mom.

Lisa sat up in surprise and took the book, opening it up eagerly. She smiled sadly at the pictures and turned the pages quickly as if she couldn't see them all fast enough. She got to the last picture of her at her husband's funeral and her smile slipped. She closed the book and leaned her head on the leather cover and cried softly.

Maggie scooted over to her mom and put her arm around her shoulders. "Oh, Mom. I didn't want to make you sad. Terry and I just thought this would be the last piece you needed to be healed," she said, feeling horrible at causing her mom even more pain.

Lisa lifted her head, shaking it fiercely. "You and Terry are sweet. But what made you think I still needed to be healed?" she asked curiously.

Maggie frowned. "Well, I remember when I was girl, I'd hear you cry in the middle of the night. Terry told me a few months ago that sometimes you still do," she said, rubbing her mom's back.

Lisa smiled and looked up at the emerging stars briefly. "Oh, honey. When you were a little girl, I was still in the process of healing. It does take a while. And I had a lot that needed to be healed. But through counseling and a loving bishop I was able to realize that I am a child of God. It's so simple. It sounds too easy, doesn't it? That's the first song children learn in Primary. But believing it is a whole different story. It's a battle. Satan tries his darndest to convince you you're nothing, and Heavenly Father is trying as hard as he can to tell you that you're divine.

For so long I didn't believe I was worth anything. I didn't feel I was as good as anybody else. I didn't believe that God could love me the same as he did other girls who were whole and pure and innocent. But then I finally realized that he loved me. *So much.* And not only that, but that he loved me just as much as every-one else. I started to heal. I had to truly understand that Jesus died *for me.* Me, Lisa Palmer. Jesus died for me so that I could be healed. Not halfway healed. Not sort of better. But healed all the way. Maggie, when I started to take the sacra-ment and take part in the Atonement, I could feel all the cracks in my soul come together. Every pain, every nightmare, every horror was taken from me. Jesus took it from me. He did that for me, Maggie. He lived so that I could live. He died so that my pain could die. I don't have to live my life a broken, damaged shell of a woman because of one man's evil. I can't overcome what happened to me. It's not possible. Only Jesus could overcome what happened to me. No amount of counseling, no amount of drugs, nothing can erase what happened to me. Only Christ can, Maggie. He is the miracle. He makes it possible for me to wake up every day happy. I am healed. All the way, perfectly, happily healed. But I do so appreciate these pictures. You'll never know how much. But no picture could heal me, sweetie. Nothing and nobody can heal except Christ. And he did," she said, hugging her daughter back.

Maggie pulled away, still frowning. "Then why do you still cry at night?" she had to ask.

Lisa rubbed her nose and sighed. "Because, sweetie, in my line of work, I see so many abused children. Girls and boys who are like I was. Young and scared and mad and so broken. I cry for them and I pray for them. I pray that I can make a difference in their lives the same way my bishop made a difference in mine."

Maggie smiled and shook her head. "Oh, Mom, you are too amazing. What did I do to deserve having you for a mom?"

Lisa laughed and kissed her hair. "Knock it off. It's not even Mother's Day. So does that answer all your questions? Are you okay with everything now?" she asked, and picked up another rock, throwing it into the water.

Maggie frowned and looked away, almost guiltily. "Mom, I'm not like you at all. I'm still really angry at what happened to you. When I talked to your mother the other day, I yelled at her and I told her to stay away from me. I just can't get over it. How can a mother stand by and let something so hideous, so evil, happen to her child?" she asked fiercely, feeling herself get angry all over again.

Lisa blew out her breath and stared up at the sky for a few minutes before answering. "*That* was the last piece of my healing. Forgiveness. No one was ever healed without first forgiving. The thing of it is, Maggie, I don't *have to* understand her. I don't need to know why she did what she did. I can leave that up to Jesus. He's the one who went through Gethsemane so that he could understand why people do the things they do. All I need to do is give all of my hate and anger and confusion and pain to the Lord. And if I do that, then what I get in return is peace. Weightless, perfect peace."

Maggie sighed and knew she needed to work on that. "I understand what you're saying, and I can see that you've found your peace. But how do you do it? I mean, just saying it doesn't get the job done. At least not for me," Maggie said glumly.

Lisa laughed softly and stood up. "It starts with taking the first step. *Wanting to*," she said and held her hand out to her daughter and pulled her up.

Maggie stood up and threw her arms around her mom. "Oh, Mom, I love you so much," she whispered.

Lisa hugged her back hard for a few moments. "I know, baby. I know."

Lisa held the photo album in her arms as they walked back down to the road. Maggie glanced at her mom and bit her lip.

"So are you going to see my grandparents?" she asked.

Lisa glanced at her daughter and smiled. "Sure. You know before Robbie and I ran off and got married, I used to daydream that Frank and Bonnie were my mom and dad. I really loved them. They were always trying to look out for me. I'll always love them for that," she said.

Maggie winced and asked her last question of the night. "What about *your* mom? Will you see her while you're up here?"

Lisa picked up a rock and threw it as far away as she could before answering. "I'm starting to think maybe I should. Maybe if I let my mom know that I forgive her, then maybe she can find some peace too. That's the thing about the Atonement. It works for everybody," she said with a kind smile.

Maggie smiled back and reached out and held her mom's hand. "I think I'll be looking into that," she said.

They drove home, past the house her mom grew up in. Lisa glanced at it sadly, but there was no anger or hate in her gaze. And she didn't dwell on it. Maggie glanced at it quickly and away again even faster. But if her mom could forgive, maybe she could too. She sighed and glanced at her mom. Maybe it was time to turn things over to the Lord.

Chapter 24

Maggie slept in late the next day and woke up to the smell of bacon, eggs, and hash browns. She ran downstairs grinning. She walked into the kitchen to find Terry kissing her mom tenderly on the cheek as he hugged her from behind. Maggie stopped suddenly, not wanting to intrude. She smiled as she watched them for a moment. Her mom used to hate to be touched. *By anyone.* Even by Maggie, but especially men. And now she had a healthy, stable, warm relationship. And here Maggie was, still a little nervous around men.

Maggie cleared her throat loudly and stepped into the kitchen as Terry let go of her mom. "Well, I must have died and gone to heaven," she said, smiling at her mom.

Lisa laughed and dished her daughter up a heaping plate. "I know how much energy you need to get going in the morning. It's hard to forget," she said, handing Maggie a fork.

Terry sat down with the paper and smiled at Lisa. "I still don't know how you could afford feeding this girl on your little salary. It's just a good thing she makes so much dang money selling her pretty pictures."

Lisa and Maggie rolled their eyes together, sat down, and prayed before they started eating. "So where's Joe?" Maggie asked, grabbing the ketchup for her hash browns.

Lisa laughed and passed her the salt and pepper. "I guess he was up early and he saw a certain beautiful neighbor out walking her dogs and he insisted on helping out."

Terry groaned and turned the page of his newspaper. "I still can't believe what a fool he made of himself last night over that woman. Carrying on like he was still in high school or something," he said in disgust.

146

Maggie snorted and stared at her stepfather. "Hey, I'd rather see him make a fool of himself over a beautiful woman than to see him make a fool of himself over a little piece of pie."

Lisa laughed at her husband as he turned red in the face.

"Well, sweetie, if you don't want people making fools of themselves, then don't cook so good." Terry winked at her.

They all finished eating breakfast and cleaned up the kitchen together before Joe made it back.

"Hey guys. I'm taking Gwen out to breakfast. We've worked up an appetite," he said, and grabbed his keys and ran right back out the door.

Lisa raised an eyebrow at her husband. "Looks like Joe's about to fall hard," she said happily in a singsong voice.

Terry groaned long and loud. "Joe has the worst taste in women. They all think they're little starlets and Joe's their servant. It's pathetic. And now look at him. Has he learned? Nope. The first model he sees and *boom*. I don't care if that woman says she raises dogs for a living. I don't buy it. She made her money modeling, and I'd bet my new Ford truck on it," he said with a sneer.

Maggie and Lisa looked speculatively at each other. "Should I, Mom? You know how much I've been wanting a truck," she said, biting her lip.

Lisa pursed her lips. "But if you do, then I won't get to drive it. Better not," she said, smiling in commiseration as Maggie's face fell.

Terry stared at the two women in irritation. "You know I'm right. Don't pretend I'm not," he said hotly.

Lisa took her husband's hand and looked up into his eyes. "Sweetie, Gwen just got a makeover yesterday morning, thanks to Maggie. Before that, she hadn't worn makeup in about fifteen years and her hair was short, spiky, and *gray*. She hasn't been out on a date in ten years and she's so nervous being around your brother all she can do is giggle. Which is really embarrassing for her. She really does raise and breed dogs for a living. And she really doesn't believe that she's pretty. So go easy on her," Lisa said gently.

Terry rolled his eyes and hmmed and hawed and then when Lisa just stared at him, his shoulders fell in defeat and he looked at Maggie. "Thanks for not taking my truck, Maggs."

Maggie leaned up and kissed him on the cheek. "You're welcome. Now, what's on the schedule for today? Anything fun?" she asked.

Terry glanced at Lisa who smiled encouragingly at him. "Well, if it's all the same to you, Lisa and I were talking last night and we were thinking about maybe looking around Alpine for a house. We've lived in St. George long enough, and we figured it's time to spread our wings and try something new. Especially if you think you might be settling here," Terry said, his smile growing bigger and bigger.

Maggie's mouth fell open as she stared at her stepdad and her mom. "Are you kidding me?" she whispered, raising her hands to her mouth.

Lisa shook her head. "Terry's already put in for a transfer. He's willing and ready. And there's plenty of work for me to do wherever I go, it seems. What do you think?" she asked worriedly. "I mean, I know you're an adult now, and you probably want your space, but I thought it would be nice considering the fact that in a few years I could be a grandma," she said, biting her lip nervously.

Maggie screamed and threw her arms around her parents and jumped up and down like a pogo stick.

"Watch my knees, Maggie! I'm an old man," he said with a laugh.

Lisa finally pulled away and took her daughter's face in her hands. "Really? Is it okay? I need to hear the words," she said.

Maggie nodded her head slowly and firmly. "I would love it. Because to be honest, I'm really starting to settle in here. I love St. George and trust me, in the wintertime, I'll be going back for very long weekends. But I just feel so much at home here. It's hard to explain," she said, shrugging.

Lisa nodded and smiled. "I know what you mean, dear. Well, we're off then. We'll catch up with you tonight sometime." She waved as they walked out the door, leaving Maggie on her own, smiling at nothing in particular.

Maggie went out on her front porch and sat down, waving at her mom and Terry as they drove away. She looked up and down the street and sighed in happiness. Everything was practically perfect. *Practically,* anyway. She leaned her head on her hands and breathed in the smell of a warm summer morning and relaxed. Gwen was happy. *Sort of.* Her mom and Terry were thinking of moving to Alpine. Luke really wasn't in love with Sage or any of his other ex-girlfriends. And she was getting to know and enjoy her grandparents. On top of that she was feeling her creative spark come back to life with a vengeance. The painting she had started yesterday with Gwen was already taking off. She couldn't wait to pry her away from Joe so she could sit for her again. Life was just as it should be, she thought, smiling peacefully.

She stretched and leaned back, resting her weight on her hands and smiled lovingly at the world. Nothing could ruin this day. Not one thing. She felt the sun warm her skin and decided on a light jog that morning. Nothing too strenuous. Maybe she'd even just walk. She was so full after her mom's breakfast, she could practically feel all the eggs and bacon and hash browns inside her jostling around. *Ookaay,* walk it was.

Maggie slipped on her shoes and locked up before walking out the door. She automatically headed toward her grandma's house and smiled, realizing that her feet knew her better than she knew herself. She couldn't wait to tell Grandma the good news about her mom moving back and how her mom had forgiven them a long time ago for all the things said at the funeral. She caught herself skipping and looked around quickly to see if anyone was pointing and laughing at her. Actually, there were. Just two grungy-looking teenage boys with ear buds hanging from their heads. She waved and smiled at them and they immediately stopped laughing and walked away. Poor things were obviously not used to much female attention.

Maggie felt so good waving, she decided to wave at everyone she saw and walked down the road doing a really good impression of Mary Poppins. She giggled at herself as she walked up to her grandma's house. She ignored her other grandmother's house out of habit and rang the doorbell. She stood for a few minutes and then knocked. She frowned and looked back behind her. Her grandma's green Range Rover was parked in front so she had to be home. She frowned at the closed door and decided to walk around to the back. She was probably picking peaches or working in her garden. She went to the left side of the Tierney house, just in case Letty was out and about, but came up against a road block. A large, tall fence. *Drat*. She walked quietly around to the other side of the house and walked toward the back. There was a fence, but it did have a door. Bonus. She lifted the latch and let herself in, closing it behind her. She walked a few feet before she heard voices—loud, angry voices.

Maggie ran toward the voices, becoming alarmed. She couldn't even imagine her grandparents fighting and not this loud. She ran to the back of the yard and stopped on a dime when she saw her grandmother Tierney standing on her side of a chain-link fence shaking her finger at her grandmother Palmer, who was standing on her side of the fence, looking furious and red in the face.

Maggie was about to turn around and walk away when she heard her mother's name.

"If I even hear that you've been anywhere near Lisa, so help me you will regret it. It's bad enough you've been making a pest of yourself with Maggie, but you have no right to go near that poor girl. I'm dead serious, Letty. I've held my tongue for far too long. What will all your friends in the D.O.P think when they find out what kind of a person you really are?" Bonnie said, her voice strong and sure.

Letty's cheeks flared out in anger. "Don't you talk to me that way. You don't know anything. You hear me? That girl has been spreading lies her whole life. She made Nathan's life a living hell with all of her lies and insinuations. I don't care if you tell everyone in Alpine your stupid little rumors, because everyone knows the truth. Nathan Palmer was a good man. A decent man and he never touched that girl. Not once. He told me so, and I believe him," she said, her voice rising to a shout.

Maggie felt herself go cold but she couldn't move. She just stood there, like a statue, listening to Letty Palmer call her mom a liar.

But Bonnie didn't. "You stupid, blind fool. Lisa never talked about it. Don't you get it? All the rumors that surrounded Lisa and Nathan were because people could look at him and see the way he looked at her. It wasn't right the way he stared at her, Letty. It wasn't right for a young girl's stepfather to look at her that way. People could see the way he treated her. He would go crazy if a boy even tried to talk to her, Letty. He would never let her date. Not because he cared about her virtue but *because he was jealous*. Lisa didn't say it. She didn't have to. People saw it. Everyone who had eyes to see knew. Everyone except you. Tell me, Letty, how do you sleep at night? Because you can scream and yell at me all day, but we both know that deep inside, way deep down, you know what happened to Lisa. And you know that you let it happen. You stepped back, shut your eyes, and turned your back on your own daughter. You let your own daughter be abused. I dare you to deny it," Bonnie spit out.

Maggie stared at Letty's face. Where before her face had been red with anger, it had gone bone white. "You don't understand. She flirted with him. I saw it with my own eyes. She tried to steal my husband away from me. She knew she was prettier than me. And she rubbed my face in it. She would swish around the house, flipping her hair and laughing just to get his attention. She wanted to take my husband from me. But don't misunderstand me. She might have stolen his heart from me, but she didn't get his soul. Because he was honorable. She came to me one time and told me he had done horrible things to her. She was just trying to drive a wedge between me and Nathan. You know what I did, Bonnie? I'll tell you. I slapped her and washed her mouth out with soap. She wanted to ruin my happiness. She wanted to wreck my life. Except she couldn't. She couldn't because Nathan was a good, strong man. So instead, she decided to ruin your life. She stole your boy from you, just like she tried to steal my husband. You know it's true, Bonnie. If it weren't for Lisa, your Robbie would still be alive," she said righteously.

Maggie felt her heart racing in fury as she saw the pain twisting on her grandmother's face. She felt her legs move suddenly and she was standing next to her grandmother. She put her arm around Bonnie's shoulders and stared her grandmother Palmer in the face.

"That is the biggest bunch of crap I've ever heard," she said acidly, watching as Letty reared back in surprise and what she thought looked like embarrassment.

"My mom didn't steal my dad. He knew he was dying. He knew it. And his last wish was to free my mom from being sexually abused by your husband. So he convinced her to run away with him and get married, so there was no way you could force her back. He saved her life. Because *you* wouldn't," she said with disgust dripping off her tongue.

Letty's face lost all expression. She stepped back from the fence, as if to put some distance between her and Maggie's words.

"Grandma, how old was my mom when Nathan Palmer moved in?"

Bonnie took a deep breath and thought for a second before answering. "She was eight or nine I think. Just a young thing," she said softly.

Maggie turned back to Letty and stared her down. "Are you seriously standing there, telling me and my grandma and the whole world that an eight-year-old girl tried to steal your husband? You know there are laws now that have been passed that punish mothers who knowingly allow their children to be abused. Your husband might be dead, but you're not. I would love to convince my mother to take you to court. That's a picture I'd love to paint. You behind bars," she said and took her grandmother's arm and pulled her back toward the house. They walked quickly away, leaving Letty standing in her yard, staring after them with what could only be horror.

Maggie with her hand still on her grandmother's arm, opened the stiff sliding glass door and led Bonnie inside, turning to shut the door firmly. And then Maggie started to shake. And she couldn't stop, no matter what. She wasn't crying, but for some reason, she couldn't stop shaking.

Bonnie brought a warm blanket and wrapped her in it and then led her to the couch in the family room.

"Oh, Maggie, I'm so sorry you had to hear that. I was just out in my garden and she started going on and on about your mother. I tried ignoring her for awhile, but then I just got so mad that I finally threw my shovel down and gave her a piece of my mind."

Maggie pulled the blanket closer together around her chest and pulled her knees up so she could suck in as much warmth as she could get.

"I'm sorry too. My mom was just talking to me last night about forgiveness and there I go shouting at Letty that I would love to take her to court. Oh my heck, I think I'm going to hell. That's where people go who can't forgive others," she said in distress.

Bonnie surprised them both and laughed a little. "Are you crazy? I think the good Lord's up in heaven doing a cartwheel because somebody might have finally broken through Letty's wall of self-deception. For a moment there when you said what you did, she looked like she finally got it. Oh my word, I know it's a commandment to forgive everybody for everything, but I still say it's easier to forgive somebody who's actually sorry. Don't you think so?" Bonnie grabbed a throw pillow to hug.

Maggie smiled weakly. "So true. I think that's the worst thing. Having to forgive somebody who will never admit they're wrong. I really don't know how my mom did it. We were talking last night, which is why I came over here this morning, and she was telling me how she had forgiven her mom and her stepfather and you guys too. I'm just amazed. And then I told her that I was going to try to forgive Letty and then the first thing this morning I come over here and feel like jumping over the fence and kicking her," she said with a touch of self-disgust.

Bonnie smiled compassionately at her granddaughter. "Life is so complicated and for some reason, it's just never easy. Forgiving people is a hard mountain to climb. One of the hardest things in this life to do, really. Lucky for you, you're still young. You have a lot of time to work on it, dear. Not as much time for me, I'm afraid," she said with a wry smile.

Maggie smiled and leaned her head on her knees. "My mom said she'd like to see you and grandpa. She told me last night about how much she wished you were her mom and that Grandpa was her dad and how much she's always loved you," she said.

Bonnie looked at Maggie, her eyes shutting in pain. "Oh, Maggie. There were so many times I wished she were mine too. It's so hard to sit back and feel powerless to help somebody you know deep in your heart needs help. But Robbie didn't. Robbie always found a way to help people no matter what. I hope your mom comes by soon," she said, and tried to hide her tears by turning her face away and wiping them quickly on her sleeve.

"She also wants to see her mom. I don't think she should, Grandma. I think Letty would just open up all the old wounds and pour acid on everything. My mom is so happy and healthy and healed. She doesn't need her mom in her life. Not now, not ever." Maggie was getting angry all over again.

Bonnie frowned and patted her granddaughter's knee. "Well, honey, that's up to her. Not you and not me. But maybe Letty will go home and think about some of the things we said today. Maybe by the time Lisa goes to see her, she'll be able to see the beautiful woman that her daughter is."

Maggie smiled sadly and nodded, not believing it for a second. "Maybe."

Maggie left a few minutes later, still shaken by her confrontation with her grandmother and still reeling from the venom and jealousy that still burned in Letty's heart. She shoved her hands into her jean pockets and kept her head down as she walked home. She had been so sure that nothing could ruin her day today. She had found the one person in Alpine who was capable of doing it, though. From now on, she'd work on her forgiveness from a distance. Proximity seemed to only mess up the process.

Chapter 25

Luke surprised everyone by offering to take them all out to dinner that night. Joe bowed out, saying something about driving up to Salt Lake to see the dirt bikes. But he looked kind of sad when he said it, so Maggie wasn't sure if it had less to do with the bikes and more to do with Gwen. She made a note to herself to call Gwen later that night and find out how things were going between her and Joe.

They piled into Luke's car and drove to Salt Lake to go to The Roof. Maggie had been there once a long time ago with her mom. They had come up for general conference and had splurged on dinner there. So she was looking forward to it.

"You're a smart man, Luke. I'm impressed. You knew you needed to do an all-you-can-eat buffet for Maggie's sake, but you didn't want to be embarrassed in front of us. You hit it out of the ballpark on this one," Terry said in admiration.

Luke laughed and turned some soft music on. "I have my faults, but starving Maggie is not one of them. And yeah, it's a bonus to impress her parents at the same time," he said cockily.

Lisa smiled and patted Luke on the arm. "Luke, you don't need to take us out to dinner to impress us. We're already impressed. You're smart, you're good-looking, and you and Maggie go together like peaches and cream. We couldn't be happier," she said, smiling approvingly at the couple in the front seat.

Maggie blushed and felt her heart constrict. "*Mom*, it's not like we're engaged or anything. We're just kind of . . . actually, I'm not sure what we're doing. Luke, what is it we're doing?" she asked, feeling a little concerned suddenly.

Luke laughed at her and grabbed her hand. "We're doing what men and women have been doing since the beginning of time. It's called courtship. Enjoy it because I hear it doesn't last that long," he said.

Terry laughed, and the conversation moved on to house hunting. Luke told her mom and Terry that he'd ask around. Most of the houses in Alpine were too expensive for her mom and stepfather. And when Maggie offered to help them out, she was met with two sets of identically insulted eyes.

"Fine! But I don't see what the point in moving up here is if you live an hour away," she said, glaring at the both of them before turning around in her seat.

Terry tried to explain things to her, but she held up her hand in irritation. "Then you'll just have to move in with me. But you're buying the groceries," she said.

Terry looked horrified and Lisa laughed. "Maggie, behave yourself. Something will come up. We've only been looking for one day. Now, no fighting. We're here, so everyone put on a smile and act like adults," she ordered, opening her door and getting out.

Everyone smiled and relaxed as they made their way up to the Joseph Smith Memorial building. They spent an hour and a half talking and putting away huge quantities of food. Luke looked like he was in pain, and Lisa elbowed Terry in the ribs when he tried to unbutton the top button on his pants.

"Let's walk around Temple Square before we go. We need to burn off some calories," Maggie suggested, and stood up.

Everyone liked the idea and agreed to meet back at the car in one hour. Luke took Maggie's hand and they walked toward the water fountain as Lisa and Terry made their way to the visitors' center. Maggie told Luke everything that had happened at her grandmother's that morning and winced when she saw the disgust on his face.

"Maggie, I'm so sorry you had to deal with that. When I think of both of my grandmas and how amazing they are, it just seems so unfair that your grandma is, well, . . . *crazy*," he said, sitting on a stone wall. Maggie hopped up to join him and stared up at the temple.

"This whole families are forever stuff. I don't know, Luke. I can see how it makes perfect sense for you and your family. But for me? It's just a bad dream. I wouldn't want to be sealed to any Palmers. But at the same time, I would love to be sealed to my mom. And although I really like Terry, and he would if I asked him, I don't necessarily want to be sealed to him, because I'd feel like I was betraying my own father who it turns out is really amazing. What am I supposed to do?" She closed her eyes and tilted her head back.

Luke looked at her and rubbed her shoulders. "You start your own line. Heavenly Father will make it right for you up in heaven with your mom and your dad. I'm sure of it. I don't know how and I don't pretend to, but I know he can fix it. Now as far as you, right now, you probably need to start thinking of getting married to a worthy man in the temple so that the children you have will be sealed to you and your husband. The eternal family is one of the most beautiful, if not *the* most beautiful, concepts in the world. You'll see," he said, leaning over and kissing her on the cheek.

Maggie sat up straight and stared at him. "You sound so sure," she said, feeling her heart race.

Luke smiled and scooted closer to her. "It's like your mom said in the car. We go together like peaches and cream. It just doesn't get any simpler than that."

Maggie frowned at him. "What exactly are you saying? You've got to spell it out for me because I'm really dumb when it comes to stuff like this," she whispered.

Luke pulled a note out of his pocket. It was crumpled and it looked like it had been drawn on and someone had wiped something smeary on it. He handed it to her.

Maggie winced at it but pulled it apart and spread it out on her lap. She looked closely at the badly handwritten words.

Will You Go Out With Me? Write Me Back If The Answer Is Yes.

She giggled and looked up at Luke's twinkling eyes that had turned a light golden green.

"Are you serious?" she asked, shaking her head in amusement.

"Well, you said you wanted Remedial Relationships 101, and so I thought I'd start at the beginning. Unfortunately, I forgot to tell you something about this class. It might start slow at the beginning, but it moves kind of fast. It's sort of an accelerated remedial course. But I can practically promise you'll get an A," he said while laughing at her expression.

Maggie gave in and laughed as she threw her arms around Luke's neck and kissed him on the cheek.

Luke pulled back. "So is that a yes?"

Maggie nodded. "It's a yes. Just imagine how fun that would have been. You and me in elementary school. I could have been your girlfriend in the third grade, and you could have walked me home from school. Dang, we missed out," she said, pouting.

Luke shook his head. "Nah, you really didn't. I didn't get the whole girl thing until junior high. I would have either ignored your existence or teased you," he said, standing up and holding his hand out to her.

Maggie put the note carefully in her purse before jumping up. She'd never gotten a note like that before. She was going to frame it when she got home. They walked around and chatted with some Temple Square missionaries before heading back for the car. They drove back, all in a good mood, enjoying each other's company. Maggie smiled and leaned back. This was how she had imagined it for herself. Having a family. True, Luke really wasn't her family. But just maybe, someday, that might be a possibility. She crossed her fingers and smiled at Luke. He grinned at her and held her hand as they drove back home. She could almost see it.

When they got back, Terry insisted on seeing Luke's basement with his woodworking tools. Lisa had some phone calls to make to co-workers and the other agencies she worked with, so Maggie walked next door to check on Gwen. She walked up to the front porch and banged hard on the door. It was almost immediately opened by Gwen.

Maggie stared in surprise. Gone was the makeup. She still had the long hair, but it was scraped back in a tight, low ponytail. Gwen didn't look anything like the happy, blushing, beautiful woman from the night before. She looked exactly like she always did, minus the spiky short gray hair.

"So, uh, what's going on?" Maggie said, not sure what to say.

Gwen took a cigarette out of her back pocket and lit up, blowing smoke to the side of Maggie's head.

"Not much, you?" she asked in an uncaring, off-hand voice.

Maggie frowned at her friend and pulled her out on the porch. "Come out here where all the pollution can float away. I can't talk to you when you're blowing smoke in my ear," she said.

Gwen rolled her eyes, sighing heavily, but joined her sitting down on her front steps.

"What happened?" Maggie asked softly, jumping over Gwen's high walls of protection to get to the heart of the matter.

Gwen's head bowed and she flicked the ash into her flower bed. "Nothing happened, Maggie. That's what. I just can't do it. I can't go from being on a ten-year hiatus to dating Joe. I just can't. You grew up with your mom. You're not new to this. How long did it take her to get comfortable with Terry?"

Maggie frowned, not really sure since her mom had worked with Terry for a few years before they started dating. "Awhile, Gwen. Is that the problem? Are you uncomfortable with Joe?"

Gwen took another puff. "It's not just that. It's everything. I have my whole life set up the way I want it. I can't just let a man inside. He'll disrupt everything and I won't know which way is up or down. And I can't pretend to be something I'm not. Last night was fun, don't get me wrong. I had a good time. And then this morning when Joe took me out to breakfast, I thought I was in heaven. But Joe doesn't know *me*. He doesn't know what happened to me. You can't make a silk purse out of a sow's ear. And that's what he sees when he looks at me. All he sees is this woman with long blonde hair and really great makeup. If he could really see *me*, he'd run all the way back to St. George. I just can't do it, Maggie. I can't lead him on. This is me and there's no use trying to be anybody else," she said tiredly.

Maggie felt her heart break for her friend. Where was her mom when she needed her? She glanced at her house and then back at Gwen. Gwen was going to have to make do with her for the time being.

"Gwen, you dear, stupid idiot. What makes you think just because something really crappy happened to you that it changed *you* into something bad? I'm only twenty-four, and I'll be the first one to admit that I don't know everything. But there's a few things I do know. I know that you're a beautiful woman, and it doesn't matter if you have long blonde hair or short spiky gray hair. Nothing is going to change the fact that you are what you are. The same way that tragedy doesn't change the fact that you are a daughter of God. God is your father. He loves you. He thinks you're beautiful. He thinks you're amazing. He knows you've been hurt. Jesus was right there with you when it happened. He knows everything. And he also knows that hiding your light behind a bushel, or ten dogs and a pack of cigarettes, is a waste of time. Be who you really are, Gwen. And stop being so dang scared," she said, clenching her hands on her knees.

Gwen leaned her head on her hand and flicked her cigarette into the bushes. "He asked me if we could start seeing each other, you know, date and stuff, and I told him no. I told him I wasn't ready for a relationship right now," she said, wiping her eyes on her sleeve.

Maggie sighed and put her arm around her friend. "So just tell him that you've changed your mind. Tell him that you're not ready to jump into a relationship, but that you're ready to get to know him at your own pace. This is your life. You do the best you can. If he can handle taking things slow, then he will. And if he doesn't want to take the time, then good riddance. But it's just plain dumb to throw away a chance at love because you're nervous."

Gwen rubbed at the nicotine stains on her fingers. "He was talking about me coming down to St. George next week to meet his kids. I kind of freaked out. And it's not because I don't like kids. You know I love kids. It was his eyes. He had this look, like he could see us twenty years down the road or something. I just couldn't deal with it. It was too much too fast," she said, rubbing her temples.

Maggie nodded, thinking of Luke, who could move a little faster than she wanted him to.

"Well, what do you do when you're walking one of your dogs and he gets ahead of himself?" she asked, smiling to herself.

Gwen sat up and looked interested. "I pull him back."

Maggie nodded. "You don't get rid of him though, do ya? You don't just take him to the pound, right?" she asked casually.

Gwen smiled. "Of course not. How stupid do I look? You know what, Maggie my girl? You're not half bad. I think I'll keep you," she said, standing up.

"Hey, where are you going?" Maggie asked as Gwen headed for her door.

"I think I'm going to ask Joe to go out for an ice cream cone with me. But first I've gotta do my hair," she said, sounding only a little worried.

Maggie smiled at the empty porch and stood up herself. She was a genius, pure and simple.

Chapter 26

The next day Maggie hung out with her mom while Joe and Terry went out to the Salt Flats to test drive dirtbikes. They even dragged Gwen out with them for lunch. Maggie casually mentioned the mall and Lisa and she were able to manhandle Gwen into Dillard's for a quick peek. Gwen gave in gracefully after she caught sight of herself in a mirror and she really saw her raggedy sweats and stained T-shirt.

"It doesn't really work anymore, does it?" she asked Maggie and Lisa.

Lisa walked up behind her and smiled into the mirror. "It still works. For you and your dogs, this is great. For going out on a date? Not so much. But isn't it great that you don't have to leave your old self behind? You just bring her with you."

Gwen smiled slowly in the mirror and nodded. "Okay then. Hypothetically, if I do decide to date Joe, and hypothetically if things go well and all that stuff, what kind of outfit should I buy to meet two wild and crazy teenage boys in?" she asked.

Maggie spotted some basic Levi jeans that were slightly flared at the bottom and worn on the tops of the thighs. "You know, those jeans with a killer pair of boots and new shirt would give them just the right image, I think. I mean, if you consider teenage boys. Especially teenage boys who've been living in bachelor heaven for a while. I bet they'd be scared to death that some ultra femmy chick will come into their lives and make them clean up and comb their hair and dress nice and stop swearing and all that stuff teenage boys do. This outfit would definitely put them at ease and at the same time, let them know that you're cool and that you can hang," she said, looking to Lisa for back up.

Lisa grinned and grabbed a silk screen T-shirt with Calamity Jane on it and the words *Scandalous* spread across the front. "Now I know for a fact that Joe is just a simple cowboy at heart. If he could see you in jeans and boots and a cool shirt like this? I don't know. I think you'd have him eating out of your hands," she said, laughing at Gwen's frightened expression.

Gwen gulped. "That's the problem. He's already eating out of my hands and I'm not sure what to do with him."

Lisa rubbed Gwen's shoulders and smiled encouragingly at her new friend. "Gwen, don't make it harder than it is. Joe's a simple man who is infatuated with a pretty woman. It doesn't get any easier than that. You don't have *to do* anything with him. You just have to sit back and enjoy it," she said, watching Gwen's expression ease a little.

"Maybe if you keep telling me that over and over I'll start believing it."

Lisa laughed and pushed her toward the changing rooms. "I'll cross stitch it on a pillow for you, I promise. Now go see if that fits," she ordered kindly.

Maggie and Lisa turned and smiled at each other. "I just love Gwen. She is going to be such a cool sister-in-law someday," Lisa said.

Maggie grinned. "Would that make her my stepaunt?" she asked hopefully.

Lisa laughed and walked over to a rack of clothes. "I'm pretty sure it would. What do you think about this shirt, Maggie? Does it look nice enough to go see my estranged mother in?" she asked lightly.

Maggie cleared her throat nervously and walked over to see the shirt. It was really ugly. It had lace and sequins and some kind of patchwork theme. She smiled as best she could.

"I think it's perfect."

Lisa laughed and threw the shirt at her. "No, seriously, help me pick something out. I was thinking of going over tonight and saying hi. Then I figured on going over to Robbie's mom and dad's. You know, get it all over at once," she said casually.

Maggie stared at her mom. She didn't look tense. She didn't look scared or sick or upset at the thought of seeing her mom again. *Wow.*

"Well, if I were you, I think I'd forget about buying a new outfit and wear something you already own. I wouldn't dress up for it. Just go as yourself. If you want to buy something, buy something for Gwen's wedding. That's what you should be looking for." Maggie glanced around for the formal section.

Lisa laughed. "You are so right. Dang you're wise for such a little baby."

Maggie stuck her tongue out at her mom but noticed Gwen walking out of the changing room. She grabbed her mom's arm and turned her to look at Gwen. "Gwen, I can't believe I'm saying this, but you're kind of hot," she said in surprise.

Lisa nodded in agreement. Maggie had only ever seen Gwen in baggy sweats, a baggy skirt for church, or even baggier pajamas. Except for the skirt the other night, which had been kind of loose, she'd never seen her in anything that showed off her figure that much.

Lisa nodded in agreement. "If I had a figure like that I'd dump Terry and go be a model," she said, laughing at herself.

Maggie snorted and turned back to Gwen who was blushing brightly now. "I'm not used to wearing tight stuff. I don't know. I don't think I can," she said, inching back toward the changing room.

Maggie shook her head. "Uh-uh. Not so fast. Those jeans aren't tight, Gwen. They just fit you. Big difference. I'm in awe. Really. Now hurry and go change so we can go find you some boots to match," she commanded and watched with enjoyment as Gwen turned and ran back to the changing room.

"This is kind of fun," she said, grinning at her mom.

All three women spent the next three hours shopping. Maggie almost didn't want to go home. But as they drove up and saw all three men sitting on her front porch, she knew it was past time. Luke, Terry, and Joe all had that *I'm hungry* look on their faces.

Lisa looked from Maggie to Gwen. "Gwen, I think it's your turn to cook."

Gwen's face crumpled. "I really don't cook very well. I just open up cans most of the time. Sometimes I order in pizza. I'm sorry."

Lisa looked at Maggie next. "What do you have in the fridge? Anything good and fast?" she asked as they all sat in the car, refusing to get out. The men were looking at them expectantly.

Maggie frowned out her window and shrugged. "Not really. Besides if it's anyone's turn to cook, it's theirs. Tell them I'm in the mood for homemade hamburgers, baked beans, and homemade ice cream," she said, licking her lips.

Lisa smiled. "You are something else, Maggie. I'm so stuffed, just the thought of dinner makes me ill. I've got plans anyway," she said, still not making a move to open the door.

Gwen sat up and pointed out the window to Luke's driveway where two cars had just pulled up. "Looks like Luke won't have to worry about dinner after all," she said, her voice filled with amusement.

Maggie whipped her head around and stared at three beautiful women getting out of the cars and carrying dishes with them. "I can't believe this. Jennie Benchley just won't give up. She's a machine."

Lisa looked at the women and back at her daughter. "You know you better do something about this, Maggie."

Gwen leaned forward and rested her head on the front seat. "It's called marking your territory. I've already gone over this with you."

Maggie turned and glared at Gwen. "Oh, you are such a big talker, Gwen. I don't see you marking any territory."

Gwen shut up.

Maggie watched as Luke practically ran from her front porch over to meet the beautiful women bringing him hot steaming dishes of food like he really was King Solomon. This just had to stop. She opened her car door and slammed it pretty hard. She stomped over to Luke's yard and up to his front porch where everyone was congregating while Luke was in the process of opening his front door.

"Hold it. I have had enough of this. All three of you pageant queens can just take your food and leave right now or so help me I'm going take your dishes and cover you with whatever is inside them. I seriously hope they've had time to cool for your sakes. You have until the count of ten to be gone," she said, watching as Luke's mouth fell open in surprise.

The women, however, didn't look scared at all. She held up her first finger and glared every single one of them down. She hadn't taken ten years of Jujitsu for nothing. She was not bluffing. She held up a second finger. The girl closest to Luke put her arm around his shoulders.

"Luke, I'm kind of impressed. She's tough."

Maggie frowned even more fiercely and held up a third finger. The girl who had spoken was the prettiest and if she didn't move her arm off Luke she was going to be first. The second girl, standing on the first step, had the gall to smile at her.

"You mentioned she was tall and athletic but I'm pretty sure I could take her," she said, flipping her hair and putting her hands on her hips.

Maggie smiled back, her eyes narrowing dangerously and held up a fourth finger. *As if.*

The third girl who still stood on the sidewalk, holding what must be a cake, just kind of smiled at her in a strangely encouraging way.

"Hey, if she can scare off Jennie Benchley, I wouldn't underestimate her. We kind of owe her our thanks, don't you think?" she said looking back to the first girl, who still had her arm around Luke.

Maggie held up a fifth finger and started tapping her foot. She was aware that her mom and Gwen were standing in her yard, watching everything along with Joe and Terry.

"I hate to break it to you girls, but the fun and games are over. Luke is now off the market. It's official. I've tried to be as clear as I can be. You only have four seconds left to get your cute little rears out of here, or there's going to be leftovers from here to Highland. Last chance." Maggie held up seven fingers.

Luke was shaking his head and grinning from ear to ear, his eyes glowing bright green. "This is what I've been waiting for. Before, when you tossed Jennie out of my life, you were just doing it out of pity. But this? I will remember this moment for the rest of my life," he said, walking down to her and grabbing her stiff fingers and pulling them around his waist as he bent and kissed her in front of everyone.

Maggie kissed him back quickly and then pushed him away. "So glad I could help you out there, now go order a pizza because all that yummy food is going nowhere near you," she said walking purposefully toward the women who were smiling and trying not to laugh.

Luke grabbed her around the waist and held on tightly. "Please don't hurt them, Maggie. They're my sisters. My mom has them cook for me every now and then because she's convinced I can't take care of myself. They're just trying to be nice," he said. Maggie's body went limp with shock and a special type of embarrassment that only happens once in a lifetime, when you honestly feel like moving to Jamaica is your only hope of survival.

Maggie closed her eyes and turned into Luke's chest, bowing her head and covering her face with her hands. "I'm moving back to St. George tonight. It was really fun knowing you," she said as her mom and Terry started laughing. But hearing Gwen's cackle of delight made her cringe even further.

"Oh, don't be a drama queen. Come and meet them. They're very curious since I've been telling them all about you." Luke dragged her toward his sisters who were laughing right along with everyone else.

Maggie forced herself to look into the faces of three women who were laughing at her with delighted giggles and outright glee.

She cleared her suddenly tight throat. "Um, I apologize for threatening to throw your food at you. I'm truly sorry if I have offended or upset you. I really am pretty normal. I'm not psychotically possessive or crazy or even violent. It's just that seeing women constantly being thrown at Luke kind of wears on a person after awhile. I guess I just snapped. Sorry," she said meekly, knowing that all three of these girls would be on the Internet as soon as they got home, letting their mom know what a psycho Luke had attached himself to.

Luke patted her back soothingly. "Maggie, this is Sheila. She lives in Cedar Hills with her husband and four kids. Lindsey lives in Alpine down by the elementary school. And this is Torie. She lives down in American Fork with her husband and baby," he said, looking at his sisters expectantly.

The sister who had put her arm around her brother stepped down and smiled at Maggie. "Apology accepted and forgotten. It's good to see Luke happy again. If you're the one putting that smile on his face, then that's good enough for me," she said, and then gave her a hug.

The other two sisters hugged her and welcomed her to the Petersen family, kindly even, though they did continue to erupt into giggles off and on. Maggie's face stayed a perpetual bright red for the next fifteen minutes before she could excuse herself and flee back to her home. She ran inside and right into her mom's arms.

"Oh, sweetie. It's my fault. Blame me. I told you you had to go and do something about it. It's Gwen's fault too. All that talk about marking territory just got you riled up."

Maggie pulled away from her mom and stared at everyone who was staring right back at her with laughing smiles.

"How can I possibly live that down? It's not possible. I should call Jennie right now and tell her to bring her nasty cookies over because I'm giving Luke back to her," she said miserably.

Terry shook his head and walked over to rub her arm. "Don't be an idiot. Luke obviously doesn't want Jennie. He's obviously in . . . I mean, he really likes you. He has a say in all of this. And I was watching that boy's face when you were getting ready to take on his family and I've never seen a happier man in my life. I bet Luke's head is the size of Texas now."

Joe laughed and agreed. "I'd just about die of happiness if a woman made as big of fool over me as you did over Luke," he said, looking at Gwen eagerly.

Gwen rolled her eyes. "Keep dreaming, Joe," she said, and blushed as everyone laughed.

They all sat around the kitchen while Terry and Joe looked up Domino's phone number. Lisa stepped out of the room to go brush her hair and her teeth. Maggie frowned. Her mom was determined to go see her mother. And she didn't want her to.

Gwen got up to leave to. "I need to go check on my dogs and feed them."

Joe stood up quickly. "Do you need any help walking the dogs later? I'd be happy to go on a walk with you," he said hopefully.

Gwen blushed and looked away. "Okay. I'd like that," she said, and smiled at everyone in the room quickly before leaving.

Maggie went and stood by Terry as he hung up the phone. "Terry, Mom's going to go see her mother now. I don't think she should," she said worriedly.

Terry frowned and leaned against the counter. "Honey, this is your mom's deal. She feels really strongly about making peace with her mother. If this is what she needs and wants, then she should do it. I know you love her and you don't want her to get hurt, but sometimes getting hurt is just part of the process."

Maggie sighed and looked away. "Yeah, but I know Letty Palmer. At least as well as I want to. Mom won't be able to find any peace with that woman."

Lisa walked back into the kitchen with a relaxed smile on her face. "Hey Maggie, will you give me a ride?" she asked.

Maggie nodded and grabbed her keys.

"Enjoy your pizza, boys," Lisa said before kissing Terry on the cheek.

"I love you, Lisa," Terry said, grabbing her hand briefly before letting go.

Lisa and Maggie walked out to the car. Both cars belonging to Luke's sisters were still in his driveway. She could only imagine what they were talking about. *Or even more likely, laughing about.*

"Stop dwelling on it, Maggie. There's nothing you can do to take it back. It was done and now it's over. Just laugh it off like everyone else, or you'll make it into something bigger than it is," she said wisely, getting in the car.

Maggie joined her and drove quickly away. "Have you ever done anything that embarrassing before?" she asked hopefully.

Lisa raised her eyebrows and clicked her tongue. "Of course not. But I'm not like you. You're like your dad in that way. Robbie would say or do anything if he felt it was right or true. He was Alpine's version of Captain Moroni. You just happen to be the female version. Trust me, this will blow over. Those girls are telling Luke right now how lucky he is to have someone willing to stick up for him. Believe it or not, that's kind of rare, Maggie."

Maggie smiled and sighed out a little of her stress. "Maybe you're right. His sisters did seem kind of cool. Torie said she could take me, can you believe that?" she asked with a laugh.

Lisa looked sideways at her daughter. "Honey, did you see her arms? She might be able to. I bet she can bench press twice her weight. She was ripped."

Maggie sneered. "Yeah, well, I have skills. I'm not worried," she said as she drove up to her grandparent's house and parked her car. *Now* she was worried. She turned off her car and turned toward her mom, grabbing her hand before she could get out.

"Mom, you don't have to do this. I don't know why you feel you have to see her, but just don't. She'll only say horrible, mean things to you. Please, just come talk to my grandparents. Ignore her," she pleaded.

Lisa sat back and squeezed her daughters hand with a small, sure smile.

"Honey, I appreciate your concern. But this needs to be done. It's for me. Not for her. I'll be all right, I promise. Now why don't you go in and see your grandparents while I pop in next door. I'll be back before you know it," she said reassuringly.

Maggie nodded her head but wasn't reassured in the least. She got out of her car and watched as her mom walked next door to the house she grew up in. She didn't walk slowly or fearfully. She walked with purpose and strength. Maggie shook her head in wonder and walked slowly up to the front porch of her grandparents' house. She stood still and listened. She knew she was being nosy, but if Letty started screaming at her mom, all bets were off. She was going to go over there and stand up for her mom.

She heard her mom knock three times on the door loudly. She heard the door open a moment later and then nothing. Total silence for the space of five heart beats. Then her mom said something too softly for her to hear. Maggie crept over to the edge of her grandparents' porch in the hopes of hearing any of the conversation.

"Lisa. You came to see me," Letty said in surprise.

"Yes. I always knew someday I would. And I'm glad I did. I won't take up much of your time, but I wanted you to know that I forgive you. I truly from the bottom of my heart forgive you. I don't begin to understand why, but for whatever reasons you stood back and let your husband rape and molest me day after day and year after year, I forgive you. And just to warn you, I'm thinking of moving back to Alpine. So if we see each other at the store or at a parade or anywhere at all, it's okay. I realize that having me here will probably make you uncomfortable, but this is my home too. So if you see me and feel like waving, just know that I'll wave back. And if you see me wave at you and you don't feel like waving back at me, then that's fine too. If you ever want to talk, I'm open to that. Good-bye, Mom," Lisa said, and stepped back and turned away.

Maggie couldn't see Letty's face but she could see her arm snake out and grab Lisa's arm. Maggie felt her whole body stiffen with alarm and knew she could hop off the porch and be to her mom's side in seconds if needed.

"Wait, Lisa. Please, just wait a second. I'm sorry, but it's just a shock seeing you after all these years. I just . . . I just want to look at your for a minute," she said, her voice catching.

Maggie frowned. This didn't sound like the Letty she had heard the other day, screaming and yelling, so full of hate and viciousness. This Letty sounded small and unsure and almost . . . aching.

Lisa stood still and let her mother touch her arm. She still didn't look afraid, but she did look wary. However strong Lisa was, she might not be to the point where she was ready to be touched by her mother.

"Have I changed any?" Lisa asked her mom, so that the awkward silence was broken.

Maggie waited patiently to hear Letty's reply. "Please be kind, please be kind," she whispered.

"You look just like my older sister Renae. You have the same look about you," Letty said softly.

Lisa stepped back, causing her mom's hand to drop off her arm. "I'd like to hear about her sometime. So are you doing well health-wise?" Lisa asked politely.

Letty's answer came quickly. "I'm fine. I'm fine. I saw your girl, Maggie. She doesn't care much for me," she said, her voice sounding more like the voice Maggie was used to.

Lisa laughed. "Oh, that's Maggie for you. She says what's on her mind, and she does what she thinks needs doing."

Maggie smiled at her mom's laughter.

"I'd like to get to know her, Lisa. She's my only grandchild," Letty said petulantly.

Maggie frowned and prayed her mother wouldn't promise something she wasn't willing to deliver.

Lisa paused before answering. "Mom, you need to understand that Maggie knows what happened to me. I didn't tell her everything, because I don't want her scarred emotionally the same way I was. But she knows what happened. Someday she'll be able to forgive you. Or she won't. But if she does, then I'm sure you'll get to know her then. And she is amazing. She's very special and very bright. Sometimes I look at her and I can see her spirit glowing, she's so bright. I really hope for your sake that you do get to know her someday."

Maggie bit her lip and felt her love for her mother quadruple. Her mom rocked.

Letty shuffled around a bit before answering. "What would it take for her to forgive me, do you think?"

Lisa folded her arms across her chest and looked away. "I think you know the answer to that, Mom. I'm leaving now. It was good to see you again. Good-bye," she said, and turned and walked down the steps.

Maggie jumped and flew across the porch to knock on the door. The door was already open though and her grandma grabbed her and pulled her inside quickly.

"What were you thinking eavesdropping like that, Margaret Tierney? Your grandpa should spank your britches," she said. She motioned for Maggie to take a seat in the living room and pushed a plate of chocolate cake into her hands.

Maggie stared in surprise as her grandma sat down with her own cake and looked nervous.

"Well, for heaven's sakes take a bite before your mom sees. Hurry!" She ordered as the doorbell rang.

Bonnie stood up, putting her cake down and flicking nonexistent lint off her pants before going to the door. She called over her shoulder loudly. "Frank! We have company!"

She opened the door swiftly and before Lisa could say one word, Bonnie pulled her into her arms and hugged her tightly. Maggie stared in distress as her mom, her superhero mom, burst into tears. Bonnie rubbed her back as the two women rocked back and forth. Bonnie rubbed Lisa's hair and told her over and over that it was okay.

Maggie stayed where she was, not quite understanding what was going on. Frank came into the room and stopped short when he saw his wife comforting Lisa. Frank walked up to Lisa and his wife and put his arms around both women and patted both their backs silently.

Maggie put her cake down and felt like she was behind a plate glass wall, staring into a scene that she had no business witnessing. A few moments later, Lisa pulled away, wiping her eyes and smiled at Bonnie and Frank.

"Well, Mom and Dad, I'm home," she finally said.

Frank looked down as he started tearing up. "Now you've gone and done it, Lisa. Now you've gone and done it. Once I get started, there's no stopping me," he said, grabbing a handkerchief out of his back pocket.

Lisa laughed and hugged him tightly.

Bonnie wasn't any better, with her mascara smeared haphazardly across most of her face.

"Lisa, do you really forgive me?" Bonnie asked, gripping Lisa's shoulders and staring into her eyes.

Lisa smiled and nodded. "You were forgiven a long time ago. When I had Maggie, I realized what it meant to be a mother. If I had been in your shoes and it was Maggie's life at stake, there's no telling what I'd say or do. Please, don't think any more of it. I should have brought her to you a long time ago, but I was worried that you still hated me. What matters now is that we're all together," she said, smiling through her tears.

Bonnie shook her head fiercely while Frank blew his nose again. "Of course we don't hate you; we never did. We couldn't. We loved you too much. Oh Frank, if Robbie was here right now, wouldn't he be so happy?"

Frank blew out his breath and shook his head. "Now my eyes are going to puff up. I'm ruined for the whole night," he said, making Lisa smile.

"Here, come sit down, Lisa. I made your favorite. Chocolate cake with sour cream chocolate icing. Here, have a piece." She ushered Lisa over to sit by Maggie.

Lisa gave a watery smile to Maggie and took her cake gratefully. "You know, when Maggie was around two, I tried all day one time to make a chocolate cake just the way you did. I figured if I was going to be a really good mom like you, then my little girl deserved the best chocolate cake in the whole world. But I could never get it right. It made me so mad." Lisa took a large bite and closed her eyes in contentment.

Bonnie laughed and blushed. "Well, you just come over next time you're in town and you and me are going to a make a cake together."

Maggie smiled happily. "You'll have to get in line, Mom. I've already scheduled out Grandma for the next year on cooking lessons."

Lisa shook her head. "Age before beauty. I've been waiting a long time to eat chocolate cake like this."

Bonnie smiled in pleasure. "You'll both come!"

Frank grinned at the three women surrounding him. "It's so good to have the family together. I can't tell you how happy I am that you're finally back home, Lisa."

Lisa smiled back at Frank and took another bite. "Well, there's more to the family now too. I remarried a couple years ago. My husband's name is Terry, and Frank, you would love him. Hunting is his life," she said, rolling her eyes.

Bonnie grinned at her husband's look of interest.

"You don't say. Fall's coming up. I know some of the best hunting spots in Utah," Frank said casually.

Lisa laughed. "Oh, please don't tell Terry that. He'll be after you until you spill all your secrets."

Frank grinned happily. "Well, send the boy over. As a matter of fact, what are we doing tomorrow night, Bonnie? Let's have the whole family over for a real sit-down dinner. What do you say?" he asked, looking at his wife expectantly.

Bonnie looked hopefully at Maggie and Lisa. "I'm game if I can get some help from these two girls in the kitchen. I bet we could have some fun. Come tomorrow around four, and we can have dinner on the table by six. What do you say?" she asked.

Maggie and Lisa smiled happily at each other. "Well, it's a good thing it's for tomorrow night. Terry and I have to leave the day after tomorrow to get back home."

Maggie frowned, and Bonnie's and Frank's faces fell too. "Mom, I don't want you to go yet. We're having so much fun with you here," she said plaintively.

Lisa leaned over and kissed her daughter on her cheek, leaving a small smear of icing. "Honey, I'll be back before you know it. Terry and I both feel strongly we should move to Alpine. So when we go home, it's just to put a for sale sign in the yard and start packing," she said, laughing at the joy she saw on Bonnie's and Frank's faces.

Bonnie jumped up and ran to hug Lisa. "It's perfect, Lisa. Just perfect. Frank and I will even come down and help you pack. We've been needing to go on a little trip anyway. It might as well be to St. George. This is perfect," she said clapping her hands.

Lisa laughed and looked at Maggie with her eyebrows raised as if to say, *Is this really happening?*

Maggie grinned and took a huge bite of cake. It was.

"Oh, Grandma? Can I bring Luke tomorrow night?" she asked.

Frank and Bonnie exchanged glances. "Well, we heard you got in a fight with all of Luke's sisters. Are you sure he's not still mad at you?"

Lisa and Maggie burst out laughing. It had to have been the Buhlers staring out their window who had told on her.

Lisa and Maggie told Bonnie and Frank everything that had happened and had them laughing so hard Frank had to leave the room. Outside, Letty Palmer sat on her porch, listening to the laughter. And as she rocked in her rocker, she thought.

Chapter 27

By the time Maggie drove her mom home, it was past dark, and Luke had been sitting on her porch for a long time waiting for her. Lisa gave Luke a quick kiss on the cheek before going inside and shutting the door.

Maggie sat down next to Luke on her porch and leaned her head on his shoulder.

"What a day," she said tiredly.

Luke nodded silently and put his arm around her. "Ready for this? My sisters like you and approve of the whole *us* thing," he said in amazement.

Maggie lifted her head and looked in Luke's face to make sure he was telling her the truth. "*Seriously*? Are they crazy?"

Luke nodded. "Yes, actually. Definitely crazy. And yes, they are serious. And just to warn you, they're already planning the wedding. I don't want to freak you out, because I know you get freaked out really easy about stuff like that, but that's all they talked about after you took off. They're convinced that any woman willing to take on three Petersen girls at once had better become a Petersen herself. My sisters don't like competition. Something along the lines of if you can't beat them, join them? I don't know. It was hard to make sense of everything they were saying after awhile, but I'm pretty sure they'll be calling you soon to do lunch," he said worriedly.

Maggie smiled and cuddled into Luke's side. "Your poor mom and dad. I know they're getting three emails right now about how I tried to beat up half the family. Your sisters might be weird enough to approve of me, but no sane mom will want someone as crazy as me in the family. Be ready to be warned off," she said, feeling kind of sad about it.

Luke shook his head and stood up. "I already talked to my mom on the phone tonight and she knows everything and she says she already likes you. She says she's putting my sisters in charge of making sure this relationship works and that if I screw this up, I'm officially disowned. Or something along those lines," he said, grabbing her hand and pulling her up too.

Maggie shook her head. "I don't get it. It just doesn't make sense. Why would your family want me anywhere near you? Jennie's blacklisted me in Alpine, whatever that means. Most people think I have a smoking problem. And I threaten people with bodily harm. That's not exactly normal!"

Luke led her down the porch and over to his house. "I'll tell you why they like you and are already trying to figure out what our kids are going to look like. Four words. You—make—me—happy," he said, slinging his arm around her shoulders.

Maggie smiled up at him and let her breath, stress, doubt, and anxiety out all at once.

"Well, that's a relief then. Wait, where are we going?" she asked as Luke opened the door to his house and pushed her inside.

"Oh, I just figured you'd want to try homemade apple fritters. They're amazing."

Maggie rubbed her stomach and smiled. Who could turn down a fritter? "Sounds good to me."

They watched *Dan in Real Life* and talked and laughed and relaxed together until she was too tired to move. Before she fell asleep, Luke walked her home, holding her up most of the way. Terry and Joe were still up arguing about some rodeo on cable they had been watching. They promised to lock up, so she stumbled up to her room and collapsed on her bed. She didn't move until ten the next morning.

She woke up to the faint smell of breakfast and smiled. She was going to hate it when her mom left. She loved food, but cooking it for herself all the time was not as fun as your mom making it for you and having it ready when you walked down the stairs. She took a much-needed shower and walked blearily into the kitchen to see that there was no breakfast. It had all been cooked, eaten, and put away. She stood looking at a clean, empty kitchen with a note on the table.

Had to meet the realtor. See you at four at your grandma's house.
Love ya, Mom

Maggie groaned and reached for a box of cereal. It was too early for such disappointment, she thought.

She walked over after breakfast to see if Gwen could model for her again, but she was gone. Probably with Joe or at the vet's. She glared at Gwen's closed door before turning around and walking dejectedly down the stairs. She saw Cheyenne across the street and waved. Cheyenne waved back half-heartedly as she pushed the lawn mower across the slightly brown grass. Maggie walked over and smiled. Chores. So much fun.

Cheyenne cut the power to the mower and waited for Maggie to walk over.

"So did you ask your mom and dad if you can model for me?" she asked with a smile.

Cheyenne nodded and frowned. "They said no. They said they don't know you very well, and from what they've seen and heard from the Buhlers, they're not sure they want me around such a bad influence," she said apologetically.

Maggie's mouth hardened, and she glared at the Buhlers' house. "*Really*. Is that so? Wow, the Buhlers have been pretty busy lately staring out their window. That's so rude, don't you think?" Maggie said with a glare.

Cheyenne surprised her and laughed. "Well, my dad was home last night and we both heard you in the front yard with Luke's sisters. My dad had the phone out ready to call 9-1-1 if you threw a punch," she said with awe in her voice.

Maggie gave in and laughed. "Oh, that was nothing. I was just trying to scare them off. I thought they might be Jennie Benchley's minions out doing her evil deeds. I wasn't going to hurt anybody. I might have hurt a few casseroles and a couple fritters to be honest, but I'm really a gentle person," she said, looking earnest.

Cheyenne laughed and shrugged. "I thought it was cool. Luke did too. Are you guys like falling in love with each other or something?" she asked shyly.

Maggie winced and put her hands in her pockets as she looked at her feet.

"I don't know. I've never really been in love before, unless you count Johnny Depp, which most women I know do. So, maybe? I guess," she said lamely, wishing she wasn't blushing in front of a young teenage girl.

Cheyenne smiled brightly. "That is really cool. You guys could get married. But where would you live? Your house or his?" she asked, looking back and forth between the houses.

Maggie bit her lip and turned to stare at her house that she loved more than anything now, and then at Luke's house, which she knew he loved. How could he ever give up his wood shop?

"Wow, I hadn't thought that far ahead. I guess that's a good question. But if I were guessing, I'd say we'd probably stay at my house because Luke's just watching his mom and dad's house while they're gone. At least that's what he said," she muttered, starting to worry about it.

Cheyenne shrugged. "Keep them both. The Petersens always use that house as a rental. It's nice having neighbors you can get used to and get to know."

Maggie smiled and nodded. "We'll work on the logistics. In the mean time, tell me all about this hair thing you've got going on. Is this a new style? Should I know about it?" Maggie asked, causing a huge smile to bloom on Cheyenne's face as she gave her step-by-step instructions on how to get the same exact hair style as Hannah Montana.

Maggie walked home a few minutes later, hoping she didn't let Cheyenne down when she tried it later that night.

Maggie spent the day up at Cemetery Hill painting scenery and doing what she loved best—painting. There was a connection she made with God that she never felt when she was doing anything else. Only when she had a paintbrush in her hand did she feel completely at one with her purpose in life. She had to be at her grandma's at four, and she needed at least an hour to get her hair just right, so she packed up at two thirty in the afternoon and headed home. It had been a very productive day so far and she was really looking forward to helping her grandma cook dinner. She knew her mom was excited too.

After getting ready, she realized that she had forgotten to tell Luke about dinner that night. It was three thirty, and he wouldn't even be home for a couple hours. So she'd call him. No big deal. She took her cell phone out of her pocket and went to punch in his number and stopped. She didn't even know her boyfriend's phone number. She stood still and tried to think. He'd given it to her. On a business card. Which she had put in her jeans pocket. *And washed.*

Maggie groaned. Well, she knew he was a banker. But which bank? She banged her head on the counter. She could just call one of his sisters, but she was still embarrassed about the other night. She grabbed an old phone book and looked up the Petersens and then realized that all of his sister's had different last names. Okay then, his brother . . . *was unlisted.* She remembered Jaden telling her that.

Fine, whatever. She'd just ask Sophie. Sophie knew everything and everybody. She would for sure know at least where Luke worked. She ran outside and down the street to Sophie's salon. She opened the door and looked around. No Sophie. She saw two older women and one of them was working on Jennie Benchley. Of course.

"Um, hi. I was just looking for Sophie," Maggie said, calling out to the two stylists and trying to ignore the laser beams of hate pointed right at her.

One of the older ladies, who looked a little like Sophie, walked over. "Hi, I'm Candy. Do you need to set up an appointment with Sophie? I can schedule you in if you'd like," she said, smiling professionally.

Maggie shook her head frowning. "Nah, I just need to talk to her. She did my hair the other day, but now we're kind of friends. I just have a question for her. My name's Maggie Tierney, by the way."

Candy's eyes widened, and she glanced back in shock at Jennie Benchley who was sitting, steaming in her chair, waiting for Candy to return.

"*You're* Maggie?" she asked as if she didn't believe it.

Maggie glanced at Jennie briefly, narrowing her eyes as she wondered what Jennie had been talking about before nodding. "That's me. And no I don't smoke," she said loudly enough for everyone in the salon to hear. Jennie turned her head away, ignoring her.

Candy cleared her throat. "Oh, well, I'm so glad to hear that. Why don't I write down Sophie's cell number for you on the back of her card?" she said, writing quickly.

Maggie leaned down closer to Candy so no one could hear and whispered. "Hey, you wouldn't happen to know where Luke Petersen works, do you?"

Candy straightened up and nodded. "Of course. He works at the bank right across from Kohler's," she said, handing her the card.

Maggie beamed and took it. "Thanks. You've been a huge help. Bye, Jen!" she called out with a little wave before leaving.

She smiled as she ran home and grabbed her car keys. She drove quickly out of Alpine and into Highland and right into the bank parking lot. She stuck her keys in her back pocket and ambled inside, shivering at the cool air conditioning. She looked around for Luke, but didn't see him so she walked up to a teller and smiled.

"Hi, is Luke Petersen around?" she asked the cute girl with short brown hair.

She smiled and pointed to one of the side offices. "He's right in there with a customer. If you'll just have a seat he'll be right with you," she said, motioning to the chairs set up around coffee tables with magazines.

All of the offices had windows so she could see him plainly. He looked so different at work. His hair was combed back perfectly. Not one hair out of place. He was even wearing glasses. He looked so professional. So out of reach. Maggie frowned. She was really dating a banker. If someone had told her as a young teenage girl that someday she would grow up and date a banker, she would have laughed herself silly. She watched him talk to his customer and couldn't help smiling. He was so cute, it just didn't matter what he did for a living. She did prefer him when he was messy though. He must run his hands through his hair as soon as he got in his car after work.

The woman Luke was talking earnestly to turned her head for a moment and Maggie caught her profile. Luke was talking with *Letty Palmer*. Maggie felt her blood cool and her face stiffen. She stood up immediately and walked quickly back to the teller. "Could you just tell Luke to call Maggie at this number," she said, writing her number down on a piece of paper. "I've gotta go," she said, and turned to leave.

But as she was leaving, Luke opened the door to his office and Letty walked out. They were caught in a head on collision. Maggie stared, unsmiling at her grandmother who looked surprised and a little shaken at seeing her too.

"Maggie," she said.

Maggie didn't know what to call her. Grandmother or Grandma just didn't want to roll off her tongue. "Hi. What a coincidence seeing you here. *With Luke,*" she said, finally glancing at him.

Luke shook his head just barely, as if warning her about something. Maggie frowned. He probably didn't want her making a scene in front of all of his employees. Fine. She could act normal. She did it all the time.

"Well, Luke, I'll be off. Thanks for all of your help." Letty then walked quickly out of the bank.

Maggie turned and watched her pensively. She looked like she was up to something. She turned back to Luke who held out his hand to her. She grabbed it gratefully and walked into his office, where she sat in the chair that her grandmother had just vacated.

"So tell me what's going on, Luke? Why was my grandmother here?" she asked, avoiding polite chitchat and getting to the heart of the matter.

Luke raised his eyebrows in a bankerish way and shook his head with a small smile. "Now, Margaret, you know that's confidential. But I will say this. Letty Palmer might just have a heart after all. And that's all I'm going to say about it. Now, to what do I owe this wonderful, incredible privilege?" he asked, smiling at her with his magical eyes.

Maggie relaxed and smiled back for a moment before answering. "I wanted to see you, of course. And I realized I don't have your phone number, and I wanted to invite you on behalf of my grandparents over for an official Tierney family dinner tonight at six," she said, folding her hands demurely in her lap.

Luke leaned back in his swivel chair and tapped his lips with his finger. "Are you telling me that my own girlfriend doesn't even know my phone number? I'm hurt."

Maggie shrugged and looked away. "I realize you gave me your business card a while ago, but that's when I thought you were just a mean, cranky neighbor that I wasn't going to have to call. It sort of got washed with my jeans. I think. Anyway, give me your digits," she said, taking out her cell phone so she could plug them in.

Luke sighed and gave her three numbers where he could be reached. Maggie flipped her phone closed and slid it back into her pocket. "Now, just so I know you know. What is *my* phone number?" she asked with a grin.

Luke blinked and sat up straighter. "Hmm, cell or home?" he asked, looking a little nervous.

Maggie tilted her head and sat back. "Either."

Luke laughed and grabbed his cell phone. "I have no idea what my girlfriend's number is. That's the nice thing about living next door. You don't need it," he said, punching in the numbers she gave him.

Maggie stood up and grabbed her car keys. "So are we on for tonight? Food, family, fun, and all the crazy stuff that goes with me and my family," she said, standing by his door.

He stood up and walked over to her. "Of course I'm on for tonight. I'm on for the rest of my life," he said, pulling her in to his arms.

Maggie grinned as she was hugged breathless and wondered why that didn't make her nervous anymore. She squeezed Luke back happily before letting go. Maybe, just maybe, she was making progress.

"Dinner's at six. See you tonight," she said, blowing him a kiss.

She walked out the door and to her car and laughed. All of his employees had congregated in the front area so they could peek at her. For some reason she got the feeling that they approved of their boss hugging his girlfriend at work. She glanced at her watch and squeaked. She was late for her grandma's, so she jumped in her car quickly and hurried, breaking every speed limit Alpine had. She drove up to her grandma's house and noticed her mom was already there. *Oops.*

She ran in the house, not even bothering to knock and stopped immediately when she saw her mom sitting on the living room couch with Bonnie's arms around her shoulders. She was crying. Maggie ran to her mom and sat next to her.

"What is it? What happened?" she demanded of both women.

Bonnie grabbed another tissue, handing it to her mom before answering. "Oh, it's nothing, Maggie. I guess when Letty found out that your mom and stepdad were moving back to Alpine, she decided to make it easy for them and she signed her house over to your mom. Letty says that she's been wanting to move to St. George, and she'd like to buy your mom's house. *Sight unseen.* I think she's trying to be nice. I think she's trying to make a grand gesture."

Lisa sniffed and pushed her hair back from her red eyes. "I know why she's doing this. She wants Maggie to forgive her. She told me that if she gives the house to me, then she expects Maggie to be open to visiting her in St. George a few times a year."

Maggie stared over her mom's shoulder at the wall. That's why Letty had been at the bank. She was really doing it. Maggie shook her head and sighed.

"You don't want to live there do you, Mom? I mean, how could you, after everything that has happened to you. Doesn't your mom realize that living there would be a nightmare for you?" she asked.

Lisa nodded vehemently. But Bonnie looked thoughtful. "I think there's a way Lisa. I say you take the house. It should be yours. But I say we tear it down. I say we burn it down. *And rebuild.*" She looked back and forth between Maggie and Lisa.

Lisa sat up and grabbed another tissue. "I could. I could tear that sucker down and build something beautiful. And when my mom buys my house, I'll have the money to do it. It could work. *Or not*," she said, looking doubtfully at Maggie.

Maggie groaned and slouched down on the couch. She was like most people. She didn't like being forced to do anything.

"I don't want to," she said, crossing her arms over her chest.

Bonnie and Lisa exchanged glances before they moved to sit on both sides of her.

"Sweetie, I know how you feel about your grandmother, but think of your mom. She'll be right next door to me, and you know I'll take good care of her. And she'll be just down the road from you. It couldn't be more perfect," Bonnie said, rubbing her knee.

Maggie closed her eyes. "Why does she even want to get to know me? I've done nothing but yell at her since I've met her. She needs to be connecting to *you*. Not me."

Lisa winced. "Maggie, there's too much under the bridge for me and my mother. There are too many memories and too many disappointments to get past. For her anyway. I've told her I'm open to connecting with her again. I think it would just be too hard. But she's very curious about you. You're her only grandchild and she wants to get to know you for some reason. Maybe start fresh. This is totally up to you, honey. If you can't, then you can't. Terry and I will work something out," she said, nodding her head firmly.

Bonnie looked into her eyes and smiled encouragingly at her. Maggie looked back, silently pleading. Bonnie smiled. Maggie sighed.

"I was figuring on doing all that forgiving stuff on my death bed or even later if possible. This is not on my timetable," she said in irritation.

Lisa and Bonnie laughed.

"You are so much like your dad," Bonnie said with a grin.

Lisa smiled too. "That's just what I was thinking!"

Bonnie stood up and grabbed Maggie's hand. "Come on. Let's go get some aprons on and cook up something good. You mull it over in your own way. Letty can wait for an answer. There's no hurry," she said, giving her a one-armed hug.

Lisa followed them into the kitchen, and they got started on squash casserole, mashed potatoes, corn on the cob, and roasted chicken. Maggie tried not to think about Letty Palmer while they cooked, but she kept sneaking in at the worst times, putting a pall over what should have been a wonderful day. Her grandma put her in charge of beating the egg whites for the lemon meringue pie, so she took all her frustration out on them, making the tallest, stiffest peaks Bonnie said she had ever seen.

Lisa grinned at her as she peeled potatoes and shook her head. She knew her daughter too well.

Bonnie announced that they would eat outside on the back patio since it was such a nice evening. She put Maggie in charge of setting the table. Maggie was glad to get some fresh air. She glanced over at Letty's yard and felt kind of bad for her all of sudden. It seemed so empty. Almost lonely. Maggie frowned and forced herself to think of something else. She worked on trying to picture Gwen in a wedding dress. She snorted at the thought and smiled cheerfully. Her mom joined her a few moments later, carrying tablecloth weights. Maggie had never seen them before, but Lisa explained how they hung on the corners of the table cloth so everything didn't blow away in the wind.

"So are you okay?" Lisa asked softly.

Maggie shrugged. "I wasn't the one crying, Mom. You were."

Lisa attached the weight and stood up, moving to the next corner. "Oh, honey, I'm human just like everyone else. It was just hard to be handed my dream on a platter and then after lifting the lid, realizing that I couldn't take it. You're right. I couldn't live in that house. And I knew you'd say no to seeing Letty."

Maggie put the last fork down and sat down, kicking her feet up on one of the other chairs. "But Mom, Grandma had a great idea. Tearing down the house and building one you liked. One *you* designed. Wouldn't that be okay? Or would it still be too hard?" She studied her mom as Lisa moved slowly around the table.

Lisa paused and smiled at the mountains surrounding her. "I've missed Alpine so much. This really is my home. So yes, I think if I could tear down that house and build a new one, I would be happy. Heck, I'd be thrilled. *But,* not at the expense of your happiness. I could never be happy knowing that coming home meant your misery," she said seriously.

Maggie sighed and closed her eyes, leaning her head back and wishing life could just be easy for once.

"How many times a year?" she asked without opening her eyes.

Lisa shook her head and smiled at her daughter. "Knock it off. Nobody likes a martyr. You know you wouldn't be able to sit in the same room with my mom three times a year. Bonnie told me what happened the other day out in the yard. I can't believe you told her you wanted to paint a picture of her behind bars," she said, laughing as she clipped a weight.

Maggie's mouth twitched, but she didn't smile. "Well, don't give up hope. I'm still thinking about it, okay?" she said, opening her eyes and looking at her mom.

Lisa smiled at her only child and nodded. "The only reason I think this would be a good idea is because it really would be good for you to forgive her.

Forgiveness is the soul's sunlight. I'd hate to see such a beautiful soul like yours darken even a little bit because you refused to forgive." Lisa was not smiling anymore.

Maggie frowned and looked away. "Great. Now my soul is dark, and I have to hang out with your mom. This day is just getting better and better."

Lisa laughed and threw a napkin in her daughter's face. "Stop whining. Now let's get back inside and help Bonnie before she thinks we're slacking," she ordered.

Maggie yawned and thought slacking sounded really good, but she followed her mom anyway. They finished the last details for all of the dishes and were carrying them outside as Frank, Terry, and Luke walked in the front door. Everyone sat around the table while Frank said the prayer, and then they all ate with such relish that the complete lack of conversation was the biggest compliment Bonnie could have asked for. Ten minutes later Luke lifted his head and remembered his manners.

"This is the best dinner I've had since I ate your roast at Maggie's house," he said, looking at Bonnie with something like awe.

Bonnie grinned and passed more mashed potatoes down his way. "You just eat up, Luke. You're too thin," she said.

Luke laughed and shook his head. "I've gained three pounds in the past month. Hanging out with Maggie has done wonders for my appetite," he said.

Bonnie smiled sadly at him. "Dear, I know how hard this last year must have been for you to lose Melanie the way you did. I'm so glad Maggie found you. I was telling Frank just the other day, the last time I saw you at Kohler's you were just trudging down the aisle looking like the most defeated man in Alpine. And now look at you. So happy and laughing, eating, and enjoying yourself. Our Maggie has a way of bringing joy to people," she said, smiling fondly at her granddaughter.

Maggie blushed but felt mortified for Luke. He looked stunned and embarrassed like a bunch of people just saw him walk out of the shower without a towel.

"Now honey, you went and embarrassed the poor man. Nobody likes to think other people have noticed their low days. We're not supposed to have emotions. We're men!" Frank pounded on the table, getting a laugh and turning the attention away from Luke, to his eternal appreciation.

"Speaking of men," Terry said, and then expertly turned the conversation to hunting.

The men's side of the table talked about hunting, while the women's side talked about Maggie's new Hannah Montana hairstyle she had copied from her neighbor. Lisa and Maggie tried to talk Bonnie into getting extensions so she could have the same look. Bonnie fought off the suggestion with a tough-ness Maggie had to admire. Bonnie then brought out the lemon meringue pie to the men's delight. There was just something about mounds and mounds of meringue that brought smiles to people's faces.

Maggie kept stealing glances at her grandmother Palmer's backyard. It was still empty, but she could feel her grandmother watching them. She couldn't see her, but for some reason, her presence was strong. Maggie sighed unhappily as she thought about what she was getting ready to agree to. But as she glanced around the table at her family, she felt a moment of pity for Letty. Because of the choices she had made in her life, she would never have this. She would never experience a table full of family who loved and appreciated each other. *But she could have a few visits a year.*

Maggie sighed and wondered just how long those visits had to be. She would have to meet with her grandmother and go over all the details. She wanted everything made perfectly clear so there were no misunderstandings and no loopholes.

Luke leaned over and whispered in her ear. "Why so somber?"

Maggie tried smiling back. "I'll tell you later. Are you ready to go?" she asked quietly.

Luke glanced at Terry and Frank who it seemed had fallen in love with each other at first glance and at Bonnie and Lisa whose heads were close together talking about something that had her mom smiling. They could leave.

Luke and Maggie stood up and thanked her grandparents for the won-derful meal and said their good-byes. Luke pulled her toward his car and opened the door for her.

"What about my car? I can just follow you home. I don't want to leave it here," she said, pulling back on his hand.

Luke stopped pulling. "I just wanted to take you for a little ride so we can talk. I'll bring you back to get your car. I promise," he said.

Maggie gave in and hopped in the car. Luke drove her up toward his parents' house but kept going past the rodeo grounds. They got out at a little clearing in the middle of some scrub oak. Luke got out and motioned for her to follow him. They hiked up a little trail to where a small lookout was nestled in the trees and rocks. Luke sat down and patted the ground next to him.

"Have a seat. You need a little color therapy," he said.

Maggie grinned and sat down next to him, leaning toward him auto-matically.

"I haven't had decent color therapy since this afternoon. This is beau-tiful," she said, looking out over all of Alpine. The water from Utah Lake looked like a mirror, so still and achingly poetic. The colors reflected on the water made her yearn for her paints almost instantly. She promised herself she would paint here someday.

"So what's weighing you down? You look like you have the weight of the world on your shoulders." Luke was looking closely at her.

Maggie sighed and pulled up her knees. "Just the weight of my mom's new house is all."

She told him everything, which he pretty much already knew, but acted as if he were hearing it for the first time.

"I didn't know about the visit stipulation. Letty made it seem as if the gift of her home was free and clear, not based on any other consideration," he said musingly.

Maggie snorted. "Yeah, well, there is one. *Me.* How can she even do this? I mean, most people can't just give their houses away and then turn around and buy another one. It's not like she even has a job."

Luke leaned back on his hands and looked out at the small valley. "Nathan had a large life insurance policy when he died. Letty's actually a very wealthy woman. So I wouldn't worry about her giving her house to your mom. She could give a few houses away and still be fine. I really think she's trying to make up for what happened, Maggie. I know it's nothing compared to what happened to your mom, but I think she's really, honestly trying here," Luke said, staring at her with concern.

Maggie sighed and hugged her knees tighter. "This whole forgiveness thing is killing me, Luke. I know I'm supposed to do it. I know I need to do it. I just can't seem to force myself to do it," she said.

Luke sighed too and moved his leg away from a bug. "I think it's harder sometimes when people hurt the ones we love. I'm not saying it's easy to forgive, but I agree with your mom. It's something that you need to do. Pray for help. Pray for the desire to forgive. Just make the first step, Maggie." He reached over and pushed her hair over her ear.

Maggie looked at the Mount Timpanogos Temple and thought of all the "forever families" surrounding her in Alpine. "Why couldn't she have just been strong, Luke? Why couldn't she have believed my mom and stood up to her husband? Why didn't she call the police and turn him in? Moms are supposed to protect their children from the world. Why didn't she protect my mom?" Maggie asked, feeling the hurt, disappointment, and disgust boiling inside her sit on her heart heavily.

Luke put his arm around her shoulders. "It's always hard for strong people to understand others who aren't. I don't know why Letty did what she did. All we need to know is that you are going to be one amazing mom. I hate to see what happens the first time someone pushes your kid down at the park. I get shivers just thinking about it."

Maggie laughed and felt her heart ease a little. "Do you think I will be able to let this go, Luke? Do you really think I can?" she asked.

Luke nodded. "Of course you will and *I know* you can. When you go see Letty, just look at it as if you were going to the hospital and seeing a cancer patient. You don't need to know how she got the cancer or why she got the cancer or even if her cancer will be cured. But you do need to understand that she's sick and in need of healing. And people who need healing or are in the process of healing, *or repenting*, however you want to look at it, tend to need flowers to remember that the world is beautiful. They might need a little treat so they don't forget that pleasure and happiness are still to be had. And they need a little friendship so they don't feel so alone." Luke rubbed her arm where goose bumps were forming.

Maggie bowed her head and thought about what Luke had said. Luke had just given her the key to visiting her grandmother.

Maggie raised her head and turned to Luke. "Luke, I love you," she said simply, laughing as he jumped up and pumped his fist toward the bright orange sky.

"I knew it! I knew you did, Maggie. Ha! Yes!" he shouted before collapsing back down next to her, tired out by his own excitement.

"Next time you tell me that, make sure my stomach isn't so full. I think I just gave myself a cramp," he said, breathing hard and holding his stomach.

Maggie laughed and hugged him. "Who says there'll be a next time?" she said, her eyes twinkling down at him.

"I do." He was confident, his eyes glowing a dazzling bright blue.

They watched the sunset together for the next half hour before they walked back to his car. He leaned up against the door before opening it for her.

"You know, I was thinking of buying the house I live in from my parents." He said in that casual way of his that made her ears perk up.

Maggie nodded her head. "That's probably a wise investment," she assented, not really knowing a wise investment from a dumb one.

Luke shook his head. "Nah, not for investment purposes. I was thinking of opening up a little art gallery. I'll have to tear down a few walls and raise the ceilings of course. I think a loft area would be good too for someone who wanted an art studio to work in. And of course the basement would need to remain a wood shop," he said carefully.

Maggie stared at Luke with a grin breaking out. "Luke, my love, you are a genius, aren't you?" She threw her arms around his neck tightly as he laughed happily with joy spilling out into the clearing surrounding them.

"You just said a mouthful," he said and kissed her gently. "By the way, in case you were interested or wondering, I love you too."

Maggie shook her head, laughing, and messed his hair up. "I so wasn't wondering. You fell in love with me the first night we met. Don't even deny it," she said.

Luke grinned and twirled her around. "I couldn't deny it even if I wanted to."

Chapter 28

When Luke dropped her off at her grandma's to pick up her car, she noticed a note sticking to her windshield. Luke was already driving away as she picked it up and felt a moment of foreboding. She knew who it was from before she even saw the scratchy handwriting.

Come to lunch tomorrow at noon.
Grandmother Palmer.

Maggie glanced at the Palmer house as she shoved the note in her pocket and got in her car, driving away as quickly as she could. Tomorrow was going to be the pits. Her mom and Terry were leaving and she had a lunch date with Letty.

The next day, Maggie helped her mom and Terry haul their suitcases out to the truck. She felt like grabbing onto the door and refusing to let them leave, but she was twenty-four now and adults would never act so immature.

"Maggie, stop hanging on the door. You're going to scratch my paint job," Terry admonished, patting her shoulder as he walked by.

Lisa threw her purse in the front seat and sighed. "Well, that's that then. We're off. I'll call you when we get home. Now I want you to stay out of trouble, young lady. No getting into fights or smoking or yelling at people. You hear me?" she said with a grin.

Maggie laughed and hugged her mom good-bye. "Trouble and me are good friends. Sorry, but we're inseparable. If you want to give some advice out, I'd suggest giving Joe some," she joked, turning to watch as Joe talked earnestly to Gwen on her front porch.

Terry came to stand by Lisa and Maggie as they watched the scene soberly.

"I know you two girls like Gwen, and I do too if I'm being honest, but if just one more woman breaks my brother's heart, I'm just going to get bent," Terry said grimly.

Lisa sighed and put her arm through her husband's. "Joe's a big boy. And Gwen is just trying to protect herself. Your brother coming in and trying to sweep her off her feet scares her is all. I bet as soon as Joe's down the road, she'll miss him. Don't write her off yet. This romance just needs to be put on a slow simmer. You know what that's like, Terry." Lisa smiled up at him.

Terry laughed and hugged her. "Don't I ever. I simmered for three years. *Poor Joe.* Well, give me a hug, Maggie girl. We need to hit the road," Terry said, opening his arms wide.

Maggie hugged her stepfather tightly, kissing his cheek before hugging her mom.

"Drive safely," she ordered, and waved as they drove down her road and disappeared around the corner.

They were gone. She sat on her front porch and watched the people walk and the occasional car drive by as she waited for Joe to go. She had a feeling Gwen would need to chat a little after she said good-bye. Fifteen minutes later, she watched as Joe got in his truck and drove swiftly away. Thirty seconds later, Gwen was sitting beside her.

"So can you model for me today?" Maggie asked when Gwen remained silent.

Gwen glanced at her and frowned. "Do I look like I want to smile at the clouds going by? I have a date next weekend with Joe and his two kids down in St. George. And *you're* watching my dogs. And yes, that means feeding and walking them and cleaning up their poop," Gwen said in a caustic voice.

Maggie grunted but didn't say no. Gwen immediately relaxed and Maggie smiled slightly. One obstacle out of the way. Now what else could she think of?

"Dating is the biggest magic show there is. It's all mirage and smoke and, and . . . nothing! None of it's real. Dating and all this romance crap is just some hormonal, chemical thing that wears off after a few months and then you're stuck with some guy you can't stand who talks about hunting all the time," she said irritably.

Maggie snorted. "I bet for every word he said about hunting, you had two to say about your dogs."

Gwen smiled but then changed her mind and glared at her. "Hey, whose side are you on? Now hush and let me complain. I'm not done. Where was I? Oh, and Joe is younger than me! Did you know that? He's thirty-seven and I'm forty. No way would that work."

Maggie's face squinched up in disbelief. *"Are you serious?"* she asked, staring at Gwen.

Gwen blushed and looked away. "Hey, I'm drowning here. I'm grasping at straws. Because if I don't, I'll be heading down to St. George next weekend and fall in love with those rotten teenagers and then I'll be done for. And then what? Huh? Then what?" she demanded.

Maggie sighed and thought of her own situation. She was done for too. "Well, then you let yourself be happy. That's what," she said simply.

Gwen groaned and shook her head. "Don't you get it? I'm *already* happy. I could be throwing all this away, betting on a relationship and then turn around and be divorced and truly miserable a year from now."

Maggie scratched her leg with her big toe and frowned. Gwen was getting a little depressing. Pessimism was only bearable for so long.

"Look, Gwen. You're a big girl now. Make up your mind and go for it. None of this half crap. Either look at Joe and see all the wonderful possibilities that come with him, or stick with what you got. *But enough with the moaning and groaning.* If you can't make up your mind, then go home and read the Proclamation on the Family. It's all spelled out perfectly for anyone to read. God created you to be in a family unit. Yeah, yeah, I know that goes against most feminist thinking, but tough. *And no, he wasn't talking about dogs.* He wants you to be married to a man who will respect you and love you and provide for you. He already provided the two kids, but who's to say you and Joe can't make a couple of your own? Now start smiling or get off my porch." Maggie then closed her eyes and leaned her head back to get more of the sun rays coming her way.

She listened carefully to hear Gwen stomping away, but no sound came from her. Maggie opened one eye and peeked at her friend. She was turned toward Maggie and was smiling grimly. Maggie opened both eyes and grinned at Gwen.

"Now that's more like it."

Gwen rolled her eyes and stood up. "By the way, I'm out of nicotine patches. I'd appreciate some more by the end of today. Or did you forget our bargain?" Gwen asked, glaring at her.

Maggie smiled and stood up. "You'll have them before dark tonight. On my honor."

Gwen sighed loudly and walked back to her house, leaving Maggie to her own devices.

Maggie puttered around the house and went through some more boxes. She couldn't concentrate because she knew she had a lunch appointment with her grandmother and just thinking about it gave her a stomachache. But knowing that her grandmother Tierney was close by made her feel a little better. She could always stop by afterward for a quick hug and a snack. Maybe lunch would only be a quick fifteen-minute deal. Maggie cheered up at the thought.

She gave up on the dusty boxes and went upstairs to shower and get ready.

She wasn't sure what to wear to lunch, but she knew she wasn't dressing up for it. That would be sending the wrong message. *Like she cared or something.* Maggie frowned and sighed morosely as she fell on her bed instead of getting in the shower. Would it be so bad to let herself care for this bitter, old, hateful woman? Would the world stop? Would her life as she knew it change forever?

Maggie frowned moodily at the faded wallpaper and closed her eyes. Just maybe, it would.

An hour later she got in her car and backed out. She drove exactly the speed limit down the road to her grandmother's house. She parked in front of the Tierney's house though. She just felt better that way. She walked slowly onto the Palmer property. She looked over her shoulder one more time, hoping to see her grandma in the window waving at her, but no. She was on her own. She walked heavily up the stairs and paused for a long moment before ringing the doorbell. She stood with her hands shoved in her pockets as she waited for her grandmother Palmer to answer. Less than a few seconds passed before the door opened. Letty Palmer stood before her, smiling.

Maggie winced. "Hi. Your note said to come by for lunch," she said, in case Letty had forgotten.

Letty nodded regally and opened the door wide for her granddaughter to join her inside.

Maggie walked in and felt a slight chill. She tried to not think of what happened to her mom in this house so long ago, but it seeped in slightly here and there in the shiver she felt down her spine and in the shadows of the house. She followed her grandmother down the hallway and into the kitchen. The house was very similar to the Tierneys', but different in the paint color, furniture, and basic feel. The Tierneys' home always felt bright and sunny. This house had an old, dark, sad feel to it. Maggie couldn't wait to leave.

"Have a seat at the table, Maggie. I made a pasta salad and rolls," she said proudly.

Maggie smiled automatically and seated herself, placing the napkin on her lap. When her grandmother was seated opposite her, they both dished up their plates and waited. Letty shifted in her seat awkwardly and then said a quick blessing on the food.

"You probably know the reason I wanted you to come today," Letty said, pushing her food around slowly on her plate.

Maggie stared at the pasta salad, not feeling hungry. She looked up and answered instead of eating. "Something about you giving my mom your house if I promise to visit you three times a year in St. George," she said bluntly.

Letty's cheeks reddened and she looked away for a second before looking back to meet her granddaughter's direct stare.

"That's pretty much it in a nutshell. I feel that I do owe your mother in some ways, and at the same time, you need to get to know the other side of your family," she said with a firm nod of her head.

Maggie sighed and crossed her legs, as she pushed her pasta around her plate in the same way Letty was pushing hers.

"I'll think about it if it's just twice a year and the visits are short," she said, resting her hands in her lap.

Letty frowned and put her fork down too. Neither woman even pretended to eat now.

"That's not the deal. I'm giving your mom a house. Doesn't that mean anything to you?" she asked angrily.

Maggie's expression didn't change at all when she replied. "Can you give my mom back her innocence? Can you give her back her childhood? What is an old house compared to that? Don't you know that I could buy my mom as many houses as she wants?" she said in a quiet, hard voice.

Letty looked down, burned by the subtle fierceness of her granddaughter.

"You can't judge me, Maggie. You don't know me. You didn't know my husband, and you weren't there. So don't sit there and judge a situation you know nothing about."

Maggie closed her eyes and prayed for patience or whatever it was she needed to get through this conversation.

"I may not have been there. And you're right, I didn't know your husband, *thank heavens*. But correct me if I have the facts wrong. My mom was sexually abused by your husband," she said simply.

Letty started breathing quickly and looked agitated. Maggie frowned but didn't take her eyes off her grandmother's.

Letty cleared her throat. "Yes," she whispered, no longer denying the truth.

Maggie blinked and sat up a little straighter. "If I'm going to agree to this arrangement, I want the entire truth. Tell me why you let it happen," she said calmly, ready to leave if Letty refused to answer her.

Letty twisted the napkin in her hands almost painfully, but she kept her gaze on Maggie.

"I don't know. In all honesty, I'm not sure. Half the time, I convinced myself it wasn't happening. Sometimes I thought I was just imagining it. Most of the time though, I was just terrified. I didn't know what would happen to me. I didn't know where I would go or how I would live or survive. I couldn't get a job to support myself, let alone a daughter. I had no family to turn to. I had no choice," she said vehemently.

Maggie felt truly ill as the words tumbled out of her grandmother. "You had this whole community. You had everyone in Alpine ready to step in at a moment's notice. So I don't buy it. You *would have* survived. And my mom would have been safe. So what's the real reason?" She prodded, crossing her arms over her chest.

Letty twisted her wedding ring around her finger and looked away. "It must be so easy, being twenty-four years old and standing in judgment on your grandmother. It must be so nice being perfect and having the perfect life. You're not God. I didn't ask you here today to hear my confession. And you have no right to demand it," she said stiffly.

Maggie stood up and gently pushed her chair in. "Good-bye," she said, and started walking out of the room.

"Wait one second, young lady. Weren't you raised to respect your elders? This is no way to treat your grandmother," she said furiously as she stood up.

Maggie rubbed her forehead before turning around. "Don't you see, you're *not* my grandmother. You're just someone my mother had the bad luck to be born to. I was here today to see if having a relationship with you was a possibility. But I can see it's not. I was willing to agree to drive down to St. George and visit with you twice a year in the hopes of getting to know you and you me. *But* that was conditional on starting out with the truth. You can't be honest with me. Heck, I still don't even know if you're remorseful. This was just a bad idea all around," she said in resignation.

Letty puffed out her cheeks and looked at her feet for a moment before answering. "I didn't want anyone knowing. It was embarrassing. It was nobody's business. I couldn't stand the idea of my neighbors and friends knowing that my own husband preferred my daughter to me," she said in a hoarse voice, not meeting Maggie's eyes.

Maggie breathed in deeply and let it out slowly. She finally had the truth. And it was ugly. But now that she had it, could she really go through with her part of the bargain? She walked back to the table and sat down in resignation. Letty sat down slowly, as if Maggie would bolt if she made any fast moves.

"That's the truth," Letty said somewhat nervously.

Maggie nodded but continued to look at her plate full of noodles before she could find her voice.

"And the remorse? Did you ever feel any?" she finally asked, sick beyond words.

Letty shrugged and picked up her roll, tearing off pieces of it and laying them on the plate.

"Of course. Don't you think I get lonely? I would have loved to have had a daughter to talk to these last few years I've been all alone. I go to church every Sunday and see all the families sitting together. I see them at Easter and Christmas when their grown-up children come to visit them. Do you think I want to go home to my empty house all by myself? *Of course* I feel bad," she said.

Maggie groaned in frustration. "I hear a lot of 'I's' in what you just said. Let me restate the question. Do you ever feel remorse for what your inaction did to my mother? Do you know how hard it is for people to heal after sexual abuse? Do you? It's not something they can just forget. A lot of people who were sexually abused as children suffer depression and feelings of suicide. I know my mom did. Some even suffer post-traumatic stress disorder. Some develop multiple personalities to deal with the horrors of the abuse. Sometimes they cut themselves. Some end up turning into abusers themselves. Don't you understand that a chance for a normal happy life was stolen from my mother? She didn't have a childhood! She was too busy being molested by your husband. She didn't have any friends growing up because she felt too different too dirty too damaged. And even if she had been able to make friends, your husband wouldn't let her have any because he was too terrified she would let his secret out. Did you know she kept quiet and denied everything because he told her he would kill you if she told anyone? She gave up her precious childhood to save *you*. And you weren't willing to save her. *Because it was embarrassing.* Do—you—feel—any—remorse?" Maggie asked, her voice rising and her eyes blazing.

Letty sat there stunned, her mouth hanging open and her eyes stricken. Her face was so pale, she looked gray and lifeless. Maggie refused to feel pity for her. She stood up and pushed her chair in firmly. She was done.

"Until you can tell me yes to that question, I would prefer not to hear from you. And when the answer to that question *is* yes, I expect you to apologize to my mother. When those two things happen, I will be happy to come visit you. Thrilled, even," she added before walking quickly down the hallway, out the door, and into the fresh air.

Maggie ran to her car and didn't bother going to her grandmother Tierney's house. She was too upset and needed to be alone. She felt like screaming; she felt like throwing something. She felt like crying her heart out for her mother. Tears fell down her cheeks as she drove down the road. She didn't want to go home though. She didn't want all of the icky feelings inside her polluting her house. She drove up American Fork Canyon and up to Tibble Fork Reservoir. She parked her car and stared at the deserted lake. She got out and walked out to a large rock in the shade of a tree and sat down, bowing her head and just wishing all the sick, horrible, angry feelings would just leave.

After she calmed down, she prayed. She prayed for her mom and all the kids out in the world who had no one to stick up for them. She prayed for all innocent children and their safety. She prayed that she could find peace. And finally, lastly, she prayed for Letty Palmer. She prayed that Letty's heart would be softened.

She ended her prayer and thought about God for a moment. She knew if she had been in God's shoes, agency would have been impossible. She could never sit back and let horrible evil things happen to children. It was bad enough when they happened to adults. But beautiful, innocent, pure children would never be harmed in her world.

She paused and wondered how God did it. What was so important about agency, that he was willing to allow people the choice to be as evil as they wanted to be? She bowed her head and prayed quietly to know. She truly needed to know this.

She lifted her head and sighed unhappily as she focused on the lake. Some thought, some feeling came to her as she sat quietly and pondered, that maybe we knew how evil this world was before we came to it, but that we were willing to come down here to prove ourselves to God. Her mom had used her agency to choose to forgive, to live a good, happy life despite what had happened to her as a child. She had used her agency to choose God. She shuddered, feeling bad for Nathan Palmer for the first time as she realized what he had chosen with his agency.

And Christ, how had he borne all the sins of mankind? She couldn't even comprehend it. And then she thought of her mother. Jesus had born her sadness and pain as well. And not just hers, but the pain of everyone who had been sexually abused. She shook her head in awe. God had provided the agency, and Christ had provided the healing.

Maggie massaged her temples. She couldn't understand everything. She couldn't comprehend everything, but she knew in her heart that it came down to the first two commandments. Love God and love our neighbors. She had to find some way to love Letty. Maggie frowned at this thought. It was an impossible commandment. Heavenly Father couldn't possibly have known Letty Palmer when he had commanded Moses to write it down. But in her heart, she knew. He knew everybody. And loved them.

But what was love? She knew love was respect. Love was kind. Love was patient. Maybe she didn't need to have the same relationship with Letty as she did with her grandmother Tierney, but maybe she should have been a little more open at lunch. She could have definitely been more patient. Any maybe more respectful. Okay, a lot more respectful. And kind? She hadn't exactly tried that with Letty yet.

Maggie clenched her hands. *But how?* How could she feel respect or patience or kindness for someone who didn't even feel remorse for the horrible acts they allowed their child to experience? And out of pride, at that?

She got up and walked up and down the small sandy beach, picking up rocks and throwing them as far and as fast as she could. It was too much. Heavenly Father was asking too much of her.

She stopped as the Spirit let her know that wasn't true. Christ had forgiven the men who had nailed him to the cross. Was it really asking so much of her to give her grandmother a chance at a relationship? She picked up the largest rock she could find and hucked it with all the strength she had. It didn't go very far. She sighed in misery. She was tired of misery. She was tired of the incessant weight on her heart. She was ready for life to be happy and normal again. She just wanted Letty to move away, for her mom to move back to Alpine, and for everyone to be happy and nice. That couldn't be asking too much out of life, could it?

Maggie reached down and picked up a small, smooth stone and threw it from her side, watching as it skipped four times over the water. The heavy rock hadn't gone far at all. The lighter rock could sure move though. Basic gravity. She had a feeling that spirits worked the same way. She knew how heavy her heart felt. She couldn't move on with it. She couldn't grow because of it. She would be stuck where she was, feeling this way for a long time if she didn't get the weight off. She had been taught from Primary days that forgiveness was the key to that problem. But nobody in Primary ever mentioned once how hard it would be to forgive someone who had hurt her mom so badly.

Maggie walked back to her sitting rock and leaned against it. Could she forgive Letty without the stipulation of forced remorse? And then, could she go ahead with the deal and visit Letty a couple times a year, knowing she was who she was and that that was never going to change?

Maggie prayed again. This time, the prayer was longer, deeper, quieter. This time, she opened her heart. An hour later, she drove back to Letty Palmer's house. She got out and knocked on the front door and waited for an answer. She waited a few more minutes, but no one came. She walked to the back of the house and peaked in the window. Their lunch plates were still there, sitting on the table still full of food. She walked back to the front of the house and looked in the garage window. Her car was gone.

Maggie kicked a stick out of her way and put her hands on her hips. Wouldn't you know it? Here was the one time she sincerely wanted to make amends with her grandmother and extend the olive branch, and Letty was no where to be found.

"She left just five minutes ago. She asked me to pick up her mail for the next few days."

Maggie's head swiveled in the direction of the voice. It was her grandma Tierney.

Maggie shaded her eyes with her hand. "Did she say where she was going?" she asked.

Bonnie smiled and nodded. "She said there was something she needed to tell your mom. I think she just drove down to St. George," she said, looking as surprised as Maggie felt.

Maggie stood very still. *Huh.* And then she smiled. She wondered if she should call her mom and warn her or let it be a surprise.

Maggie winced, remembering all the things she had just said to Letty and thought it might be better to leave it up to Letty to explain to Lisa. Her mom wouldn't be too happy with her if she knew everything that she had said at their little lunch. She actually had been raised to respect her elders.

"Care for some homemade ice cream?" her grandmother asked.

Maggie felt incredibly light as she walked toward her grandma. "So much, you wouldn't even believe it," she said, walking into her grandma's open arms.

Chapter 29

The two spent the afternoon talking. Maggie was dragged outside to help with some weeding and was surprised at how therapeutic it was to rip weeds out from among the beautiful flowers. If life could only be that easy.

She left her grandma's an hour later and drove to Kohler's. As she stood in line with three boxes of nicotine gum and patches under her arm, she grew aware of some loud whispering coming from behind her.

"Bonnie keeps swearing up and down that her granddaughter doesn't smoke, but look right there. Read what that box says she's carrying. Why would she need all that if she's not a smoker? I tell you, that girl's trouble. And the way she's stolen Luke out from Jennie, I say she's nothing but bad news."

Maggie's eyes turned to slits as she turned slowly to see who it was whispering so loudly for everyone to hear. As soon as she turned, the person in question stopped talking. She studied all the ladies behind her. Most of them were bright red in embarrassment. Either from being caught gossiping or just as uncomfortable bystanders. She zeroed in on the one lady who looked slightly self-righteous. She had a beautiful head of big, super-puffy caramel brown curls. She obviously had never been to Sophie. She was dressed nicely and had the same put-together look of almost every woman in Alpine. Except for the angry, sizzling eyes, she looked like your average Relief Society president.

Maggie smiled in a friendly way and stepped out of line with her boxes still clutched under her arm and went to stand in front of the woman.

"Hi there. You seem to know a lot about me, but I don't seem to know you. I'm Maggie Tierney, and you are?" she said, holding out her free hand to shake.

"Carol Asher," she said, shaking Maggie's hand quickly.

"I see you've noticed my patches here. If you have any questions about it,

I'd be happy to answer them," she said, still smiling as brightly as the local PTA president.

Carol sniffed and looked to her friends for back up, but none of the women were looking at her. Everyone was staring straight ahead in line, not one muscle moving.

"I just think it's strange how someone like you can breeze into town and cause so much havoc. You obviously don't have the same standards as we do. I'm sorry but you just don't fit in. I honestly feel sorry for all the Petersens. Their poor mom and dad off on a mission while you sneak in and ruin everything," she said stoutly, grasping her purse tightly to her chest.

Maggie nodded her head in agreement. "Change can be hard. I understand that. But explain to me something. How is my buying this box of nicotine patches for a dear friend of mine who is struggling to quit causing havoc? And what really gets me, is how is my dating Luke Peterson going to ruin everything? Really, I would love for you to explain it to me."

By this time the store manager had walked quickly up to Maggie and tapped her politely on the shoulder.

"Miss? I would appreciate it if you wouldn't mind taking your conversation outside. I feel that the personal nature of this confrontation is upsetting to our other customers," he said, turning red.

Maggie, still smiling, handed the boxes of gum and patches to the manager and smiled once more at Carol.

"It was super nice making your acquaintance, Carol. Hope to run into you sometime soon," she said, and walked out of the store. She fumed as she stomped to her car and drove twenty minutes to American Fork to buy all of Gwen's supplies at Walmart. She was getting so tired of always fighting with people. It seemed like people either hated her on sight or loved her. There was no middle ground here. She had gone practically her whole life blissfully ignored by the world, and now she couldn't make a move without someone calling someone else who told someone else something entirely different. It was starting to really tick her off.

She stomped back out to her car and threw her bag in the passenger seat and then headed straight to Bajio Grill. Only gargantuan amounts of Mexican food could help her mood. She stuffed herself on nachos before she had the strength to head back to Alpine. She drove slowly past the city limits, looking on both sides of the street for banners that said, *Maggie Tierney, Stay Out!* No signs yet. But give her a week, and she wouldn't be surprised to see a hot air balloon telling her to leave while she had the chance. She drove home and immediately went to give Gwen her stash. Gwen wasn't answering so she stuck it between the screen and her door and stomped back home, where Luke was standing on her porch waiting for her.

"What in the world has happened to you today?" he asked with an exasperated grin.

Maggie sighed and then surprised herself by tearing up. She sniffed back the tears before they could explode, and looked away before answering.

"Oh, just everything. I yelled at my grandmother again, I got into a fight with Carol Asher in line at Kohler's, and I'm thinking of moving back to St. George. No one in St. George would dream of telling me off for buying nicotine patches," she said, getting mad all over again, which didn't sit well with the Mexican food lining her stomach.

Luke nodded sympathetically. "Sorry, but you can't move back to St. George."

Maggie felt like stomping her foot. "And why not? I just don't fit in here. I only fit in with you and my grandparents. Well, and Gwen and maybe the bishopric and a few of your family members. Oh, and Sophie too. And I really liked Jacie. But that's it, Luke. That's it," she said in a strained choked voice.

Luke shook his head. "Margaret, Margaret, Margaret. You can't move away, because you'd be leaving me behind. And we stick together," he said, stepping closer and wrapping his arms around her as he rubbed her back soothingly.

Maggie felt some of the stress and strain evaporate almost immediately. "Maybe you're right. I would hate to leave you at the mercy of all the beautiful, single women in Alpine. Would you like to live in St. George?" she asked, hopefully.

Luke shook his head. "I hate seeing my skin melt when it hits 112. It's just something I don't want to get used to. Come in, put your feet up, and tell me all your troubles," he said, grabbing her keys and opening the door for her.

They went inside where Maggie told him her conversation with her grandmother Palmer. His eyebrows stayed raised for most of the conversation. That kind of worried her. She ended by telling him about Letty driving down to St. George and sighed when she saw his eyebrows lower slightly. As she finished, she rested her head back on the couch cushion and felt exhausted.

Luke hmmed for a moment before saying anything. "Sweetie, you certainly have a way with words, don't ya?"

Maggie kept her eyes closed and groaned loudly. "You think I'm going to hell, don't you?" she asked in a small voice.

Luke's mouth turned up slightly, and he ran his finger down her cheek. "Maggie, you aren't going anywhere without me, so no. You're definitely not going to hell. I hear it's just as hot there as in St. George. But tell me again why you went back to Letty's house," he said, trying to understand exactly what happened.

Maggie blinked at him and sat up a little. "I told you. I went up the canyon and did some praying and thinking. Well, I came to the conclusion that in spite of everything I don't like about my grandmother, it's a commandment that I forgive her and that I somehow love her. And by love, I don't mean matching sweaters. I mean love by showing respect, kindness, and patience," she said clearly.

Luke nodded his head calmly. "Okay, yeah, I get that part. So you were going back to tell Letty that you were going to agree to the three visits a year down in St. George?"

Maggie frowned but nodded. "Actually, two visits a year. One hour each," she said.

Luke frowned at her. "That's only two hours a year, Maggie. Do you think that's enough time?"

Maggie shrugged and grabbed a pillow protectively around her stomach. "Hey, she hasn't even seen me in twenty-four years. Two hours a year is oodles," she said with a firm nod of her head.

Luke shook his head to say what he thought of that. "Margaret, Margaret. What am I going to do with you?" He grabbed her hand and massaged her fingers.

Maggie sighed. "I don't know, but figure it out fast, because I feel like I'm going crazy. I just wish my life was different. I guess everyone says that, but right now, I'm really feeling that maybe just normal and boring regular lives are the way to go," she said, closing her eyes again and leaning against Luke's chest.

"So do you think Letty went down to St. George to apologize to your mom?" Luke asked with a frown on his face.

Maggie winced and shrugged. "I'm not real sure. I peeked in her window and she left without even cleaning up her kitchen. The pasta salad was still on the plates. She didn't even have time to pack or anything. It looked like she just grabbed her keys and ran for the car. So she's either had an epiphany or she wants to see what kind of house she's buying from my mom. Either way, my mom is having company tonight," she said worriedly.

Luke grabbed his cell out of his pocket. "Call your mom," he ordered.

Maggie was scared but she took the phone anyway. She hated getting in trouble. She dialed her mom's number and waited. On the fourth ring she picked up. "Hey Mom, listen, don't get mad at me, but your mother is on her way to see you. She should be there in about an hour or two."

Lisa was quiet for a moment. "And why is that, Maggie?" her mom asked softly.

Maggie bit her lip and looked at Luke, but he was sort of frowning at her too. She was on her own.

"Um, well, she invited me to lunch today to discuss my visiting her in exchange for her house. So I showed up," she said, feeling kind of proud of herself for just doing that.

Lisa sighed loudly. "Maggie. What did you say that would have my mother driving down to see me?" she asked more firmly this time.

Maggie paused and bit her finger nails for a second. "Not much really. She just seemed to think that her nasty old house was so amazing and that I should be so grateful on your behalf, and I just happened to mention that I wasn't all that grateful because an old nasty house doesn't exactly pay back the nine years of hell you went through because of her. I might have said something about how if she ever felt remorse for what she allowed you to go through, then I might be tempted to visit her. Or something along those lines."

Lisa was silent for a moment and then burst out laughing. "Maggie, you are one wild woman, you know that? How did I get a daughter like you?"

Maggie felt some of the pressure in her chest ease slightly and she smiled nervously. "So you're not mad at me? I mean, I swear I had no idea that she would jump in her car and head to St. George. Seriously. She's had the last thirty-odd years to feel remorse. Maybe it was building up all this time and it took just a little shove from me in the right direction to send her down the right road," she said, looking hopefully at Luke to see if he might agree with her. Luke rolled his eyes.

"Honey, you're no little shove. You're a tornado and you know it. So what time did she leave?" Lisa asked.

Maggie breathed in a little easier. Her mom was taking this way better than she would have. "Um, I'm not really sure. After lunch I kind of drove up the canyon to cool off and when I came back to talk to her and tell her that I would try a little harder to be accommodating, she had left already. She asked Grandma to get her mail and paper though. I think it might have been around two. But I'm not sure," Maggie said.

Lisa sighed. "Well, this should be interesting. And Terry's working late tonight too. Dang. Well, I am curious to hear what she has to say, that's for sure."

Maggie frowned. "Mom, if she's not there to apologize or whatever, it's okay. Don't let her hurt you anymore than she has," she said, starting to tense up again at the thought of her mom on her own with Letty.

Lisa laughed again. "Oh honey, you worry too much. I'm a big girl now. I'll call you later and tell you how it goes. Okay?"

Maggie sighed. "Okay. I love you, Mom. Bye."

Maggie disconnected and looked at Luke who was staring at her with a half smile. "Okay, that's one down. Now why did you get in a fight with my aunt at Kohler's?" he asked seriously.

Maggie gasped and covered her mouth with her hands. "Carol Asher is your aunt?"

Luke nodded and looked away. "Not my favorite aunt by any means, but she is my mom's sister. She's best friends with Marlene Benchley by the way."

Maggie groaned and shut her eyes. "Now your mom's going to get that e-mail I was telling you about."

Luke nodded his head in agreement. "Oh, I'm sure of it."

Maggie opened one eye and glanced at him. "So how close is your mom to Carol?" she asked softly.

Luke sighed and leaned his head back on the couch. "Oh, pretty close, if you call identical twins close."

Maggie pulled a pillow over her face and screamed loudly. She pulled it down a moment later when she felt better. "So listen. If you want to break up with me, I totally understand," she said, looking away from him.

Luke laughed and pulled her into his arms. "Just kidding," he said and laughed when she tried to strangle him. "I don't even know any Carol Asher."

Maggie threw Luke off and then put a choke hold on him that had him begging for mercy.

"You're teasing me after the day I had? Oh, you are so in for it. I'm calling Cooper Christiansen right now. I bet he'll drive up and help me pack up and move back to St. George. No forget that, I'll call Jennie up and have her help me pack. She'll do it faster," she said with a glare. Luke grinned as he pulled her hands away from his throat. "Margaret, now stop being childish. I told you, you're not going anywhere. Now why don't you come over to my house? I want to show you something," he said, standing up and pulling her up with him.

Maggie glared at him, but followed him to his house. He walked down to his basement and into the room with all of his tools. He picked up a large plaque that had writing on it. He turned around, holding it up so she could read the words. It had been hand chiseled in beautiful calligraphy and stained a cherry red. *Families ARE Forever.*

Maggie smiled and looked at Luke. "And why is the word *are* so big compared to the other two?" she asked, reaching out and tracing the words with her finger.

Luke glanced down and up again, smiling. "I had to stress the word *are,* because you seemed to have a little trouble with that one. I made it for you." He handed it to her.

Maggie's eyes widened in surprise. It was beautiful and obviously expensive. He had to have spent many hours on it. "Wow Luke, this is amazing. I can't believe you made this for me. I'll put it up in my house as soon as I get back," she said, rubbing her hands over the smooth wood. As she turned the wood to look at it, she noticed there was more etching on the back. She moved past Luke and laid it on the work bench so she could look more closely at it. She bent down and read out loud.

"Margaret Tierney, Love of My Life and the Joy of My Soul. Please Be My Wife." Her eyes widened and she turned to look at Luke in shock.

"Are you serious? *Really?* Me, for real?" she asked, looking at him as if he were crazy.

Luke looked at her without smiling and nodded. "Yes, you, Maggie. Nobody else," he said quietly.

Maggie looked down at her feet and shook her head. "How can you ask me to marry you? I mean, I cause so much trouble. I'm always getting into fights with people and rubbing people the wrong way and doing crazy things. Why would you want to marry somebody like that? I mean, dating, sure fine. But marriage? *Forever?"* she asked, still in shock.

Luke leaned up against the work bench and crossed his arms over his chest. "If I wanted to marry a woman based on how little trouble she caused, I'd already be engaged to Jennie. That's not my number one criteria in a wife. I only have one, which is that I love her," he said.

Maggie's face melted into a grin and she threw her arms around Luke's neck. "Thanks, that's so sweet. And I'll think about it," she said, kissing him on the cheek.

Luke pushed her away and glared at her, his eyes turning a silvery brilliant blue. "Excuse me? *You'll think about it?* Oh, that's great. I can't wait to tell our kids that one," he said in irritation.

Maggie laughed and picked up her plaque. "Come help me hang this," she said and walked out of the room.

Luke stared after her and then smiled. He walked slowly out of the room and shut the light off. She wasn't the most predictable woman in the world.

Chapter 30

Lisa called Maggie later that night around eleven thirty. Maggie had been sitting on her bed, staring at the phone, willing it to ring for the past half hour.

"Hey, there you are. How did it go?" she asked her mom.

Lisa sighed. "As good as anything like that can go, I guess. But she did apologize, like you said. She said that she was sorry."

Maggie frowned. "Is that it? She just said she's sorry and that's it? End of story?" she exclaimed.

"Well, you sort of know what my mother's like. Don't you think that's pretty huge for her?" Lisa asked with a smile in her voice.

Maggie played with the yarn on her quilt. "I guess. Maybe you guys should think about family counseling? You know some really great counselors. Maybe they could help your mother work up to being open to a real relationship or something," she said hopefully.

Lisa made a humming sound. "That's actually a really good idea. I think she might even be open to something like that now. Before it would have been impossible. But now? Who knows. And Maggie? I just want to say thanks. I know if your dad had lived, he would have said all those things to my mother. Thanks for sticking up for me. I know that's hard for some people to do. But you're different. You don't care what the consequences are, you tell the truth, and you say what needs to be said. I love that about you. Don't ever change," she said seriously.

Maggie grinned and lay back on her bed. "Thanks, Mom. And I can promise you I won't. I've tried and it's impossible. Oh and guess what? Luke proposed to me tonight," she mentioned casually.

Lisa screamed so loud in her ear Maggie had to rip the phone away from her face. She stared at it in horror as her mom kept screaming. She finally calmed down sufficiently for Maggie to put the phone back to her ear.

"Mom, are you crazy? Are you having a breakdown?" she demanded.

Lisa laughed. "No, dear, I'm not crazy and I'm not having a mental moment. But my only daughter and only child has just told me she was proposed to. Do you know how much work I have to do now? Oh my heck, I need to call your grandma. We are going to plan you the biggest, most beautiful reception in the world. Yeah!" she yelled again.

Maggie grinned. "Mom, I didn't say yes."

Lisa stopped yelling. "What? What do you mean you didn't say yes? *Did you say no?*" she asked in confusion.

Maggie sighed. "Of course not. I just told him I'd think about it. I don't see what the hurry is. We both have time. We don't need to rush an important decision like this."

"Oh," was all Lisa said.

Maggie told her mom all about Luke's proposal and Lisa got excited again.

"I don't care what you say. I know you're marrying that boy, Maggie. You can say you're thinking about it all you want, but I'm still calling your grandma. I'm getting started right now," she said determinedly.

Maggie laughed. "What if I put Luke off until his mom and dad get home? That's a year away," she said warningly.

Lisa sputtered. "You can't put that poor boy off for a whole year. That would be cruel. Why don't you go ahead and say yes to the proposal and then just be engaged for awhile. At least then he's not sitting there, worrying about it every day. You know you love him, Maggie." Lisa said sternly.

Lisa smiled and looked up at her ceiling. "I do, Mom. I really love him," she said dreamily.

Lisa laughed. "Is this where you start singing a Celine Dion song?" she asked.

Maggie snorted. "You're the one screaming your head off. If anyone's singing Celine, it's you and you know it."

Lisa laughed. "You're right. I can already see your wedding video. Nothing but Celine Dion music. You'll love it."

Maggie grinned and talked to her mom for a few more minutes before hanging up.

The next week passed by quickly. Maggie even convinced Gwen to sit for her one more time before she left for St. George.

Gwen sat in the same old sun dress as before and stared out over Alpine.

"I'm leaving tomorrow. So are you ready for my dogs? Did you read all the instructions I wrote out for you?" she asked with a frown.

Maggie rolled her eyes and dipped her brush. "Don't be such a worrywart. I've read everything, and if it makes you feel any better, Luke and Cheyenne are going to help me too. Besides, you're just going to be gone three days, not three years," she said, looking back at her canvas.

Gwen sighed. "I'm going to miss them. I'm going to miss Alpine. But you're right. It's just three days. What can happen in three days?" she asked in a tense voice.

Maggie raised her eyebrows. She didn't say it, but she knew a ton could happen in three days.

"So you don't sound very excited. Is everything okay?" Maggie asked gently.

Gwen looked at her and then away. "I should be excited, huh? An old spinster lady like me having some gorgeous man interested in her. But I'm so nervous and sick about it, I can't even enjoy it. I used to have a therapist I talked to a while back. I'm thinking of calling him up and going again. I really don't want to mess this up, but I just feel like all my old baggage is right with me, going everywhere I go and getting in the way. I think maybe I should cancel until I get my head on straight," she said, as the wind gently moved her hair around her face.

Maggie put her brush down and walked over and sat next to Gwen. "I think seeing your therapist is a great idea, Gwen. But why would you need to cancel your trip to St. George?" she asked curiously.

Gwen shrugged. "It's like I keep telling you, but you're not hearing me. I'm not a normal woman. You know that. It's nice to pretend I am, but I'm not. Even if everything went great with Joe and his kids, and I fell in love with him and he fell in love with me and we got married and the whole fairy tale, I'd be cheating him. Joe's expecting a woman who will give him one hundred percent. Mind, body, and soul. Honestly, I feel like all I have left to give anyone is maybe thirty-five percent," she said, ripping grass out and watching the wind dance it away on her hand.

Maggie sighed and ripped some grass herself. "I'll tell you what Terry told me when he started dating my mom. He knew she had been abused. He knew everything. But I was giving him a hard time about dating my mom. I didn't trust him not to hurt her. And he told me that my mom's love was her widow's mite. If she gave him all she had to give, no matter how little that was, then it would be enough for him. Maybe when you go see Joe this weekend, maybe you should think about telling him how you feel. Tell him what happened so he understands why you're so nervous. Otherwise, he'll just assume it's something he did or said or didn't do or didn't say. He might surprise you," she said.

Gwen smiled crookedly. "Why am I sitting here listening to a twenty-four-year-old baby? That's what I want to know," she said, throwing her grass up in the wind.

Maggie laughed and stood up, walking back to her paints. "Because you're dang lucky, that's why."

Gwen snorted and went back to her pose. "Thanks, Maggie. Thanks for pushing me in the right direction all the time. Oh, and I'm out of patches again," she said.

Maggie groaned. "I'm getting tired of buying those things. How many can you use in one week?"

Gwen laughed again. "I'm kidding. I was just hoping you'd get in another fight at the store again. I heard you got assigned home teachers," she said, laughing even louder.

Maggie sighed loudly and glared at Gwen over the canvas. "Yeah, *the bishop*. He's heard so many rumors about my smoking habits, he's worried about me now. When are you quitting, so I can quit?" she asked.

Gwen smiled proudly. "I haven't smoked a cigarette in one week."

Maggie jumped up and down and clapped her hands. "Gwen, that's fantastic! You're amazing."

Gwen smiled and nodded her head slightly and said so softly that Maggie couldn't hear, "I am. I am amazing." And when the warmth filled her heart and the wind caressed her cheek, Gwen knew it was true.

Chapter 31

Letty Palmer returned home on the same day Gwen left for St. George. In the time she spent down south, Letty spent part of every day with her daughter, trying for the life of her to reconnect in some way with Lisa. Lisa was able to convince her easily enough to meet with her and a family therapist. And although Lisa wouldn't tell her daughter what was said in those sessions, Maggie could tell that no matter how painful it had been, some good had come of it. They were both learning how to be mother and daughter again.

Maggie had given her grandma Tierney strict instructions to tell her the moment Letty got home. And right when she got the call, she got in her car and went over. She knocked on the door and waited only half a second before it was opened by Letty. Letty looked at her for a moment and then smiled.

"I'll talk to you on the porch. My house reeks of rotten pasta salad for some reason," she said dryly as she walked out to join her granddaughter.

Letty sat in the rocker and Maggie sat on the top step. "So you've been down to see my mom, huh?" Maggie asked, clasping her knees with her hands.

Letty nodded and looked out over her yard. "It was about time. I'm glad I did. I'm grateful I did," she said in a voice Maggie hadn't ever heard before. It was almost humble and gentle.

Maggie blinked in surprise. "I'm glad. Thank you."

Letty glanced at her granddaughter and smiled. "No, Maggie. Thank you. You know in the Book of Mormon when it talks about being hard-hearted? That was me. For a long time, I had hardened my heart. It took a battering ram like you to help me see the truth."

Maggie blushed. She'd been compared to a tornado and now a battering ram. Most girls were compared to nice things like flowers and pearls.

"I'm just glad you and my mom are working things out. Are you still set on moving to St. George and giving your house to my mom?"

Letty rocked and nodded. "Yes. I am. And don't worry, you don't have to come visit me. Of course you're welcome to, anytime. But it's up to you," she said.

Maggie's eyes opened in surprise. Things had changed. A lot.

"Well, I think I can promise you right now, I'll be down to visit you. Maybe more in the winter time than the summer time, but I'll be down for sure," she said kindly.

Letty smiled and held her hand out to Maggie. Maggie stared at her grandmother's hand and paused, but then she smiled and lifted her own hand to grasp it warmly in hers. As Maggie let go of her grandmother's hand moments later, she could almost feel a weight lift off her heart. She was free.

She sat and talked to her grandmother for almost thirty minutes before leaving to meet Luke for dinner. She gave Letty a quick hug before leaving and smiled as she waved good-bye. She waved at her grandmother Tierney who stood in the window of her house, looking out at her too. She drove away feeling good. She felt good to be living in Alpine. She felt good for having grandparents in her life. And she felt good that she was able to do something she had been scared she'd never be able to do. Forgive.

She drove into Draper and met Luke at a little steakhouse right off the freeway. She walked into the restaurant and saw him immediately. He stood up as she walked to him and walked right into his hug, feeling the immediate warmth that she loved so much.

"You know what, Luke? I love hugging you. It's the best feeling in the world," she said as she sat down.

Luke smiled delightedly and handed her a menu. "Just don't you forget it."

Maggie smiled as she looked at the menu. "I think I'll have the . . . hmm . . . yep. I think I'll have Luke. Forever. And ever," she said and put her menu down.

Luke lowered his menu and stared at her. "What did you just say?" he asked in surprise.

Maggie laughed and grabbed his menu out of his hand. "I'll take the forever families please. With a couple of kids on the side," she said, grinning at his expression.

Luke started to smile. His eyes started to glow brightly and then he was standing up and swinging her around the restaurant in front of everyone.

When everyone had stopped clapping and they had ordered and were sipping their water, Luke leaned over and grabbed her hand. "By the way, that order of kids on the side? It only comes in fours."

Maggie raised her eyebrows at that. "I think the menu specifically said it came in a two-pack," she said firmly.

Luke shook his head slowly. "I talked to the manager in charge and he says no way. They do make exceptions, but not for you. Sorry."

Maggie laughed and threw a roll at Luke. "We'll see how the first one goes, okay?"

Luke grinned happily. "The first one. You and me, Maggie. Getting married and having a family. And to think when I first saw you I thought you were a hemp-wearing vegan obsessed with Tuscan architecture."

Maggie snorted and made room for the large steak being put in front of her.

"Life can surprise you, huh?"

Luke watched his fiancée dig in to her food as if she had been starving for the last twenty-four years and sighed in pure happiness. He was so grateful for surprises.

Epilogue

Gwen ended up having a great time in St. George. And she was right. She fell in love with those teenage boys of Joe's immediately. Joe asked her to marry him eight months later and surrounded by her friends and family she was sealed in the St. George temple for time and all eternity. She decided to sell her house and move down to St. George permanently to live on Joe's ranch. Her dogs couldn't be happier. Gwen has officially given up wearing her pajamas all day. She now has a wardrobe full of jeans and boots and the occasional dress. She got rid of her extensions and now has a cute, shoulder length hair style, with blonde highlights. Joe still thinks she's the most beautiful woman he's ever known.

In the meantime, Lisa and Terry moved up to Alpine and stayed with Bonnie and Frank while they built a two-story, old-fashioned Victorian home with wide wrap-around porches. It took a year for the construction of the new home but Bonnie and Frank both cried when Terry and Lisa moved into their new home. Next door.

Cheyenne's parents finally let her model for Maggie and were shocked when the painting sold for $375,000. Maggie gave fifty thousand dollars to go toward Cheyenne's college fund. Cheyenne is still trying to choose between becoming a lawyer or a having career in the music business.

Jennie Benchley ended up moving to Seattle, where she now works as a nanny for a wealthy family. She misses her family, but at least she doesn't have to see Maggie every day of her life. She's still having a problem with that second commandment.

And Luke and Maggie? They're doing great. They were engaged for a year so they could be married when Luke's mom and dad got home from their mission. They decided to get married in the Mount Timpanogos Temple on a beautiful summer morning. All of the flowers were blooming and there was a smile on every face. The photographer couldn't have been happier. The only snag in the entire day was when Letty Palmer and Bonnie Tierney couldn't decide who should be the one to straighten Maggie's veil for her. And in the individual family shots, one of Maggie's favorites was the one where she was surrounded by her mom and both grandmas. At the reception held in Frank and Bonnie's backyard, the picture Maggie painted of her dad in her backyard was put on an easel right next to her bridal portrait. She insisted on having her dad with her on the most important day of her life.

The reception lasted late into the night, but right before they left for their honeymoon in Greece, Maggie had one more surprise for her husband.

"Luke! Come over here and open up your gift!" Maggie yelled across the yard.

Luke hugged Marlene Benchley quickly and went to join his wife.

"Hey, you got me a present. That's so sweet," he said, kissing her lovingly on the forehead.

Maggie grinned and put the heavy present in his arms. Luke looked at her curiously as he put the box on a table to open it. Everyone at the reception quieted down to see what Maggie looked so excited about.

Luke pulled the paper off and lifted the top. He laughed as he pulled out a beautiful china plate and held it up for everyone to see.

"You got me china. How did you know that's the one thing I wanted from you?" he said, shaking his head.

Maggie grinned and shrugged and ignored everyone's confused expressions. Inside jokes were inside for a reason.

"But that reminds me. I bought you something too. You are going to love this," he said, motioning for Tim to give Maggie a box beautifully wrapped in silver paper.

Maggie smiled in pleasure. She really loved opening presents. She ripped the paper off almost violently and opened the lid of the box. She lifted out a bright, lime green helmet.

Maggie frowned.

Luke laughed. "It's for four-wheeling. I knew after spending all day with you in the sand that you were the woman for me. Look at the back."

Maggie turned the helmet over and read in bright neon pink lettering. "Mrs. Petersen."

Maggie sighed and put it on so the photographer could take her picture.

Luke slipped it off her head and tried to pat her hair back into place.

"Thanks for taking a chance on me, Margaret," he said for her ears only.

Maggie smiled in total contentment. Taking chances was the only way to live life.

Book Club Questions

1. What do you think is harder for victims of abuse: Forgiveness? Or learning to trust again?

2. Was Lisa right to have kept Maggie away from Alpine and her grandparents?

3. Gwen sees life through canine vision. Is this a coping technique or is she on to something?

4. Lisa's belief that no one can be healed without Christ's atonement goes against mainstream thinking. What do you think modern psychologists would think about Lisa's views?

5. Why was Luke unable to stand up to Jennie Benchley? Do you know anyone like Jennie?

6. Is secondhand victimization a reality? And how does today's media play a part in it?

7. Maggie was worried that the Proclamation on the Family might offend Gwen. Why is that?

8. What would you have done differently if you were Lisa? What would you have done differently if you were Letty?

9. Why is the song "I Am a Child of God" so important for victims of sexual abuse or any type of abuse?

10. Forgiveness was a big theme in this book. Are there times when forgiveness doesn't necessarily mean having a relationship with someone?

Helpful Information

How Can I Protect My Child from Sexual Assault?

1. Communicate! Tell your children that you are always there to talk about anything. Tell them that you are there to help them solve problems and protect them.

2. Teach your children that it is against the "rules" for adults to act in a sexual way with children and use examples.

3. Teach your children that their bodies are their own and that it is OK if they don't want a hug or other contact that might make them uncomfortable.

4. Teach your children that it's OK to say NO and it's OK to leave the situation.

5. Trust your own instincts! If your instincts tell you something is wrong, follow up!

6. Stay calm. If a child discloses abuse to you, or hints at possible abuse, don't overreact. Believe the child and communicate that belief to him or her.

7. Thank the child for telling you and praise his or her courage for speaking up.

8. Emphasize that what happened to the child was not his or her fault and that the child did not deserve to be treated like that.

9. Tell the child that it is your responsibility to keep the child safe and that you will do the best you can to protect him or her.

10. Report your suspicions of abuse to the local police or child protective services agency (www.rainn.org).

Statistics

1 in 4 girls is sexually abused before the age of 18.

1 in 6 boys is sexually abused before the age of 18.

1 in 5 children are solicited sexually while on the internet.

Nearly 70% of all reported sexual assaults (including assaults on adults) occur to children ages 17 and under.

An estimated 39 million survivors of childhood sexual abuse exist in America today.

30–40% of victims are abused by a family member.

Another 50% are abused by someone outside of the family whom they know and trust.

Approximately 40% are abused by older or larger children whom they know.

Only 10% of children are abused by strangers.

Most children don't tell even if they have been asked.

Over 30% of victims never disclose the experience to anyone. (www.darkness2light.org)

Helpful web sites

www.darkness2light.org

www.rainn.org

Information quoted exactly from these sources:

Darkness to Light, "Statistics." www.darkness2light.org.

Rape, Abuse & Incest National Network, "How Can I Protect My Child From Sexual Assault?" www.rainn.org.